Praise for *Something*

"Weaving between the past and the present of all three women, *Something Wild* creates a compelling, believable, and upsetting portrayal of how trauma ripples through a family. . . . Good books sometimes cut to the bone, and this one feels like a scythe."

—Scaachi Koul, *The New York Times Book Review*

"Rarely has an author taken the time and demonstrated such honesty with the complexity of girls' desire and how they act on it, how it can sour the sweetest relationship. . . . At a time when many novels rely on intricate plots or eccentric narrative voices, *Something Wild* eschews literary pyrotechnics and relies instead on the power of truth. We may not like what we see, but we know we're being given an opportunity to change the way we look at sexual dynamics."

—Bethanne Patrick, *The Washington Post*

"This wise, brilliant novel is so special, so overflowing with honesty and love—about motherhood, sisterhood, what it's like to be a woman—that every paragraph feels like an epiphany. Hanna Halperin knows the fierce love that can exist especially among broken things. *Something Wild* moved me deeply."

—Glennon Doyle, #1 *New York Times* bestselling author of *Untamed*

"What if you found out your mother was being abused? Tanya and Nessa head back to Boston to help their mother move out of their childhood home, only to find out that she's in an abusive relationship with their stepfather. The sisters want to tackle the issue in different ways, colored by a secret experience they've lived through."

—Zibby Owens, *Good Morning America*

"A first novel that weaves its spell subtly . . . As *Something Wild* builds to a climactic ending, we feel more and more connected to the fixed points of life, which Halperin places for us throughout the book like stepping stones. . . . For although this novel takes us on a troubling journey to the edges of wildness, the tender, intimate, and honest bond between Nessa and Tanya manages to carry us to the safer shores of love."

—Sonia Taitz, The Jewish Book Council

"A searingly wild ride with emotional depth . . . Halperin's talent as a writer makes the book one of the year's must reads."

—*The Martha's Vineyard Times*

"A deceptively easy read of a gut-wrenching story . . . It's rare to find so nuanced and accurate a fictional take on intimate partner violence as author Hanna Halperin manages to pull off in *Something Wild*, to say nothing of the complexities of sibling relationships and family dynamics."

—*Madison Magazine*

"Bold and surprising . . . unflinching and brave, Halperin's story lays bare the characters' nuanced and complicated responses to domestic violence. This haunting portrait of a broken family will stay with readers."

—*Publishers Weekly*

"When sisters Tanya and Nessa Bloom travel to the Boston suburbs to help their mom pack up their childhood home, they reckon with their past while discovering a disturbing truth: their mother is in an abusive relationship. Now, they must figure out what comes next for all of them." —*Marie Claire*

"The true joy of the characters in this novel comes from the choices the sisters don't make, how they learn from the mistakes of their family. . . . [Halperin] shows how adept she is in her understanding of abuse: so ubiquitous in today's society that, despite how it ravages a family through generations, is unsurprising to the characters, and therefore, presented calmly to the audience. . . . With its delicate depiction of domestic abuse, *Something Wild* becomes a truly harrowing story." —*The Jewish Exponent*

"In this compelling debut that examines overt violence and buried pain in the lives of a mother and her two adult daughters, Hanna Halperin explores the injuries that can and cannot be healed, the wrongs that can and cannot be forgiven, and the times when love is and isn't enough. *Something Wild* is an unflinching look at what happens when closed doors and hearts are at last flung open."   —Judith Claire Mitchell, author of *A Reunion of Ghosts*

"*Something Wild* is a profound and intimate novel that follows two sisters' evolving identities in the wake of personal tragedy. Though its main characters are survivors, this book is not just about the cost of violence; it is a nuanced look at the power dynamics nestled deep in our homes, our conversations, and the makeup of our society. Halperin writes the Bloom family with rich specificity, creating characters alive with vulnerability, beauty, and rage, all the while telling a greater story of how one generation of women can inherit trauma from the last. An unforgettable debut that I'll be grappling with for years to come."

          —Lucy Tan, author of *What We Were Promised*

"*Something Wild* is a brave, harrowing novel, beautifully written and unflinching in its examination of spousal abuse, sexual exploitation, divorce, and legacies of trauma. It is also, miraculously, a tender-hearted examination of sibling love and betrayal, of the wounds we suffer and inflict on those we need the most, and the mercy required to endure them. Hanna Halperin possesses the courage of all great novelists: she is able to stare down the truth without judgment. I was spellbound while reading her remarkable debut, and haunted long afterward."

          —Steve Almond, author of *All the Secrets of the World*

ABOUT THE AUTHOR

Hanna Halperin is a graduate of the MFA program at the University of Wisconsin–Madison. Her stories have been published in the *Kenyon Review*, *n+1*, *New Ohio Review*, *Joyland*, and others. She has taught fiction workshops at Grub Street in Boston and worked as a domestic violence counselor.

Penguin Readers Guide available online at
penguinrandomhouse.com

SOMETHING WILD

A Novel

Hanna Halperin

PENGUIN BOOKS

PENGUIN BOOKS
An imprint of Penguin Random House LLC
penguinrandomhouse.com

First published in the United States of America by Viking,
an imprint of Penguin Random House LLC, 2021
Published in Penguin Books 2022

ISBN 9781984882080 (paperback)

THE LIBRARY OF CONGRESS HAS CATALOGED THE
HARDCOVER EDITION AS FOLLOWS:
Names: Halperin, Hanna, author.
Title: Something wild : a novel / Hanna Halperin.
Description: New York : Viking, [2021] |
Identifiers: LCCN 2021010040 (print) | LCCN 2021010041 (ebook) |
ISBN 9781984882066 (hardcover) | ISBN 9781984882073 (ebook)
Subjects: LCSH: Sisters—Fiction. | Mothers and daughters—Fiction. |
Psychological fiction.
Classification: LCC PS3608.A54865 S66 2021 (print) |
LCC PS3608.A54865 (ebook) | DDC 813/.6—dc23
LC record available at https://lccn.loc.gov/2021010040
LC ebook record available at https://lccn.loc.gov/2021010041

Printed in the United States of America
1   3   5   7   9   10   8   6   4   2

Designed by Amanda Dewey

For Sofia and Gabe

When they were young, Nessa and Tanya Bloom played a game where they chased each other up the stairs of their house. Whoever was doing the chasing would get close, just at the heels of the other, reach out and grab her ankles, pinch her sides, smack her butt. It was fun at first, the thrill of running away, the thrill of chasing. They'd laugh, giddy with the fight or flightiness of it, until the one being chased would scream out, *Stop, I'm getting the Wild Thing!*

The Wild Thing was the kind of feeling they had in dreams—of not being able to run fast enough, of somebody's long, grabbing, proprietary fingers, right there, on the verge of reaching them. They didn't actually hurt one another; they weren't the tackling type and they didn't wrestle. They fought all the time, just not physically—over who got to go first, who got the pink one, who got the blue. They would scream over what was fair, what was just, who was more deserving. Their mother used to hold out her index finger. "Do you two want to fight over this speck of dust?" she'd ask. Usually they did.

They didn't fight when they were on the stairs, though. It was a game, until one of them got the Wild Thing, and then, just like that, they'd stop.

On a car ride from the Berkshires back to Arlington—their parents up front, sisters in the back—Nessa and Tanya watched an old man cruise by in a red convertible. The man caught the girls' gaze, and then, like he'd been planning it, grinned and lifted one finger to his lips: *Shhh*. They began to shriek—out of surprise, out of embarrassment, out of rage—out of what exactly, they didn't know. It was electrifying. Feeling the Wild Thing out there on the highway.

"Aren't you going to *do* something?" they implored their parents. "Don't you want to *kill* the creep?"

This was when their parents were still together. But their mother and father just laughed. Tucked away in the backseat, Nessa and Tanya had felt safe enough. Their little family car had seemed as secure and foolproof as a spaceship, speeding down the highway. Nessa remembers it, every time she drives down the Mass Pike, the way the man in the car had looked at them, like he knew he was going to get away with it.

IT HAD RETURNED over the years—the Wild Thing—and not just on the stairs, but out, at other places, with other men. Nessa can't help but think that her body must have anticipated a certain kind of danger before she herself had understood it.

The worst the Wild Thing had ever gotten, and the time she and Tanya never talk about—not even to acknowledge it happened—was the night at Dan's house fourteen years ago. The worst mistake, Nessa thinks, of her life. But in her darkest moments, the whole thing feels like an inevitability. That somehow, she was meant to end up on that decrepit porch with the sagging sofa, her little sister in tow. All her life, that was where she'd been heading. That when she and Tanya chased each other up the stairs of their house when they were young, they'd been preparing one another for what was to come.

I.

Frankly, Tanya Bloom doesn't have time to drive up to Massachusetts and clean out her childhood house. She has dozens of cases to work on and though she'll bring her computer, the chance of getting anything done is slim. Moving her mother out of 12 Winter Street is a daunting job, and Nessa will be no help. Really, it would be easier to send her mother and her sister off into Boston for the day, so Tanya could do it herself, go through the house with industrial-sized trash bags, throw the majority of everything away. Her mother has a hard time saying goodbye to almost anything.

The move makes no sense. The so-called property in New Hampshire that her stepfather, Jesse, recently inherited is nothing more than a dusty patch of rubble. The house itself is so bleak and dated Tanya could barely scroll through all six photos on her phone before calling her mother to talk her out of it.

"Jesse's going to fix it up. We have big plans for it!" Lorraine kept repeating in such a psychotically cheerful voice that Tanya realized Jesse must have been sitting right there beside her mother. The conversation hadn't lasted more than three minutes.

Tanya is taking two personal days off from work to make the trip—Thursday and Friday, the first personal days she's taken since starting her job as ADA in the Manhattan District Attorney's Office, one year ago.

"What will you do without me this weekend?" Tanya asks Eitan, her husband, that morning. "You should take Will out," she says. "Help him meet somebody new." It's six thirty, the latest they've both stayed in bed together for a long time—months, at least. On any other Thursday, Tanya would've already been coming home from the gym by this time, ready to jump in the shower and begin the mad dash of getting dressed in order to get to the Seventy-Ninth Street subway stop no later than 7:50 a.m.

Eitan makes a face. "It's too soon," he says. "Besides, Will's too soft for New York women."

"His ex was from New York." Tanya rolls over on her side and looks at Eitan. She likes him best this way: before he's showered or shaved or brushed his teeth, blurred around the edges with sleep. No one else in the world gets to see him like this.

"Even so, he needs someone kind," Eitan says. "Maybe someone from the Midwest."

"Do we know any kind people?"

"Not really," Eitan says, smiling. He reaches for her hand. "Hey, what about your sister?"

"I think she's seeing some deadbeat she met at work. And, there's no way I'd let you set Will up with Nessa."

"Why not?"

"He's too nice for her. Or maybe she's too nice for him." Though *nice* isn't exactly the word Tanya's looking for.

"What's wrong with that?" Eitan asks.

"Two really nice people can't be together. They'd get bored. There'd be no tension."

"So I take it I'm the nice one in our relationship?"

"Of course you are. You're one big giant pushover." Tanya pats his stomach.

Her phone vibrates on the nightstand and Tanya leans over Eitan to check. It's a text message from Nessa.

Fuck I think I have a UTI

An ellipsis appears and several more texts follow in quick succession.

Is it normal to pee 7 times in 1 hour???

My vagina feels like it's going to fall off

Not normal, she texts back. *Do you want Eitan to write you a rx?*

Yes please!! Nessa responds.

K, Tanya writes. *Hydrate*

Tanya puts the phone down. "Nessa needs you to write her a prescription for antibiotics. She has a urinary tract infection."

"She should really get a urine sample before—"

"Eitan, a woman knows when she has a UTI."

"It's so that she can be prescribed the correct type of antibiotics."

"Write what you usually write," Tanya says. "Don't be annoying about it."

"Fine." Eitan pulls Tanya's hand to his mouth and kisses it. "So," he says. "You're really not going to tell them. Not even Nessa?"

Tanya shakes her head.

"You don't think they'll be able to tell?"

"No," she says flatly. The only person who knows Tanya's body well enough to notice anything different is Eitan. She'll start showing soon, though, according to the books and to her doctor, and the thought terrifies her.

TANYA MET EITAN THREE YEARS prior while she was in her second year at Columbia Law and he was in his third year of medical school at Mount Sinai. She'd been taken with Eitan Abrams right away. He was gentle and solemn. He was Jewish, like her father, his Semitic features handsome and familiar. She liked his eyes, long lashed and heavy lidded, the color of green Kalamata olives; sharp. There was something noble about his nose.

They hadn't been trying to get pregnant. They were both twenty-eight, practically a decade too young to have a baby these days, in Tanya's opinion. Their lives were full and busy and satisfying; they didn't need a child on top of everything else.

But then last month her period was late, and on a whim she bought a pregnancy test from Duane Reade during her lunch break. She wasn't expecting anything. In fact, the impulse to buy a test had surprised her. She normally didn't get nervous about these things; she was always careful and she didn't have a lot of sex, anyway. She chugged a water bottle, took the test into a single-person bathroom in Starbucks. Double pink lines appeared promptly in the window. Her first thought had been: Will I have to miss work to get an abortion? Her second: There's a person—half me, half Eitan—in my uterus right now at this very moment.

That evening on her commute home, packed onto the 1 train with barely enough room to breathe, Tanya glanced at the seats closest to the doors, the ones reserved for the elderly, the handicapped, the pregnant. Something akin to anger passed through her. She didn't want special treatment. She didn't want to be expected to sit. She'd have an abortion, she decided; no question.

When she arrived home half an hour later, the hallway of their building smelled like garlic cooking on the stove. It was Eitan, making dinner. He would want it, she knew. Fucking Eitan would want it more than anything.

He'd broken away from his Orthodox upbringing years ago—he was no longer a religious man. He was not moralistic, and he was certainly not pro-life. But he was a family man. It was something about him that Tanya knew she was supposed to covet.

He'd been raised Modern Orthodox, the youngest, and only boy, in a family of five kids, and even as a child he'd been aware of the sect's hypocrisies. In shul, while he and his father prayed downstairs with the other men, his four older sisters and mother sat in the balcony, where it was hot and crowded; where in the summertime, the fans were so loud that the women could barely hear what the rabbi was saying downstairs.

Really it was his anger toward his parents, much more than any archaic rule or ritual, that led Eitan away from Orthodoxy. Still, though, Tanya sometimes saw flashes of traditionalism in her husband. They'd be walking down the street and pass a family and Eitan would smile approvingly in their direction—and Tanya could feel herself tense up. And not just any family; it was the big, conventional families that Eitan liked. A mother and a father, a gaggle of kids, all those genes mixed up and shaken out into different yet related forms. It annoyed her, the way his face brightened at the sight of a young couple pushing an infant in its carriage, or a father carrying a child on his shoulders, his pregnant wife dutifully by his side.

Eitan insisted this wasn't the case, but she knew that he didn't just want babies with her—he wanted Jewish babies.

When Tanya was young, her own family had done the Jewish thing, too. Hebrew school, lighting the menorah, going to services on the High Holidays. But when her father left her mother, most of that ended. Her mother was technically Catholic—although Lorraine hadn't set foot inside a church since she was a girl—but without Jonathan around, they all gave up on being Jewish. There was no longer a point.

"WHAT ARE YOU MAKING?" she'd called, stepping inside the apartment, gearing up to tell him about the test.

"The eggplant thing," Eitan called back from the kitchen.

Tanya set down her purse and laptop and found Eitan in the kitchen. They kissed quickly. "How was your day?" Eitan asked, returning to the stove.

She stepped out of her heels. "Interesting."

"How'd the meeting go?"

"Not bad. But I'll tell you about it later." She took a glass from the drying rack and filled it with water. She was visibly shaking. "It was interesting for another reason."

"Yeah?" Eitan adjusted the heat on the burner and prodded at the simmering eggplant. "What's that?"

"I'm pregnant."

She hadn't planned for it to come out like that—so blunt, so un-prefaced. She didn't even know how she felt, saying it out loud.

Eitan whirled around. He looked almost comical, his eyes taking up half his face. "You're kidding me, right?"

"Does that seem like the kind of joke I would make?"

"You're *pregnant?*"

"According to the First Response test I bought at Duane Reade."

Then Eitan smiled so huge that Tanya actually groaned. She was surprised, though, to find that she was holding back tears.

He threw down the spatula and practically lunged at her. "Holy shit!"

"That's what I said," she laughed, hugging him back.

"Oh, Tanya." He squeezed her then, so tight that she yelped: "Eitan, you're going to kill it."

Eitan, naturally, began to cry.

"Babe, the eggplant," Tanya said.

"Who cares about the eggplant?"

She knew then that there would be no abortion. There would be a baby. There already was one.

THERE WERE SEVERAL REASONS WHY Tanya was not going to tell her mother and sister that she was pregnant. She would tell them eventually, of course. She had no choice. But her plan was to put it off as long as physically possible.

Tanya did not enjoy attention, particularly when it came to her body. Well, that was not entirely accurate. She liked attention, though only at certain times and by certain people—namely Eitan, though sometimes she liked the feeling of being admired by other men, and even other women, as long as it was from a distance, and they were subtle and not crude about it; and only if they themselves were attractive, too, in some way.

But she was wary about showing. She saw the way people behaved around pregnant women. Suddenly their stomachs were open for public gawking and the inner workings of their bodies fair game for questioning: *Are you nauseous? Do you have cravings? Is this your first? Will you have more?*

When Tanya was younger, she'd shared a physical closeness with her sister and mother that was comfortable and natural, and now difficult for her to imagine. There'd been a time when it was easy to be naked around one another. They went skinny-dipping; they hung out together in the bathroom while one of them showered. They used the toilet without closing the bathroom door. When Tanya got her period at age thirteen, Nessa had done a live demonstration of how to insert a tampon. And when Nessa decided one day that she was going to shave off all her pubic hair "just to see what it looked like," she had shown Tanya immediately. They'd laughed and named it the Naked Mole Rat.

Things had changed, though—with their bodies and with each other. Certain details about herself that at one time seemed harmless—underarm hair, pubic hair, those mysterious little bumps around her areolae—she now kept private. To Tanya, these things screamed of sex.

Her mother and sister had a habit of staring—at themselves, at each other, at her. *What are you looking at?* she found herself wanting to yell sometimes, when they were looking too hard. But she never did because when it came down to it, she didn't want to know the answer.

Nessa Bloom doesn't believe in God, but when she gets a UTI this severe, sometimes she feels as if she's being punished for something, by someone. Sitting on a bus for four hours isn't going to help. She would have preferred to drive to Arlington, but Henry persuaded her to lend him her car for the weekend.

"Marvelous day," her seatmate announces, seemingly to Nessa. Nessa glances over. The woman's face is wide, dappled with age spots, purplish lipstick gathered at the corners of her smile. She smells of clothing that's been sitting in a closet for many years.

"It is," Nessa agrees. She smiles back, which takes effort, considering the pain she's in.

"Summer is just around the corner." The woman shifts in her seat to face Nessa head-on. "Let's hope the air-conditioning works properly."

"Right," Nessa says. She has to be careful with women like this, lonely women, hungry for conversation and connection. She has a way of attracting them.

"The last time I was on one of these Peter Pan buses, the air-conditioning broke halfway to Boston."

"Oh no."

"It wasn't too terrible because the day was cool to begin with. But on a day like this? We'd melt into our seats." The woman mimics melting by throwing her arms and head back dramatically. Then she chuckles.

"Are you going home or leaving home?" she asks, and when Nessa opens her mouth to respond, she realizes she doesn't know how to answer.

MINUTES LATER THE BUS pulls out of the depot and starts its journey down Elm Street before merging onto the Mass Pike toward Boston. Nessa gets that familiar rush in her stomach. It's not a purely bad sensation, exactly—the Wild Thing—but it's unsettling, and paired with the UTI, it produces a feeling of intense homesickness in Nessa.

Nessa returns more frequently than Tanya. It's not often that they go back to Arlington together, to the house they grew up in, and this will be the last time they ever do. Nessa crosses her legs together and squeezes.

She glances behind her at the awful little restroom at the back of the bus; wonders how long she'll be able to hold out before going back there. The woman next to her will probably get suspicious after Nessa's third or so trip. She'll think it's drugs, or maybe just diarrhea. At the very least, Nessa is grateful not to be sitting next to a cute guy, or any guy at all.

Nessa resists the urge to text Tanya again, even with an update on the UTI.

Instead she texts Henry. *Did you make it to Dr. Janeski's on time?*

She stares at her phone. He is the type to either respond immediately or not for hours, sometimes days, later. When ten minutes goes by with no response, she tucks her phone into a pocket of her backpack and leans her head against the darkened glass window and closes her eyes.

Nessa met Henry at Dr. Janeski's and she knows she has to end things with him soon if she wants to keep her job with the psychiatrist. But despite Henry's clumsiness in bed, despite the gruff way he handles her—her body and her emotions—she looks forward to seeing him.

It started a month ago when Nessa bumped into Henry at the bus stop on the corner of Main Street. At first Nessa couldn't place him. She recognized his camo hoodie, his posture—slumped. He was tall, well over six feet, but he stood as if he was in a room with low ceilings, even though he was outside. It was Henry Alden, from Dr. Janeski's office, she realized, as he flicked ash from his cigarette.

As she approached, she waited for Henry to notice her, but he didn't until she was standing right in front of him. He gave her a funny smile, as if to say, *Do I know you?*

"Henry, right?" she said.

He nodded, still smiling.

"Nessa," she said. "I'm the receptionist at Dr. Janeski's office."

"Oh," he said, nodding. "Right, right." His eyes jumped from her face, down her body. "You waiting for the bus?"

Nessa nodded even though she was only a few blocks from home, no more than an eight-minute walk. "You too?"

"Yup."

"Can I bum one?" she asked.

Henry reached into his back pocket and pulled out a pack of Camels and held it out for her.

For a moment they stood smoking, not talking, and Nessa could feel Henry looking at her. She thought back to Henry's file in the office and tried to remember what was written there. She'd been the one to create the file, to make photocopies of Henry's insurance card, write ALDEN in capital letters on the tab, put a hole-punched intake sheet in the front of the file for Janeski to take notes on during the initial consultation.

He'd been arrested that fall for stealing a taxi, she remembered then. It was his parents, who were housing and feeding him, who insisted he see a psychiatrist. *Anxiety,* Dr. Janeski had written in the diagnosis section. Janeski used an inky ballpoint pen to take notes, her spidery lettering like eyelashes clumped with too much mascara. But Nessa didn't think Henry seemed anxious.

It was inappropriate that she approached him—a HIPAA violation—and if Dr. Janeski found out, she'd be angry. It was probably the type of thing Nessa could get fired for.

Henry pulled out his phone and glanced at it. "The bus was supposed to be here ten minutes ago," he said. "I fucking hate the bus."

"Yeah," she said. "You don't have a car?"

"I do," he said. "My license was revoked, though." He rolled his eyes and smiled at her and she thought he had a nice smile. "I get it back in six weeks."

"Why'd it get revoked?" she asked.

"You're gonna think I'm crazy."

"I won't," she promised.

"I was really wasted," he started. "There was this taxi sitting there; it was over on Spring Street." He pointed in the direction of Spring Street. "The driver had gotten out, was helping this old lady carry her bags up the stairs. He left the car unlocked and running and I got in and drove away." He smiled, bashful and proud at the same time.

"Why'd you do that?" Nessa asked, smiling.

"I have no clue," he said. "It was stupid. I had to spend the night in jail and now I have to rely on fucking public transportation."

"I can give you a ride home if you want."

He raised his eyebrows. "Yeah?"

"We just have to walk to my apartment, but it's not very far."

"Sweet," Henry said.

They started down Main Street and Nessa liked the feeling of walking next to somebody so tall. It made her feel small and delicate, two things Nessa rarely felt.

She'd been living in Northampton for two years and she knew that tangle of streets around her home well—the uneven sidewalks; the houses painted unusual colors like lilac, pale green, sunny yellow; the gardens out front, which were just beginning to bloom again—but walking with Henry, she saw everything afresh.

"This is me," she said, turning into her driveway, where her car was parked. She lived alone in the upstairs of a small house. The owners lived downstairs with their Doberman.

"This is where you live?" Henry asked, looking the house up and down, the same way he'd looked at her fifteen minutes before.

Nessa nodded and clicked her fob, unlocking the car.

For a moment they both stood by the car, Nessa on the driver's side and Henry by the passenger's, though neither one of them got in.

"What's it like inside?" Henry asked.

"Do you want to see?" Nessa said, and Henry nodded.

SINCE THEN THEY'D met up once or twice a week to have sex. Usually Henry spent the night and Nessa would drive him back to his parents' house in the morning.

He was one of Janeski's psychopharm patients—he came in twice a month for his Xanax prescription and that was it. No talk therapy, so there was little chance of his sex life coming up, and he had promised Nessa he wouldn't say a word. But Dr. Janeski was smart and Nessa was easy to read. For his last appointment, Nessa hid in the bathroom on Thursday morning when Henry was scheduled, so she wouldn't be in the waiting room when Dr. Janeski came to get him.

It wouldn't be the worst thing in the world if she was fired, she reasoned. She'd been at it for two years now, and the job had gotten old. Nessa answered the phone, faxed in prescriptions, managed the billing. It was fine; mostly boring, with brief bouts of excitement, and Henry, with his boyish eyes and incredible height, had been the latest bout.

"WHAT DO YOU THINK OF DR. JANESKI?" she'd asked Henry the night before, in bed. The symptoms of her infection hadn't developed yet—they'd come on suddenly, only after Henry had dropped her off at the bus depot that morning.

"She's nice," he'd said, shrugging, and it occurred to Nessa that Henry didn't care about his psychiatrist—what he thought of her, or what she thought of him.

After she slept with Henry the first time, she'd revisited his file on several occasions. He was thirty-three, three years older than her, and worked as a landscaper. He'd been fired from most of his jobs, usually for coming to work drunk or high. Growing up he got in trouble at school and was diagnosed, incorrectly, with ADHD. According to a prior school psychologist who'd faxed over notes, when Henry was eight his mother left the family unannounced and came back a year later with a mysterious burn on her arm and the word *respect* tattooed on the inside of her bottom lip. These details touched Nessa. Not because of Henry's mother, but because they were things Henry noticed and thought about and said out loud.

SOMEDAY, when she has the money, Nessa will go to therapy. She understands herself well enough to know that she's probably a little mentally ill. She doesn't hear voices or anything like that. She's just sad a lot of the time—most of the time—not that you'd know it, necessarily, by looking at her.

TWO HOURS INTO THE DRIVE, the bus pulls into a rest stop and Nessa grabs her bag and slides past the old woman, frantic to use a real bathroom. In line, she checks her phone again. No text from Tanya or Henry, but she does have one from Jesse, her stepfather.

Bus in at 12 at South Station right?

Jesse is usually the one to pick her up or drop her off to things—he'd been doing it ever since he entered their lives, when Nessa was fourteen and Tanya was twelve. She knows that he enjoys it, helping out in these concrete and distinctly paternal ways. She can picture him now. Standing in a crowd at the station, hands in pockets, scanning eyes until he finds hers, then pulling one hand from his pocket and raising it—smiling—while walking toward her. He always insists on taking her bag, even if it's a backpack and it's already on her back. He's always on time.

Yes 12, she confirms. She adds a smiley face.

Then a stall finally opens up and Nessa hurls herself inside, almost knocking a woman over in the process. She slams the swinging door behind her, her fingers trembling as she slides the lock in place. She's taken Tanya's advice and has been drinking water all morning, and this time when she pees, she's actually able to produce something. It's such a relief, her eyes well up.

Lorraine Bloom pulls left into the parking lot for Menotomy Beer & Wine and lights a cigarette. It's nine in the morning and the liquor shop is closed, the lot empty. Menotomy is on Broadway, which is perpendicular to Winter, just around the corner from their house, out of sight. A breeze passes and the grass by the sidewalk quivers, catching light. The girls will be home soon, Nessa by bus, Tanya by car. There are things to do before they arrive.

Her phone chirps. Jesse. *Where are you?*

Traffic, she writes back. *5 min away.*

She watches the ellipsis appear on her phone, Jesse typing a response. Then the ellipsis disappears, appears again, then goes away for good. Lorraine puts her phone in the cup holder and tosses the cigarette out the window. She keeps mints and mouthwash in her glove compartment, along with a jar of peanut butter, to cover up the mint.

Lorraine rinses her mouth, eats a glob of peanut butter, and pulls out of the lot and drives slowly down Winter Street. She no longer knows any of her neighbors except for the O'Briens, the elderly couple who shares the two-family house with her and Jesse. Most of the people who lived on Winter Street when the girls were little have moved out, and at some point, Lorraine went from being the young mom of two pretty little girls to a middle-aged woman who avoids eye contact with her neighbors and sometimes smokes in their driveways before pulling into her own.

Her girls are still pretty, of course, but they're grown up now, busy with their own lives. Tanya is beautiful in the way she's always been—long, silky hair, wickedly high cheekbones, green inscrutable eyes like a cat's. Her beauty is sharp and in focus, the first thing you notice about her. She looks like their father, Jonathan. And Nessa has grown into her beauty, though her daughter still doesn't know it. Lorraine sees the way Nessa moves through the world, seeing everything except for herself—no idea that anyone might be looking at her, too. Her older daughter wears her vulnerability on her face like a milk mustache—unknowingly, cute, and just a little bit pitiful.

Lorraine can't pinpoint exactly when she was booted out of her daughters' inner circle, but it happened sometime when they were teenagers. *Normal*, is what other parents said about this sort of detachment from their mother— not that Lorraine spoke to many other parents about her relationship with her daughters. She wasn't the type of mother to befriend the other moms or host many playdates. Was that the problem, she wonders sometimes.

But no, whatever happened during those teenage years hadn't felt exactly *normal*, though nothing, she supposes, felt normal after Jonathan left.

In just a matter of months Lorraine will leave Winter Street behind. For the first time in her life, she won't live in Arlington. She was born and raised in this town. She knows it the way you know a close family member—how it smells and what its moods are, what it's like at its worst and its best, all the details that a visitor would overlook. She's watched it change over the decades, from when it was a dry town with only a handful of restaurants, back when it was mostly big, Catholic families. People seemed to know each other then.

Now Arlington has everything—Lebanese food, Indian food, Mexican— Arlington's become a *destination*. It has Starbucks. When Menotomy opened, the first beer and wine store since Prohibition, Lorraine and Jesse walked there on opening night and bought two bottles of the most expensive wine she'd ever drank and finished both of them on their front porch.

In 1985 Alewife Station was built and suddenly Cambridge and Boston were just a train ride away. People in Cambridge who couldn't afford Cambridge anymore started to move to Arlington—professors, artists, students, professionals. "Snobs," Lorraine's mother complained, back when her mother was still alive.

One of those people had been Jonathan Bloom. A corporate lawyer, Jewish, originally from New York. "Not the city, though," he'd clarified to Lorraine on their first date, as if it was something to apologize for.

"I've never been," she said.

"Where? To New York, or New York City?"

"Neither."

"I'll have to take you. We'll eat better food than this." He nodded to the pasta on their plates, and Lorraine smiled, not knowing whether to be excited or insulted. She'd brought him to her favorite restaurant in Arlington.

SHE AND JESSE can't afford to live in Arlington any longer, especially now that Lorraine is unemployed. At first Lorraine resisted when Jesse proposed the move. She doesn't know anyone in New Hampshire and she'll be farther away from her daughters. Besides, Arlington is home. She can't imagine herself anywhere else. Now, though, she's getting more used to the idea. Maybe starting somewhere new is exactly what she and Jesse need.

Jesse's car is in the driveway and Lorraine pulls in by the curb, behind the O'Briens' Volkswagen. She wants another cigarette badly, but she puts the pack back in the glove compartment where she keeps the mouthwash and the peanut butter. Jesse knows she smokes, but he's also under the impression that she's trying to quit. Their latest fight, the one they're still coming down from, was about Lorraine's smoking. Jesse came home early from work to find Lorraine in the side yard chain-smoking, a graveyard of cigarette butts scattered in the grass in front of her. Ever since she was fired from Stand Together, she's been going through a pack a day. On a bad day, sometimes more. Recently, it seems, she's always either smoking or brushing her teeth.

She was listening to music, earbuds snug in her ears, and didn't hear Jesse approach. When she felt his hand on her shoulder, fear shot through her stomach. She jumped and cried out, dropping her iPhone into the grass.

"How many of these are from today?" Jesse demanded. She'd considered lying, but the risk of being caught in a lie wasn't worth it.

"All of them."

Jesse knelt in the grass and gathered the stubs in his palm, counting. "Eight cigarettes in one afternoon." He looked up at her. "Why would you tell me you were quitting?"

"I am," she said. "I'm trying. I'm *addicted*."

He looked at her sharply.

"Sorry," she said.

He let out a harsh laugh. "Don't apologize to me. I'm not the one who's going to die of lung cancer." Then he tossed the cigarette butts back into the grass and stood. "You owe me ten bucks."

"For what?"

"What the hell do you think? The pack." He held out his hand. "Give me the rest."

Lorraine pulled the pack from her back pocket and gave it to Jesse. There were only a few more in there anyway, and she had two unopened packs in her glove compartment.

INSIDE SHE HEARS JESSE in the kitchen. He's singing and the weight lodged in Lorraine's chest lifts and floats away.

"Baby," he calls out.

In the hallway, Sally is asleep on her belly, tail twitching, so Lorraine knows she's dreaming. She reaches down and gently scratches behind the dog's ears.

"Hi, Sal baby," she whispers, and Sally stirs, opening her huge, bloodshot eyes without lifting her head. She blinks sleepily at Lorraine before closing them again. She's an old woman now, fourteen people years, ninety-eight dog years. And that's how Lorraine thinks of her: an impossibly old woman.

"She's sad personified," Nessa had said wistfully, the day they'd brought the little basset hound home as a puppy, when the girls were teenagers.

"Not everyone is *sad*," Tanya had countered.

In the kitchen, Jesse's at the stove in his boxers, and across the room, a giant bouquet sits on the table.

"Lorrie," he says, glancing over his shoulder. "I'm sorry."

She walks over to the table and touches a silken petal, ducking her head into the bouquet, inhaling. Flowers mean forgive me. Flowers mean sex. She closes her eyes and tries to make her body relax. She thinks of the woman's voice on the meditation tapes she's been listening to. *Let go of the tension in your toes. In your calves. Your knees. Breathe the negative energy out.*

She can sense him before he touches her—a tightness in the air. He buries his face between her shoulder and her jawbone and she feels the wetness of his eyes on her neck, then the pad of his lips in that same spot, and she almost laughs out loud, that he's kissing away his own tears. *What an idiot,* a voice in her head cries out, loud and mocking—though her face reveals none of it.

His kisses move from her neck to her collarbone and then he kneels down in front of her and kisses her stomach and the front of her jeans, sliding his hands up her legs.

She hopes the sex goes quickly; she has so much to do. She goes through the list in her head as Jesse picks her up and carries her to the living room. It's been days since she's washed her hair. They need more packing boxes. They're almost out of toilet paper. She imagines Tanya's repulsion at finding no toilet paper in the house.

Jesse lays her down on the couch and undresses her, removing each piece of clothing as though unwrapping a fragile gift. He folds her jeans and T-shirt neatly, pulls off her underwear, unhooks her bra, and guides her arms out through the straps.

Jesse sits on the floor beside her and begins to touch her. He's so good at touching her, and she hates him for it. He moves his hands over her, softly and tenderly. "I love you," he says, his voice like a buoy across a dark, calm sea.

For a moment she opens her eyes. From the couch she can make out the top of Sally's head, her droopy ears splayed out like pigtails on either side of her. Lorraine is glad the dog is asleep. She feels guilty having sex with Sally close by, the way she wouldn't want to have sex knowing Nessa or Tanya were in the next room.

"What?" Jesse asks.

"Sally," Lorraine says.

"Sally's fine," says Jesse.

Lorraine closes her eyes again. She lifts her hips off the couch and Jesse tightens his grip on her thigh, the other hand still moving patiently. She squeezes her eyes tighter and clenches her muscles and feels that double-sided pang of wanting and not wanting it to be over.

But it ends and she gasps and lets her hips drop.

There it is—home. The brown peeling paint, a faded chocolate, pale yellow trim on the windows and railings and doors. It's a color combination so familiar to Nessa, so native to Arlington, that a physical sensation accompanies the colors, especially today—coming home for the final time. She knows the gentle slope of the telephone wires against the pale, spring sky; the forest-green trash bins along the side of the house, the way they blend into the chocolate brown.

A Realtor's sign protrudes from their small lawn, which is barely a lawn at all. A big blue banner across: SOLD. A bunch of red balloons are tied to the porch railing, bouncing and bobbing off one another. Someone, the real estate agent probably, has put flowerpots leading up the front steps.

Inside, at first Nessa doesn't recognize her mother. From the back Lorraine looks old and small. Mostly it's her shoulders, the way she's curled into herself, her neck bent as if she's praying, though all she's doing is washing a dish. Her jeans are too big for her and the seat of her pants sag, the band of her underwear exposed.

"Mom," she says, walking up behind her, and Lorraine whirls around, a flash of alarm in her eyes. She smiles and Nessa is shocked to see that there are braces on her mother's teeth.

"Sweetie," Lorraine says, hugging her. When she pulls back, she covers her mouth with her hand. "Aren't they awful? Dr. Nathan recommended them."

"They're not so bad," Nessa says, horrified. "But I don't get it, your teeth were fine."

Jesse appears in the kitchen then with Nessa's bag. He walks over and puts his arm around Lorraine's waist and tugs her shirt down a little. Jesse has always towered over Lorraine, but today they look exorbitantly mismatched—like they're existing on two different scales. Jesse, ten years younger than Lorraine, has never quite lost his boyishness, and even though there is gray in his stubble now, and a softness in his belly, he has the look of an overgrown kid—bright-eyed and rosy-cheeked.

Nessa feels a swell of sadness at her mother's sloppiness—that she's allowed her shirt to ride up like that, that she lets her underwear show. Tanya, she's certain, will feel irritated by Lorraine's appearance, and therein lies some fundamental difference between her and her sister. Although Nessa could guess, she doesn't know how this difference came to be—that Tanya ended up one way and Nessa another.

"I can't believe it," Nessa says, glancing around. "The house already feels so empty."

Lorraine looks around the kitchen as though seeing it for the first time. "It's felt empty for a while," she says, and then she leans into Jesse, who squeezes her shoulder.

NESSA BEGINS TO WADE through the piles of clothing in her and Tanya's old bedroom. Most of it should have been thrown out years ago—bell-bottom jeans from elementary school, training bras with fraying straps, period-stained days of the week underwear. There's the denim jacket with red roses embroidered onto the back that Nessa wore almost every day in middle school, Tanya's faux-leather jacket from Limited Too, a metallic blue. Among the clothing are Ellie the Elephant and Lisa the Monkey, their fur worn and faded, their bodies limp.

Each item feels loaded and slightly magical to Nessa, the way the smell of Elmer's glue might transport you back to a specific classroom, or the opening chords of a song to a specific childhood crush. Holding the stuffed animals in her hands, Nessa is glad that Tanya isn't here yet: Tanya, who isn't drawn to nostalgia, who looks forward with a vengeance, and never back. Her sister would have rolled her eyes at Nessa, cradling these forgotten animals.

Nessa takes out her phone and snaps a picture of the room, then sits down beside the piles. She opens her texting thread with Henry and types a message: *My childhood bedroom,* she writes, and attaches the photograph. But she deletes the text and writes another: *My mom got braces, it's weird.* But she deletes that one, too. She doesn't want to scare him off, and talk of families means you want someone to understand you.

Nessa types another message: *I'm still sore from this morning.* Clicks send.

A few seconds later she gets an emoji back: a winking smiley face sticking out its tongue. And then: *Come back I miss your body.*

She smiles and puts her phone down beside her and collapses onto the floor. Then gets back up and goes to the bathroom; tries to pee but nothing comes out.

She texts Tanya from the toilet. *Mom has braces.*

Tanya's response, dictated by Siri, appears immediately: *What the actual fuck.*

A LITTLE WHILE LATER there's a knock on the bedroom door. Nessa is expecting Lorraine, but it's Jesse. "I'm going to take Sally out," he says. "Want to come?"

Nessa holds the leash—it's a new one, bright magenta patterned with paw prints. Sally plods ahead of her and Jesse at a snail's pace, each step labored and deliberate. Even as a puppy, Sally had been a subdued soul, with a melancholic bark and a tendency to fall asleep in the middle of chaos.

The year they got Sally, 2003, had been bad for Nessa, the night with Dan a looming shadow they now lived in but pretended not to. That night, when it occurred, was like turning a corner from one reality into another. But as time went on, the fuzzier it became, and the chance of ever talking about it—of going back in time and making things right—seemed to disappear completely. Tanya was barely speaking to Nessa then, and Lorraine was spending all her free time at Jesse's, and often it seemed that the only ones at home were Nessa and the puppy. Nessa used to lie with Sally after school, stroking her long, soft ears and quietly singing songs as though the dog was an infant who might one day learn the words herself.

Nessa and Jesse make their way down Winter Street, stopping every few minutes for Sally to smell a patch of lawn or study a crack in the sidewalk.

"How's work been?" Jesse asks.

"It's okay," Nessa says. "I'm pretty bored there, but it pays the bills."

A neighborhood kid on a bike teeters past, clutching the handlebars in a death grip, staring ahead with intense concentration. Up the street a man who must've been the boy's father is yelling instructions.

"You think you want to do what that doctor you work for does?" Jesse asks.

"Be a therapist?" she says, glancing at him. She feels as though she might have to pee again, but they just left the house; she wills the urge away.

Jesse nods.

"I think so." There's not a lot Nessa can picture herself doing, but she does know how to listen.

The boy's father jogs past them, holding his hand up in greeting, and she and Jesse nod hello. "There you go, buddy!" the man calls to his son. "Nice and steady."

"You get people," Jesse says to Nessa.

She shrugs; she doesn't know if he means it as a question or a statement. "Well. Kind of."

"And you're easy to talk to."

"Am I?"

"Oh yeah," Jesse says. "I've always found it easy, anyway. You listen. You were like that as a kid, too. You listen closely, and not just to the things people say, but to the things they don't say."

"Thanks. I'm glad you think so." Nessa attempts to hide how happy this makes her, though she's sure it's all over her face. Lately she's been thinking about quitting her job at Janeski's and applying for social work programs. Smith has a good one. But thinking about something isn't the same thing as doing it.

It took her until she was twenty-four to get it together to apply for college. Before that, she'd spent a number of years aimlessly following around boys. There'd been a cross-country road trip with Trevor that had ended in Montana when they ran out of money. For a while she'd lived in a dorm room at Bennington College with her boyfriend, Max, until the RA had caught on and she was kicked out. There was a year-long romance with a married man who she still received texts from sometimes. The truth was, those years were mostly boring and lonely.

At Tanya's college graduation, Nessa was overcome by the beauty of Smith's campus—the tree-lined paths, the stately brick buildings, Paradise Pond. The girls graduating called themselves Smithies and hugged one another tightly—even Tanya, who hated to hug. Nessa applied early decision to Smith and didn't tell anyone when the small envelope showed up in the mail. *We are sorry to inform you.* So she accepted an offer from UMass Amherst— the state school twenty minutes away—and started her undergraduate degree just as Tanya moved to New York City to begin law school. Nessa did well enough in the classes she was interested in and blew off the ones that bored her. She didn't graduate with honors or plans or a boyfriend.

She decided to move to Northampton, Tanya's old stomping grounds. When she saw the Smith students around town—going for coffee or brunch, or for drinks at the Green Room or Packard's, she liked to picture Tanya— happy and well-adjusted, arm in arm with another girl.

"What's this gap on your résumé?" Janeski had asked Nessa during her interview. The psychiatrist was looking for an assistant who was "detail oriented, with a psych background and a warm disposition." Nessa figured she sort of fit the bill.

"I was traveling," Nessa said.

Janeski raised an eyebrow. "Abroad?"

"I spent a lot of time in Vermont."

Janeski moved on to the next question.

It occurred to Nessa that she might have no business being a therapist. She understood sadness—often this made people feel safe around her. But she hadn't yet figured out what to do with this sadness, or how to make it go away.

Sally stops and sniffs, pattering around in a circle on the sidewalk, looking for a place to relieve herself. Nessa and Jesse stop, too.

"I've always found it easy to talk with you, too," Nessa says to Jesse. "I've been seeing this guy," she goes on. "He's one of her patients."

Jesse's eyebrows shoot up. "One of the shrink's patients?"

Nessa nods and tries to read Jesse's face. He looks amused, but something sharper, too.

"So he must be nuts, then?"

"Not any crazier than the average person."

"Oh yeah?"

"He stole a taxi," Nessa says. "The key was in the ignition, just idling. I guess the driver was carrying a woman's bags up the stairs for her. He got in and drove away."

Jesse bursts out laughing, and Nessa starts laughing, too.

"Jesus," Jesse says, "that couldn't've ended well."

"No. He got arrested."

Nessa looks down at Sally, who has just deposited four golf ball–sized turds in the middle of the sidewalk. She glances at the house they're in front of. This one looks brand-new, also a two-family home, but unlike hers, with the two front doors adjacent, like a couple holding hands, the two entrances are located on the far ends of the house, for optimal privacy. Nessa can picture the house it replaced perfectly. Small and maroon, paint peeling so bad it was spotted.

"You be careful, though," Jesse says. "This taxi thief—is he nice to you?"

"Sometimes."

"What's his deal?" Jesse asks, his voice suddenly serious. "He doesn't hurt you, does he?"

"No, no. It's nothing like that. Do you have a bag?"

Jesse pats his pockets, front and back. "Shit. No."

They smile at one another, like two kids getting away with something.

"Oh well," Nessa says, and all three of them keep walking. "He can just be kind of an asshole sometimes," Nessa goes on. "It's fine, though. I'm going to end it with him."

It's not that she needs Jesse to persuade her to stop seeing Henry. She doesn't actually care about Henry. He won't be in her life for long—she's always known that. But it feels nice when Jesse gets like this, a little worked up. Her own father has never been protective; mostly, she figures, because he just hasn't been around. Her father has always been content seeing only the top layer of things, as though digging any deeper might turn up a mess he'd prefer to avoid.

Jesse, on the other hand, sees everything.

"You think he'll listen?" Jesse asks. "Take no for an answer?"

"What choice does he have?" Nessa asks, as they cross the street to the other side, where the private school is, a brick building with a half-moon driveway out front. At one point it was a therapeutic day school for kids with emotional problems. Now it's just a normal K–8.

Up ahead, the boy on his bike barrels toward them, a terrified look frozen on his face. His father is running behind him. Nessa glances again at Jesse, who appears deep in thought and doesn't register the boy on the bike. She wonders if Jesse is thinking about her.

"If he's anything like the men I know," Jesse says, "he'll think he has all the choices in the world."

"I'm not worried," Nessa says.

"Still, if you ever need someone to tell him to get lost, you'll call me, right?"

Nessa pictures Jesse showing up at her house in Northampton, telling

Henry to get lost. There's something equal parts exciting and mortifying about this picture. "Yeah," she says. "I'll call. But I promise you it's not going to be a problem."

Jesse nods. "Good."

The boy on the bike has started to scream. "Dad!" he yells, and it surprises Nessa how high-pitched the boy's voice is, how vulnerable. "How do I stop?" he wails. "How do I brake?"

"Pedal backwards!" the father calls back. "Backwards, son!"

Nessa and Jesse and Sally stop to watch. For whatever reason, the boy seems unable to pedal backwards, seems unable to do anything at all. He continues to belt forward, his shoulders hunched up by his neck, his helmet huge and askew on his small head.

"This kid's about to eat shit," Jesse says quietly to Nessa, and though it's subtle, there's a hint of excitement in her stepfather's voice.

WHEN TANYA ARRIVES LATER that evening, Nessa and Lorraine greet her outside in the driveway.

"The traffic was horrendous getting out of the city," Tanya announces, as she embraces Lorraine and then Nessa. "It took me literally two hours to go twenty blocks."

Tanya has always had the mysterious ability to look fresh, even after a five-hour drive. Her hair is pulled up into a neat ponytail, a few dark strands framing her face, and when Nessa leans in to hug her, she gets a whiff of Tanya's shampoo—coconutty and feminine. She's wearing black linen pants and a fitted black T-shirt and tiny diamonds sparkle in her earlobes. Her face is clean, free of makeup except for her lips, which are painted a matte pink, and the slightest suggestion of blush on her cheekbones. She looks, as she always does, prettier than Nessa remembers.

"You must be starving," says Lorraine, tucking a strand of hair behind Tanya's ear.

"I snacked in the car," Tanya says, recoiling just the tiniest bit from their mother's touch. Nessa waits for Tanya to mention Lorraine's braces, but Tanya doesn't say anything. Her sister seems to be avoiding looking at their mother at all.

When they go inside, Jesse appears in the front hall. "Hi there, Tanya," he says.

She shoots him a one-second smile that doesn't reach her eyes. "Hey."

"Want me to grab that?" He reaches for her suitcase.

Tanya holds tight to her bag. "I got it."

A reaction flickers across Jesse's face before disappearing. "How was the trip?"

"Long and uneventful." Tanya pushes in the retractable handle of her rolling suitcase with a click and starts to make her way upstairs. "Ness," she says over her shoulder, her voice warming. "Want to come up?"

NESSA AND TANYA DRIVE to the Walgreens on Mass Ave. to fill Eitan's prescription. It's nice being in the car with her sister, driving past the Capitol Theatre and Quebrada Bakery; the convenience store on the corner of Mass Ave. and Everett where they used to walk to as kids to buy candy. Most things are the same. Mass Ave. is lined with apartment buildings, a mix of prewar and affordable housing—boxy buildings from the 1960s and '70s. Colonial houses interspersed among the dozens of small businesses.

They drive past the side street leading down to Spy Pond, where when they were little, their mother and father used to take them on picnics. Then, past their old high school—big, brick, and domineering with white columns and a steeple on top like a church. Nessa glances at Tanya, but her sister does not look over to the school on their right, not even for a second.

Nessa takes the first dose of antibiotics in the car, in the Walgreens parking lot.

"You really should go see your doctor."

"I know what a UTI feels like."

"Yeah, but it matters what kind of antibiotics you take."

"Did Eitan not want to write the prescription or something?"

Tanya regards Nessa with unmasked exasperation. She seems to be deciding what to say next. "The responsible thing is to go to the doctor, Nessa."

"What I really need to do is start peeing after sex."

Tanya looks out the window and Nessa wishes she hadn't said the last thing about sex.

"That place looks nice," Tanya says.

"What?"

"That café." Tanya gestures out the window, across the street. "With the yellow awning. Mom's leaving Arlington just as it's getting kind of cute."

Nessa looks at the darkened storefront with the pretty yellow awning, *Louisa's* in white script across the front. She can't imagine her mother and Jesse in a coffee shop like Louisa's, one that sells five-dollar cookies and plays mellow, indie music, a bulletin board by the front counter advertising yoga and guitar lessons.

It's the kind of place her mother might admire from outside the window, but if she suggested going in, Jesse would scoff.

"I could make you better coffee in our own goddamn kitchen," he'd say.

"It's for the atmosphere, Jesse," her mother would protest.

"I'll give you atmosphere, baby." Then Jesse would put his arm around her and squeeze tight, pulling Lorraine away from the shop.

Those were the kinds of conversations they had. She knew that Tanya found them cheesy—maybe disgusting. It reminded Nessa of teenage love. Always showing off for one another. Always flirting, always fighting.

"So what's his name again?" Tanya asks. "This guy?"

"Henry."

"Are you guys in love?" Tanya smiles at her sarcastically.

"I don't love him," Nessa says. "Sometimes I don't even like him."

"What don't you like about him?"

"He's kind of gross, actually. He picks his nose in front of me," Nessa says. "I don't think he even realizes he's doing it. Once I saw him wipe it underneath the seat in my car."

Tanya laughs. "Ew, Nessa. Did you call him out?"

"No, we don't have that kind of relationship yet."

WHEN THEY GET HOME, Nessa and Tanya and Lorraine sit on the front stoop together. The sun has set and the sky is a deep blue, punctuated by the milky streetlights up and down Winter. Across the street, a neighbor's big-screen TV flashes color in the downstairs window. When Lorraine lights a cigarette, Tanya leans back, fanning the air in front of her. "Mom, you have to quit." When Lorraine doesn't respond, Tanya shields her nose and mouth with her hands. "It's selfish to smoke."

"How do you mean?"

"You're essentially committing suicide. We want you around. We don't want to watch you—"

"Jesus, Tanya," Nessa says. "Chill." Nessa tends to forget how critical her sister is, how quick Tanya is to feel disappointed by everyone, as though each of their flaws is a direct and personal attack on her.

Lorraine puts her cigarette out on the porch step and tosses it in one of the flowerpots. "How's your dad?" she asks.

"He's good," Tanya says, her voice rising in pitch, content to change the subject now that the cigarette is out. "They're all doing well. They're going on a vacation soon, to Maine or something. Ben broke his arm a few months ago, but he just got his cast off."

Hurt tugs at Nessa. She hadn't known about their half brother's arm or the vacation in Maine.

"It's so interesting, to imagine your father having a son," Lorraine muses. "I bet he's good with him. Jonathan's always been confident enough to not get competitive with other males. I always liked that about him."

"Is Jesse like that?" Nessa asks, though she knows the answer.

"Jesse gets competitive with the mailman, for God's sake. *Why does he always wave at you like that?*" Lorraine mimics, shaking her head. "Jesus Christ. I'm glad you two are girls. He adores you."

"What about Eitan?" Nessa asks.

"He's secure," Tanya answers shortly. She seems bored by the conversation, or annoyed with it; Nessa can't tell which.

"He's so handsome, Eitan," Lorraine says to Tanya, in a low, confiding voice, like a girl at a sleepover.

Tanya doesn't respond, but she leans her head on Lorraine's shoulder and closes her eyes. "I'm tired, Mom," she says, suddenly soft and childlike, and Lorraine puts her arm around Tanya's shoulders. Nessa envies that about her sister, Tanya's ability to be nurtured by Lorraine.

"I'm so happy my girls are home," Lorraine says. She puts an arm around Nessa, too, and Nessa sinks into it, and for a moment there's a feeling of closeness, like they might all sit there for a while—but then Tanya lifts her head and says, "It's too cold out here."

"Go inside, honeys," Lorraine says. "I'll be in in a minute."

Nessa and Tanya stand up and go inside, leaving Lorraine on the steps so she can smoke in peace.

That night, Nessa wakes up suddenly from a nightmare—it's a recurring tooth one, where her teeth crumble in her mouth and she spits the bones, practically dust, into her palm. She sits up, swiping her tongue along her teeth, which are still there, tight and whole in her gums.

The house is humming with something—Nessa doesn't know what, but she realizes then that she was woken by a loud noise. A door slamming. Next to her, Tanya is asleep, curled on her side, holding a pillow. Nessa eases out of bed and makes her way down the hallway, her bare feet cold on the wood floors. Lorraine's door is open and Nessa steps inside. The walls, blank and naked, stare out into the room. No one's in bed.

Downstairs, she follows the light from the kitchen, and when she turns the corner, she sees her mother. Lorraine is on the floor, leaning against the cabinets in her nightgown, knees up. Her head is tilted, so that her right ear is almost touching her right shoulder, and she's holding her neck. When she looks up at Nessa, Nessa sees that the white of her mother's left eye is no longer white but a deep, wet red and the other one is marbled with red freckles.

Nessa runs to her. Up close Lorraine smells. It's strong and nauseating—an artificial floral mixed with rot and sweat. It's not a familiar smell, and that, for some reason—even more so than her mother's eyes—frightens Nessa. Lorraine slides one of her hands to the front of her throat and gently tenses her fingers, and immediately Nessa understands that Jesse has done this to her.

"Where is he?" Nessa says.

"He left."

Nessa starts to stand. "I'm calling the police," she says, but Lorraine grabs her violently by the wrist and, despite herself, Nessa sits.

"I don't want the police involved." Lorraine glances around the kitchen, the blood in her eyes glimmering brilliantly.

Then there are footsteps and they both look up, terrified, but it's only Tanya in the doorway. "Oh my God," Tanya says, her eyes wide. She looks at Nessa for an answer, but Nessa shakes her head, speechless.

"I need you to bring me to the hospital," Lorraine says, not to Nessa or Tanya but to the empty space between them.

Tanya rushes over and they each put an arm under Lorraine and together all three of them stand, the smell so strong it's embarrassing. Nessa has a vision then, of the future, when Lorraine is old and she and Tanya will have to help their mother go from sitting to standing.

"We'll take the rental," Tanya says. "I'll grab my purse."

Tanya drives and Nessa sits in back with her mother, holding her hand, which is soft and surprisingly cool. Lorraine keeps her eyes open and stares straight ahead out the front window. In the rearview mirror Nessa sees that Tanya's eyes are clear and her face is steady, but her sister's knuckles are white on the wheel and she's driving fifteen miles over the speed limit.

It's the middle of the night and the roads are nearly empty, Mass Ave. a smooth, black ribbon unfurling before them. They sail through green light after green light, as if the city knows what's going on and is ushering them through. Nessa looks out the window at the other night travelers—mostly trucks. She wonders where Jesse is. At a bar, most likely, or driving. She pictures Jesse with his hands around her mother's neck. Imagining it makes something in her own throat tighten, so that for a moment she's unable to swallow or take a breath, her throat is so thick with panic.

She thinks about the time a Tinder date she brought home put his hands around her neck during sex. "Do you like this?" he said, applying pressure. It was the only question he'd asked her the entire night to which he sounded genuinely interested to know the answer. It surprised Nessa; he'd seemed so mild.

"Yes," she told him.

His name was Nick and they'd continued to have sex for the rest of the summer. They never went on a date, though. He wasn't interested in anything serious, he told her.

She kept waiting for him to do it again. He hadn't, and she'd been too embarrassed to ask. There was always the possibility of it, though, and that was what made it interesting. At the end of the summer, he told Nessa that he had a girlfriend and he couldn't see her anymore.

Nessa glances again at her mother. Then she rolls down the window and the cool spring air whooshes into the car, filling up the silence and masking the flower rot.

WHEN THEY LIMP into the emergency room at the Somerville Hospital, a nurse walks briskly over, pushing a wheelchair. "Easy now," she says, helping Lorraine into it. The nurse looks neither surprised nor alarmed by Lorraine's eyes or the red marks that have started to appear around her neck. "It's quiet tonight," she says to Lorraine. "You shouldn't have to wait long to see the doctor."

"Thank you," Lorraine says. "These are my daughters," she adds, lifting her hand. "I'd like them to come with me."

The nurse looks at Nessa and Tanya and smiles. "Pretty, just like their mom."

Nessa and Tanya follow them down the hallway, the nurse pushing Lorraine along in the wheelchair. It gives Nessa a weird feeling, the fact that her mother seems to know who the nurse is, and how small Lorraine looks in the wheelchair—how comfortable she seems easing into it, like she's done it before.

Tanya is having trouble breathing. Something smells strange in the hospital room—bad—and every time she looks directly at her mother, the blood in Lorraine's eyes sends a wave of nausea so powerful up through Tanya's gut that she almost has to run out of the room to vomit. In order to avoid direct eye contact, Tanya looks at her mother's forehead and blurs her vision whenever she turns in Lorraine's direction. Luckily Nessa is doing the hand-holding. If Tanya was forced to touch her mother in this state, she is almost certain she would vomit.

"Where the fuck is the doctor?" Tanya says for the third time, glancing at her phone. It's 1:14 in the morning. Eitan is definitely asleep.

"I'm sure he'll be here soon, honey," Lorraine answers, her voice a painful rasp, and Tanya regrets asking.

"Excuse me for a sec." Once Tanya is in the hallway, she breaks into a run. She makes it to a single, handicap-accessible bathroom just in time, slamming the door behind her.

When Tanya was little, she used to cry when she threw up. Not afterward, but while it was happening. As if one action triggered the other. She doesn't know why it happened this way, only that it did. She's grown out of it, though, vomiting and crying simultaneously. But now, as she hurls into the pristine hospital toilet, hot tears leak out, like some sort of physiological reaction.

"Fuck," she mutters into the toilet bowl, once the contents of her stomach have emptied. She looks up. Above the toilet there's a laminated flyer: *It hurts to call but it hurts more not to. Call our 24/7 hotline to speak with a trained domestic violence counselor if you or someone you know . . .*

She flushes, then stands to examine the damage in the mirror, but her face isn't as bad as she thought it would be. She hasn't cried enough for her eyes to have puffed, and after rinsing her face and mouth with cold water, she appears presentable.

She pulls out her phone and calls Eitan.

He answers on the second ring. "Are you okay?" His voice, half-asleep, is laced with alertness and concern. He's used to waking up quickly from being on call.

"I'm okay, but my mom's not." For a moment her own voice catches and she wonders if she's going to cry again, but she regains control. "Jesse strangled her. We're in the emergency room waiting for the doctor."

She glances at the flyer above the toilet and thinks of tearing it down— as if it might be bugged, as if it might be watching her.

"Oh my God, Tanya." She pictures him sitting up in bed. "Do you want me to come?"

"No," Tanya says. "I mean yes, of course. But I don't think it would be a good idea."

"What the hell happened?"

"I don't know. We're still trying to figure it out." Tanya turns away from the mirror and begins pacing the bathroom. "To be honest, Eitan, I'm not surprised this happened. I mean, of course I'm shocked. You don't expect to wake up in the middle of the night and see that—but Jesse is a classic abuser. Manipulative, controlling, insecure, power-hungry. God knows he's been emotionally abusing her for years. It should come as no surprise that he beats the shit out of her, too. I just thought I would have picked up on something like this, or that if it had gotten to this point, she would have left him, you know?"

As she says the words, she wonders if they're honest. It is true that she hadn't been aware of Jesse's physical abuse. But also, Tanya has never allowed herself to think about such possibilities. She hardly goes home. She calls her mother once a month, if that, and they don't talk about anything personal. Tanya never asks about Jesse.

"Tanya—"

"Unless this is the first time this happened, in which case, let's just get him arrested and be done with it as quickly as possible. Photograph the injury—there are witnesses of course, we went to the ER; we have literally all the evidence we need. We'll get a restraining order; he'll be out of our lives forever, and we'll never have to see his hideous fucking face again."

"Tanya—"

"What?"

"Are you okay?"

"Yeah."

"You're talking really, really quickly."

"Is . . . this . . . better?"

She can hear Eitan gather his breath. "You must be really frightened." He's using his soft voice, the one she associates with his religious side, with his desperate wish to be a father, with the effortless, practically ridiculous way he seems to love her.

"I don't have time for therapy," she says. "I need to get back to my mom. I'll call you later, okay?"

"Please do. Tanya, tell me if you change your mind and you want me to come up."

"I'll let you know," she says, but she knows with certainty there is no chance of this happening. Her life with Eitan is a separate thing from her life with her family. She doesn't want to mix the two. She doesn't want to take the chance of contaminating something sweet with something insidious.

I'm done with him," Lorraine says. She's sitting up in bed in her hospital gown, and Nessa is beside her on a rolling stool. Tanya, who has just come back from the bathroom, rolls furiously closer to the bed on another stool.

"We should have him arrested," Tanya says, pulling out her phone. "Like, now."

Lorraine makes a sharp movement with her head and then winces. "No."

"Why not?"

"It will only make him angrier."

"Well, will he leave?" Tanya asks.

Her sister is wearing her coat over her pajamas, but there's still something professional about the way Tanya looks, leaning forward with her legs crossed, her phone securely in her hand, like a weapon. Nessa feels herself begin to shrink in her younger sister's presence.

"Leave where?" Lorraine asks.

"The house."

"He lives there, Tanya."

Tanya balks. "Well, he needs to get the fuck out. We're not going home if he's going to be there."

"I can't just kick him out, Tee."

"Fuck yes, you can. If you don't want to report it to the police, which, by the way, you absolutely should, you can get a restraining order, in which case he will be legally obligated to leave."

In the harsh hospital lighting, her mother's face is washed out, with streaks and crumbles of mascara surrounding her blood-red eyes. "I don't want to make a scene," Lorraine says.

"He's the one who made the scene, Mom," Tanya cries. "Look at you!"

Lorraine doesn't respond. The floral rot smell has intensified and Nessa realizes that she's been holding her breath, trying not to inhale.

"Mom, has this ever happened before?" Nessa asks.

"No," Lorraine says forcefully. "We got into an argument. It's complicated."

"What's complicated about that?" Tanya points at Lorraine's neck.

Lorraine lowers her gaze. "I hit him first."

"I don't care." Tanya's eyes are wild. Something shifted since her sister came back from the bathroom. She has gone from stunned to furious, and Nessa feels a little frightened of Tanya—of what might possibly come out of her mouth. She doesn't know Tanya in the same way she did when they were younger. Or rather, Tanya doesn't let herself be known. In moments like these, Tanya goes elsewhere—and Nessa is left guessing and useless.

"He strangled you, Mom," Tanya says. She looks viciously to Nessa for help, but Nessa feels frozen. She's experienced this before: paralysis born from shame. That she hadn't known Jesse was capable of doing this. That she should have known. And even worse: that Jesse was somebody who she trusted. Someone she felt close to, maybe someone she loved. All of it feels unbearable.

"How long has this been going on?" Nessa finally asks, Tanya's eyes boring into her. Though it doesn't make sense, Tanya's rage seems directed at her.

"There is no *this*, Nessa," Lorraine says, but she's still looking at Tanya. "We got into an argument and we both lost control. It happens sometimes."

"This is more than an argument," Tanya says. "I can't believe I'm having to say this to you. You'd be stupid to let him back in the house."

"Tanya," Lorraine says. "Don't talk to me like that."

"Talk to you like what?" Tanya bursts back. "Talk to you like I don't want you to die in your own kitchen? Do you understand how fucked up this is?"

"What was the fight about?" Nessa asks.

"He heard what I said about him," Lorraine says, her voice breaking—the most emotion she's shown the entire night. "The thing about the mailman. And your father being confident. I can't believe I said that, like a fucking idiot, when he was just inside."

There's a single knock on the door then, and a doctor wearing a white coat strides in without waiting for a response, a man so thin he's almost concave. "Lorraine," he says, his voice deep for how slight he is. He makes his way to their mother's bed and Nessa and Tanya both roll their stools away to give him room.

"Dr. Reimer. These are my daughters, Nessa and Tanya."

Dr. Reimer turns his attention briefly to Nessa and Tanya, shaking both their hands before turning back to Lorraine. "How are you feeling?"

Lorraine smiles wryly and Nessa's stomach churns at the sight of her mother's braces. "I've been better."

"I'd like to ask you a few questions about tonight. Would you prefer your daughters to stay here or wait outside?"

Lorraine looks at Nessa and Tanya skeptically. "They can stay."

Dr. Reimer glances at the electronic chart that is open on a standing computer in a corner of the room, then sits down beside their mother. "Can you tell me the events of what happened this evening?"

"My husband. We got into an argument," Lorraine starts. She reaches up to touch the top of her head and Nessa notices then how greasy her mother's hair is. She's not sure how she missed it before. "He threw a bottle of soap at me. He poured it over me. Then he choked me."

Nessa feels nauseous. She glances at Tanya, whose face is stripped of emotion. Now that the doctor is in the room, Tanya seems oddly reticent, willing to take a backseat.

"Did you lose consciousness?"

"No."

"You didn't see stars or anything like that?"

Lorraine squints her eyes. "A little, maybe."

Dr. Reimer nods. "Describe it to me. The stars."

"In my peripheral vision. Kind of like a head rush. Flashing lights."

"How does it feel to swallow?"

Lorraine holds a hand to her throat and swallows. "It's alright. It hurts a little."

"Any ringing in your ears?"

Lorraine shakes her head.

Dr. Reimer stands. "Look up for me?" he says, and Lorraine cranes her neck. Dr. Reimer examines her, touching her glands. "Any pain?" he asks, and when Lorraine swallows, Nessa can see in her mother's eyes that he's hurting her.

"A little," she says.

"You have subconjunctival hemorrhaging," he tells her, and when Lorraine looks at him blankly, he says: "The blood vessels in your eyes burst."

Lorraine looks surprised and glances over at Nessa and Tanya. "They did?"

The doctor nods. He sits down again, beside her, and when he speaks again his voice is softer than before. "Lorraine, I'm wondering if you'd like to speak with a counselor. We can get one here, right now." He's asked her this before. It's clear.

Lorraine shakes her head. "I don't need a counselor," she says.

"Excuse me for pushing, Lorraine, but I have to tell you—you do."

THEY LEAVE THE HOSPITAL an hour later with instructions to rest, and with a phone number for a domestic violence hotline, should Lorraine change her mind.

They don't speak on the car ride home, though the silence in the car feels different this time: strained. Lorraine and Nessa don't hold hands. Tanya still speeds, but her turns aren't as gentle. Nessa rolls down her window and lets her hand surf through the air until Lorraine asks her to close it because she's cold.

When they pull into the driveway, it's three a.m. and Jesse's car isn't there.

"What if he comes back?" Tanya asks, putting the car in park.

"He won't," Lorraine says. "I texted him. He's going to stay at a friend's house."

"And what about tomorrow?" Tanya presses.

Lorraine sighs. "We'll deal with it tomorrow. Let's just go to bed."

THAT NIGHT NESSA cries as quietly as she can into her pillow. She hates how Tanya had looked at her in the hospital room; how frustrated her sister had seemed at Nessa for not knowing what to say, or for saying the wrong things. Her sister hasn't come back to bed, and Nessa thinks it must be because Tanya is angry with her.

Nessa wishes she had never gone on that walk with Jesse. She's embarrassed by how good it had felt when he complimented her, when he offered to tell Henry to get lost. She's ashamed that the first feeling she had when Tanya brought up the restraining order was one of loss. That she might never see Jesse again.

But Nessa is frustrated with Tanya, too. It's easy to peer into other people's relationships—to make judgments and adjustments—when you have someone who loves you waiting for you at home. Women like Tanya never have to worry about being alone.

Nessa pulls out her phone and composes a text to Henry. *I miss you,* she writes. She knows she won't send it, but she lets the words sit there in the outgoing box.

Then, something astonishing happens. An ellipsis appears. Henry is writing her a message. Immediately, Nessa stops crying and waits, her heart pounding. The ellipsis disappears.

She waits up for an entire hour, but his message never comes.

T anya doesn't go back to bed that night. She sits on the stairs with her phone in her hand, waiting for Jesse.

A car pulls in front of the house at five a.m. and Tanya stands, her heart doing such violent, out-of-control things, her entire body is palpitating. She holds her phone in one hand and her keys in the other. She took a krav maga class a few years back, and she rehearses the moves in her mind. She remembers the fighting stance, one leg behind the other, the jutting out of her elbow. Jesse wouldn't hurt her, though. He's too smart, too calculating to do something that stupid. That was the thing about Jesse that her mother didn't understand. His outbursts weren't bursts at all. They were entirely controlled.

She thinks about Eitan and what he would say if he knew she was waiting up to fend off Jesse. She's sure her husband would have thoughts about it. *Let me at least come up and help you,* he'd say. But Tanya learned a long time ago that the only person who can really protect her is her.

Jesse stumbles in. He pulls the door shut and then his head snaps up, registering Tanya. He smells like a brewery.

"You can't stay here," she says quietly. She doesn't want to wake up Lorraine or Nessa.

He glances around. "I'll sleep on the couch."

"No."

He sighs. "Tanya."

She hates it when he says her name. "What?"

"How is she?" His face crumples then, and Tanya sees that he's been crying, that his eyes are red, his face blotched.

"How the hell do you think?"

He slides to the floor and puts his head in his hands.

"You have thirty seconds to get out," Tanya says. "If you don't I'm calling the cops."

JESSE LEAVES, but Tanya's heart does not slow. She lies on the couch, clutching the blue throw blanket, her eyes wide-open. Images play through her mind, images she doesn't want to think about. Things she hasn't thought about in years. She tries to focus on stupid shit like the color of the walls and the wool of the blanket against her chin and her forearms. She tries to visualize Eitan—his eyes, his nose, his arms—her apartment back in New York. But she keeps seeing the hungry expression on his face as he walked toward her that night, the dim light of the bedroom; space restricting.

Tanya sits up. She goes to the front door and jiggles the doorknob. Locked. This makes no difference, of course; Jesse has a key. Still, it calms her. She goes to the kitchen and flips on the lights; avoids looking at the spot where just a few hours ago Lorraine was sprawled on the floor. Opening the refrigerator and the freezer, she surveys its innards. Processed foods, takeout containers, frozen dinners. Dismal but unsurprising.

She settles on an apple with peanut butter. Her mother buys Skippy, Super Chunk. The kind a child would choose. Then again, she reasons, it could be Jesse's. As she eats, early morning sun drifts in through the windows in soft, warm patches. She thinks of the light in her mother's room upstairs and wonders what Lorraine's face will look like that morning—whether it will have changed shape and color with the passing hours.

Tanya's crunching and the hum of the refrigerator are the only noises in the house. The quiet here, in comparison to the city, is unsettling. Downright frightening. Tanya wonders how she handled it as a child, all those hours at night of uninterrupted silence. She had Nessa, though, right above her in the top bunk. Breathing and sighing and murmuring. That was the thing about sharing a room with a sister. It was never actually silent. Sometimes Tanya could practically hear her sister think.

She finishes her apple and goes upstairs to find her running clothes. Upstairs Nessa is asleep. The shades are drawn and their bedroom is a soft sapphire blue, the same blue morning light from girlhood.

Nessa stirs on her side of the room. When they were teenagers they'd disassembled their bunk bed and put each bed against opposite walls. "What time is it?" she asks.

"Early," Tanya says, as she rummages through her suitcase. "Go back to sleep."

Nessa turns over, pulling the covers with her.

Downstairs Tanya sits on the bottom step and ties her running shoes. He appears again in her mind. Not just his face but his entire body. And this time she can smell him. Smoky, washed hastily, but underneath, something putrid, like ham gone bad. Tanya jumps up, pressing her palms to her eyes, and shakes her head as if to shake away the thoughts.

She runs outside and immediately she feels better, out of that stifling house. The day has hardly begun—the sun low in the sky, the homes on Winter Street quiet and still with sleep. Tanya takes off in the direction of Mass Ave., past the empty tennis courts and playground on the school grounds, past the school itself, which is reassuring to Tanya—it always has been—even when the attending students had behavioral problems and she could hear them yelling all the way from her house.

The closer she gets to Mass Ave., the nicer the houses become. A number of the homes from her childhood have been knocked down and replaced with bigger, more modern versions. She reaches Mass Ave., the artery that runs all the way from Boston out to the suburbs. If she were to turn left on Mass Ave., pretty soon she would reach North Cambridge—gritty and not much to look at, perpetually noisy with the stop and start of traffic, the feeling of being both populated and abandoned—before moving deeper in where eventually Cambridge becomes lush with brick and ivy, bridges over the Charles, crawling with students. That little cushion of Crimson safety.

And then there's Central Square. When she thinks of Central Square, she thinks of an exposed scar, how it grows darker and uglier in sunlight. She avoids Central whenever possible.

Tanya turns right, runs in the direction of Arlington Center, and beyond that, the wealthier suburbs—Lexington and Concord. Hometown of the Revolution. Spacious houses with nice yards, the best public schools in the state. She pictures her father and Simone and Ben, still asleep in their big, quiet bedrooms in Lexington.

Tanya picks up speed, runs past the bus stop and a row of mailboxes and a teenage boy, high out of his mind. Pretty soon all of it bleeds together. The world's a blur, and Tanya's breathing steadies.

Nessa wakes to find Tanya is out and Jesse hasn't come home. She borrows her mother's car. She doesn't know the exact address, but she knows it's on Inman in Central Square. Once she finds the street, Dan's house is easier to locate than she thought it would be. It's quick, too, only a twenty-minute drive. She takes Mass Ave., passing Porter Square then Harvard Square, driving farther into the city. It's alarming, how close he was to them all those years. She wonders, with horror, if she's ever passed him on the street or been on the same subway car with him without realizing. And if she were to see him now, she wonders, would she recognize him?

She's drawn there, it seems, by some force outside of herself. Once she arrives, she sits parked across the street, staring. The Christmas-striped couch is still on the porch and there's one car in the driveway, a silver Honda, splattered with dirt, Rhode Island license plates.

Time has a way of warping dimensions. The duplex is smaller than she remembered it and closer to the street. The tiny lawn out front is no more than a narrow strip, a bit like their own, but it's a vibrant green—cared for. The entire property is neater and healthier than it is in her memory, almost as though the house itself has gotten a haircut, lost some weight. It occurs to Nessa that Dan might no longer live there, though she can't imagine somebody new choosing to keep that damp, weathered couch on the front porch.

It's the first and only time she's been back since that night fourteen years ago with Tanya, and she doesn't know why she's here, except that last night, after they got home from the hospital, she dreamt of him for the first time in years. She fell asleep thinking about Jesse and woke up thinking about Dan. Somehow the two meshed into one. Even in her dream, they were interchangeable, one turning into the other, again and again. In the dream it seemed logical, the way things do in dreams. She didn't question it. When she woke up, it seemed to her a sort of answer or clue.

Something is happening inside Nessa. She's sweating and her stomach is making noises. It's guilt, she realizes; she's steeping in it. She imagines him inside, slumped in the La-Z-Boy, head back, feet up, unsuspecting. She wonders what Tanya would think if she knew Nessa was here. If Tanya would hate her for coming here, or if she would understand completely. She wonders if Tanya dreams of Dan, too. Nessa would never ask her. Even the thought of such a question makes her weak with shame—but still, Nessa wonders.

Nessa stays parked there for fifteen minutes, watching the duplex for signs of life. It remains still enough to be a photograph.

1999

Nessa was about to turn thirteen when her father moved out of 12 Winter Street. Their home, which had always felt like a nest to Nessa, in the non-negotiable way it held her and her family, suddenly seemed flimsy and unreliable. Certain things that had always been there took on a new meaning. For example, the small swamp out back.

"Check out our water view," Lorraine would say to the men she brought home, in a voice that was supposed to be funny.

Nessa and Tanya could hear them talking from the living room, where they spent most of their time those days, watching television and movies. When they heard the front door open after one of her dates, Nessa turned down the TV and listened. She liked to know what the man's voice sounded like, to hear what Lorraine's voice sounded like with him.

Before bringing him to the kitchen Lorraine always poked her head in to check on them. "How's it going, girls?" she asked. "Did you eat enough?"

They would nod and smile her away. Their mother felt guilty about leaving them alone, but Nessa understood Lorraine needed those men. Since their father left, Lorraine's loneliness had taken root and bloomed into something wild and frightening.

Lorraine was always in a better mood when she was seeing someone—that was when the best parts of their mother came out, and she was goofy and affectionate and laughed at all of Nessa's and Tanya's jokes. But her moods could come crashing down with no warning, and then she'd disappear into her room for days, where she'd complain on the phone to her friends about the latest breakup, and sometimes to Nessa, too, when Nessa would bring her up snacks and chilled bottles of seltzer.

As odd as it was having strange men in the house, their mom was happier with them, so Nessa preferred it that way, too. Tanya never liked it, though. It didn't matter to Tanya who the man was or what kind of mood Lorraine was in around him. "They all suck," she commented to Nessa, "compared to Dad."

NESSA WAS TALL enough then that she no longer needed to hoist herself up on the counter to see the water view from their kitchen window. In the night, the swamp looked black and soft, like a hole you could fall into. This was the spot where Lorraine kissed the men she brought home. She showed them the water, then turned around and let them press her against the counter, let them run their hands up and down her sides and her back. Nessa didn't know how she knew this was what happened, but she did. Their voices stopped and a certain kind of silence radiated from the kitchen into the living room that only Nessa could hear. She could tell by the way Tanya sat beside her, not bothering to breathe quietly, that her sister didn't notice it.

Alone in the kitchen, Nessa would turn around so her back was pressed against the counter and lean back, pretend that she was about to be kissed. She would close her eyes and wrap her arms around herself, let her hands linger over her brand-new, miniature breasts. She loved them, more than anything else about herself. The soft way they felt under her palms, but especially the way they looked, hidden but not hidden, beneath her shirts.

BECAUSE NESSA WAS OLDER, she slept on the top bunk. She liked being up there, in her cocoon, where the wall met the ceiling and she couldn't sit up straight without hitting her head. When she leaned over the side of the bunk she could reach out and touch the ceiling fan. She used it as her own personal place to store her things. Whenever she needed something, she just leaned over and spun the fan until the blade she wanted was closest. She kept her lip gloss and nail polish and compact mirror on one blade, her art supplies on another, and a pack of cigarettes she found in her mother's purse on the third. Lorraine started smoking after their father left because she thought it would help her lose weight. Her mother would've been upset if Nessa knew about the smoking, so Nessa pretended not to notice when her mother's breath and hair smelled of it, or when she disappeared into the side yard for five-minute spurts. Sometimes when Nessa was alone in the house she would take a cigarette out of the pack and purse it between her lips, blow pretend smoke into somebody's pretend face, and whisper her name to the ceiling. *I'm Nessa,* she'd say, as though someone had asked her who she was.

Lorraine's bedroom was down the hall, but ever since their father moved out, she didn't like sleeping in there alone. Sometimes she slept in their room, on the bottom bunk with Tanya. She said she would sleep up top with Nessa, but she always had to pee in the middle of the night and she didn't like climbing down in the dark.

LORRAINE WORKED IN A CENTER for adults with developmental disabilities, called Stand Together, helping them do things like dress and eat and bathe. Some of them needed support to make meals or apply for jobs, and she helped them do things like that, too. On Fridays they went out on trips, to local parks or to Dunkin' Donuts. Lorraine's days were long, but she said her work was meaningful, helping those in need live happier lives.

Lorraine said there were two types of people in the world: givers and takers. She was a giver, and their father, apparently, was a taker. "That's what made it work, at first," Lorraine explained, "but also what made it fall apart."

The way Lorraine talked to Nessa, like she was an adult, Nessa knew her mother thought Nessa was a giver, too. Lorraine thought they were the same that way and it made Lorraine feel connected to Nessa, in a different way than how she was connected to Tanya. What her mother didn't realize back then was that Nessa *was* a taker. She took more than anybody realized.

Sometimes it was little things: dollar bills in Lorraine's night table drawer, or hats and mittens she found in the school lost and found. During art class she slipped glitter glue pens and erasers into her pockets, and one time she walked out with an entire box of markers and no one noticed. After Halloween that year she snuck Tanya's candy so she could save hers, make it last longer.

In the free hour she had after school, before Tanya or her mother got home, Nessa really went crazy. She liked to eat an entire microwave pizza, plus a handful of cookies, and then she'd take a bag of goldfish up to her room with her to snack on while she did her homework. By the time dinner rolled around, Nessa was stuffed and bloated, but she still ate whatever her mother put on the table, even if it was another microwave pizza. They had to go to the grocery store twice as often those days.

Recently, she'd taken something bigger: a watermelon-flavored lip gloss from the convenience store, even though she had the money to pay for it in her pocket. It was easier than she expected it to be, just a matter of curling the little thing into her jacket sleeve and walking out, dumb and innocent, which was how she looked anyway. Every morning she took it down from the fan and dabbed it on her lips before school. It made her lips shine in a soft, pink way that reminded Nessa of the way flowers looked in rain. When Tanya asked to borrow some, she went back to the store the next day and took one for her, too.

LORRAINE MET HER men on a dating website that her friend Wendy helped her sign up on. Nessa snooped on her mother's computer sometimes—the dating site was usually open—just to see what might be coming. There were three pictures of her mother up there, two of them photos she'd seen before in the albums they had downstairs, one of them unfamiliar. In the first one, Lorraine was wearing her favorite leopard-print blouse, and she had her hand on her hip. She looked clean and pretty and a little bit annoyed, like whoever was taking the picture had made a stupid joke. Nessa imagined her father saying, *Flash those pearly whites, babe,* which was something he'd said before, back when he still called Lorraine babe. Then there was a close-up of Lorraine's face, in midlaughter, her eyes squinty and sparkly. Nessa recognized it from a photograph her father had taken of her and Tanya and their mother on the beach, but the photo had been cropped so that all you could see of Tanya and Nessa were the tops of their tanned shoulders.

The third one barely looked like Lorraine at all. She was wearing a black dress Nessa had never seen before and was gazing at the camera with big eyes and lips that were just barely touching, like she was about to lean in and tell you a secret.

Nessa clicked around and saw that Lorraine was messaging back and forth with a man named Raymond. Raymond was balding and had a soft bulgy nose and a smile that was nice but hesitant, like he wasn't sure if he should show his teeth or not. He had asked Lorraine if she would like to get dinner with him, and she had answered that yes, she would. Then he listed four different restaurants they could go to, and though Lorraine hadn't responded yet, Nessa knew that his list was probably disappointing to her mother. Lorraine didn't like making decisions like that; she preferred the man to take charge.

IT WAS A FRIDAY, which meant they were spending the night at their father's. Nessa and Tanya packed overnight bags to bring over to the new apartment complex where Jonathan now lived. His building had an indoor pool and an elegant lobby downstairs with big comfortable chairs and vending machines and, to Nessa, the feeling of staying at a nice hotel.

SOMETHING WILD · 59

Their father had been away for work in Salt Lake City, and it was the longest that she and Tanya had ever gone without seeing him—six weeks.

Nessa was in the kitchen with her mother when they heard him pull up and honk. Lorraine, who was chopping vegetables, shook her head and smiled angrily.

"Nessa," she said, without looking up. "Will you tell your father to please come in?"

"Sure," Nessa said, and she ran outside to get him.

Her father's car was out front, humming with heat and music. His windows were tinted and when he saw her he rolled his down and stuck his head out. "Hi, Ness."

Nessa waved. His face was shaved clean and his hair was shorter than the last time she'd seen him. She tried to smile, but it turned out feeling ugly, like when you smile for a photograph and you know without even seeing it that it came out poorly.

"Mom wants you to come in," she said.

Jonathan smiled a little, like he was expecting Nessa might say this, and he turned to the passenger seat and that was when Nessa realized that someone else was in the car with him. "Give me two minutes," he said. And though she couldn't see who he was speaking to, Nessa knew by his tone of voice that it was a woman. The idea of her father with another woman made something painful tighten in Nessa's chest. The truth was, it was an entirely different matter than her mother with another man, mostly because Jonathan was someone who knew what he wanted while Lorraine was someone who was still trying to find what she needed.

Nessa ran ahead so that she could watch from the front hall as her father walked up to the house. It wasn't often that she got to see him coming home anymore, and she wanted to commit it to memory.

When he came inside, Lorraine appeared in the hallway with a fresh coat of lipstick and a spatula in her hand. "How was your trip?" she asked squeakily. "I wanted to touch base with you about Tanya's medication."

"Still taking the heartburn stuff?" He stuffed his hands in his coat pockets. "The trip was good, thanks. Busy."

Lorraine nodded. Her face was serious, the one she used when she spoke about her clients. "Yes. She should take it thirty to fifty minutes before eating. Not after she eats, otherwise it's not as effective." She glanced at Nessa. "Nessa knows the drill."

Her father smiled and rubbed his hands together. "Yup. Great. Same as last time."

"Tanya's still packing. Want to come in?" She nodded toward the front door, which he had left open. "You're letting in the cold air."

"Sorry about that." He shut the door. "Is she almost ready?"

"I don't think so," Lorraine started to say, but then Tanya appeared at the top of the stairs, her backpack so stuffed it was practically exploding off her back. "Hi, Daddy," she said, and then without warning she swung the backpack off her back and pitched it down the stairs where it landed with a thud at the bottom.

"GIRLS, THIS IS SIMONE," Jonathan announced as Nessa and Tanya climbed into the backseat, Tanya singing, *Jingle bells, Batman smells, Robin laid an egg.* When Tanya realized there was another person in the car she stopped singing and froze.

"My friend from work," he added.

Simone turned around and smiled. She was pretty, not in the soft, flowery way their mother was pretty, but in a gorgeous way—in the kind of way that you can't quite believe you're looking at a real person. Her skin was olive toned, her features lush and dramatic—rosebud lips, eyes the shape and color of almonds, hair that was somehow brown and gold and bronze all at the same time.

"I've been looking forward to meeting you two," she said. She stuck out her arm to shake hands, but they both just stared at it.

"Nice to meet you," Nessa said, because someone had to say something.

Simone tucked her arm back in the front seat with the rest of her. "You too, Nessa," she said, and Nessa was surprised that the woman knew her name. Then Simone and her father shared a smile that made Nessa's stomach hurt.

Next to her, Tanya was squirming, trying to heave the backpack off her back and pulling at her scarf, which was knotted in the straps. Nessa reached over and helped untangle her. There was a heaviness in the car, coming mostly from Tanya, and Nessa knew how her sister was feeling. How stuck Tanya was and how much she wanted to cry but how useless that would be because this was their life now.

"What do you want for dinner, girls?" her father asked. "Pizza?"

Simone looked back at them and Nessa wondered if she thought by *girls* he was referring to her.

"We always have pizza," Tanya said darkly.

"Pizza's just an option, Tee. We'll have whatever you want."

"There's an excellent Indian restaurant right around the corner from your dad's," Simone said then. "Do you two like Indian?"

Tanya stared harshly at Simone and then turned to Nessa and whispered, *Pasta*.

"Tanya would like pasta," Nessa repeated to her father. Then she smiled at Simone, who was still peering back at them. Part of Nessa felt proud that somebody so beautiful was looking at her the way Simone was, but Nessa had a feeling it had more to do with how handsome her father was than something to do with her.

Their father was the kind of handsome that made women laugh and made girls shy. He had a smile that made you want to smile back. Nessa understood then that having that kind of handsome in your life meant something—it meant something huge to her mother. Without it, Lorraine was floundering, always looking around, trying to figure out who she was without it.

"Pasta it is," Jonathan declared, and suddenly the car was speeding up and they were on the highway that would bring them across town to where his apartment complex was waiting. They all went silent, and Nessa thought of her mother back home, still with that dark lipstick on and the spatula.

AFTER THEY ATE, Jonathan asked who wanted to go swimming and Tanya jumped up and yelled, *Me me me.* Nessa and Tanya went into the bathroom to change into their suits. They peeled off their clothing and left them in a pile on the floor, then danced around and made ugly faces in the mirror.

At one point Tanya stopped dancing and stared at Nessa's chest in the mirror. "Boobs," she announced.

Nessa smirked. "Jealous?"

"No," Tanya said, but Nessa saw the way she was staring at them.

Nessa pulled on her bikini top and threw her hands behind her head and made a come-hither look in the mirror. Tanya copied her, but her face looked more like she had a burp stuck in her throat.

"Do you think Simone is pretty?" Nessa asked.

Tanya slipped her arms through the straps of her pink one-piece. "Simone looks like this." She furrowed her brow and crossed her eyes and made buckteeth all at once and her face transformed into something so revolting that they collapsed on the floor laughing.

THE ROOM WITH THE POOL was warm and echoey in a way that made winter outside seem far away. The water was a bright candy-colored blue that turned a shade darker in the deep end and shimmered a little under the dim ceiling lights. Nessa and Tanya were barefoot, just in their suits, and Nessa followed her sister to the edge of the pool.

Tanya sat and dipped her feet in, slowly swished her legs back and forth. Nessa knelt beside her and dipped her fingers in, touched the back of Tanya's neck, and Tanya shrieked.

Their father and Simone came over, him in his navy blue trunks and her in a yellow bikini.

"How is it?" Simone asked Tanya.

Tanya fluttered the water with her feet. "Cold."

Nessa lowered herself into the pool, sending shivers up her spine. She took a deep breath, squeezed her eyes closed, and dunked her head under. In the thick quiet of the water she stretched her arms and legs and propelled herself forward, sleek and weightless as an eel.

Nessa was gliding toward the deep end when she felt a hand grab her foot. She lunged upward and burst out of the water, ready to pounce on Tanya, but when she opened her eyes, Tanya was still on the edge of the pool next to Simone and she saw it was her father who was in the pool with her, treading water and grinning.

She gave him a look and dove toward him, searched blindly for his foot underwater. She found it and squeezed hard, felt his toes buckle inside her palm. She wriggled toward the surface, smiling. Bubbles exploded from her mouth and nose, like her happiness leaking out of her.

When she opened her eyes, though, Simone and Tanya were both in the water paddling around and her father was no longer just hers. Tanya pinched her nose, took a big breath of air, and went under. Simone was drifting around as though in a bathtub, her long hair wet up to her neck but the top still dry and soft.

"Marco!" Jonathan shouted, and he made a big show of closing his eyes and spinning around in the water, but the only person who said "Polo" was Simone.

"Marco!" he said again. Tanya doggy-paddled up to Nessa and splashed her hard in the face. Nessa splashed back and Tanya laughed.

"Polo," Simone said again, her voice soft as a wisp, but Jonathan still heard it. He paddled toward her, his eyes closed, and suddenly Nessa understood what her mother meant when she'd said her father was a taker.

SIMONE STAYED THE NIGHT. Their father tried to pretend this was normal, but Nessa could see him stealing glances at Tanya and her, trying to see if this bothered them. Nessa and Tanya slept on the pull-out sofa bed in the living room with the blankets and pillows that their father had bought especially for them to use when they stayed over. When he kissed them good night he asked if they wanted him to sing the moon song, a song their parents used to sing to them when they were little. The idea of her father singing the moon song made Nessa's skin hurt, but Tanya said yes, so Nessa turned over and stared at the wall and dug her fingernails into her palms while Jonathan sang. The room was dead quiet except for his voice and the song seemed to go on forever.

IN THE MORNING while their father made breakfast, Nessa locked the bathroom door and looked through Simone's makeup case. It was like a treasure chest in there, with dozens of silver tubes, pink powdery palettes in plastic cases, and various metal instruments whose functions she didn't know. She liked the way the different tubes and wands felt in her hands—expensive, and mysteriously feminine.

Then a picture appeared in her head—a picture of Nessa and Simone. It was vivid, fully formed, as though it had always existed, even though this was impossible, since she'd only met Simone yesterday. Simone was showing Nessa how to put on makeup. She was bending down, pressing a brush to her cheeks, blowing the stray flecks from her face. "Close your eyes," Simone said, while she applied mascara. In the picture, Nessa was herself, but she was older and prettier. It was as if she had taken all her good qualities and gotten rid of all her ugly qualities, and there she was: Nessa, but better.

In the picture she was getting ready for a date. "Don't let him try anything you don't want," Simone said to her. "Now dab those pretty lips together." And Simone dabbed her own lips together to show. Though her father wasn't in the picture, Nessa knew that he was right outside of it, just behind the bathroom door, waiting for them to come out.

The picture was soothing to imagine and she let herself melt into it. She played it over in her head—the cheeks and the eyes and the lips—the things

Simone said to her. But after a few minutes she felt that she should stop. She opened her eyes and forced herself to look at her reflection without warping it in her imagination to look any happier or prettier or skinnier than it actually was.

She didn't try the makeup out—she wasn't so stupid as to paint the evidence all over her face—but she slipped two tubes of lipstick, one shimmery pencil for eyes, and one of the soft rose blushers into her pocket. She fished through the case some more and pulled out a little suede pouch with silver script letters across the front: *Salt Lake City, Morgan Jewelers.* Inside was a gold chain so light and fragile that when she lowered it into her palm it just felt like a soft tingle before disappearing completely, as though dissolving into her skin. She held it up to her neck to see how it looked, then sat down and took off her sock, and slipped the necklace in before pulling her sock back on her foot.

JONATHAN HAD MADE WAFFLES for breakfast and Nessa ate three of them before anybody else even started their second.

"Slow down, Ness," Jonathan said. "You'll make yourself sick."

Nessa shrugged and took several slow bites, opening her mouth wide so that Jonathan could see all the mushed-up waffle inside. She made a point of swallowing hard and that was when she remembered Tanya's medication.

"Dad," she said. "You didn't give Tanya her pill."

"Oh, right. Thanks, Nessa." Jonathan drizzled more syrup over his waffles. His hair was sticking straight up on one side and the pillow lines tracing his jaw made him look strangely bare, like Nessa was seeing a part of him that should have been covered up. "Tee?" he said. "Let's get you your pill."

And in that moment, Nessa hated her father. "Are you a moron?" she said.

Jonathan and Tanya and Simone all turned to look at Nessa.

"Are you a fucking *moron*?" she said again.

"Nessa, language—" Jonathan started to say, but Nessa cut him off.

"Mom *told* you that she has to take it before eating, otherwise it's not effective." She was shouting. "Now if her chest burns it's all your fault and if she throws up it's because of you."

"Calm down, Nessa. This is not the end of the world." He turned to Tanya. "Tee, you can take the pill now and you'll be fine."

Tanya nodded and stared down at her half-eaten waffle and Simone stood up in her seat, as though she was about to offer to get Tanya's pill.

"You don't know that," Nessa said.

"Excuse me?" Jonathan looked at her and Nessa could see that she was embarrassing him in front of Simone.

"You don't know she'll be fine," Nessa said. "You act like you know everything, but you don't." She stood. "Now if you'll excuse me," she said. "These waffles taste like shit." She waited for Tanya to laugh or for her father to yell, but they both stayed quiet. As she hulked out of the room she could feel them watching her and she tugged her shirt down to cover the flabs of skin on her hips that Lorraine called love handles, though Nessa didn't know why, because there was nothing lovable about them.

NOBODY TOLD LORRAINE about what happened during breakfast. Not Nessa, not Tanya, and not their father. Nessa couldn't tell if they didn't say anything because they didn't want to humiliate Nessa or because they thought that if they told Lorraine, they'd also have to mention Simone.

THAT NIGHT, when Nessa was sure her mother and Tanya were both asleep in the bottom bunk, she pulled out her new makeup from her pockets and turned the ceiling fan so that the cosmetics blade was closest. She put the eyeliner, the lipstick, and the blush next to her watermelon lip gloss. In the dark, she admired her collection, how pretty each item looked, how perfect they all seemed, huddled together like a little family. She imagined how she'd look the next morning in the mirror, how she would watch her face transform from something plain into something beautiful.

As for the gold necklace that was still hidden in her sock, she decided that she'd give it to her mother. She would sneak it into Lorraine's bedroom when her mother wasn't home, put it somewhere visible enough so that Lorraine would find it, but carelessly enough so that she wouldn't be sure how it got there. At first her mother might be confused. She wouldn't recall ever having bought a gold necklace and she'd rack her brain, thinking maybe it was a gift from a long time ago that she'd simply forgotten. She might ask Nessa and Tanya if they knew where it came from, and because Tanya actually wouldn't know, she'd just shake her head and forget about the whole thing.

Nessa would shrug and say, "I have no idea, Mom, but it looks really nice on you."

"You think?" Lorraine would say, touching the shimmer of gold on her neck.

And Nessa would smile and maybe she'd even hug her mother and then she'd say, "Yes, look in the mirror, Mama. See how beautiful you are."

W hen Tanya gets back from her morning jog, Nessa is out and Jesse still hasn't returned. Tanya tells Lorraine that she has to run an errand for work, and then leaves in her rental car to meet Simone at their usual spot. Tanya and Simone discovered Rosie's during Tanya's junior year of high school, back when she and her stepmother started getting together, just the two of them. Rosie's is private—a coffee shop tucked away down a side street in Harvard Square. In the warm months, there's a patio set up out back where they've planned to meet today. Their visits aren't secret exactly, though neither one of them has told anyone else in the family about them.

When Tanya arrives, her stepmother is already there, sitting at an outdoor table. Simone is wearing a long yellow dress that clings to her slender body, and wedge sandals dangle from her feet. Her hair is shorter than the last time Tanya saw her, cut right at her jawbone, parted on the side. When they're out, people often mistake them for mother and daughter, and though Tanya never lets it show on her face, she finds pleasure in those moments; the brief charade the two of them play together, standing a touch closer than they usually stand, Simone paying for the both of them.

Today Simone's beauty is something of an offense. It practically seems to mock Lorraine.

That morning, Tanya texted Simone briefly about what happened, so when Simone spots Tanya from across the courtyard and stands to embrace her, there is panic in her stepmother's movements.

"I'm glad to see you," Simone says, kissing Tanya on the cheek. Simone's worn the same scent for as long as Tanya can remember, a fragrance called Rose Noir that comes in a little glass bottle that sells for one hundred and ninety dollars at Nordstrom. Tanya looked it up.

"You too," Tanya says, and she feels a twinge of guilt then, keeping her secret. It was easy not saying anything to Nessa and Lorraine, but keeping the pregnancy from Simone feels more like a lie.

They both sit, pushing their sunglasses up on their heads. "Ben's arm is feeling better?" Tanya asks.

"Fine," Simone says, waving her hand. "Tanya, how is she? How are *you*?"

"Her face looks like hell. But that'll go away. He came back last night at, like, five a.m."

Simone's eyes grow wide with shock and outrage, and Tanya can't help but feel comforted by this. "I got him to leave the house, though," Tanya says.

"Honey, he's dangerous," Simone says. "You shouldn't be doing this all on your own."

"We're going to get a restraining order."

"Good. Oh, thank God."

"She's not being very cooperative."

"Your mom?"

Tanya nods.

Simone purses her lips. She's careful not to say anything about Lorraine. She's always been careful about this. "How's Nessa?" she asks.

"She's in just as much denial about Jesse as my mother is," Tanya says. "Always has been."

A waitress comes with their coffees then, gently setting down two mugs and a small pitcher of cream.

"May I bother you for some soy milk?" Simone asks the waitress.

"And a peppermint tea," adds Tanya. "Thank you."

The waitress nods and hurries away.

"I'm avoiding caffeine these days," Tanya explains to Simone.

"Oh, I didn't know. I shouldn't have ordered without asking you first."

"Don't worry," Tanya says. "It's a new development."

"Trouble sleeping?" asks Simone.

"Not really. Just trying it out." She doesn't break eye contact with Simone when she says it, and it occurs to Tanya that she's a skilled liar. It would never occur to Simone that Tanya might not be telling the truth.

"Is Eitan coming?"

Tanya shakes her head.

"He couldn't get off work?"

"He could have, I guess. But it's too hard for me, balancing everything. Everyone. It would just be more stressful for me, having him here. It's better this way—keeping things separate."

Simone looks as though she's going to say something, and Tanya knows she's trying to come up with a gentle way to probe this. "Have you told my dad what happened?" Tanya asks, before Simone has the chance.

"Not yet," Simone says. "I will, when I get home. But I wanted to talk to you first."

"Thanks. And Ben is doing okay?"

"He's fine, honey. He got his cast off just in time for the end of baseball season."

"Do you have pictures?"

Simone smiles a little and pulls her phone from her purse, then hands it to Tanya.

Tanya scrolls through the photographs. "I like this one," she says, turning the phone to show Simone: Ben in his baseball uniform, cheering from the sidelines. His left arm is in a cast tattooed with autographs, and his right arm is up above his head, triumphant. It surprises Tanya, every time she sees a photo of Ben, and even more when she sees him in person, that he's her little brother. He doesn't feel like a brother in the way that Nessa feels like a sister. Tanya loves him, but it's a distant and simple love; a lesser one. It's the way Tanya loves her father.

It's taken a long time—a decade really—for Tanya to feel comfortable speaking to Simone about her family, but now that she does, her conversations with her stepmother have become a critical piece in enduring her visits with her family. She can be honest with Simone, and when she wants to cut the conversation short, Simone always takes the hint.

The waitress comes with Tanya's tea and the pitcher of soy for Simone, and Tanya watches Simone pour the milk into her coffee, white spiraling elegantly into brown.

When Tanya and Nessa were kids, Tanya hated Simone. Given the circumstances, that was expected, and eventually Tanya got over her hatred toward her stepmother—or maybe it was hatred toward her father that she'd outgrown. Simone was different from her mother. She was polished and confident, with a law degree from Harvard and a summer house on Martha's Vineyard. She came from a wealthy family and you could see it in the way she interacted with the world. She was used to getting the things she asked for, and when Tanya was around her, she grew used to getting those things, too. When Tanya was applying to law schools, Simone's father, a retired family court judge, wrote her a letter of recommendation and made a phone call to the dean of admissions at Columbia to "put in a good word." When Tanya was accepted, Simone was the first person she called with the news.

Simone was the sort of Jewish, Ivy League–educated, intellectual woman that her father must have always thought he was entitled to, because once he got Simone, he held on tight and never looked back. He committed himself to his life with Simone in a way that Tanya didn't remember him ever doing with Lorraine. It took Tanya a while to realize this wasn't Simone's fault, but a reflection on Jonathan.

Simone and her family, from Manhattan, were the kind of people with enough social grace not to flaunt their good lot in life—but you could sense it right away when you spoke with them. Their intellect, their quiet confidence—it was like good hygiene. It was just there. But Tanya knew it was more complicated than that. The kind of life that Simone and her father led in Lexington now—the kind of life they were giving Ben—it was expensive, and it was passed down from generation to generation.

Simone would never say this out loud to Tanya, but she would never raise her son in Arlington in a two-family house, where the schools were good but not great. Ben would probably grow up to go to Harvard and discover a new type of diabetes or be a world-renowned cellist. He'd started taking lessons at age four. "Soon he's going to have to choose to focus on baseball or the cello," Simone had told Tanya recently. "Colleges want to see mastery." Ben's bedroom is double the size of what hers and Nessa's was growing up. It's baseball themed, with baseball wall decor and a collection of signed baseballs displayed on the top shelf of his bookcase. Tanya doesn't resent Ben for this, and she doesn't resent Simone. She gets it. It's natural, she knows, to want to give your kid what you had, and more. The person in all this she resents is her father.

After the divorce, her mother had stayed in the house on Winter Street with Nessa and Tanya. Her father paid Lorraine his part of the mortgage as well as alimony—he continued to for many years—but Lorraine was the one who ended up with less, and therefore, so had Nessa and Tanya. Looking back on this, Tanya isn't surprised, given her father's career and the shark he hired as his divorce attorney.

Her parents both found new partners quickly—and significantly younger. Simone was fourteen years younger than her father and Jesse was ten years younger than her mother. For a while, Tanya had felt personally offended by this: as though her parents had wanted to delete the last decade of their lives and start again with someone who was practically a kid themselves.

At Tanya's graduation from law school, all four parents and stepparents sat together, along with Nessa and Eitan and Ben. When Tanya found them afterward in her cap and gown, the women had lunged at her with their phones to take pictures, so eager they had seemed to get away from one another. As she posed for photographs, she watched Jesse and her father make conversation several feet away, both with their arms folded across their chests. Her father was comfortable on the university campus, but Jesse appeared out of place. It was cold that day and over his suit jacket he had on a bright red windbreaker and a Red Sox hat. At one point a student walked by and called out, "Fuck the Red Sox!" and Jesse promptly yelled back, "Fuck you, asshole!"

Immediately Tanya glanced at her father. Jonathan, she could see, was horrified and amused. He was looking to Simone to share the moment with. He wanted to roll his eyes or quietly laugh, but Simone was avoiding her husband's gaze, pretending she hadn't heard Jesse's comment at all.

"Don't start," Lorraine muttered to Jesse. "Why you're wearing a Red Sox hat in New York is beyond me."

Tanya didn't know who she despised more in that moment. Jesse or her father.

IT WAS WHEN TANYA was in high school that she began to seek out Simone, when they started to form a relationship separate from the rest of the family. At the beginning, Tanya didn't talk to her stepmother about anything huge. She didn't tell Simone about what had happened, that night with Nessa and Dan; it was years before Tanya told anyone about that.

But she spoke with her stepmother about her high school boyfriend, Dylan Starr, and her friends at school whom she'd met through Dylan. She told Simone about the classes she was taking, where she wanted to go to college, what she wanted to do when she grew up. She talked to Simone about Nessa. It had taken a long time for Tanya to understand that there was a sadness inside her sister, a sadness that had a way of rubbing off on Tanya, that seemed to leak down from the top bunk to the bottom bunk each night.

Before she understood that, she'd been furious with her sister. Falling asleep and waking up had started to feel impossible with Nessa right above her. Something as harmless as hearing her sister yawn might set Tanya off. And when she heard her sister moving above her, the faint rock of the mattress—Nessa went about it quietly, as though Tanya wouldn't be able to hear what was going on just above her—Tanya felt the urge to throw her feet up, kick hard onto the bottom of her sister's mattress, scream at her to stop.

Tanya oscillated between feeling angry at Nessa and sad for her, and it was the feelings of sadness that wrecked Tanya, that made her want to run as far away from home as she possibly could—away from Nessa and their mother and the claustrophobic air that lived, bottled up, in their house on Winter Street.

A decade passed before Tanya told anybody about what happened at Dan's house. To this day, she's only told two people.

First, she told Simone. This was several years ago, around the time Tanya started to fall in love with Eitan. She didn't tell Simone very much. Just the bare bones: the email address, the beers in the living room, the bedroom he brought her to. She didn't talk about *him* at all—about the things he did or said. She didn't tell Simone his name and when Simone asked for it, Tanya said she didn't know it.

"You have to tell Eitan," Simone had insisted, afterward. "Not for him, but for you. For your relationship."

"It's humiliating."

"You have nothing to be embarrassed about, Tanya." She leaned in and took Tanya's hands in her own, which had surprised Tanya. Usually they didn't touch one another, except to hug hello and goodbye. *"Nothing,"* Simone had repeated. It was the first time Tanya wondered if this might be true.

"You can't tell anyone." Tanya was trying hard not to cry. "You can't tell my dad."

"I won't." Simone squeezed her hands. "I love you very much."

And though she didn't say it back, she knew that Simone understood that Tanya did love her. That she'd gone to her for a reason.

So she did tell Eitan, a few weeks later—and it was Eitan to whom she told the details.

Now, she looks at her stepmother, sipping her coffee and soy milk, and imagines what it would be like if she were Simone's daughter, and not Lorraine's. She wonders how her life would be different; how she would be different. It's a pointless line of questioning, of course. She wouldn't be Tanya at all, if that were the case. She'd be an entirely different person.

Tanya is her mother's daughter. There's no getting around that. The same undeniable way that she is Nessa's sister.

They share more than just genetic material, more than just history. When she and Nessa were little, they called it the Wild Thing; a certain intuition for danger. Though now Tanya wonders if it was less of an intuition and more of a predisposition—maybe even a wish. Tanya reaches up and fingers the scar on the back of her head, the slight divot invisible to the eye—discernible only by touch—a physical manifestation of the Wild Thing. Like so many things, she and her sister don't talk about the Wild Thing anymore, not after what happened and not after Tanya got hurt. Though Tanya is certain that Nessa must still get it sometimes, just as Tanya does. It isn't the kind of thing that simply disappears.

1999

The song playing in the orthodontist's office was one of those bouncy love songs that made Nessa want to dance. Inside her sneakers, she flexed her toes to the beat, while keeping the rest of her body still.

Dr. Paterson was pressing down hard on her bottom molars and a small animal noise escaped from the back of her throat.

"Bite for me," he said. "Good."

With one eye Nessa took a peek. Dr. Paterson's face was just inches from her own. Up close she could see the pores on his nose, zillions of pinpoint dots, all moist with oil. He leaned in closer, one of his eyebrow hairs squirreling out, almost touching her cheek. It was longer and coarser than the rest, like a pubic hair.

"Almost done," he said.

Nessa closed her eyes and squeezed her hands together, inhaling through her nose. Dr. Paterson smelled like soap from a doctor's office and something else all his own.

"These are going to be sore for a few days, Nessa. You're going to want to stick to soft foods for about a week." He snapped his gloves off and tossed them away, then slid his wedding band back on his finger.

Nessa swiped her tongue over her teeth and pretended not to be upset. The inside of her mouth felt too small with all this new equipment. Dr. Paterson held up a hand mirror and Nessa gave it a fake smile. She looked like a machine.

"Two years," he said. "If things progress the way I want them to, maybe less." Then he waved his hand and she walked out and down the hallway toward the waiting room where her mother and Tanya were waiting.

She noticed it right away when she walked in: the shimmering curve against her mother's collarbone. It had been three days since she'd hung the necklace on her mother's bedside lamp and she'd started to think Lorraine would never notice it.

As though she could hear her thoughts, her mother's hand flew up and briefly touched the chain. Lorraine set her magazine down, smiling. "Hi, sweetie. Let's see 'em."

Nessa bared her teeth.

Tanya glanced up curiously from her book and Lorraine came closer to get a look. "How do they feel?"

"Kind of sore." Nessa didn't dare look at the necklace directly, but as she stared into her mother's face, she could see it, a little ways down.

"What color did you pick?" Tanya asked.

"Pink and green," Nessa said. "Every other." Nessa closed her lips over her mouth. She was going to have to learn how to smile without teeth.

ON THE RIDE HOME, Nessa sat up front with their mother. "I'm going to make noodle soup for dinner," Lorraine said. "The receptionist gave me a list of braces-friendly foods. Jell-O, mac and cheese, ice cream. Soup, of course." She listed them on her fingers. "All your favorites."

"I don't want soup," Tanya said from the backseat.

"Today is Nessa's day, Tee."

Nessa glanced behind her. Tanya was hunched over her book, her hair spilling onto the pages. One of her thumbs rested at the base of her nose.

Nessa didn't want soup either, but she didn't say anything. She liked the sound of *Nessa's day.* Her mother glanced over at her. They caught eyes with each other and smiled.

THERE WEREN'T ENOUGH NOODLES in Lorraine's noodle soup to make it seem like real food, so Tanya found saltines from the cabinet and dunked them into the broth, ate them like cookies in milk. "Want some?" her sister asked, offering up the sleeve of crackers. Nessa shook her head. Maybe the upside of braces would be that she'd eat less.

After dinner Lorraine asked them if it was okay if she went out for a drink with a friend. A drink with a friend meant going on a date. They both said sure and Nessa followed her mother upstairs to watch while she got ready. Lorraine undressed and put on a new pair of underwear, then disappeared into her closet. The dress she emerged with was the black one Nessa had seen on the dating website.

Lorraine shimmied it down over her hips and adjusted the fabric so that it fit snugly over her chest. Years before, to make them laugh, Lorraine used to lean over so her breasts hung like coconuts. "This is Mommy," she would say, squeezing one. "This is Daddy. And they kiss together." And then she would press her breasts together as though they were kissing, turning her cleavage into a deep ravine. "Do the boob thing!" they commanded sometimes, and she would do it, and all of them would laugh. Since their father had moved out, Lorraine had stopped doing the boob thing and Nessa and Tanya no longer asked her to.

Lorraine examined her reflection in the bathroom mirror and Nessa waited for her eyes to flicker over the necklace, but her mother's gaze moved from her hair to her face down to her chest without stopping to linger anywhere in between.

"What do you think?" Lorraine asked. "Up or down?" She pulled the clip out so that her hair fell in waves over her shoulders.

"Up," Nessa said, though she wasn't sure why. Her mother looked prettier with her hair down. And then, unable to stop herself: "I like your necklace."

"Thanks, sweetie." Lorraine gathered her hair again and held it in a clump on top of her head, made her eyes big, and flared her nostrils. "You really like this better?"

"Yeah." Nessa paused. "Where'd you get it?"

"CVS, I think."

"No. The necklace."

"Oh." She touched it again, like she'd done at Dr. Paterson's office. "Dad gave it to me a while ago."

Her mother's lie came out so quick and easy Nessa wondered if Lorraine really did think it was a gift from her father. Maybe he had given her a gold necklace at one point.

Lorraine cupped her hands over her mouth and exhaled, then poured mouthwash into a cup and whirled it around.

"Who are you going out with?" Nessa asked.

Lorraine spat into the sink, wiped her mouth with the back of her hand. "A man named Raymond." She made a face at Nessa in the mirror. "He's a doctor. Well, a chiropractor. I don't know if that counts."

Nessa nodded. She didn't know what a chiropractor was.

"How do the braces feel, Ness?"

"They feel normal now," Nessa said. "I can't remember how my mouth felt without them."

NESSA AND TANYA watched *The Sound of Music* while their mother went out with Raymond. Halfway through they paused for ice cream and Nessa put the carton in the microwave to soften it, while Tanya got the whipped cream and the chocolate fudge and the jar of maraschino cherries from the refrigerator.

They settled back into the living room under the blankets with their ice cream. Nessa liked the second half of the movie better, when the Nazis come and all of a sudden everything feels dangerous. It had only occurred to her recently that she might have been involved in all this, if she had been born during a different time in history. The thought made her feel a mix of shame and pride. She'd started tutoring for her bat mitzvah just two weeks before her father had moved out. Though nobody had told her directly, Nessa's bat mitzvah had been called off. Tanya was no longer going to Hebrew school.

Nessa knew this should be a relief; she no longer had to go to tutoring, and she didn't have to learn a Torah portion or write a speech. Truthfully, though, she was devastated. She was never going to be a real Jew—not in the way she'd started to think of herself.

"You know what the Holocaust is, right?" Nessa asked Tanya, during the scene when Rolfe brings Captain Von Trapp a telegram from the Nazis.

"Yeah," answered Tanya, in such a way that Nessa wasn't sure she did. Her sister hadn't gotten to the part in Hebrew school where they learned about the concentration camps or read *Number the Stars*, and now she never would.

"It's when the Nazis made all the Jews go to these camps, and they had to shave their heads and get tattoos of numbers on their arms, and then they—"

"*Nessa,*" Tanya whined. "I'm trying to watch."

Eventually Tanya fell asleep, her face pressed against the back of the couch. When the movie ended, the clock on the DVD player read 9:51. Nessa felt too tired to walk upstairs. She was about to put in a second movie when she heard the front door open and her mother's lilting voice. "I had a great time, Raymond."

"Please," the man's voice said. "Ray."

"Ray," Lorraine repeated silkily.

"I did, too. I'm sorry again about your linguine, though."

"Oh, don't worry. It's not your fault."

They both laughed. It was Lorraine's fake laugh, the one she used with adults.

"I'd love to see you again," Raymond said.

"I'd like that, too." Then her mother lowered her voice and Nessa had to strain to hear. "I'd invite you in, but my girls are asleep."

Then there was silence, the kind where Nessa could feel them kissing. Her back and hips tingled where she imagined Raymond's hands were touching her mother. Nessa slipped one hand between her legs. She could feel it there, too. The sensation was like being on a roller coaster—the moment when you drop and everything inside your body feels like it's floating.

Then the front door closed and Nessa heard her mother's footsteps. She curled over and pressed her face into the back of the couch like Tanya and closed her eyes. A few seconds later she could feel her mother looking at them. Then Tanya farted in her sleep, a loud unapologetic pop, and Nessa stuffed her face harder into the back of the couch to stifle her laughter. She waited for her mother to laugh, too, but she didn't.

There was the sound of her mother's footsteps, the soft feeling of a blanket over her back—the blue woolen throw blanket, she could tell by the smell—and her mother's hand, cool on her hair. Nessa listened as Lorraine walked into the kitchen. The kiss of the refrigerator door opening, then closing, the snap of Tupperware, the beep of the microwave. The smell of soup. Over the whir of the microwave, she could hear Lorraine crunching on saltines. When the microwave beeped, Nessa opened her eyes. Quietly, she pushed back the blanket and tiptoe-ran from the living room into the front hallway, then upstairs to her bedroom.

A FEW NIGHTS LATER when the phone rang, she could tell by her mother's tone—her girlish *What's up?*—that it was her father on the line. The extension was in her mother's bedroom, so Nessa ran upstairs and picked up just in time to hear her father say, "It's about Nessa."

"What about her?" Lorraine asked.

Nessa moved the mouthpiece away so they wouldn't be able to hear her breathing.

"I think she may have taken something from my apartment the other week."

"Okay?" her mother said. Nessa could hear the disappointment in Lorraine's voice, that he was calling about Nessa and not her.

"A necklace," he went on. "A gold necklace."

Nessa pictured her mother's hand flying to her neck.

"Have you seen it?" he asked.

"No."

"You're sure?"

"Yes, I'm sure." Then Lorraine's voice turned sarcastic. "Since when have you started wearing jewelry, Jon?"

"It's not mine."

"Obviously."

"I wouldn't have bothered you with this, but it was expensive, and I think Nessa may have taken it." He paused. "I'm worried about Nessa, Lorraine. She's gained a lot of weight. Don't you think?"

"Oh, fuck you," Lorraine snapped, as though he had just called Lorraine fat instead of her. "Nessa doesn't have your girlfriend's necklace, okay?"

Nessa slipped her hand under her shirt and squeezed, assessing her flesh, the way she'd seen her mother squeeze fruit in the grocery store.

For a long moment her father was quiet. Then he said, "Lorraine, this is what I mean when I say you make things inappropriately about yourself. May I speak with Nessa?"

There was a sharp intake of breath, and when Lorraine spoke again, her voice was so small and young she sounded like a whole different person. "Did you introduce the girls to this woman?"

When her father didn't answer, Lorraine started to cry. It was quiet at first, lots of watery sniffs. But then it got louder and she was crying the way she must have cried as a little girl, holding nothing back.

Nessa started to cry then, too. She put her hand over her mouth and tears slid down her face and over her hand, into the crease of her neck.

"I'm sorry, Lorrie." Her father's voice tumbled out. "I'm sorry."

Lorraine choked a little bit and made a sound like she might throw up and that was when Nessa forced herself to put the phone down in its cradle.

AT DINNER LORRAINE was no longer wearing the necklace, and when she didn't speak to Nessa or look at her, Nessa got the queasy feeling that she'd messed up badly. Tanya was blabbering. Neither one of them was listening, but they were both pretending to, and Nessa was relieved that Tanya was there, that her little sister gave them somewhere to look besides at one another. When Tanya asked if she could be excused to watch TV, Lorraine nodded, but when Nessa stood to follow, Lorraine pinned her with her eyes. "Stay for a minute."

Lorraine waited until the sound of the TV came on in the other room before speaking. "Why didn't you tell me that your father has a girlfriend?"

It wasn't the question she'd been expecting. The truth was, she didn't know why she hadn't told her mother about Simone except that to have said the word *girlfriend* to Lorraine would have been frightening. "I don't know," she said.

A splotch of red bloomed on Lorraine's chest and Nessa watched it travel up her neck and into her face. "Do you realize how foolish I feel?" Lorraine said. "Knowing that everybody besides me knew about her? That I was the last one to find out?"

Nessa looked down at her thighs and wondered if it would make things better or worse if she started to cry.

"It didn't occur to you that maybe you should have told me?"

Nessa squeezed her eyes and tried to conjure tears, but nothing came.

"Look at me."

She looked. Her mother's face was hot and it was quivering in strange spots—above her eyebrow, in the cushion of her chin. The thought came to Nessa before she had the chance to will it away: her mother looked ugly.

"I'm sorry, Mama."

Lorraine's eyes gave way, like something frozen puddling. She blinked fast. "It's not your fault," she said, her voice softer.

Lorraine pulled her chair closer and leaned over the table. "What's her name?"

"Simone."

"Do you know how long they've been seeing each other?"

Nessa shook her head, relieved not to know the answer.

"Do you know how they met?"

She shook her head again.

"Do you know what she does? Like, what her job is?"

"No."

"What does she look like?"

Nessa shrugged.

"What color hair does she have?" Lorraine's eyes were bright with impatience.

"Brown?"

"Curly or straight?"

"Straight," Nessa said.

"How long?"

Nessa touched her arm to show.

"How old is she?"

"I don't know."

"If you had to guess?"

Nessa turned different numbers over in her head. "Twenty-nine?"

"Jesus," Lorraine said.

Then her mother's face broke, and she covered it with both hands.

"I don't know, though," Nessa said, hating herself. "I couldn't tell."

Lorraine exhaled hard and whispered *Jesus Christ* into her hands.

"She's not very pretty, Mom," Nessa said, and Lorraine looked up. "Tanya says she looks like this." Nessa did the face—the buckteeth and the cross-eyes and the furrowed brow—and her mother laughed. Nessa did it again, even uglier, and Lorraine started to cry.

"Nessa, sweetheart," her mother said, wiping her eyes. "I need to tell you something. And you can't tell Tanya about this, okay? She's not old enough to understand."

Nessa nodded. It felt so good to hear her mother call her sweetheart that she thought about reaching out and grabbing her mother's hand. Instead she leaned over the table and tried to show Lorraine how much she loved her with her eyes.

"Your father was cheating on me. When we were still married. Do you know what that means?"

Nessa nodded. Cheating. It was one of those things she knew about, though she had no memory of ever being told what it was.

"Asshole," Nessa muttered. It was a word she'd never used before, and she thought her mother might chastise her—or laugh at her—but all Lorraine did was smile sadly and shrug. "I thought you should know," she said. "I thought you should have the full story."

THAT NIGHT NESSA thought about Simone in her bathing suit. She pictured the yellow knot at the base of her neck, and she imagined Simone reaching back to pull the string, the bikini top dropping to the floor. She imagined Simone's breasts, smaller than her mother's, and just as beautiful; her nipples dark and sharp; the flesh around them cold and goose-bumped. Nessa re-wound the picture and this time she imagined it was her father pulling the string at the base of Simone's neck. She pictured his hands skating down Simone's sides to the bikini bottoms and sliding them off; Simone stepping out of them. She imagined Simone naked, lying on a bed with her legs open, the dark triangle of hair between her legs similar to the hair Nessa now had—hair that sometimes excited her and sometimes embarrassed her.

As she thought about it, her body began to pulse impatiently. She turned over on her stomach and slid her palm between her legs, and pressed. Slowly, quietly—so that Tanya wouldn't be able to hear from the bottom bunk—she moved against her palm, meeting each pulse with pressure. She closed her eyes and pretended that her hand belonged to somebody else—not her father or Simone or anyone she knew—but some unnamed, faceless man who she imagined loved her very much.

Nessa breathed hard. The roller-coaster floating feeling spread from between her legs to the rest of her body—her arms and her legs and her fingers and toes—warm and tingling and so perfect she had to stuff her face into her pillow to stop herself from making noise.

When Nessa returns to 12 Winter Street after driving to Dan's house, Tanya and Lorraine are sitting on the front steps. Lorraine is smoking, lazily holding a cigarette in one hand. They're both wearing sunglasses and from a distance they look stylish and dreamy, like two teenage girls with all the time in the world to kill.

When Nessa approaches, they look up at her from behind their sunglasses and she gets the uneasy feeling they've been talking about her. Lorraine taps her sandaled foot on the step. "Sit," she says, and Nessa sits, settling on the step below, leaning against her mother's legs.

Tanya reaches out and pulls a stray hair from Nessa's shirt. "Where were you?"

"I took a drive."

"*I took a drive,*" Tanya mimics, making her voice low and theatrical.

"Jesus. I can't say anything right with you people." She pulls Tanya's big toe and Tanya flinches, yanking her foot away.

"So we've decided something," Tanya says. "Mom's going to get a restraining order."

Nessa turns around and looks at Lorraine. It's impossible to read her mother's expression from behind her sunglasses.

"Against Jesse?"

"No, against you," Tanya says. "Of course against Jesse."

"How do we do that?" Nessa asks.

"We'll go to the courthouse," Tanya says. "Fill out the paperwork. We were waiting for you."

"Okay."

"It's the right thing to do," her mother says then, her voice tense and defensive, as though Nessa has disagreed.

THE COURTHOUSE is a modern-looking building in Medford, right on the Mystic Valley Parkway, between a Gold's Gym and a Bertucci's Pizza. They enter through a metal detector and send their purses into X-ray machines. The security guards who usher them through get annoyed when Lorraine forgets to take her iPhone out of her pocket.

"Your *phone*, Mom," Tanya says, from the other side of security.

"Shit," Lorraine says. She rummages in her jeans pocket, looking up at the guards, panicked, and Nessa wishes they could turn around and walk back out the way they came. She has a terrible feeling about this restraining order—how determined Tanya seems on getting it, like it's a simple solution to a simple problem.

They make it through. Once inside, Tanya leads them to a long counter with a sign above: CLERK MAGISTRATE.

The woman behind the counter studies them through a pair of green reading glasses propped up on the bump of her nose. "Good morning." She phrases it warily, as though they're about to prove her wrong.

"Good morning," Tanya answers. "My mother would like to apply for an emergency 209A." She touches Lorraine briefly on her shoulder.

The clerk turns her attention to Lorraine. "I'll need the names and dates of birth for both you and the defendant." She puts a piece of paper on the counter and Lorraine steps forward to write, glancing sideways at Tanya.

Lorraine writes: *Lorraine Bloom 10/10/58* and *Jesse Wright 5/22/68*. Nessa can tell by her mother's handwriting that her mind is somewhere else.

"What sort of relationship do you have with Mr. Wright, Ms. Bloom?"

"He's my husband," Lorraine says.

The woman nods and hands Lorraine a clipboard with some forms. "You'll fill out these questions here, regarding what sort of protective order you'd like." She eyes Tanya, waiting for her to interject. "There's no abuse, vacate premises, stay away, no contact. You can choose any of these—any combination, or all of the above. On the last page is where you'll write your affidavit explaining to the judge why you're in fear of imminent serious physical harm. You'll want to go into detail, and be specific, starting with the most recent incident." She turns the page over and points. "When you write on this last page here, your affidavit, be sure to flip the page so you're not writing on the carbon paper. Do you have any questions?"

Lorraine shakes her head.

"Alright. Let me know if you do and once you're done you can bring this back to me."

They find a free bench in the hallway, and Nessa and Tanya sit on either side of their mother. Other people are filling out paperwork on benches, while some mill around aimlessly. There are people dressed professionally, like Tanya, and others in jeans and sweatshirts. Nessa watches a mother and her young daughter walk quickly across the open lobby, hand in hand. The woman looks as if she's about to burst out crying. The child looks catatonic.

Tanya explains each section to Lorraine in a low voice, prompting her what to write and where. It's the most relaxed Nessa has seen Tanya since they've come home and Nessa feels suddenly irritated at her sister—how comfortable she is telling their mother what to do and how to do it. When Lorraine gets to the final lined page, she asks, "So what exactly do I write here?"

"This is where you'll tell the judge why you're getting the order. He wants to see that you're scared of Jesse. You'll start with the strangulation last night, and that we went to the emergency room."

Lorraine shakes her head. "I don't want to include that."

Tanya raises an incredulous eyebrow. "Why the hell not?"

"Because." Lorraine looks down at the blank form. "I don't want to get him in trouble. And I'd rather talk about his yelling and anger anyway. He's never done anything like that before."

"You have to include the physical abuse," Tanya says firmly. "That's the whole point."

Lorraine puts a hand through her hair and glances down the hallway.

"Mom," Tanya says. "Were you frightened last night?"

Lorraine closes her eyes and looks as though she's counting silently in her head. Then she opens them. "It's complicated, Tanya. I know you don't see it that way. But it's not so black and white."

"If someone strangles you to the point where you almost black out, that's pretty black and white."

"I don't want him to go to jail."

"He won't," Tanya says, exasperated. "Not if you don't report it to the police. But you have to include it in your affidavit."

"Will Jesse read it?"

"If he shows up at the two-party hearing, yes, most likely he will."

Lorraine's eyes widen. "What's a two-party hearing?"

Tanya nods patiently and all at once, Nessa is scared. She hadn't realized Jesse would have to show up to some sort of hearing.

"So how this works," Tanya explains, "is that today the judge will decide whether or not to grant you an emergency restraining order. If he does grant the emergency order—which he *will*, if you write that Jesse strangled you—he'll set a date for a hearing, sometime in the next ten days. In the meantime, Jesse will be served with the emergency order, and if he chooses to, he can show up at the two-party hearing and say his side of the story. He is not obligated to show up, however. After the two-party hearing, the judge will decide whether he wants to extend the emergency order. Usually it's for a year, but sometimes he might extend it for a shorter period of time— three or six months." Tanya's voice is calm. "Having a restraining order taken out against you is not a crime. It does not go on your permanent record. He'll only get in trouble *if* he violates the order. Violating a restraining order is a criminal offense—it's grounds for arrest—and that's what makes it effective." She pauses. "For law-abiding citizens, at least."

Lorraine's eyes dart toward the front entrance and Tanya follows her gaze. "Mom, if you're frightened for him to read it, if you're scared what he might do in retaliation, that's all the more reason why you need this order."

Lorraine nods and then leans over the clipboard and starts to write. Her hair falls around her face like shields, blocking the paper from view.

"What are you writing?" Tanya asks.

Lorraine doesn't answer.

"Mom?" Tanya says.

When Lorraine doesn't respond, Tanya exhales emphatically.

Lorraine writes the last sentence and dots it with an ambivalent period. Then she leans back so they can read.

I have been with Jesse Wright for sixteen years. He is a good-hearted person but he comes from a sad family. His parents were abusive. His father hit his mother and as a little boy Jesse would be the one to intervene and stop his father. So sometimes Jesse was hit, too. He carries around a lot of anger. Sometimes he takes it out on me. He calls me names and yells at me and gets in my face. Sometimes it gets so bad that I leave the house. Once I slept in my car. He always apologizes afterward but in the moment, he loses control. One time he was so angry that he ran over a cat with his car. The cat was in the middle of the road and it was hurt so it couldn't really move. It was bleeding. Jesse ran right over him. I don't know if he meant to do it, but he also didn't try to go around it. He was driving really quickly. He didn't stop at any of the stop signs. I felt extremely scared.

Nessa feels sick—not because of what her mother has written—but because of what she's left out.

She glances at Tanya. Her sister's face is stony. "The only relevant thing here is that he murdered a cat," Tanya says.

"What about the yelling and the anger?"

Tanya shakes her head. "The judge isn't interested in your psychological evaluation of Jesse. It doesn't matter if he grew up in a Russian orphanage or was raised by terrorists. It still doesn't make it okay that he hurt you. Do you understand that you could have died last night? You're in denial, clearly, but—"

"Tanya," Nessa says. "Stop."

"Stop what?"

"Stop yelling at her."

Tanya throws up her hands. "I'm not yelling at her. I'm telling her basic facts. Neither one of you seems to realize the extreme lethality of this situation."

"You're talking to us like we're stupid," Nessa says.

"That's because you are," she says. "I've seen millions of restraining orders get denied. I know what the judge wants to see."

"*Girls.*" Lorraine's voice cuts through the hallway and a man on another bench glances over curiously. "Stop."

Tanya looks pointedly in the other direction and Lorraine stands with the clipboard and takes it back to the clerk magistrate. Nessa and Tanya follow. The clerk flips through the pages, surveys the affidavit, her eyes moving quickly, betraying nothing. Then she nods. "You can go to the courtroom now. You're going to be in courtroom 1." She points. "Make a left and then straight down that hallway. There's a sign on the door. Please turn off your cell phones before going inside."

Court is already in session when they enter courtroom 1—a large room with butter-yellow walls, adorned with paintings: portraits of old white judges in black robes, the knots of their ties peeking through like little fists. Tanya leads them toward the middle of the room.

The benches are scattered with people: some alone, some in twos or threes. The lawyers, seated at large desks in the front, are dressed better than everyone else—their hair, especially, is nicer than everybody else's. Suddenly, Nessa feels relieved that Tanya is there with them, that her sister blends in with the other attorneys, with their polished looks and their aloofness.

The judge, an older white man with a head full of white hair—his portrait would fit in among those on the wall—is in dialogue with a boy standing in front. "Mr. Mahoney," the judge is saying in a thick Boston accent, "do you understand the charges against you?"

The boy nods. He is lanky and slouched, his hands deep in his pockets. "Yes, Your Honor." He has been charged with a DUI. Nessa thinks about Henry then, and what he must have been like in court. She imagines him in a button-up shirt, his hands clasped behind him, nodding deferentially to the judge. For some reason, the thought excites her.

When the judge calls Lorraine's name, her mother stiffens and turns to Tanya.

"Right up there, Mom," Tanya says quietly, nodding toward the front of the room. She squeezes Lorraine's arm. "You'll be great." Her sister's voice is reassuring; it must be the voice she use with her clients.

Nessa and Tanya watch their mother walk quickly down the carpeted aisle, her fists balled at her sides.

"Hopefully the judge notices the hemorrhaging," Tanya whispers to Nessa. Lorraine's hair is down, matted against her head, and the tag of her shirt is peeking out in the back. Nessa moves closer to Tanya and they hold hands. Tanya's palm is warm and sure against her own.

"Ms. Bloom, raise your right hand."

Lorraine's hand goes up.

"Please state your full name for the court."

"Lorraine Abigail Bloom."

"Do you promise to tell the truth, the whole truth, and nothing but the truth, so help you, God?"

Lorraine nods. "I do," she says, the words swallowed up by the room.

"Alright, Ms. Bloom, I'm going to take a minute to read this over." The judge is holding her papers in his hand and they watch him read. He regards the paper with such indifference that Nessa feels sick to her stomach. Then he puts it down.

"Ms. Bloom, you've been married to Mr. Wright for sixteen years?"

"We've been together for sixteen years. Married for ten."

"And how long has the verbal abuse that you mention here been going on?"

Lorraine tilts her head. "I guess from the beginning," she says.

Nessa is ashamed. She never considered it verbal abuse before, though now she wonders what she thought all that yelling and fighting was.

The judge nods. "And why now? What made you decide to come get this order today?"

Lorraine pauses.

Next to Nessa, Tanya is on the edge of the bench, her back so straight, it's as though she's trying to stand up without actually doing so.

"Lately it's been getting worse," Lorraine says.

"Can you be more specific?"

"Well. He's quicker to get angry. He loses his temper over the smallest things."

"And the incident with the cat," the judge says. "When did this happen?"

"About a month ago."

"So why did you wait to come in until today?"

"I—I had to take some time to think about it."

Tanya exhales.

"Ms. Bloom, do you feel scared of Mr. Wright?"

For a full thirty seconds Lorraine is silent. Then she nods her head, and it becomes clear that her mother is trying not to cry. "Yes," she says, this time louder. "I do."

The judge nods. "Well, I am not going to grant this order today. From what I can see, it's not an emergency. What I will do is set a hearing for next Monday so that Mr. Wright can have a chance to talk, too. At this point I need more time and more information to make a decision. Mr. Wright will be served over the weekend and the hearing will be set for Monday, April twenty-fourth, at ten a.m. Make sure you show up, Ms. Bloom, otherwise the matter will be dropped."

Lorraine nods.

"Okay," he says. "Thank you."

Nessa and Tanya look at each other. They've always had the ability to feel identical feelings, but this—this feeling is unlike any they've ever experienced. Nessa has the strange sense then that Tanya knows where she was earlier today; that she's been thinking about him, too.

Lorraine is walking toward them. She looks blank. Nessa can't tell if she's trying to soothe them with her face—*I'm okay, girls*—or if her face has nothing to do with them at all.

THEY DRIVE TO THE ARLINGTON DINER for lunch. While Lorraine is in the bathroom, Tanya turns to Nessa, businesslike. "I don't trust Jesse not to lash out when he gets served. I think we should leave this weekend."

"Seriously?"

"This is a vulnerable time. When he realizes she's applying for this order and leaving him, he's going to freak."

"But what's he going to think if we all just disappear?"

"I don't care what he thinks. I just don't want to be around him, and I don't want Mom to be around him. We have to convince her to include the emergency room visit on her affidavit. She has to do that."

"Tanya."

"What?"

"I went to Dan's house today."

Something passes over Tanya's face then, like a net. For a moment she looks stuck, unable to move, to change expression. But then it lifts, and Nessa sees that her sister is furious. "What the *fuck*, Nessa."

"Tanya, I think we should press charges. You were fourteen, how could he not see that you were—"

"Shut up, Nessa." Tanya's voice is low and clipped, but there's something hysterical in her eyes—a childlike terror. "Mom's coming back. Just stop talking, okay?"

"Okay." She'd been wrong; Tanya had not been thinking about Dan at all. She wants to reach over and hug her sister, but she sees that Tanya does not want to be touched.

Lorraine slides into the booth and Tanya rearranges her facial features to look calm and unruffled, then puts one hand firmly on Lorraine's wrist. "Mom, we're going away this weekend."

Lorraine smiles sourly. "Somewhere tropical?"

"No," Tanya says. "Somewhere safe."

This was not supposed to be a weekend about Dan. But everywhere Tanya goes, she can smell him. He's there on her clothes, on her hands, in the smells of food cooking. As she and Nessa pack to go to Vermont, where they've decided to take Lorraine for the weekend, Tanya buries her nose in each of her shirts. Initially, there's the scent of her detergent and their apartment in New York, and there's also the slightly more stale smell of her suitcase, but underneath she can detect it—the smoky, meaty stink of him.

"This is disgusting," she says into her French Connection sweater.

"What?" Nessa says.

"My clothes reek. I hope the bed-and-breakfast has laundry."

Nessa doesn't respond.

They're alone in their bedroom. They haven't really spoken since the thing Nessa said in the diner. It's the closest they've ever come to talking about what happened. It had been so surprising to hear Nessa say his name—so surprising and, at the same time, disturbingly normal. But more than that, it had felt mean for Nessa to whip it out like that—crude, almost—without warning Tanya first. That something as small as a name—three harmless letters—has that kind of effect on her, horrifies Tanya.

"You're not allowed to say that," she'd wanted to scream. But that would have been absurd.

So, they're running away, as though this might solve their problems.

Tanya understands that nothing is as simple as throwing a sheet over it and pretending it's not there. But she also knows that her mother is more likely to go back to Jesse if she sees him before the hearing. And then there's the fact that Tanya can't stand the smell of her own house; that each time she walks up and down the stairs, a feeling of dread builds like heavy grit in her stomach. It's not the Wild Thing exactly, because no one is chasing her; rather, it's the memory of being chased, of being stuck, and that's how Tanya feels—like she's stuck inside her own mind, encased in her own body. All she wants to do is move.

She wants to get away from Arlington, with its troves of Dunkin' Donuts and gas stations and car dealerships and white-steepled churches. She doesn't want to clean out this messy house, sort all the junk into piles—*keep, throw away, donate*. She doesn't want to walk the dog up and down Winter Street, or do all the old things they used to do "one last time." She doesn't feel nostalgic for this place the way her sister and mother do. The smallness and whiteness of Boston's inner suburbs, the way everyone is stuck in their ways. Especially the men—the macho men, the arrogant men. The strong silent types who drink themselves into oblivion every night but still insist they don't have feelings. The self-important intellectuals—*I'm getting my PhD . . . in Cambridge?* The beat of silence, as they wait for the inevitable follow-up questions so they can launch into their autobiography.

Oh, men like this exist everywhere. New York is swarming with misogynists, some who call themselves feminists, others more straightforward about it. But home is where Tanya feels it most acutely. It's where she feels smallest. She's reminded of what it felt like, growing up with a mother who divorced one asshole but quickly found herself another, smiling all the while, as if she was the luckiest woman alive.

II.

2001

Nessa was in the car when it happened. There was the blare of a horn, one long continuous blast. The impact—the tightness of her seat belt across her chest—metal scraping metal, her mother's scream.

"Shit, shit, *fuck*," Lorraine cried, as they pulled over behind the car they had just slammed into. A man burst from the driver's seat, yelling. It was dark outside and on the shoulder of the road he looked frightening, illuminated by Lorraine's headlights. He was coming toward them, spittle spraying from his mouth.

"Should I get out, too?" Nessa asked as Lorraine opened the car door, but her mother didn't respond.

"I'm sorry," Lorraine said breathlessly to the man. "I'm so, so sorry." She was crying already, clutching her jacket close to her.

The man threw up his hands. "Did you not see me?"

Lorraine shook her head. "I didn't. I don't know what happened. Are you hurt?"

"No." He rubbed his jaw. "Are you?"

"I'm alright," she said.

"Well, that's good." His voice had become softer.

Nessa watched as they walked over to the front of their car and knelt, and then over to the side of his. When they stood, the man disappeared into his car for a minute and came out with a pen and a piece of paper, which he gave to Lorraine. Her mother took them and began to write, using the hood of their car as a surface. Nessa watched the man watch her mother write. He was handsome.

Lorraine finished writing and when she glanced back at the man, she tucked her hair behind her ear. He smiled at her, and Nessa felt her own stomach dive. His smile transformed his face from something cold and perfect into something urgent and enchanting.

Lorraine handed him the paper and then, unbelievably, the man pulled her mother in for a hug. The top of her head barely reached his shoulder. A minute later, when Lorraine climbed back into the car, she began to laugh.

"What?" Nessa asked. Her hands were still shaking from the crash.

"He wants to take me out to dinner," Lorraine said, shaking her head in disbelief. She was shining.

WATCHING HER MOTHER fall in love with Jesse was like watching a movie. Nessa was on the outside looking in, though neither one of them seemed to know she was paying any attention.

Lorraine became happy and distracted, a permanent smile etched into her cheeks. She hardly ate, those first months, but she made elaborate dinners for Nessa and Tanya, listening to music while she cooked. She cleaned the house compulsively. She sang. When her daughters spoke to her, she nodded along, but she wasn't really listening.

When Lorraine wasn't spending time with Jesse she was talking about him on the phone to her friends. Her voice and her eyes changed when she spoke about Jesse. Nessa could feel how bored she was, looking at anybody's face whose wasn't his.

Jesse was the manager of an Italian restaurant in North Cambridge called Angelo's and those first months he brought them take-out containers of chicken parm and breaded mozzarella sticks and Lorraine would swoon. It annoyed Nessa how happy the food made her mother, but it annoyed her even more that Lorraine barely ate any of it. Nessa didn't like eating Jesse's food in front of Lorraine, but usually she'd sneak down to the kitchen to eat it on her own after everyone had gone to bed. The food from Angelo's was good.

Nessa didn't want to like Jesse, but she did. The first time they met he said, "Nessa, I owe you an apology. I really do. For yelling like an asshole. When your mom told me you were in the car when that happened, oh my God, Nessa, I wanted to die." He shook his head. "I was such a jerk. I really was. I'm sorry."

"It's okay," she said, stunned. No adult had ever spoken to her like that.

"It's not, though. I'm going to make it up to you, okay? I don't know how, but I'm going to make it up to you. I promise."

Nessa shrugged. Then she waited. Weeks passed and nothing happened. She never brought it up with him again, but she began to live with Jesse's promise like a stone deep inside her pocket. Something cool and smooth to hold, to pass absentmindedly between her fingers, something to keep tight in the center of her palm.

ONE DAY AFTER SCHOOL, Nessa found Jesse watching TV, the volume turned up higher than they ever had it. He was the only one home.

"Hi," she said.

He looked over his shoulder. "Hey there." He reached for the remote and turned it down.

Nessa shrugged her backpack off and dropped it to the floor, then wandered into the kitchen to wade through their messy fridge.

"Nessa," Jesse called from the living room. "Come here a sec."

Nessa walked back into the living room.

"Has anyone ever told you that you look like her?" Jesse nodded toward the television screen, where two men were yelling back and forth at each other across a parking lot. "Hold on," he said. "She'll be back."

Several moments later a woman appeared on the screen. "There," he said. The actress that he was referring to was so pretty that Nessa wondered if he was making fun of her.

"No."

He shrugged. "Something about the eyes."

"Really?"

"Yeah. Looks a little like your mom, too."

Nessa studied the woman's face. "I guess so," Nessa said. She sat down on the arm of the chair.

"Have you seen this movie before?" Jesse asked.

She shook her head.

"It's good. You'd like it."

"What's it about?"

"Those two guys are friends. They just robbed a bank together. The taller one is pissed because his buddy, Vic, slept with his girlfriend. Vic had no idea that's who she was, though."

"That's why they're yelling at each other?"

"Yup."

"And the girlfriend is the lady who kind of looks like me?"

"Right. Michelle. She knew *exactly* who Vic was," he said. "She's gorgeous but a bitch. The pretty ones always are."

Nessa blushed, wondering if Jesse had just called her gorgeous, or a bitch, or both. She watched, waiting for the actress to come back on the screen.

The front door opened then, and Lorraine's voice rang out. "Hi, honey!"

"Hi!" Nessa and Jesse called back at the same time. Jesse grinned at Nessa. "You're definitely the honey she means," he said.

Lorraine appeared in the living room with grocery bags in her arms.

"Babe," Jesse said, jumping up. "You should've left them for me."

"There's more in the car." She eased the bags onto the floor and flexed her fingers. "Thanks. Take the keys."

Jesse took the keys from her and kissed her mother on the side of her smile. "I missed you," he said, in a voice Nessa wasn't supposed to hear, and she realized then that she was jealous.

LATER THAT WEEK on the school computers Nessa found the actress from the movie on the internet. She scrolled through photo after photo, trying to locate herself in the beautiful woman's face. On the TV screen that day—through Jesse's eyes—she'd started to see the resemblance. Now it felt like a cruel joke. She looked nothing like that woman.

"Looking at porn?"

Nessa spun around in her seat, her face hot.

It was Tommy McKenzie, a loudmouth kid in her grade—taller than most boys, with a shock of orange hair and teeth that always looked like they needed to be brushed. He was grinning, looking over her shoulder at the computer screen filled with images of the actress.

"I didn't know you were a lesbo," Tommy said, his voice too loud for the library.

Quickly, Nessa x-ed out the browser window. "I'm not. I was looking up a movie I watched with my mom's boyfriend." She could feel her blush all the way up in her skull.

"Sure, lesbo," he said, giving her another perverse smile, before leaving her alone at the computer.

THAT NIGHT WHEN NESSA touched herself, she thought about the actress. In her fantasy, she was the actress, and she was beautiful and untouchable and she was a bitch. She was allowed to be a bitch *because* she was beautiful. Nessa understood that a boy like Tommy McKenzie would never have spoken to her that way in the library if she really was pretty. He would have been too scared to talk to her. He might have a crush on her. At the very least, he would be attracted to her.

Nessa had no idea what that felt like—to have a boy like her. She imagined it was the kind of feeling that made everything else bearable about life, worth living for.

They're an hour outside of Arlington, heading toward Vermont, when Lorraine cries out, "Shit!" and slaps a hand down hard on the dashboard.

"What?" Tanya yells back, startled.

"Sally," Lorraine says. "We have to go back for Sally."

Inwardly, Tanya curses. She is shocked that her mother is actually going along with her plan. She'd expected Lorraine to protest, but Lorraine had agreed almost instantly when Tanya suggested driving out of state for the weekend. Nessa had suggested Bennington, where an ex-boyfriend of hers had gone to school, a small college town three hours from Boston, out of the way enough that Jesse would never think to look for them there.

"Mom," Tanya says. "We're almost halfway there."

Lorraine shakes her head. "We have to go back."

"Sally will be fine for a weekend."

"But, Tee," Nessa says from the backseat. "What about what he did to that cat?"

Tanya throws Nessa a death glare in the rearview mirror.

"I don't think it's a good idea for us to take the dog anyway," Tanya says. "That might provoke him. Right now we need to maintain a safe distance until Monday."

"Tanya, honey," Lorraine says. "You have to turn around now. I'll drive if you want. But we can't leave Sally alone with him."

"Has he ever hurt Sally?" Tanya asks.

"Once," Lorraine says tightly. "Take that exit coming up." Her mother points.

Tanya signals and gets into the right lane.

Immediately they hit heavy traffic on Route 2 toward Boston. They inch forward as the sun sets and the muscles in Tanya's face start to clench. A band of tightness is forming across her eyebrows and forehead: the start of a migraine.

"I don't know if the bed-and-breakfast even accepts pets," Tanya says, but nobody responds. In front of them is an endless sea of taillights, glinting cherry red. The fact is, at this rate, they're barely going to make it to the bed-and-breakfast in time for the nine p.m. check-in.

After twenty minutes of minimal movement, Tanya hits the wheel with her palm. "Was there an accident or something? Why the fuck is it so slow?" She's close to tears.

"Rush hour," Nessa offers unhelpfully from the backseat.

"Thanks."

"Can we listen to music or something?" Nessa asks.

Tanya tosses Nessa the auxiliary cord. After a minute, something depressingly bleak blasts out from over the speakers.

"Are you trying to make me slit my wrists?" Tanya yells over the dramatic crooning.

"Do you have a specific request?" Nessa asks.

"Maybe something a little less emo?"

"Hmm," says Nessa. "What do I have here that's devoid of emotion."

Tanya rolls her eyes in the rearview mirror, but Nessa isn't looking.

By the time they pull onto Winter Street, it's almost dark out and Jesse's car is in the driveway. All the lights on their half of the house are on. The O'Briens aren't home.

"Fuck," mutters Lorraine, as they sit across the street in the car.

"Well, what did you expect?" Tanya can't help saying. "That he was conveniently going to be out?"

Lorraine unbuckles her seat belt.

"No," Tanya says. "I should do it."

"I don't want you to, Tanya. We don't even know if he's gotten the summons yet. He could be worked up."

"Which is exactly why you shouldn't go inside."

"Let me go with you, Tee," Nessa says from the backseat.

"We need to make this as undramatic as possible," Tanya says. "I'll go in, okay?"

"I don't know, Tee," Lorraine says.

"Mom," Tanya snaps. "Just trust me."

Tanya gets out of the car and soundlessly closes the door. She walks up the driveway past the real estate sign and the red balloons and the idiotic flowerpots. The front door is closed but unlocked. Tanya eases it open, anticipating the squeak. She was hoping Sally would be in the front hallway where she usually is, waiting for whoever's coming through the door next, but the hallway is empty. She can hear the television from the living room.

She'll play this cool and casual, she decides, walking in quietly but not sneakily, with nothing to hide. Jesse's on the couch in front of the television. She sees a swatch of fur on the floor next to the couch, Sally's tail.

At the sound of her footsteps, Jesse whirls around and looks at her over the back of the couch. He seems surprised.

"Hey," she says. "What's up?" She can tell by his face that he hasn't been served yet.

"Where have you guys been?" he asks. "I was starting to get worried."

"We got caught up," she says. "Hey, Sal," she calls, raising her voice and kneeling. "Come here, girl."

Sally gets up, tail wagging, and patters over to Tanya.

"Where's your mom?" Jesse asks, standing.

Tanya stands, too. "I'm not sure. I was out with Nessa. We were just coming by to pick up Sally for a walk."

"What are you talking about?" he says, glancing at the darkened windows. "It's late. I already took her out."

"Midnight stroll," Tanya says. "Come on, Sally." She pats her thigh and starts making her way to the front of the house, avoiding Jesse's eye.

"Tanya, where is Lorraine?" Jesse's voice is strained and when Tanya doesn't answer, it rises in volume. *"Tanya!"*

Tanya whirls around, heart banging. "Don't *yell*, Jesse."

"Then answer me," he says. He strides toward her and she realizes then, by the lurch in his gait, that he's drunk. "Where's Lorraine?"

Tanya is trembling. She hates him, for making her feel terrified in her own house, for chasing them out this way. It seems preposterous that this is the same house where she woke up every morning of her childhood. And here she is, trying to reason with a drunk man who has taken over; looming in the living room like he owns it.

She feels a brief flash of fury toward her father, one town over, snug in his home with his wife and child—unaware, as always. She tries to dismiss it. Behind that anger is hurt and Tanya is tired of being hurt by him.

At this point she has just as many memories of Jesse in their house as she does of her own dad. Jesse sprawled on the living room couch, Jesse coming out of the bathroom, checking that his fly is up, Jesse in her parents' bedroom—in her parents' bed. Her father living at 12 Winter Street is more hazy than real—all those early memories meshed together into a conglomerate: when Dad was theirs. When Mom was less shaky.

Tanya takes a step toward Jesse to give him the illusion that she's not afraid. "Stay away from us," she says, keeping her voice low and steady, the way she does in the courtroom, even when she knows she's losing. "I'm holding you accountable for what you've done." And then she leaves, the dog at her heels.

Once Tanya's outside, she breaks into a run and, despite Sally's age, the dog keeps up. Just as she's climbing into the driver's seat, a police car coming from the other direction pulls into the driveway—quiet, no lights.

"That's them," Tanya says.

They all watch from the car as Jesse is served. A police officer rings the doorbell and Jesse appears in the doorway. He looks scared when he sees the officer. He steps outside on the front porch in his socks, and when the officer hands him a manila envelope he looks at it, bewildered, as though he's been handed a mango or a music box.

He opens it right away, in front of the officer. His face twists. The officer says something and, remembering that he's being watched, Jesse retreats back into the house and slams the door in the officer's face. Then Lorraine's phone starts ringing and doesn't stop for the next two hours.

2002

Nessa and Tanya were flower girls in their father's wedding. Simone chose matching lilac dresses for them to wear, with off-the-shoulder necklines and cool, silk skirts that swished like water against their legs.

The dress looked good on Tanya. Her sister's shoulders were as small and pale as flower petals against the lilac color, and the style showed off her delicate collarbone. Tanya sauntered around the backyard, beaming at anyone who looked in her direction. And people were looking—at both of them.

The lilac silk clung to Nessa's stomach, and the neckline pinched her back and shoulders, leaving red marks. The dress had looked better on her in the dressing room, where the lighting had been low and apricot colored. She regretted not getting a bigger size. The only part of the dress she liked was the bodice, which hugged and bolstered her chest. Nessa's breasts were large now, bigger than both her mother's and Simone's, and she was proud of them. Tanya, who was only just starting to develop, didn't have anything you could see in a dress.

THE WEDDING TOOK PLACE at Simone's family's summer house on Martha's Vineyard, in a backyard the size of a football field. Before the ceremony, Jonathan and Simone posed for photographs in front of an old stone wall surrounding the property. In the distance, three white horses grazed in a field, and beyond that, waves crashed on a private beach. The photographer called out directions in a monotone voice while the assistant arranged them in different positions as the photographer shot. Nessa and Tanya standing in front of Jonathan and Simone; all of them in a row; one with just the girls and Simone, and another one with just their father—each of them planting a kiss on either of his cheeks.

"Excellent," the photographer said. "Now, just the smaller one with Dad"—and the assistant ushered Nessa off to the side.

Everybody cooed as Tanya put her arms around their father. Nessa blinked hard, trying not to cry. She was frantic to disappear before the photographer called out the next inevitable direction. *And now the bigger one.* That was what she was, she thought, red-faced and mortified. She remembered a word on her vocabulary test the week before: *mammoth.*

Once he was done with Tanya, the photographer nodded toward his assistant and called out: "Now the older one with Dad."

The older one. Nessa almost laughed with relief. She took Tanya's place and her father wrapped his arm around her. Jonathan smelled like shampoo and deodorant and a breath mint, but underneath it all, he smelled like her dad, and Nessa remembered what it used to be like waking up on weekends and finding him downstairs, still in his pajamas, and how good he'd smelled like that, warm and soft like his old sleep T-shirts. She squirmed closer to him and closed her eyes, resting her cheek against his arm.

"Lovely," the photographer said, but Nessa's eyes were still closed and the photographer's voice sounded far away. There was the fast succession of clicks, like shuffling a brand-new deck of cards, and then the voice again: "Now look at each other and smile."

Nessa opened her eyes and looked up.

"Love you, Ness," Jonathan whispered, giving her shoulder a squeeze, and Nessa wished then that she was still a little girl, that she could stuff her face into her father's chest and tell him that she wanted to go, she was ready to leave—and together they might walk away from the crowded tent, forget about the ceremony and the party afterward, forget about all these people, and simply go home.

"Wonderful. Now I want the groom and the mother of the bride."

BY THE TIME the reception started, the sun had set and the ceiling of the tent was sparkling with hundreds of soft white twinkle lights. When Nessa looked up, it was like floating in a sky full of stars. On each table, tea lights drifted in small baths of water, and white candles, all lengths and widths, glistened everywhere, their creamy wax melting into intricate, elegant shapes. Beyond the tent the backyard gleamed a velvet green-black. The evening was the kind of beautiful Simone was—so pretty it hurt.

Nessa was sitting at her table alone, the tablecloth littered with plates of half-eaten cake and used silverware, glasses of water, the ice cubes melted down to slivers. Everybody else at their table—Tanya and six of Simone's nieces and nephews—was on the dance floor. Nessa glanced behind her to the center of the tent where a vibrating mass of people were dancing to "Hot in Herre." It was a song that embarrassed her, even from a safe distance.

Earlier, Nessa had allowed Tanya to pull her out of her seat and onto the dance floor. She'd swayed her hips and moved her feet a little, but that was all she'd been able to manage. Next to her, Tanya was dancing the way kids at school did, grinding her hips, as though moving against an invisible person behind her. Nessa had closed her eyes and tried to trick herself into moving the way she was able to do in the privacy of her bedroom, but it had been impossible surrounded by so many people. She felt stuck and ugly, like a parent chaperone clumsily bobbing her head to a song meant for younger ears.

Near the front of the dance floor, her father was dancing with Simone and their new friends. Nessa had observed them from afar for several minutes. Watching her father dance was like watching a stranger dance. She couldn't imagine going up to him, inserting herself in the unfamiliar circle of people. When he'd caught her watching, he'd waved at her, motioning her to come over, and it had been embarrassing for both of them. Nessa in her tight lilac dress—she could feel how ugly she looked—her father pretending to want her to join. She shook her head and walked away and he hadn't followed her.

Now she was back at the table. She nudged Tanya's plate closer to her and ate a glob of frosting. Then she finished one of the nieces' plates.

Restless, Nessa stood up and made her way through the maze of tables toward the drink station. Most people were up out of their seats dancing, and the rest of the tables looked similar to hers: plates of cake crumbs, jackets slung over chairs, high heels peeking out from beneath tablecloths. When she caught sight of a pack of cigarettes peeking out of a silver handbag at table 13—Marlboro Gold, the same kind her mother smoked—she grabbed it without thinking. She thrust her hand into the bag and snatched the box, then pressed it close against her leg. She skipped the minibar and walked straight through the tent to the back, then out into the dark stillness of the backyard.

SHE DIDN'T HAVE A LIGHTER, and part of her was relieved. She was scared to smoke and she didn't know how.

But when she turned around and saw one of the servers from the catering company a few yards away, smoking a cigarette of his own, Nessa felt she had no choice. If she did nothing—if she simply went back into the tent and watched people dance from her table—she knew she'd be miserable. She was growing dangerously tired of herself.

So Nessa opened the pack and pulled out a cigarette, held it between her pointer and middle finger. She wet her lips with her tongue—her mouth was suddenly dry—and approached the server with what she hoped was nonchalance.

"Excuse me," she said. Her voice came out so quietly that the server didn't hear. "Excuse me," she said again, and this time he jumped, his free hand flying up to push his glasses up his nose. "Holy shit." He laughed a little. "I didn't see you there. You scared the shit out of me."

"Sorry. I didn't mean to." Her voice sounded too high and her fingers holding the unlit cigarette quivered. "Do you have a lighter?"

The server raised an eyebrow. He was short, just a few inches taller than her, but his shoulders were broad beneath his uniform. He was older, Nessa could see that, but probably not by much. There was a shadow of facial hair on his cheeks and chin. He wore square glasses, and both of his ears were pierced, but instead of earrings he had two black rings through his earlobes, each one with a hole the size of a dime. Nessa could see straight through them, into the darkness of the woods.

She put the cigarette between her lips as she'd done dozens of times in her bed with her mother's unlit cigarettes, and stepped closer. She lifted her chin.

The server took a lighter from his pocket and flicked it so that a dollop of flame appeared. Nessa leaned in, touching the end of her cigarette to the fire, then inhaled deeply. Scratchy heat filled her chest and she began to cough.

"You okay?" The server glanced behind her as though somebody might be watching from the trees.

Nessa nodded, but her eyes were watering and heat was rushing rapidly to her face. She turned to the side. "Sorry," she choked out.

"Nothing to be sorry about."

She waited until the coughing stopped and then took a second puff. When she inhaled this time, it went smoother and her heart started to beat at a normal rate again.

"You look too young to be smoking."

"How old do you think I look?" Nessa asked. She was emboldened by the fact that she was no longer hacking, and it was easier to talk with a cigarette in her hand. For the first time Nessa understood why people got tattoos and dyed their hair blue and pierced their eyebrows. It was a way to hide and be seen at the same time.

"I don't know," he said, glancing at Nessa in a way that would have made her blush if she wasn't standing in the dark. "Fourteen?"

"I'm sixteen," she said. It was almost true.

"Oh. Huh." He nodded toward the tent. "How do you know them?" From their spot in the yard, the party looked far away, like a warm, glowing, pulsing planet unto itself.

"My dad's the groom."

He laughed, surprised. "No way."

"Yeah. It's weird."

She watched him take a puff from his cigarette, then blow smoke from the side of his mouth. "What is?" he asked.

"That I have a stepmother. That all those people in there are supposed to be my family now. I barely know anyone."

The server nodded. "I get it. My stepdad's a real dick. You don't have to listen to what she tells you to do. They like to think they have control, but they don't, and they know it."

Nessa decided not to tell him that Simone had never once told her what to do. It was better like this—both of them suffering the same way. "How old were you when your parents got divorced?" she asked.

He dropped his cigarette butt into the grass and nudged it with the toe of his shoe. "They were never married," he said. "I was a mistake."

"What do you mean, a mistake?"

He smiled. "Like, the condom broke. My mom had me when she was seventeen. Whoever the dude was, she never told him about me. Or maybe she did and he just didn't want anything to do with it. Her story changes a lot."

"Wow," she said. "So you don't know who your dad is?"

The server shook his head. "Nope. For all I know he could be some guy in that tent."

They both looked at the tent, as though the server's father might emerge.

A bubble of something quivered in Nessa's throat—sadness? Joy? She couldn't tell if it was good or bad, only that she felt extra alive. "I'm sorry," she said, and she hoped it was the right thing to say.

The server shrugged. "Don't be," he said, and when he looked at her his eyes and his half smile were so soft that Nessa felt light-headed. "Hey, do you want a drink?" he asked. "I can sneak one out here for you, no problem."

Nessa laughed, shocked. "That's okay," she said quickly, and immediately she regretted saying no.

He smiled. "I should get back." He nodded toward the house.

"Okay."

"See you around?"

"Yeah," she said. "See you."

Nessa watched as he walked away, one hand in his pocket and the other dangling by his side, his fingers tapping something out on his leg. Halfway across the lawn he stopped and turned around. "Hey!" he called out, and he pointed right at her. "Careful. Those things will give you cancer." Then he grinned, and her entire body exploded with happiness.

She waited until he disappeared into the house before she dropped her cigarette on the ground. She stamped it out with the toe of her shoe, just like he had, and headed back into the party with a new, unexpected kind of armor.

The Bennington bed-and-breakfast won't allow dogs, but it turns out the place across the street, the Paradise Motel, will. Nessa is relieved to be sitting in the backseat with Sally's head nestled in her lap, and not up front with Tanya and her mother, where the tension is sharp, practically pungent.

When the texts start up, first it's just a few chirps from Lorraine's phone, but soon there are dozens coming in, another one every few minutes, each one shriller and more urgent sounding than the last.

"What's he saying?" Tanya asks.

Lorraine doesn't answer.

"Don't write back," Tanya says. "Better yet, block him."

Lorraine just stares out the window.

At some point, either Jesse stops texting or Lorraine puts her phone on silent, and the car goes quiet. When they cross the Massachusetts border into Vermont, the roads out in the country are darker, windier. The mountains appear, but in the night, they're just murky shapes—ink-black mounds against a wool-black sky.

Nessa had always associated those mountains with the boyfriend in Bennington. She'd convinced herself they were in love, that when he sang Neil Young songs on his guitar, he'd been singing about her. And that when he forgot to pick her up at the bus station, or he was an hour late, or he showed up stoned or drunk, they were all honest mistakes.

Now, seeing the mountains, she feels a sharp pang of heartache. It's not for him, and it's not for Henry, or even for her mother, who seems unable to stop glancing down at her phone. It's just a feeling that begins in Nessa's chest and rises all the way up to her throat. And then—just like that—it passes.

BY THE TIME they pull up to the motel, it's almost ten. There's a sign out front by the road, lit up: VACANCIES, COMPLIMENTARY BREAKFAST, PETS ALLOWED, WIFI.

There are hardly any other cars parked outside the motel, and Nessa doesn't know if this makes her feel more safe or less.

In the lobby, a silver bell sits on the desk with a handwritten note: *Please ring for assistance!* Tanya rings the bell and moments later a young woman stumbles out of a door. She blinks at the light and pushes her hair back from her eyes.

"Good evening," she says huskily. Her name tag reads *Erica*.

"We'd like a room for three, please," Tanya says.

The woman yawns and fiddles with the mouse, rousing a very old computer to life. "Three, three, three," she mutters. Nessa glances around. The lobby is homey and poorly decorated, like a grandmother's living room filled with thrift-store clutter. The sofas are dated, not matching, though they look comfortable. There's a wooden coffee table with stacks of the Vermont local papers and a pot of fake flowers. A large-screen TV is playing the Weather Channel in the far corner of the room. The ceilings are low, the lighting a mixture of fluorescent ceiling lights and warm, yellow floor lamps. Deep purple curtains hang in the windows. The peculiarity of the place is calming. No one will find them here.

"Any pets?"

"One."

Erica glances over the desk and smiles at Sally, who is sitting at Nessa's feet. "Cutie." She looks back at Tanya. "Smoking or nonsmoking?"

Tanya glances at Lorraine. "Smoking," she says. Tanya's way of being warm.

"Alright. I have one room with two double beds or one with a queen-sized and we could pull in a cot."

"Two doubles is fine." Tanya opens her purse, and Lorraine puts her hand on Tanya's wrist. "Honey, let me."

"Don't you and Jesse share a bank account?"

Lorraine drops her arm and then nods. "Shit."

"Don't worry," Tanya says. "Better safe than sorry."

Nessa glances at Erica, but the woman hides any reaction or curiosity she might have and Nessa wonders how often people show up at this little motel in the mountains to hide.

Tanya hands Erica her credit card and in exchange Erica gives them three plastic swipe keys. "You're in room 164," she says. "Right down that hallway there. There's breakfast in the morning."

THEY WAKE UP hungry and leave Sally in the room to find the breakfast lounge, then watch while Erica rolls in a cart of food and arranges everything on a long card table beneath a checkered tablecloth. "Enjoy," she says, after all the food is spread out. She gives them a little wave before disappearing.

They survey the spread: mini boxes of cereal, pastries, small doughy bagels, oatmeal, yogurt with berries and granola, Vermont-made honey and syrup. They take some of everything and fill mugs with coffee, bring it all back to their table. They're quiet at first, eating as though they haven't eaten for days.

After the initial burst of hunger is satiated, they slow down, take stock of the accumulation of empty dishes. They sip from their mugs and dunk bits of pastry into the coffee.

Tanya is the first one to push her plate away. She wraps one arm around her face, smelling the crease of her elbow, and lifts her arm, taking a whiff of her armpit. "I stink," she announces. They haven't showered since before going to court the morning before.

This prompts Nessa and Lorraine to lift their arms, too.

"It's not a great situation over here either," Nessa says.

Tanya leans in, sticking her nose close to Nessa's armpit. "Not as bad as mine."

"Girls!" Lorraine laughs, as Tanya offers her armpit to Nessa.

"Ew, Tee." Nessa yanks her head away from Tanya.

"I get the clinical stuff and it still never lasts."

"Mom, you should smell it."

"I'm not going to *smell* it—"

A couple walks in then and this makes all of them shut up. Tanya, whose arm is still raised, quickly drops it. She starts to laugh and this makes Nessa laugh, too. Lorraine puts both hands over her face and shakes her head.

AFTER SHOWERS, LORRAINE falls back asleep immediately on one of the double beds and Tanya and Nessa share the other. For a while the sisters lie quietly, listening to Lorraine's breath, monitoring the rise and fall of their mother's chest.

Then Nessa rolls over to face Tanya and they stare at one another the way they used to do when they were younger, when it seemed they were quite possibly thinking and feeling all the same things. At one time, it had seemed magical. The unexplainable mix of sounds and smells and colors and feelings that made up the Bloom girls. It was no longer that simple. They'd grown up with the same mother and the same father. They'd grown up sleeping an arm's length apart from each other. But somehow, they'd still had entirely different childhoods.

"Tanya," Nessa says.

"Hmm?"

"Will you give me a massage?"

To Nessa's surprise, Tanya nods. Nessa rolls over onto her stomach and

Tanya climbs on top, straddling her. Nessa pulls off her T-shirt and brushes her hair off her neck.

"Where does it hurt?" Tanya asks.

"Everywhere. My shoulders."

Using her thumbs, Tanya kneads Nessa's back, moving in circles around her shoulder blades. She finds the knots and works at them, applying slow, patient pressure.

"Thank you," Nessa says after several minutes. "Do you want one?"

"Relax," Tanya says, and she continues to rub Nessa's neck. Nessa breathes deeply and closes her eyes.

Tanya works thoughtfully down Nessa's spine. It hurts in a good way, and Nessa feels herself melt into a different thing altogether—just a body, a puddle of sensations—muscles, bones, pressure points. Everything else evaporates. There's pain and pleasure, and that's it; everything on a spectrum.

She misses Henry. She thinks how nice it will be, to go home to someone who will hold her.

When tears come it's neither happiness nor sadness. It's just wet in Nessa's eyes and when she blinks, wet on her cheeks.

Tanya touches Nessa's cheek but doesn't say anything. She moves her fingers into Nessa's hair and scratches lightly at her scalp, all the millions of little nerve endings sparking under her nails.

2002

At first Tanya thought it was shit. It was a brownish-copper color and in her underwear of all places. But it didn't smell like shit and it wasn't in the seat of her underwear. Alarmed, she pulled Nessa into the bathroom. "Look," she said, pulling down her pants, showing her sister the stained mess.

"Tee," Nessa said, her eyes growing wide. "You got your *period*."

"But why is it that color?" Tanya asked.

"Because the blood is dried. Oh my God. We have to tell Mom."

But Lorraine was downstairs with Jesse, and Tanya did not want to involve her mother's boyfriend in this in any way. Tanya did not like any of her mother's boyfriends, but Jesse was especially bad. It was something about the way he smiled at Tanya. Like he was trying to win her over, like he might be able to trick her if she relaxed too much.

"No," Tanya said. "Not now." She turned toward the bathroom mirror and looked herself up and down. Her pants were still bunched at her knees. "I'm menstruating," she announced, businesslike, to her reflection.

Nessa giggled and tried to hug her, but Tanya ducked. "Don't touch me, I'm ovulating!" she cried, this time in a slightly hysterical tone.

"You're going to need a pad."

"Fuck no." Tanya shook her head. "I'm not wearing a diaper. I want to wear a *tampon*." The word was ridiculous to say out loud.

"You realize you have to stick it up your vagina, right?" Nessa asked.

"I know."

"It took me, like, a year to figure out how to do it."

"Will you teach me?" Tanya asked.

"Let's go to Mom's bathroom."

They migrated bathrooms and Nessa turned on the bright overhead lights, locked the door behind them, and rifled through the cabinet under the sink for the box of tampons. "We're going to be needing more of these," she said, glancing inside the box, and Tanya felt a flutter of excitement, along with a burst of pride, that she'd joined the ranks of tampon-wearing women in the house.

"Okay," Nessa said, handing Tanya an oblong-shaped package. "Here you go."

Tanya held it out in front of her. "What do I do with it?"

"Open it, dummy."

Tanya opened it and examined the bulbous head of the tampon, the patch of cotton peeking out from behind pink plastic, the embarrassing string hanging down, making the whole thing look fishlike.

Nessa discarded her own pajama pants so she was standing in her underwear. "So you want to stand like this . . ." She modeled. Her legs were widespread and she was bending her knees a little, like she was playing defense in a basketball game. "Then you just find the hole and slide it up there. When it's in, you push the applicator thingy with your finger, then pull the plastic out."

"Okay." Tanya removed her stained underwear so she was naked from the waist down. She stood in the defensive position, and, keeping her eyes on her sister, she probed around for "the hole" with the tip of the tampon. Once she felt an opening, she pushed. "It's hitting up against something," she said.

"What do you mean?"

"Some sort of wall."

"Try at a different angle."

Tanya readjusted the angle of the tampon and pushed, but the tampon wouldn't budge. "I don't think it's the angle."

"Are you sure you're putting it in the right hole?"

"Isn't there just one?"

"Tee! Are you serious?"

"What?" Tanya yanked the tampon away from herself, frightened suddenly by the idea of sticking a foreign object inside a hole she hadn't known existed.

"There's more than one hole. You know you don't pee and poop out of the same place, right?"

"I'm not sticking the tampon up my butt, Nessa. I'm not an idiot."

"Well, did you know there's a third hole?"

"Yes, I know there's a third hole," Tanya said, looking away. She did not. "Will you just show me?"

Nessa sighed. "Fine. But it's not going to work very well on me because I'm not bleeding."

Nessa pulled down her own underwear and flicked them off her ankles.

Her sister's vagina looked different from Tanya's; it always had. There was something more external about Nessa's vagina. The inner lips were longer and peeked out—you could see the pleats and the folds, whereas Tanya's were more hidden; shyer. Now her sister had pubic hair that covered a lot of it. Tanya had hair, too, but not as much as her sister—though Tanya knew more was coming.

Nessa took a tampon from the box and then spread a towel down on the tiled floor. "I'm going to do it lying down," she said, "so you can see where it goes, and then when it's inside, how I push in the applicator."

Her sister lay down and spread her legs. Using one hand, Nessa opened the inner lips, exposing pink, shiny, hairless flesh. It was not how Tanya imagined a vagina to look up close. In fact, she'd never before imagined what her own vagina looked like up close. In her mind she'd always thought of it more as a surface than something multifaceted, with various textures and openings.

"See the hole?" Nessa asked, pointing with her finger.

"Yes," Tanya said.

"Okay, so you put it here . . ." Nessa slid the tampon inside, wincing a little.

"Does it hurt?"

"Not too bad. Okay, so once it's here is when you push. See how I push with my finger and the cotton part goes up, but the plastic part comes out?"

"Yeah, I see."

"And the string just hangs so when you want to take it out all you have to do is pull." Nessa pulled. "*Ow*. Dry cotton." She sat up.

"I think I can do that," Tanya said. She resumed the defense position and this time felt around with her fingers for the right hole. When she found it, she held the lips open like Nessa had, and prompted the tampon inside. "It's going," she said. Tanya moved her finger to the plastic applicator and pushed, and, to her surprise, the plastic came out, but the tampon stayed securely inside her. "Oh my God," she whispered, looking up at Nessa. "It's fucking inside me."

Nessa smiled. "Weird, right?"

Tanya looked at herself in the mirror. The string hung between her legs and she pointed at it. "Nasty." She did a little dance.

"Just wait until the second day."

"What's the second day?"

"It's like the worst bloody nose you've ever had, but it's inside your vagina."

"Nessa," Tanya said, laughing.

Nessa began to laugh, too. "You'll see what I mean when you pull the tampon out. It's like a murder happened."

"I can't wait," Tanya said, and she meant it.

LATER THAT NIGHT Lorraine came up to say good night. "Sweet dreams," she said, sticking her head in the doorway.

"Guess what I got today," Tanya said, unable to keep the news from her mother any longer.

"What?" Lorraine asked.

"You have to guess."

"An A on your math test?"

"Well, yeah, but that's not what I was talking about."

Lorraine came into the bedroom and sat down on the edge of Tanya's bed. Instinctively her mother reached for Ellie the Elephant, running her hands down the animal's floppy ears. "Give me a hint."

"It's red."

"A pimple?"

"My period."

Lorraine put Ellie back down on the bed and a stern expression came over her mother's face. "Tanya, are you serious?"

"Yeah, earlier tonight."

For a moment Lorraine looked like she was going to burst out crying and then she lunged forward and pulled Tanya into an urgent hug. "Oh my God. Why didn't you tell me?"

"Mom, you're pulling my hair."

"Sorry," Lorraine said, sitting back a little. "Why didn't you tell me, sweetheart?" She was smiling now, brushing Tanya's hair off her forehead and tucking it behind her ear in quick, furious motions.

Tanya couldn't tell if her mother was happy or upset, or some combination of the two. She hadn't been expecting a reaction like this. When Nessa had gotten her period, her mother had barely blinked. It had been no different, really, from when her sister had gotten braces.

"My baby got her period," Lorraine said, still stroking Tanya's hair. "Want me to show you where the pads are?"

"Nessa did."

"Oh, good. Do you need help with how to use them?"

"Nessa helped me."

For a moment they were quiet, waiting for Nessa to say something from the top bunk, but Nessa was silent, didn't even shift in her bed.

"Do you have cramps?" Lorraine asked. "Does your stomach hurt?"

"No."

"Honey, when did you get it?"

"A few hours ago, I guess."

"Why didn't you come tell me?"

"Mom, stop."

"Stop what?"

"Asking me so many questions. I don't know. I'm telling you now."

"You know you can tell me anything," her mother said in a low voice.

Tanya felt something toughen in her chest. It was a sensation she was getting a lot those days. She couldn't put a name to it or predict when it was going to come on—but when it did, it was impossible to ignore. For a while she thought she was having heartburn again, but this was different. It had something to do with her family. The simplest word for it might be anger, but it was a sickly, more tired feeling than just being angry.

"I'm tired," she said.

"It's late. I love you, sweetie." Lorraine leaned out from under the bottom bunk. "Love you, too, up there, sweetie."

"You too," came Nessa's voice, muffled against her pillow.

When Lorraine left the bedroom she left the door open a crack so that a ribbon of light from the hallway slinked in, bisecting the room.

Tanya waited for Nessa to say something. To make a joke or a sarcastic comment about their mother, or just to ask Tanya to get up and close the door—the light from the hallway was bothering her. But something had shifted from before; her sister was somewhere else.

STRADDLING NESSA ON THE HOTEL BED, Tanya has not been this physically close to her sister in years, probably since that day in their mother's bathroom fifteen years ago. When she feels on Nessa's cheeks that her sister is crying, Tanya pretends that she doesn't notice. The danger of getting this close, after all, is just this. People get vulnerable with touch. She no longer hugs clients for this reason; she avoids touching even shoulders and hands. For some people it's like pressing a button. That's what it's like with her sister. Touch Nessa and she'll open up, pour herself out to you. It's probably a nightmare having sex with her, Tanya thinks. She's probably the type of woman who cries afterward—or worse, during—wanting to be held and coddled.

Sickened by the thought, Tanya climbs off her sister's back. She remembers back to the diner—*I went to Dan's house today*—and this time thinking about her sister saying his name repulses Tanya. It's as if Nessa had whispered something dirty—a secret code word that only Tanya knows, only Tanya understands.

Tanya lies down, putting as much space as she can between her and Nessa, even though she knows that Nessa will notice this and probably be hurt by it. Then she pretends to fall asleep.

The first time Jesse hit Lorraine was on their honeymoon. They'd gotten married earlier that week at the town hall, just the two of them. Lorraine hadn't seen the point of having a big wedding. She'd already had one of those, and the idea of doing it again embarrassed her. Besides, Nessa was on a cross-country road trip and Tanya was finishing her freshman year at Smith and she didn't want to drag them away from their lives. Also, she and Jesse didn't have many friends. They spent most of their time with each other. There was the additional fact that Lorraine's closest friends, Wendy and Marcy, didn't like Jesse. When she announced that she and Jesse had decided to get married, her friends had written her a joint letter outlining the reasons why they thought this was a mistake. Their biggest concern, they wrote, was that Jesse seemed controlling.

And he was. Lorraine knew this; she was not blind. Jesse was hot-tempered, possessive, domineering. He was the opposite of Jonathan that way. With her first husband, he'd been present, it seemed, with everyone but her. She'd spent the second half of their marriage trying to get his attention, trying to ignite some sort of reaction in him; any reaction at all. And the reaction she eventually got was that he wanted a divorce.

Jesse cared. He gave a shit. And he was never going to leave her. She was sure of this.

To the ceremony, Lorraine wore a cream-colored dress that fell past her knees and Jesse wore dress pants and a dress shirt. He looked handsome as ever, his brown eyes sweet and full of feeling; his usually messy hair combed back. She loved the grooved lines framing his mouth, how they deepened when he smiled and laughed. He couldn't stop smiling at her. As they stood across from each other in the dingy little room that smelled like ancient filing cabinets and wet paint, all she felt was grateful.

They both took a week off from work and rented a cottage in Chatham with a view of the sound. It was May and winter was clinging to Cape Cod, colder and grayer than either one of them expected. Too cold to swim or to wear anything but jeans and windbreakers. On the first night it was pouring, and they went to a fish fry place for dinner, with paper napkins and a bar taking up half the restaurant. When Jesse announced to the waiter that they'd just gotten married, the waiter came back with shots of their best tequila, and she and Jesse drank and laughed so much, they didn't even realize when they were the last ones in the restaurant.

It couldn't have been more different from her first honeymoon. Jonathan had taken Lorraine to Paris. It would have been romantic, she supposed, if she had known French or had better style. On their first dinner out she ordered something in French and Jonathan had corrected her pronunciation in front of the waiter. Her overarching memory from that trip was feeling clumsy and overheated, and wishing she was more interested in art than she was.

The first full day on the Cape, she and Jesse walked by the ocean. It was something between a mist and a drizzle, the blank stretch of beach before them disappearing into fog. Above, seagulls wailed, drifting and diving through the stone-colored sky, and in the distance, they heard the bells of buoys, though it was too foggy to see very far past the shoreline. Lorraine insisted on walking barefoot—she liked the sand, wet and freezing beneath her feet, the romance of the cold beach. They had the entire thing to themselves.

Jesse was hungover, though, and in a mood. When Lorraine pointed to the gulls overhead, when she picked up shells and rocks, holding them out in her palm, he rolled his eyes and kept walking. She stopped at one point and dragged her big toe through the sand. *L + J,* she wrote, in huge letters, and waited for him to look over his shoulder. When he didn't, she called his name. "Look!" she said, and, begrudgingly, he turned around and walked toward her.

For several moments he stared at the initials in the sand and then looked back up at her. "What?" he asked. "Do you want a medal or something?"

"Don't be a jerk," she said hotly, right on that familiar edge of anger and playfulness, where they always seemed to be dancing. Then she pounced on him.

They'd wrestled before, usually before or after sex, rolling around on the bed, tickling one another, laughing.

They fell onto the sand and Lorraine mounted him. "Yes, I would like a medal, please," she said, pushing her palms into his chest, and he grinned, grabbing her waist and squeezing. Before she knew it, he'd flipped her so that he was on top. He pinned her to the ground, holding her wrists down with his hands.

"Get off," she cried, laughing and struggling beneath him.

"Not gonna happen," he said, staring down at her as she thrashed beneath him.

"You're hurting me!"

"Too bad." He pushed down even harder so that her wrists started to ache beneath his hands.

"Jesse, get off me," she said, and when he didn't let up: "Get the fuck *off*."

"Shut *up*, bitch," he said, and before the words even sank in, he hit her, square on the side of her head.

Tears sprang to Lorraine's eyes as pain radiated from her left cheek and ear. She looked up at him in shock.

Jesse seemed not even to be looking at her. It was as though he was looking past her, through her head and down into the sand, lost in some hateful, faraway thought.

It was then when she had the distinct thought: *I made a mistake marrying him.* She thought of Nessa and Tanya. As if by hitting her, he had somehow hit her daughters also. This was what made her furious.

His hands were no longer pinning her down, and she scrambled out from underneath him, grabbing her shoes and running back in the direction they'd come from, holding her aching ear with her free hand.

She was aware of Jesse following her, calling her name, but she didn't turn back. When she got to the parking lot, theirs was the only car in the lot, and the doors were locked. Jesse had the key. Lorraine leaned against the door, pressing her ear, which pulsed against her palm. She had never been hit before and it was as though she'd walked from one world into another.

Jesse appeared several minutes later. She didn't look at him; she was too humiliated.

There was the sound of Jesse unlocking the car.

"I want to go home," she said, when they both got in. When he didn't respond, she looked over and said it again. "Jesse, I want to go back to Arlington. Today."

Jesse returned her gaze. She expected him to be mad, to protest, but his eyebrows were peaked with worry, his eyes glassy. "I understand," he said softly, and then he put the car in reverse and pulled out of the parking spot.

When they got back to the cottage, Lorraine went straight to the bedroom and began pulling clothes out of the drawers and closet, shoving them into her suitcase. She had brought far too much clothing, most of it absurdly summery for this drab, freezing week on the Cape. She had packed a teddy—a black lace thing that she'd gone and bought for herself especially for this trip. Sexy but not too sexy. It covered her upper thighs the way she wanted it to, while still showing off her cleavage.

"Lorrie."

Lorraine looked up. Jesse was standing slumped in the doorway.

"I'm almost finished packing," she said, thrusting the teddy deep into the bag. "You should start."

"Wait, Lorrie. Can we talk first?" His voice was so soft she could barely hear him.

"There's nothing to talk about," she said. "You *hit* me."

"I don't know what came over me," Jesse whispered. "You have to believe me, I will never, ever do that again. Babe?"

She walked over to the bedside table, gathering up the clutter that had already started to build; it was amazing how quickly you could move in somewhere and make it your own. Her glasses and hand cream, a box of matches from the restaurant last night, a glass of water with dust floating in it.

"Lorrie, hold on a sec," Jesse said, and this time his voice was a little louder, though gentle still. "Can we just stop and talk, just for five minutes? Can you just give me five minutes to talk to you and then I promise we can finish packing and leave?"

She looked up at him. "Five minutes," she conceded.

"Thank you," he said, visibly relieved. "Lorrie, thank you."

She sat on the bed and he came over and knelt in front of her. "Lorrie, sometimes I have these urges," he said, his eyes huge. "It's embarrassing to talk about, like I feel so ashamed. I haven't even really been able to make sense of it in my own mind. But I get these cravings." He looked down at the floor and then straight at her. "To dominate you. Not in a *real* way, of course. But sexually. It's like a fantasy. There's something about you that turns me on in this way I've never been turned on by anyone before. Like I'm almost scared about how attracted I am to you. I want to try all these things, things I've never done. When we were on the beach and I was on top of you, I got excited. I never meant to hit you like that. It was a complete accident. I got carried away. An urge gone wrong. I feel like a monster." He gazed up at her.

"You really hurt my ear," she said. She could feel herself beginning to cry, and she knew, then, that crying would change things—this would be the beginning of her forgiving him. She felt relief. To be sad and not angry. That he was being soft.

"Can I see it?" he asked.

She shrugged and Jesse stood, leaning in to examine Lorraine's ear. Gently, he touched the tender skin around it and then lightly kissed her earlobe. "Do you need to see a doctor?" he asked.

"I don't think so."

"Because if you do, I'll take you there right now. We can go to the emergency room right this second if you want."

"I don't think that's necessary, Jesse. And what would we even tell them?"

"We would tell them the truth."

"The last thing I feel like doing on my honeymoon is sitting in an emergency waiting room." She was really starting to cry now. She squeezed her eyes shut and took a deep breath.

"I have an idea," Jesse said. He sat down beside her on the edge of the bed. "Let's take a bath. Let's take a steaming hot bath in that gigantic bathtub until we're wrinkled all over. And then I want to take you out to dinner. A really nice dinner. We'll get dressed up and we'll order the most expensive wine they have and, like, all the desserts on the menu. How does that sound, Lor?"

She couldn't bring herself to answer, but she put her head on his shoulder.

"What was that you were holding a second ago?" Jesse asked, after several moments had gone by.

She glanced up at him. "What?"

"That black nightgown."

"Oh." She shook her head. "It's dumb."

"It didn't look dumb." He moved his leg slightly so that it pressed up against hers. "Can I see it?"

"I don't know, Jesse," she said, but a quiet thrill had started to build inside her. The thrill was mixed up with the relief.

Jesse leaned across the bed and reached into her bag, pulling out the teddy. He held it out in front of him, looking at it with such rapture that Lorraine could hardly breathe. Then he glanced at her. "Do I get to see you in this?" he asked.

"No," she said.

He smiled and set the black lace lightly down on the bed. "I'm going to run the bath," he said. "You rest. I'll come get you when it's ready."

WHEN LORRAINE LOOKS BACK on this day, she wonders if this was the moment when she could have changed the course of things. If she had insisted they pack their bags and leave right that instant, if she'd put her foot down—maybe things would have turned out differently for her. But she was tired and hungry and upset, and it was her honeymoon. They'd paid for the rental for the entire week. They hadn't used the Jacuzzi yet. A bath and a romantic dinner—it had sounded so nice. So in that moment, she'd leaned her head on Jesse's shoulder. She'd allowed him to make things right.

JESSE HAS BEEN TEXTING her endlessly since they left the house last night with Sally. Lorraine put her phone on silent so the girls wouldn't hear the incoming chirps, but she's been watching his text messages come through, a new one every twenty minutes or so, though she's stopped herself from writing back.

HIS LATEST: *Lorrie, I made an appointment with a couples therapist. Dr. Louis Keller. He comes highly recommended. It's for this Thursday at 6 p.m. You don't have to come but I'm going to be there. I hope you decide to come. Don't give up on us yet.*

SHE GLANCES OVER at her daughters. They're both asleep, Tanya with the pillow curled under her, Nessa flat on her stomach. Their hair is splayed out, overlapping, and it's impossible to tell whose is whose. For the first time since they left, Lorraine writes a response to Jesse.

I'LL THINK ABOUT IT, she writes. Clicks send.

THAT'S ALL I'M ASKING FOR, he writes back within seconds, and it's as though he's reached through the phone and touched her.

They all wake up in the afternoon. The motel room has transformed into a bath of rose-gold light and shadows. The sun coming through the blinds is thick and warm as honey. Lorraine is propped up on her pillow reading something on her phone, and Tanya is curled on her side beside Nessa, a pillow tucked under her arm.

"Hi," Nessa says.

"Hi," Lorraine echoes.

And Tanya. "Hi."

Nessa has the feeling then of never wanting to leave. How safe they are there, holed up together. Jesse and Henry and Eitan—their father and Simone and Ben—far away, in another world entirely, one that doesn't exist inside this womb of light. They could live here in this sun-soaked room forever, eating complimentary breakfasts for the rest of their lives. Erica can be their gatekeeper, sleeping in that back room of the lobby every night, making sure no one dangerous is allowed to enter.

Northampton is only ninety minutes away, but her world there—Janeski's office, sporadic nights with Henry, long directionless walks through her neighborhood—all of it feels disjointed, a life that doesn't really belong to her. But here, burrowed close with her mother and sister, Nessa feels right.

They get up leisurely and change, then congregate in the bathroom to freshen up. They brush their teeth and Tanya has eyeliner in her purse, which she passes around. Lorraine's bruises have changed from an angry red to a dotted plummy purple color. Lorraine pulls her hair over her shoulders, adjusting it just right to cover the bruises, like Nessa and Tanya used to do to cover up hickeys.

When they leave the room in search of food, Nessa is disappointed that a different person is at the desk this time, a man with heavy eyelids and a gold crucifix hanging from his neck. His name tag says *Chris.*

"What would you recommend for dinner around here?" Lorraine asks him, and Nessa is aware of the hint of flirtation in Lorraine's question, the way her voice raises a touch in pitch.

Chris wheezes and thuds his chest with his palm. "On Main Street you have lots of options. Bennington Pizza House——a real crowd-pleaser. Let's see. Madison Brewing Company——good burgers, good beer. There's Lucky Dragon if you like Chinese. A fish fry place. We keep a whole list of restaurants over there, if you want to take a look." He points to a small wooden table with a black binder and a pile of take-out menus.

Lorraine nods. "Wonderful."

"Just take a right out of the lot," he goes on. "Straight down Main Street."

"Where to, ladies?" Lorraine asks when they're in the car.

Tanya makes a sound of distaste from the backseat. "None of it sounds especially appealing."

"I'd do the burger place," Nessa says.

"Tee?"

Tanya plunks her feet on the console. "Whatever you guys want."

The restaurant is on Main Street nestled between Bennington Pizza House and a clothing shop. The storefront's painted green with big windows looking into the dimly lit pub, all wood and brick.

Inside there's dozens of empty tables and a bar. They're greeted by the hostess and led to a table by the window. Other than the employees, they're the only people there.

A waiter comes by with the menus, a teenage boy, his face and neck studded with infected acne. "Welcome to Madison Brewing Company," he says, pouring them water and avoiding eye contact.

Quietly they look through the menus. After a minute Tanya puts hers down. "I can't eat any of this."

"Why not?" Lorraine asks.

"Everything is fried or drenched in cheese," she says. "It's fine. I'll just get something from the supermarket after you guys are done."

Nessa's jaw tightens, agitated. She doesn't know why her sister always feels the need to put them down; to equate the oil, the cheese, with something about them. Nessa no longer eats the way she did as a child. Not that the hunger has gone away, but she's figured out other ways to curb it. She's not as thin as Tanya, who pays seventy dollars a month so that she can run herself ragged on a battered New York Sports Club treadmill every morning. But Nessa likes her body. Not every day, and not in every mirror. But overall. It's usually when she's next to Tanya that she's tempted to stuff herself again.

"Do you want to go somewhere else?" Lorraine asks Tanya.

"Did you hear his list of restaurants?"

"What about the fish place?"

Tanya rolls her eyes.

"Well, if there's nothing you can eat here it doesn't make sense to stay," Lorraine says. "You must be hungry. What if you got the eggplant dish?"

"It's fried," Tanya says. "It's fine. I'm not even that hungry."

"Oil isn't going to kill you, Tanya," Nessa says.

Tanya lets out a short laugh. "Actually, that's exactly what it will do."

"Well, don't ruin it for us," Nessa says.

Tanya holds up her hands. "I'll shut up."

The waiter returns. "Are you ready to order?" he asks, and when no one says anything Nessa nods. "Go ahead, Mom."

Lorraine squints at the back side of the menu. "I'm wondering," she says, pointing, "if it's possible to get the eggplant provençal but without frying the eggplant?"

"Um. Like, just a plain eggplant?"

"Well, a little oil's okay," she says. "Just, you know, not deep fried?"

"Um." He scratches at his pad. "Okay. I'll ask them." Then he turns to Tanya, and Nessa sees the way her sister's prettiness and forthright gaze catch him off guard. "What would you like, miss?" he stammers. Under the violent red of his acne, his cheeks burn even brighter.

Tanya smiles coolly. "I'm set with water, thanks."

"Oh, okay." He begins to write it down before remembering they already have water glasses in front of them. He turns to Nessa next, visibly relieved, and his face resumes its normal color. "And you?" he asks. Hurt tugs at Nessa's chest, followed swiftly by humiliation. How pathetic she is, to feel rejected by a fifteen-year-old waiter.

"I'll have the pulled pork sandwich," Nessa says, just to piss off Tanya. "And an appetizer of truffle fries for the table."

A tense minute passes after the server leaves. Then Tanya speaks: "So we should talk about Monday."

Lorraine sighs. "I guess we should."

"I don't see any reason why you won't get the restraining order if you tell the judge about the strangulation," Tanya says. "Jesse, I'm assuming, will show up to the hearing, and he'll have a chance to speak, but I'm not really worried about that. But, Mom, I do think you have to mention the physical abuse. And that you have documentation that you went to the hospital. I know it's hard to talk about, but the judge needs to know the full story, and that's a crucial part of the story."

"Tanya," Nessa says. "Why don't you let Mom decide what is crucial to the story. It is *her* story, after all."

"Are you pissed at me for some reason?" Tanya says, turning to Nessa. "For not ordering something?"

"I just think you're being a little condescending."

"Girls, come on." Lorraine leans back in her chair.

"Mom, the big question now is where you're going to live," Tanya says. "You don't have to move out of the house for another month or so, right? I'm sure you'll have enough time before then to find an apartment or at least something short-term until you figure out your next steps. And if you need to, you can always come and stay with Eitan and me in the city."

"Or me," Nessa says. "You can stay with me, too."

Lorraine takes a sip of water and glances toward the kitchen. "I do have a little thing here called a job."

"You can work it out with Selma," says Tanya. "Given the situation, I'm sure she'll understand."

"It's not the kind of situation I'm very keen on sharing," she says. "Oh, look, Ness, here come your fries."

"*Our* fries," Nessa says. "They're for the table. Especially Tanya."

"Let's talk about this later, after dinner," Lorraine says. "I just want to enjoy a meal without thinking about all this crap."

"It's the day after tomorrow, Mom," Tanya says. "There's not that much time to push it off until later."

Lorraine transports a handful of fries onto her plate. "Don't these look good," she says, though she doesn't eat any.

Nessa pops one into her mouth, burning her tongue, and lets it drop from her mouth back onto the plate. "Hot."

Tanya has her phone out and is texting.

The waiter comes by. "How are the fries?" he asks.

"Great," Nessa says. He nods and scurries away.

"What are you doing on there?" Nessa asks then, nodding at her sister's phone. "It's kind of rude."

Tanya looks pointedly at her. "I'm arranging with work to take Monday off so I can go to court with Mom. And I'm letting Eitan know that I'll be home by the evening and I'm asking him to cancel my hair appointment Monday night."

"Honey, you should go to your appointment," Lorraine says. "I'll be okay in court. Don't worry about me."

Tanya looks up, her eyes blazing. "I *do* worry about you," she says. "I come home and you've lost fifteen pounds and in the middle of the night you're strangled in our own kitchen." She looks at Nessa. "And you two are acting like nothing is wrong. We're not on a vacation right now."

The waiter arrives at the table and gently sets down their plates.

Lorraine's face has lost its color. "I shouldn't have put this on you girls. This is something I have to work out with Jesse."

"There's nothing to work out, Mom." Tanya is practically shouting. "You have to leave him. Period."

Lorraine stares out the window. "I know," she says.

"No one ever has the right to lay a hand on you." Tanya slams her fist down on the table. "He should be locked up. He should be held accountable, condemned, for what he's done. You can't let him get away with this. And you know, Mom, the next woman he finds, he's going to do the same thing to her, he's going to—"

And then Lorraine's shoulders fall.

Tanya's entire face changes. She speaks softly. "It's going to be okay. You're safe now. We're going to make sure you're safe."

Nessa puts her hand on Lorraine's shoulder. "Tanya's right."

"I don't—"

"What is it, Mom?" Tanya presses.

Lorraine looks at Tanya, but then she turns to Nessa. "He's never going to leave me."

Nessa and Tanya glance at one another.

"He's not going to find someone else," she goes on. Then, everything about her hardens. "I do love him."

Tanya stands, pushing her chair back so quickly that it falls over behind her, and storms out of the restaurant.

Nessa catches the waiter's eye from across the room where he and the other two servers are watching. "Check," she mouths to him, and he nods, catapulting into action.

"Jesse is complicated," Lorraine says, looking up at Nessa. "He gets really bad when he drinks. He's not like this all the time. It's like a different person comes out. He feels terrible about it," she says. "He wants help. He's agreed to go to couples counseling."

Nessa nods. "Have you gone?"

"Not yet," she says. "He has the name of this man and everything, someone who comes highly recommended." She looks out the window. "Should we go find her?"

Nessa shakes her head. "She'll text when she wants us to find her. Let's just give her some time to cool off."

Lorraine nods and takes a sip of water.

"Mom, is this the first time he's hurt you?"

"Yes."

"Really?"

Lorraine regards her tiredly and Nessa is surprised by how quickly her mother gives in.

"He's hurt you before?"

"Of course, Nessa." For a moment, her mother seems irritated.

"When did it start?"

"Not too long ago," Lorraine says. "I don't remember when, exactly."

"What happened?"

Her mother sighs. "Honey, I'll tell you about it, but I don't want to upset you more than you already are."

"I can handle it," Nessa says, but already she's bracing herself.

All those weekends she could have visited but hadn't. All the one-minute phone calls, exchanging pleasantries, promising longer conversations soon. Guilt engulfs her, the sickly way it overtakes you in a single breath.

Lorraine studies Nessa. She seems to be deciding what to say next.

2016

Things started to get bad after the party at Diane's house. Jesse hadn't wanted to go. He didn't like Lorraine's coworkers. "They're boring," he complained. "Especially that butch one," he added, meaning Diane. The party wasn't even really a party—it was more of a get-together, a gathering of coworkers and friends to celebrate Diane's upcoming retirement from Stand Together. But after some persuasion Jesse had agreed to come along, mostly because Lorraine promised there'd be alcohol there, and that they wouldn't have to stay long.

As soon as they stepped inside Diane's house, a big colonial out in Concord, Jesse smiled broadly, turning on his Jesse charm, and Lorraine relaxed a little. Once Jesse was out and surrounded by other people, his mood always seemed to lift, and Lorraine couldn't help being swept along with it.

It was over by the drinks when Lorraine stopped short at the sight of a man across the room. At first she thought she must be making things up. But no, that was him: Raymond, the chiropractor from Match.com, whom she'd gone on a handful of dates with years before, right after Jonathan left. He was by himself, a drink in one hand and a paper plate of food in the other. He looked mostly the same from all those years ago; a little heavier maybe, and balder. She'd been unimpressed with his looks when she was younger, but now, almost twenty years later, she was less interested in what he looked like and more interested in whether he would remember her or not. She glanced at Jesse. He was going straight for the beer, expertly prying the cap off a bottle of Heineken and air toasting Lorraine before taking a sip.

Lorraine reached for one of the open bottles of pinot grigio in the ice bucket and poured herself a generous glass, wondering if she should approach Raymond or if it would be better to pretend she had no idea who he was.

"Trying to get wasted?" Jesse said, glancing at her cup.

"No," she said.

"Go easy, Lor," he said, and then he walked off, leaving her alone by the drink table.

Lorraine took several long sips and then wandered into the living room in search of her coworkers. She spotted several of them, and was about to break into the conversation, when she heard her name.

"It's Lorraine, right?"

Lorraine smiled. "Hi, Raymond."

"God, I'm glad that was you. I thought, either I'm about to make a complete fool of myself or I have an excellent memory. It has to be, what . . . fifteen, twenty years?"

"Something like that."

"Well, it's great to see you." He seemed genuinely pleased to see her, and Lorraine felt a swelling in her chest.

"You too," she said. "How do you know Diane?"

"My wife, Elizabeth, is good friends with her." He pointed across the room to a small circle of women, but it wasn't clear which woman Elizabeth was. "How about you?"

"I work with her at Stand Together."

"Oh, right! I remember you did that kind of work."

"How's your practice going?"

"Oh, it's going," Raymond said. "I figure I'll put in another six, maybe seven years, then think about retiring, like our good friend Diane."

"Are we really that old?" Lorraine asked. She reached up and touched her hair, as though that might provide an answer.

Raymond laughed. "I think we might be getting there."

A woman walked over then. She was short and heavyset, dressed in an oversized silky blouse, a loud magenta, over matching silky pants. Her hair, blond and cropped, was a little long in front but short and buzzed in the back, an utterly sexless hairstyle, Lorraine noted, one that she herself would never get.

"Hi, there. I'm Elizabeth," the woman said, smiling, with the warmth and directness of a preschool teacher. She held out her hand to Lorraine. "I don't believe we've met yet."

"Lorraine," she said, shaking Elizabeth's hand.

"Lorraine!" Elizabeth repeated, as though she'd been hoping to meet Lorraine all night. "So nice to finally meet you. Diane's told me so much about you."

"Really?"

"Oh yes, of course. Honey," she said, turning to Raymond. "Did you just meet Lorraine?"

"Funny thing," Raymond said, smiling a little. He was at least a foot taller than his wife, but next to her he seemed to wither a bit. "Lorraine and I actually dated briefly about fifteen years ago. We were matched up on Match.com, if you can believe it."

Elizabeth's eyes widened and a humorous look came over her face. "You're kidding me!"

Lorraine shook her head; the wine was starting to get to her. "Isn't that crazy?"

"That's *wild*," Elizabeth said. Then she started to laugh. "Diane!" she called, turning around. Her preschool-teacher voice carried out into the house. "Diane!"

Several moments later Diane appeared.

"Guess who used to date fifteen years ago courtesy of Match.com?" she asked, smiling widely.

Diane raised her eyebrows.

"*These* two," Elizabeth said, putting one hand on Raymond's shoulder and the other on Lorraine's.

"No kidding," said Diane.

That was when Jesse appeared. He was smiling, but his eyes were cold, and Lorraine's body tensed. "What was that?" he asked, coming up behind her. He was holding a Heineken—a new one—and he slipped his other arm around Lorraine's waist, letting his thumb rest on the waistband of her jeans. "I'm Jesse," he added, addressing Elizabeth, before glancing dismissively at Raymond.

"Hi, Jesse," Elizabeth said ardently, as though each new piece of information she received just got more and more thrilling. "You must be here with Lorraine."

"She's my wife."

"Well, it's a delight to meet you both. I'm guessing you haven't heard the funny coincidence yet."

"Not yet," Jesse said, still smiling. His grip on Lorraine's waist grew tighter.

"It turns out our spouses matched on Match.com fifteen years ago. Lucky for us, it didn't work out."

Jesse laughed. "Lucky for us."

"We got out of that whole mess before it really got started." Raymond piped up then. "These days with all these new sites and apps."

"And Tinder!" Elizabeth said with a dramatic wave of both hands. "Kids are meeting each other on a website called Tinder! They get together just to, you know—dunk the dingus—and then call it a day. No more dinners or movies or meeting the parents. It's a *sex* application," she said, lowering her voice, which was still fairly loud. "Swipe and sex."

"Dunk the dingus?" Lorraine said, but Jesse spoke over her.

"It's disgusting," he said. "The way men treat women like commodities, dating the same way you'd go shopping for a car or a watch. Lorraine has two daughters and I love them like my own. It kills me to think of men seeing pictures of them on their screen, then swiping yes or no."

Lorraine's throat tightened at the mention of her girls. Tanya, of course, was married and not on any such app. But she knew it was Nessa he was talking about. Jesse had a soft spot for Nessa; mostly because Nessa had a soft spot for him. She knew that Jesse brought Nessa up to punish Lorraine, to make her jealous. And that was what he was doing right now. Jesse was angry at Lorraine. She could feel it with every ounce of her body, the same way you feel nausea coming on. He was angry at her for dragging him to this party; for having once dated Raymond; for having the nerve and the wherewithal to have gone on a dating site fifteen years ago.

"Oh, but you know the girls do it, too!" Elizabeth went on. "They swipe just like the boys do. It takes two to tango." She glanced at Raymond and grinned. "Or should I say, two to Tinder."

Raymond laughed and Lorraine watched Jesse eye him sarcastically.

"You know," Elizabeth said, turning to Lorraine. "You should tell your daughters about a dating website called Bumblebee. Or Bumbler. Something like that. The rule is the lady has to contact the gentleman first." She smiled pointedly at Jesse. "How do you like that for switching things up?"

THEY LEFT SHORTLY AFTER, but not before Jesse downed two more beers and Lorraine hid in the bathroom for ten minutes and smoked a cigarette out the window. She found mouthwash in Diane's medicine cabinet and rinsed her mouth out, and then she went back out and poured herself a few more sips of wine to cover up the mint.

They were silent on the walk from the house back to the car and Lorraine knew this was a bad sign.

"Are you okay to drive?" she asked once they reached the car, sensing before the words left her mouth that they would be the ones to ignite their inevitable fight.

"Jesus, Lorraine," Jesse burst back, red-faced. "If you don't want to get in the car with me, then have one of your fucking friends drive you home."

"I'll get in the car with you," she said quickly.

As Jesse started the car and pulled away from the curb, she imagined a scenario in which she did not get in the car with Jesse and she did, in fact, ask one of her friends to drive her home. She imagined asking Raymond.

Jesse sped the entire way, going fifty miles an hour in mostly twenty-five-mile-an-hour districts. He plowed through stop signs and screeched around curves. At one point, Lorraine asked him to slow down, but this only made him drive faster, so she shut up for the rest of the way. By the time they got home she was crying. She ran from the car into the house and Jesse stormed in after.

"You knew that guy was going to be there?" he demanded.

They were standing in the living room, Lorraine on one side of the couch and Jesse on the other.

"Raymond?"

"Who the fuck else would I mean?"

"No, I didn't know, Jesse," she said. "I haven't talked to the man for fifteen years."

"You looked pretty cozy for two people who haven't seen each other for fifteen years."

"It was small talk, Jesse. We were making small talk!" She held out her hands. "What do I need to do to convince you that I love you and only you. You're my husband. You're the only person I want."

Jesse stared at her, squinting, and for a moment it looked like he might be hearing what she was saying, like he might be reconsidering the past hour and seeing it for what it was. But then he smiled oddly and said, "Was he a good fuck?"

"What?"

"Well, was he?"

"God, Jesse. We never slept together."

Jesse scoffed and traipsed around the couch, so he was just inches away from her. "Yeah, right." Up close he smelled like beer and sweat and deodorant.

"We didn't."

"Like hell you didn't. I know you, Lorraine. Just tell me." Then he smiled. "Or what—was he, like, really small or something? And you're trying to protect him? Or what? Limp dick? What's his deal?"

"Not everything is about sex, Jesse. We went on a few dates. Four, probably, max. I never saw his dick."

"Did you show him your tits?"

"Fuck this," she said, turning away, and then he swung at her.

It had been a while since Jesse had done that. Months had gone by—almost half a year. Lorraine had convinced herself that that part of Jesse had gone away. He'd outgrown it, or maybe it was she who had changed. She'd grown stronger or more stable. A less easy target.

But there they were again. She fell to the floor and Jesse climbed on top of her, panting. He restrained her with one arm. With the other, he put pressure on her neck, not so hard that she wasn't able to breathe, but enough that she was terrified. It was the first time he'd done that, restricted her air passage, and she panicked, gasping and thrashing beneath him. "You're too old for him anyway," he said then, calmly. "No man is going to want you anymore."

When he finally let go, at first all she felt was relief. She gulped in air and rolled out from underneath him. She tried to say something, but she found that her vocal cords ached, that her entire body was trembling. She went upstairs and climbed into bed.

That was when the sorrow sank in.

OVER THE NEXT FEW WEEKS, Jesse did what he always did afterward: he turned gentle. A soft place for Lorraine to land. This time, though, Lorraine found herself thinking about Raymond. She imagined what life was like for him and Elizabeth: Raymond coming home each evening from his chiropractic practice; Elizabeth coming home from whatever she did all day. The two of them making dinner and watching television. Elizabeth chatting in that loud, excited way of hers, Raymond listening closely and chortling. She could see they enjoyed each other, loved each other. She couldn't imagine that they were intimate, though. She wondered if Raymond was the type to cheat on his wife, though the thought of it made her sad. Besides, her attraction to Raymond—if she could even call it that—wasn't really about sex.

She found him on Facebook. It was her secret account, the one she used on her work computer. Jesse didn't want her to have a Facebook. He grew too jealous, too suspicious of any new Facebook friends, so she kept it from him and used it sparingly; he didn't know it existed. Her Facebook name was Lorrie Sal—Sal for Sally—and she didn't have any pictures of herself, or identifying information available to the public. Her profile picture was a photograph she'd taken on her phone one afternoon, taking Sally on a walk. A yellow flower, sprouting up from some vines crawling up a fence. She'd liked the surprise of the flower, the unlikeliness. She'd actually shown the photo to Jesse, though he'd barely glanced at her iPhone screen. "Artsy" was all he'd said, mockery in his voice.

Raymond's profile picture was of him outdoors at some sort of tourist attraction. He was wearing sunglasses and a backpack and was pointing to something outside of the frame. She imagined Elizabeth behind the camera instructing him to smile and point. Lorraine friended him and, after some deliberation, sent him a private message. "Hi Ray!" she wrote. "Great bumping into you after all these years. I hope it's not another 15 years before I see you again! xx, Lorrie."

Every workday she checked her account for a response. After a week of silence, she told herself that maybe he wasn't an active Facebook user. He never posted anything, after all. But when a month passed, and he still hadn't responded, Lorraine came to the conclusion that any interest in her that she'd picked up on that afternoon at Diane's party—romantic or platonic— she must have imagined. She didn't know how this was possible, but she felt heartbroken.

Then one Thursday morning, she came to work and she had a notification. Heart racing, she clicked on it: "Raymond Schild liked your photo." She clicked further, and her photograph of the flower on the fence popped up.

Below it was Raymond's name with a little thumbs-up. For the rest of the day, she carried around a warmth in her chest.

IT WASN'T EVEN a week after that when Selma, Lorraine's boss at Stand Together, stuck her head into the kitchen where Lorraine was helping to prepare for that day's lunch. "Someone's up front to see you," she said.

"Who?" Lorraine asked, surprised.

Selma shrugged and made a face, indicating her irritation. Pop-in visits weren't encouraged. Lorraine nodded and checked in with the other staff on lunch duty and followed Selma back toward the front office.

At first, when Lorraine saw Elizabeth, Raymond's wife, sitting in the waiting area, a pang of anxious excitement ran through her. Her first, albeit crazy, thought had been: maybe Raymond wanted to leave Elizabeth for Lorraine and Elizabeth was there to chew her out. But when Elizabeth stood, a concerned look on her face, Lorraine knew instantly this wasn't the case.

"Lorraine, I'm Elizabeth, from—"

"I know, I remember you."

"I'm sorry to bother you at work," Elizabeth said. "I didn't know the best way to reach out to you." Her preschool-teacher voice was largely subdued.

"That's okay." Lorraine glanced at Selma, who was watching them closely.

"Use the conference room," Selma said to Lorraine, sharply. Lorraine knew she was treading on thin ice.

Lorraine led Elizabeth to the conference room down the hall and closed the door. "What's going on?" she asked.

Elizabeth leaned over the table. "Raymond got a strange Facebook message the other day from 'Lorrie Sal.'"

Lorraine could feel the start of a deep blush. "What?"

Elizabeth pulled out her phone. "We figured out pretty quickly that it wasn't you and that it was probably your husband." She handed Lorraine her phone.

Raymond, I want to see you. Meet me at the Compton Inn & Suites on
Friday at 5 p.m. I'll be in the lobby waiting for you. Don't tell anyone
else about this message.

"This isn't me," Lorraine said, at once relieved and sick to her stomach.

"I know," said Elizabeth. "We thought there was something suspicious
with this account. Look at it—there's no posts on it or anything. We realized it was a different Lorrie Sal account from yours. A double."

Lorraine clicked around and saw that other than the photo of the flower
and the fence, the account was virtually blank; it had no friends or posts or
other pictures.

"It was such a bizarre message," Elizabeth went on. "After Ray got it, he
showed it to me, and I showed it to Diane, and Diane told us that, well, Jesse
had a history of being—" Elizabeth paused and looked at Lorraine carefully.
"Manipulative."

"I don't know what to say," Lorraine said. She was mortified. "I'm not
sure how . . ." She trailed off.

"Lorraine, I've been noticing a car parked outside our house quite a bit.
It's a black Honda Civic with a license plate 134 GB2. I'm almost certain it's
your husband's."

"I—"

"If he doesn't let up I won't hesitate going to the police," Elizabeth said,
the way a parent would speak to a misbehaving child. "You might consider
going yourself." She leaned in and lowered her voice. "I have to ask. Does he
hurt you?"

"No," Lorraine said automatically.

"Even so. Impersonating you and sending out messages like this." Elizabeth raised her eyebrows. "I can't imagine it feels very good."

Lorraine stiffened. It gave her a strange feeling, thinking about Elizabeth
and Raymond and Diane talking about her marriage. She wished then, with
a sudden intensity, that she'd never sent that idiotic message to Raymond. It

was humiliating, that Elizabeth knew about it, that Diane probably did, too. "I can handle my marriage on my own," she said to Elizabeth. "I've been in it for ten years."

Elizabeth nodded curtly. "Well. I wanted to let you know." She hesitated for a moment. "I'm not sure what he's up to, but it doesn't seem good." Then she stood. "I'll let you get back to work, Lorraine."

Lorraine stood, her heart thwacking miserably. "In the future, I can't have visitors here. It's not allowed, and it doesn't make me look good."

THAT EVENING WHEN LORRAINE got home, Jesse's car wasn't in the driveway, and she was relieved. She didn't know how she was going to confront him about this.

Lorraine went inside, fed Sally, and started washing the dishes from breakfast that morning. When Jesse came up behind her, only a few minutes later, she barely had time to think, it all happened so quickly. He grabbed a fistful of her hair and slammed her face down hard into the kitchen sink. Her nose, hitting the counter with such blunt force, screamed in pain. He did it again, six or seven times, each time harder than the last.

She felt her teeth slam up against her lips, her lips slam up against the steel of the sink basin. There was the cracking of several teeth coming loose, and then the scattering sound of teeth falling into the sink. Her nose was gushing blood. It seemed to happen fast and slow at the same time. The pain was terrible, but it was the amount of blood, and the feeling of not knowing when it would end, that frightened Lorraine more than anything else. He was screaming at her about Raymond's car.

Then it stopped. Lorraine sank to the floor, holding her face, as though if she didn't, the whole thing might fall off. Everything was slick with blood—her face, her hands, her clothing. She didn't know where any of it was coming from. When she opened her eyes, all she saw was the red-black of it. She lost consciousness.

When she woke up, several minutes later, she was still leaning against the cabinet, and Jesse was holding ice to her face. "Hospital," she managed to say. He didn't respond and she stood, wincing, and he didn't stop her. She found her teeth in the sink, stained pink with blood, and put them in her pocket. Then she drove herself, one-handed, to the emergency room. With the other hand, she held a wad of paper towels to her mouth. She didn't cry because she couldn't afford to. One of her eyes was already swollen shut.

At the hospital, adults in the waiting room pretended not to stare at her, but children just looked, so Lorraine closed her eyes. She didn't have to wait very long to be seen. They attended to her wounds and took X-rays of her face. She was told she was lucky her nose wasn't broken. She remembers smiling at the word *lucky*. The most damage had been done to her mouth. They told her she was going to need to see a dentist and an orthodontist. She was there for five hours, and by the time she left, her face had morphed into something unrecognizable—her bruises had changed from reds and pinks to eggplant purple and different shades of yellow, like some sort of deranged sunset. The size of her face had doubled. When she saw her reflection in her rearview mirror, she turned away.

A FEW DAYS LATER, sitting in the dentist's office together, with three of Lorraine's teeth in a Ziploc bag, Jesse admitted to Lorraine that he had made a fake Facebook account and sent Raymond a message impersonating her.

"What would you have done if he'd shown up at the hotel?" Lorraine asked, cotton-mouthed and woozy on pain medication.

Jesse looked down at his lap. "I would have killed him."

She would leave him, she decided then. She had to. "Jesse." Her *s*'s were *th*'s.

He looked at her.

"Look at me."

"I'm looking, Lorrie."

"No. Look what you *did* to me." She started to cry then, and when he reached for her she shook her head and pushed him away.

He told her that he had discovered Lorraine's secret Facebook account and figured out a way to hack it. He'd seen her message to Raymond, and since then, he'd been following both of them—Raymond and Lorraine— certain that he'd catch Lorraine cheating. That day when Elizabeth had driven to Stand Together to talk to Lorraine, she'd driven Raymond's car; and when Jesse had spotted Raymond's car in the parking lot of Stand Together, he'd grown irate.

Lorraine missed ten days of work. When she returned, still bruised and swollen, and with braces on her teeth, Selma called Lorraine into her office. She didn't waste any time. "Lorraine, I'm sorry to have to do this, but this is no longer working out."

Lorraine's stomach sank. "Is it because of all the sick time?" she asked. "Because I can explain—"

"No." Selma cut her off. "You've been off your game for a while, Lorraine. You're only half here. With clients like ours, I need you *all* here, all the time. I need one hundred percent. Not seventy-five percent, not fifty percent."

"I can do that," she said. "I can give one hundred percent."

Selma shook her head. "I've already made up my mind." Then she sighed and for a moment she looked truly sorry. "I wish it wasn't the case."

Lorraine looked into her lap. She was doing everything she could not to cry, but the facts of her life were surfacing. She was almost sixty and unemployed. Soon she wouldn't have health insurance. Her money was tied up with Jesse's money, and they didn't have much of it. The house on Winter Street was in both their names, but the new house in New Hampshire was only in Jesse's. She tried to picture herself doing another job—waiting tables or babysitting somebody's kid, or even another social services job, if Selma would still write her a recommendation. But then she imagined herself at the interview. Swollen and reeking of smoke. Nervous. She imagined Jesse showing up at a new apartment, a new job. He would find her, and he would be furious. She hated her life with him. But a life without him would be far more terrifying.

She blinked back tears. Jesse's face came into focus in her mind. Her future was clear, and it was with her husband.

LORRAINE DOESN'T TELL NESSA all of this. She tells her most of it, though she leaves out certain details. She doesn't tell her about her teeth falling out, or that she's not allowed to have a Facebook. She tells her daughter that she no longer has a job, though she can't bring herself to use the word *fired*. Her daughter looks scared and there's no need to frighten her more. She doesn't repeat to Nessa what Dr. Nathan said to her, after the dentist finished working on her mouth.

"Get out, Lorraine," she'd said, lifting up the blue surgical face mask, panic in the dentist's voice. "I'm begging you. Woman to woman. Your life is in danger."

Tanya is running the risk of hitting somebody. She can't hit her mother, she thinks bitterly—Jesse is already taking care of that. So if she hits someone it's going to be Nessa—Nessa, who will never hit back. Tanya doesn't understand Nessa's attachment to Jesse. How it's possible for her sister to love someone like Jesse. And it *is* love. She sees the way Nessa's face softens when she's around him, the way her eyes flicker over in his direction, looking for approval.

Outside the sky is moody, copper with eggplant-colored clouds. Tanya gets in the car and drives, leaving her sister and mother stranded at the brewpub. She flies down Main Street, passing by the quaint shops, the little restaurants, not in the mood to feel charmed. When she reaches a patch of strip malls, she spots Walmart and pulls into the massive parking lot in search of something to eat.

Inside, Tanya picks out a bag of baby carrots and a thing of hummus from the grocery section, and then she walks around the store, soothed by the air-conditioning and the shelves of toothpaste and tampons, paper goods and school supplies, everything in its place. The superstore is surprisingly calm. The aisles are large and clean. Her shoes click with each step.

She hates this version of herself, the one she becomes when she's around Nessa and Lorraine for too long. She begins to feel embarrassed by them. All their unhappiness starts to ooze out in small, unbearable ways. They become caricatures of themselves—their flaws exaggerated and magnified. All three of them crawl back into old, familiar roles, as though they're playing some sort of re-creation game that's neither fun nor necessary.

Tanya finds herself in the baby aisle. She looks around at the receiving blankets, the diaper bags and creams and wipes, the pumps, the nursing pads. She doesn't know what most of it is, and in that moment she feels furious at Eitan—for impregnating her, for wanting such a conventional life. She picks up a package of infant onesies and rips it open, pulls one out. It's barely bigger than her own hand, with sleeves so small they make her gasp. Quickly, she stuffs the onesie back inside the package.

"Excuse me, miss."

Tanya whirls around. It's an employee, a middle-aged man wearing a navy blue vest over a lighter blue button-up. "Are you planning on buying those?" he asks.

Tanya shakes her head and puts the package back on the shelf. "I just wanted to see what size they were."

He smiles broadly and nods a few times, as though she's told a joke. "Here at Walmart we have a zero-tolerance policy when it comes to shoplifting." He sounds practically jolly.

"I wasn't shoplifting," she says. "But if it will make you happy, I'll buy them." She puts the package in her basket along with the carrots and hummus.

The man takes several steps toward Tanya. "May I escort you to the register?"

"I can find my way, thank you," Tanya says.

"I could use a little stroll myself. Let's walk together."

Tanya gives the man her coldest stare and turns around, begins walking toward the front of the store. Behind her, she's aware of him following her.

"Pregnant?"

She stops in her tracks. "Excuse me?"

He's caught up with her and he looks eagerly in her basket and then pointedly at her stomach. "Are you pregnant?"

"That's none of your business." She glances at his name tag. "Tim."

"Don't get upset," he says brightly. Up close his eyes are small and bloodshot, and his eyelashes are so pale they're white. "It's a happy thing, having a baby."

"I'm going to the register now," Tanya says. "Please don't follow me. Do you understand?"

The man's eyes travel the length of her body. "I'm sorry I upset you."

"I'm not upset," Tanya says. "I'm simply asking you to leave me alone." She's resolved to stay calm. Tanya turns on her heel and walks in the direction of the registers. She can feel his stare, branding her back.

She doesn't start to cry until she makes it to the front of the store where all the checkout lines are. She picks a line with a woman at the register and takes deep breaths, pressing her palms to her eyes, as if to quiet them. She's furious, but she no longer knows at whom.

Tanya leaves the package of onesies on the magazine rack and puts the carrots and hummus on the conveyor belt.

"How are you today?" the woman at the register asks blandly.

"Fine," Tanya says. "And you?"

"Good, thank you, ma'am. Will that be credit or debit?"

"Credit," Tanya says, and swipes her card.

The interaction leaves her slightly calmed and, outside, she calls Nessa.

"Hey," Nessa answers. "Where are you?"

"Walmart, down the road."

"I talked to Mom. She's going to tell the judge about the strangulation."

Tanya exhales. She hadn't realized she'd been holding her breath. "Good," she says, and then she starts to cry again.

"Are you okay?" Nessa says.

"I'm coming back to the restaurant now," Tanya says. "Let's go back to the motel. This place creeps me out." The feeling she's having is the Wild Thing, but it feels too strange—too risky—to say these words aloud to Nessa.

"Okay," Nessa says. "Come pick us up and we'll leave right away."

2003

The idea started at their father's apartment building, on the elevator ride down to the pool. Nessa was sixteen and Tanya had recently celebrated her fourteenth birthday. They hadn't bothered with clothes or shoes, and when the elevator's gold mirrored doors closed, Nessa and Tanya were faced with their own glowing reflection: Tanya in her white bikini, the length of her legs, the silky curtain of hair over her shoulder. And Nessa, taller and curvier, her breasts barely contained in her black one-piece, a bun perched on her head. They saw how beautiful they looked—not just each of them separately, but how they looked beside one another, a study in opposites. They laughed and posed and turned around to check out their backsides.

On the way down to the lobby the elevator pinged and the doors opened to reveal two men. It was their clothing that made them men in Nessa's mind, and not boys. They were dressed the way their father dressed for work—in button-up shirts and slacks, brown leather belts around their middles. They had facial hair, but not too much of it. Their eyes were bright and young.

It was only a matter of seconds, but Nessa saw it on their faces, the way the men took them in, swallowing them; assessing, cataloging, imagining. It was as plain as the hair on their faces: Nessa and Tanya excited them.

Then the men averted their gaze and stepped inside. The elevator closed again and all four of them stayed quiet—the men pretending not to look at

Nessa and Tanya in the mirrored doors and Nessa and Tanya pretending not to see them looking. The air in the elevator thinned, then disappeared almost completely. There was the sound of their breath and the width of their shoulders; the perfect smell they gave off, of men's deodorant and something musky and leafy and dark. They stood, each with a foot of space between their feet, unlike Nessa and Tanya, who stood with their ankles and knees and thighs touching. By the time they reached the lobby, Nessa's body was thrumming. The men stepped aside to let them walk out first, and she and Tanya bolted barefoot across the carpeted lobby, aware of the men behind them, watching their butts while they ran.

"HOW OLD DO YOU THINK THEY WERE?" Nessa asked after they jumped in the pool.

"Twenties?" Tanya floated on her back, her toes emerging from the water.

"How old do you think they thought we were?"

"Old," Tanya said. "You definitely. With your boobs."

"They are kind of massive." Nessa glanced down at her chest. "I don't get it. Just two lumps of fat. What's the big deal."

"I get it," Tanya said, and she gazed thoughtfully at Nessa's breasts. "They're pretty."

Nessa looked down again and pulled at her suit, so that her right breast popped out. It did look pretty, soft and plump, half-submerged in water.

Tanya watched Nessa and as though she had dared her, Tanya pulled her bikini top over her head. They both started to laugh, and in one fluid motion Nessa pulled down her suit and Tanya pulled off her bottoms and they threw their bathing suits over to the side of the pool.

"I feel so free," Nessa said, twirling in slow circles, the water kissing her all over.

Tanya hoisted herself out of the pool. She stood naked and dripping on the edge and Nessa watched her, transfixed by her sister's body—the beautiful neatness of it: the one-inch valley of space between her breasts; the gentle slopes of her hips; her belly button, a dainty moon-shaped blip. Tanya had always treated her body as something to be honed and perfected, something to be looked at and admired, but from a distance. Nessa felt not envy, looking at her sister's body, but pride.

Tanya glanced at the door and Nessa could tell her sister wanted someone to walk in. The men from the elevator. Or any man really.

Then Tanya arched her back and stretched her arms over her head. She dove, disappearing into the pool so gracefully that when she broke the water, it was almost soundless.

"What do you think those guys would do if they walked in right now?" Nessa asked Tanya after she came back up.

"I don't know." Tanya glanced again at the door. "Maybe they'd swim with us."

Nessa looked down at her naked body, flickering under the shimmering blue. The details were obscured, but her shape was there. Nobody had ever looked at her the way those men in the elevator had, as though they had wanted to touch her.

"What if no guy ever wants to have sex with me?" Nessa said, and though she meant it as a joke, out of nowhere her eyes were wet and her nose was burning and she wasn't sure how she'd gone so quickly from happy to hopeless.

"Of course guys will want to have sex with you," Tanya said. "You just have to wait and find the right one."

Nessa nodded. She was tired of waiting. She knew her imagination so well that the stories she made up in her head no longer excited her. She had thought about the server from her father's wedding too many times for him to still be an actual person. Now he was just an extension of herself—an outline of a boy she had filled in and invented, stale with her own bottomless longing. She'd spent hours, days—*years*, probably—of her life, imagining the right guy.

"I guess worse comes to worst I could become a porn star," Nessa said. "Or a prostitute."

Tanya laughed. "Yeah, right," she said, and Nessa wondered if Tanya even knew what a porn star or a prostitute was.

"How much do you think those guys would pay to have sex with us?" Nessa asked.

"A million dollars."

"No, but actually. How much do you think?"

"I don't know. A hundred bucks?"

"I was going to say fifty."

"We're definitely worth more than fifty." Tanya looked down at her naked body. "I mean, we're hot."

"We are?"

"*Look* at us."

"I kind of want to do it," Nessa said.

"What?"

"Be a prostitute." Nessa paddled to the edge of the pool and held on, treading water with her legs. "What if we did it?"

"Have sex with those guys for money?"

"No, not them. They live in Dad's building. That would be too weird. We'd have to find other guys."

"You're joking, right?"

"We could make up hooker names," Nessa said. "It would be fun. Like Crystal and Chandelier."

"Um, no." Tanya laughed.

"How about Paris and London?" Nessa said. "I could be Paris and you could be London."

"No, I think you'd be London and I'd be Paris."

"Fine," Nessa said. "Or Lola and Layla."

"I like those."

Nessa started to imagine one of the men from the elevator undressing her, but she pushed the thought away. She didn't want to imagine the life out of it.

Tanya held on to the edge of the pool and fluttered her legs behind her.

Her butt rose out of the water, two pink cheeks, smooth and wet. "Isn't being a prostitute against the law, though?"

Nessa thought about all the millions of pornos that men watched every day. She had watched one of them herself on the computer when no one was home. After watching porn the first time, she'd gone back and watched it again the next day, and the day after, and the day after that, until she knew the video so well she could play it out in her head, shot by shot. "Not in Nevada," she said.

"I guess."

"Or Amsterdam."

"How would we even do it?" Tanya asked. "We can't just go out on the street."

"We could make a website," Nessa said, and that was when it turned from a joke into a plan.

NEITHER ONE OF THEM KNEW enough about computers to make a website, so instead they created an email account, hottgirls@hotmail.com—they thought this was funny—and typed up a flyer. They settled on the names Lola and Layla and decided to slip flyers into a handful of mailboxes in Cambridge. They made the flyers at the public library, where Lorraine wouldn't accidentally find them.

They chose houses with poorly kept lawns, with broken venetian blinds instead of curtains. They checked the cars in the driveways, avoiding the *Baby on Board* and *My Child Is an Honor Student* bumper stickers, searching instead for cars that looked like they might belong to lonely men. Sometimes they peeked in windows, hoping to get glimpses of potential clients. Even the smallest movements of a person inside roused them into excited laughter.

For weeks, nobody got in touch. They checked their email every day, multiple times. "Anything?" they asked each other sometimes. After a while they began to check less frequently, and the idea, the excitement of it, started to fade.

THEN ONE DAY, a message came in. They were together, in the living room, when they discovered it, and when they saw the subject line, "Hello," along with the time it had come through, 5:03 p.m., they both started to laugh. The idea that anybody would actually respond was ludicrous—unbelievable, even.

"Oh my God," Nessa said. "Should we open it?"

"I don't know," Tanya said. "I'm scared." But of course they opened it and read it together silently, grasping hands.

"Hello," it read. "My name is Dan. I am interested in meeting up. I am a nice guy in my 20s. Please write back so I know your real and not a hoax."

"He spelled 'you're' wrong," Tanya said.

"Who cares," Nessa said. She sat up. Her entire body was buzzing. She felt more awake than she'd felt in years. *Dan,* she thought, rolling the name over in her mind.

"I think we should write back," Nessa said.

"Really?" asked Tanya. "You don't think it's weird?"

"His email sounds normal."

"Yeah, but." Tanya glanced again at the computer screen, and Nessa saw a glint of sarcasm in her sister's expression, and for some reason this hurt her feelings.

"Tanya, we can't back out now."

"Why not?"

"Because," Nessa said. "It actually worked."

So they wrote an email back and set up a time to meet Dan at his house that night.

"What are we supposed to wear?" Nessa asked.

Tanya suggested they wear the kind of outfit they might wear to a school dance—short shorts with spaghetti-strap tank tops—and it was Nessa's idea to go out and buy lingerie, since the guy, Dan, was probably expecting something out of the ordinary.

Lorraine was at Jesse's for the night and she'd left money for pizza. "We're going to need more than this," Tanya said, holding up the twenty-dollar bill on the kitchen counter.

"Follow me," Nessa said. They went upstairs to their mother's bedroom and Nessa opened the small drawer in Lorraine's night table. She knew her mother's drawers intimately, from years of looking through them when Lorraine wasn't home. There were a few twenties shoved into the back, along with a mess of crumpled receipts and business cards, coins furry with gum and lint, hair clips, lip balms. Nessa took two twenties and handed them to Tanya and then rifled around some more until she found the little blue plastic squares that she was looking for. "And these," Nessa said, holding them up, and she could tell by the way Tanya looked at them, confused, that her sister had never seen a condom before.

THEY WALKED TO T.J. MAXX to buy lingerie. "I like this." Tanya held up a pink bra and underwear set, the bra straps slender ribbons and the cups made of crushed lace. The underwear was solid pink in front but the back was gauzy and transparent. Nessa chose a second set off the rack and together they tried them on in the big, wheelchair-accessible dressing room.

The pink bra and underwear looked pretty on Tanya, but Nessa's skin was pinker than her sister's, so the lingerie just blended in with her flesh. "Black would look nice on you," Tanya suggested, so Nessa found the same set in black and returned to the dressing room. They stood beside one another in the big mirror.

"Who do you want to be?" Nessa asked. "Lola or Layla?"

Tanya stood up straighter and sucked in her tummy so that her butt stuck out. "Layla?"

"I guess that makes me Lola." The name felt soft and pretty in Nessa's mouth, and she imagined how much softer and prettier it would sound coming from a man.

"What if it hurts?" Tanya asked. She skimmed a hand over her stomach.

It hadn't occurred to Nessa to worry about it hurting, and even then, the thought of pain didn't scare her. "I think it only hurts at first," she said. She smiled at Tanya in the mirror and hip-bumped her, and the hilarity of the situation hit them all over again.

NESSA HAD WALKED to Alewife Station from Winter Street before, but it felt different this time, at night, with her sister, so close to so much traffic. Nessa kept waiting for somebody to roll down their car window and ask them what they were doing, where they were going—to tell them to go back home, *now*. But nobody said a word to them. Once they reached Alewife, that monstrosity of a building—stories of concrete, tangled in highway—Nessa experienced a surge of emotion deep in her belly: *freedom*. They were really doing this.

They bought T passes and boarded the train, easy as that. As they pummeled into the city, Nessa looked around at the other people in the subway car. There were teenagers getting off at Harvard Square, college students with their backpacks and their books, people in scrubs, homeless people. There was a loud drunken group of adults, all wearing Red Sox hats, taking up an entire row. A young family with a double stroller, two toddlers peeking out from beneath the canopy.

And of course there were the couples. Holding hands, leaning into one another, whispering things. Nessa watched them with interest. What was everybody else doing with their evening? she wondered. All these grownups with specific destinations in mind, with plans. With *dates*.

As they made their way up out of the subway into Central Square, Nessa felt like a dog with an electric leash. She was waiting for the shock, for the harsh yanking back. But as they stepped into the mild Cambridge evening, anything felt possible.

Inman was a quiet, pretty street with lots of trees and old Cambridge houses, lush gardens out front. Dan's was a ways down. His house didn't have a garden. There was a big, sagging sofa on the front porch, the kind of sofa that wasn't meant to be outdoors, red and green striped like Christmas wrapping paper. From across the street they gaped at his house, chain-sucking Tic Tacs and imagining the man inside.

"We should have a signal," Tanya said. "In case we want out."

"How about if we touch our chin, that means we leave."

Tanya considered it. "I touch my chin when I'm nervous. I might do it by accident without thinking." She demonstrated, pinching her chin between her thumb and her middle finger. "Don't you see me do this a lot? It's one of my habits, I think." She looked uncertain, grasping at her chin.

"Maybe," Nessa said, though she'd never seen her do it before. "How about our eyebrow, then?"

Tanya tested out the gesture, tracing her eyebrow with her index finger. "Okay." She nodded. "That works."

AT TEN MINUTES TO EIGHT they walked across the street, and when Tanya stared nervously at the door, Nessa reached out and knocked. From inside they heard a dog barking and then slow footsteps.

When Dan opened the door, Nessa was startled to see flecks of gray in his beard, surprised that he had a beard at all. His eyes were small and green and alert and he looked kind of baffled to see them standing there. He was wearing a plain white hat with the bill faced frontward and a button-up flannel, an undershirt peeking out. The undershirt frightened Nessa. She had spent so much time thinking about her and Tanya's bodies, she had almost forgotten he was going to have a body, too.

He wasn't cute, but he wasn't exactly ugly either, and when he smiled and opened the door for them, there was something gentlemanly about the way he stretched out his hand, gesturing for them to come in. "Welcome. Did you find it okay?" His voice was soft, like when teachers deliberately speak quietly to make you listen up.

Tanya nodded. She looked a little pale.

"We took the T," Nessa said.

Dan led them into the living room. There was a gray couch and a green La-Z-Boy pointed toward the TV. The room smelled like smoke and artificial orange. "Can I get you ladies something to drink?"

Nessa and Tanya glanced at one another. "What do you have?" Nessa asked.

"Wine. Beer." He looked at them, his eyes moving quickly up and down. "Orange juice."

"Beer for me," Tanya said, surprising her sister with her out-of-the-blue confident tone.

"Me too," she said.

"Sure thing."

They sat next to each other on the gray sofa while Dan disappeared inside the kitchen. They both felt the urge to laugh, though neither one of them did.

Dan came back in the room then, carrying three bottles. He put two down on the coffee table in front of them and then settled into the La-Z-Boy with the third. "How old are you girls?" he asked, taking a sip.

"Eighteen," Tanya said, without missing a beat. She took a swig of her beer like she'd done it a million times before, and it occurred to Nessa that maybe she had.

Dan nodded and pulled the bill of his hat down so it sat more securely on his head.

After a few sips the drink made Nessa feel warm and relaxed. "This is good," she said, holding up the bottle. She thought her voice sounded nice. Sultry even.

"Glad you like it."

She glanced at her sister. Tanya's cheeks were pink from the alcohol and she had tossed her hair over to one side so that it fell like a wave over her face. Nessa stopped herself from reaching over and tucking the hair behind Tanya's ear.

For several more minutes there was silence and then Dan set his bottle down on the table and leaned forward in the chair. "So I wasn't expecting two of you. How does this work? I just pick?"

Tanya and Nessa glanced at one another. They hadn't really thought about this. The idea of splitting up made Nessa feel shaky, a deep sort of scared, right in her gut. She thought about their mother then and wondered what Lorraine would think if she knew what they were doing right now. Then she thought about Jesse. How angry he'd be if he knew that Dan had offered them alcohol. Jesse wouldn't want them to be there; she was sure about that. She turned to Tanya and gently touched her eyebrow with her pointer finger, hoping Tanya might nod or touch her own eyebrow, but Tanya just pressed her lips together and shrugged. Then Tanya turned back to Dan. "Yeah," she said. "You choose."

"Well, in that case." He nodded toward Tanya and Nessa felt something sharp break in her chest.

"You want to . . ." He trailed off.

Nessa looked down at the beer in her hands, still half of it left, and tried not to let anything show on her face. The shaky feeling and the hurt feeling were all mixed up. She wasn't sure which one to listen to.

When Nessa looked up, Tanya looked pale again, but maybe, Nessa thought, a little proud. Tanya didn't say anything to Nessa but made a face like, *Is that okay?*

Nessa nodded. "I'll just see you later," she said. When neither Tanya nor Dan moved, Nessa stood up and pulled her shorts down a little with one hand, the other hand still around the neck of the bottle. Then she left.

Outside, she sat down on the Christmas-striped sofa on Dan's porch to wait for Tanya. The second half of the beer was easier going down and she drank it in long, slow sips. She felt bad for herself and angry at Tanya. Her sister should have listened when Nessa had touched her eyebrow. Nessa set the empty bottle down and stretched out on the sofa. It smelled musty, but it was soft and worn, surprisingly comfortable. She lay there, looking up at the rotted wood of the porch ceiling and the cobwebs fuzzed over everything like moss. From somewhere down the street, she heard the rev-ving of a car engine and the blast of a radio grow louder and then softer as it passed through the neighborhood.

Then it arrived all at once. Her fear. She stood, chest heaving, cupped her hands against the window and pressed her face to it. The room she was looking into was dark, a dining room table stacked high with mail. She pushed her ear against the glass and listened. She wasn't sure what she was listening for, but each time she heard the groan of a bus from down the block, or the wind through the trees, it sounded eerily human. The noises were frightening, but the moments of quiet—when Dan's house seemed to pulse with some silent warning—were even more so.

Nessa knocked, first softly on the window, as though Tanya might be just behind it, waiting for her signal. And then she went to the front door and knocked again, this time harder. She tried the doorknob. It was locked.

"Tanya!" she yelled, but there was no answer.

Images of her sister began running through her head like a slide show—Tanya embracing their father at his wedding, Tanya curled up on the couch with their mother. Tanya, naked and perfect, diving into the swimming pool. And then Nessa thought about the porn she'd seen—the woman with her shaved vagina and large engorged breasts, the strange sounds she was mak-ing, and Nessa began to cry. She pounded the door with her fists. "Tanya!"

Nessa ran around to the back of the house. The lawn was dark and dead, no grass, just overgrown weeds and rocks. She tripped over something—a hose—and landed hard on her hands and knees. Pain exploded in her mouth where she'd bitten her tongue. She pushed herself up. The back of Dan's duplex was dark except for one window on the second floor, which was emitting a grayish glow. She tried the back door, but it didn't budge. "Tanya!" she yelled again, waving her arms over her head.

She ran back around to the front porch and jiggled the doorknob, tried forcing the windows up. Finally, she sat on the front steps and waited. She counted in her head at first, and then out loud. She was at seven hundred and forty-two when the door opened and Tanya stepped out.

"Tee." Nessa stood, leaking with tears and snot and blood.

Tanya looked back, dazed, her makeup smeared under her eyes.

"Are you okay?"

When Nessa reached to hug her sister, Tanya took a step back, then nodded without meeting Nessa's eye. "Come on," she said.

"What happened?" Nessa followed her down the steps and onto the sidewalk.

Tanya looked left and right down the street. Then a car pulled up and her sister nodded toward it. "There," she said. "He called me a cab."

They climbed into the backseat together and Tanya gave the driver their address.

Tanya was quiet, staring out the window. Nessa reached over and touched her sister's shoulder, and Tanya turned to Nessa and smiled politely as though she barely knew her.

"Here you are, ladies," the driver said as he pulled into their driveway.

Tanya took some cash out of her pocket and handed the driver two twenties. He gave her back some change and she looked at the money bewildered, like she wasn't sure what to do with it, then slipped it back into her pocket.

Outside the air was cool and clean and smelled like home. Everything was as they'd left it: the blur of bushes out front, the trash bins leaning against the side of the house, the sloping telephone wires.

"What happened?" Nessa asked Tanya again, once the cab disappeared down the block.

"Nothing," Tanya said. "It was just sex."

The way she said *sex*, like it was something that shouldn't have to be explained, gave Nessa the feeling she had better stop asking questions.

2003

Nessa didn't sleep that night, and across the room from her, neither did Tanya. Her sister's breathing remained quick and shallow and she got up to use the bathroom five times, once every hour. Nessa kept count. After the third time she whispered *Tanya* into the darkness, but Tanya didn't answer.

Eventually light bled through the blinds, flinging stripes across the walls and ceiling. Nessa lay listening to the rhythm of Tanya's breathing—still awake—until her sister got up for the sixth time and Nessa heard the shower start.

Nessa sat up. Her body was sore from being awake all night and her eyes burned. Tanya's bed was a mess. The blanket was spilling onto the floor, the sheet dislodged, tangled and twisted like something alive splayed on the middle of the mattress. Her sister's stuffed animals, usually wedged between the wall and the foot of the bed, had been moved up by the pillows. Nessa sat down on the bed and took one of the stuffed dogs in her arms. When she pulled the blanket up to cover herself, she noticed Tanya's jean shorts shoved into the crack between the wall and the mattress. She pulled them out. Tanya's underwear was still inside, the pink lace dark and stiff with blood. Nessa sat up, dizzy.

Tanya walked in a few minutes later wrapped in a towel. Her face was clean, all her makeup washed away. She blinked at Nessa, expressionless.

Nessa thought about Dan's ruddy, pockmarked cheeks, the hint of his smile when he'd opened the door. She fell from Tanya's bed onto the floor. "I'm so sorry, Tanya." She was crying again.

Tanya didn't move or speak. When Nessa looked up, Tanya was watching her as though from a distance.

"Tanya," Nessa said. She held up her sister's bloodied underwear and then she started to hit herself. On the side of her head, on her face, her ears, her cheeks. She began to breathe slower, the slapping like a metronome.

"Stop, Nessa," Tanya hissed. She reached down and grabbed the underwear from Nessa's hand. "Stop. You're acting crazy."

"Are you hurt?" Nessa whispered.

Tanya's eyes were bone-dry. "No."

"Should we tell Mom?"

"Are you kidding me?" Tanya cried. "*Promise* me you won't tell Mom."

"But are you okay?"

"Jesus, Nessa. Just stop talking about it."

"I shouldn't have let you stay in there," she said. "I'm so stupid. This whole thing was so stupid."

"Maybe. But it's over now. There's no point in talking about it."

"Did it hurt?"

"Yes," Tanya said shortly, and something hardened in her sister's face. That was all she was going to say. Tanya walked over to the closet. Her shoulders were tense, speckled with water droplets, her hair a wet, dark sheet down her back. "Can you step out," she said with her back still to Nessa. "I want to change."

Tanya had never asked Nessa to leave the room so she could change, and it frightened Nessa, that her sister didn't want Nessa to see her body. Nessa stood and left, closing the door behind her, and waited in the hallway, listening. There was the sound of Tanya's footsteps and the click of the lock on the doorknob. Nessa thought maybe Tanya was going to cry, but Tanya was silent. The only sounds coming from the bedroom were those of clothes being yanked out of drawers and pulled on.

SOON AFTER, TANYA got a boyfriend. He was three years older than Tanya, one year older than Nessa, a senior named Dylan Starr. Tanya came up to Dylan's chin and when they walked the halls together, he kept one arm draped over her, his fingers grazing her chest.

Tanya started coming home late, usually after dinner, her hair tangled around her face, her lips so red and swollen that Nessa felt embarrassed to look at her. When Nessa asked Tanya if she and Dylan Starr were having sex, Tanya raised her eyebrows, as though that was answer enough.

"So you are?" Nessa pressed.

"What do you think," Tanya said in a voice that was neither sneering nor genuine.

"I don't know. That's why I'm asking," Nessa said, but she got no further information.

"Is sex with Dylan good?" Nessa asked once, lightly, the way she imagined girls talked about boys they were sleeping with.

"Stop asking me so much about it," Tanya said. "It's weird."

Nessa waited until her sister left the room to cry. She was crying a lot those days, after school and on weekends, the kind of crying that left her body weak and depleted. Often she fell asleep afterward, and it was that feeling, her body preparing itself to lose consciousness, that she craved. She'd wake up several hours later, the sun on its way down, almost dinnertime.

During the day her naps were deep and dreamless—hours simply disappeared. At night, though, she dreamt about Dan. In her dreams, he had chosen Nessa. She'd wake up tingling, the way she felt right after having an orgasm, and it was that, more than anything else, that made her despise herself.

Tanya had new friends—Dylan's friends, mostly older. Nessa saw her hanging out on the Ledge, a cluster of benches where the popular kids congregated before and after school and during lunch. Sometimes she'd watch

Tanya from across the quad, laughing and leaning into Dylan Starr, gathering her hair on top of her head and tying it into a messy bun—the way popular girls knew how to do, the gesture as sensuous and exotic as a dance move. Watching Tanya, suddenly popular, confused Nessa. Her little sister had surpassed her; abandoned her. And Nessa had no one to blame but herself.

One day Nessa forgot her lunch at home and when she walked out of class, instead of taking a left to go upstairs to the art hallway where she usually ate, she took a right out the back doors, in the direction of the Ledge.

Tanya was sitting on one of the benches, squished between two other girls. All six of their legs dangled, slender and bare, sandals hanging off their feet. A boy was telling them a story and Tanya was laughing, her mouth open wide. She looked happy, Nessa thought.

When Nessa approached she saw Tanya's eyes flicker in her direction before quickly looking back at the boy.

As she broke the invisible border, crossing from outside the Ledge to inside it, the girls beside Tanya glanced over. They regarded Nessa with a mix of annoyance and apathy, the way someone might eye a hungry bird loitering at a picnic.

The boy was loudly telling his story, throwing his hands around, fading out only when he realized the girls' attention had turned elsewhere. "Sorry," Nessa said to the boy, who said nothing in response. Then she looked at Tanya—her sister's smile was still pasted on her face.

"What's up," Tanya said, her voice thin and bored.

"I forgot my lunch and my wallet," Nessa said. "Do you have any money?"

Tanya patted her front pockets with her hands and then shrugged, shaking her head.

Nessa looked at her and realized she felt scared.

"I don't," Tanya said loudly, as though Nessa hadn't understood. She turned around, her face burning.

"Who's that?" someone asked as she walked away.

"My sister."

"That's your sister?"

Tanya must have nodded because Nessa didn't hear her response and she didn't want to turn around to see Tanya's expression.

THAT NIGHT NESSA AND TANYA and Lorraine ate dinner in the living room in front of the TV. On the screen a pretty woman on a reality television show spoke in an emphatic voice. "I want someone I can do the little things with." The woman's teeth were huge and white, perfectly square. She wore a pink bikini. "Grocery shopping, making dinner. Watching TV. Walking my dog, Munchkin." She gazed into the camera. "I *deserve* love." She announced it with such conviction that Nessa wondered, Were there people who didn't?

Tanya and her mother had their feet up on the coffee table, Tanya's foot grazing Lorraine's ankle. A take-out container sat balanced on her sister's stomach, rising and falling with her breath. Her face and arms were flushed, and she had that ruffled look about her that Nessa thought must be sex.

"Can we change the channel?" Nessa asked.

Neither one of them responded. On the screen another woman sniffled. "This is so much harder than I thought it would be," she said. "When I see him with the other girls it destroys me. It's the first week where I think I might be going home." She had indelicate features, hair straightened to death. The woman was right, Nessa thought. She would be going home. If not tonight, then soon.

"Can we *please* change the channel."

Tanya threw Nessa a look. "Chill out."

"Do you actually like this shit?"

Tanya frowned at the screen and Lorraine typed something into her phone, smiling from the corner of her mouth.

Nessa stood. "I'm going up."

"Good night, honey," Lorraine called after her, her voice distracted.

———

NESSA WAS ALMOST at the top of the stairs when she heard the slap of bare feet on wood, the rhythm of Tanya's breath. When she turned around, Tanya was behind her, reaching, a wicked expression on her face. Nessa jumped away, but Tanya grabbed her ankles fast and squeezed.

"Tanya!" Nessa yelled, and her sister's grasp tightened. Her fingers were working their way up Nessa's legs, to her thighs and butt, kneading her flesh like dough. It tickled and Nessa's legs buckled, her muscles suddenly useless. She attempted the word *stop*, but she was laughing too hard, jerking and flailing under Tanya's hands. The Wild Thing was strong, and it was no longer a fleeting sensation, the way it always was on the stairs. It was potent. Her entire body was the Wild Thing. She continued to laugh, tears pricking her eyes. "Stop!" she shouted, conjuring enough strength to yank one of her legs away.

Tanya's eyes shone and she lunged for Nessa's free ankle.

"Stop!" Nessa cried again, but Tanya only held on tighter, her fingers hot and angry on Nessa's leg. With her free foot, Nessa tried to push her away.

"Scared?" Tanya said, a millisecond before Nessa kicked her, hard, in the chest. Tanya's arms flailed out for balance, and for several seconds she hung there, suspended—her feet solidly on the step, and the rest of her body floating.

The rest was fast. A backwards somersault—limbs everywhere, the white of her neck, the flash of her eyes. There was a terrible cracking sound. Tanya landed on the floor at the bottom of the stairs.

Nessa raced down.

Ten steps.

Nine steps.

Eight steps closer.

She was waiting for Tanya's cry. An enraged *Fuck you*. But Tanya was silent, her body a noiseless puddle of arms and legs. When Nessa saw the blood, she went hot. It was dark, almost black, growing in girth beneath her sister's head.

Lorraine appeared in the hallway. She made a sound, something between a scream and a dry heave. "Call 911," her mother said in a voice that
wasn't hers, and Nessa nodded, finding her way from the hallway to the
kitchen. The numbers swam in front of her. She blinked fast, trying to clear
her vision. Her fingers were thick and heavy as she dialed; her hands themselves felt huge, like the foam hands they give out at sports games.

For an unbelievably long time the phone rang before a woman's voice,
calm, appeared in Nessa's ear. "Nine one one," she said. "Emergency."

"My sister fell," Nessa said, lips moving clumsily. "We need an ambulance."

"Bring me the phone, Nessa," Lorraine yelled from the hallway.

Nessa ran to her mother with the phone. Lorraine had taken off her
shirt and was holding it under Tanya's head, which lay like an object in her
mother's lap. Lorraine's hands were covered in blood and there were streaks
of it on her cheeks and neck. Nessa began to shake. Lorraine took the phone
and told Nessa to get her a clean towel, which she did, breathlessly. Then she
watched as Lorraine wrapped Tanya's head with the towel, saying, *Uh-huh,
uh-huh,* into the phone.

That was when Nessa started making promises to God. She would never
eat another cookie. She would never think about that disgusting porn while
she masturbated. She would never masturbate. She would spend the rest of
her life making it up to Tanya. She'd spend the rest of her life keeping her
sister safe.

A few minutes later they heard the ambulances approaching, far-off
wails of sirens getting closer and closer, until they were right outside the
house. Nessa ran to the front door and opened it, and men in electric-yellow
uniforms ran through the doorway.

TANYA WAS GETTING A CAT SCAN when her father showed up, Simone a
few steps behind him. He surveyed the emergency room, his eyes darting

around until they found Nessa's. He was wearing a suit and tie and Simone was done up in a black dress, her hair pulled back.

Her father brought the smell of outside, of an elegant restaurant. He hugged Nessa, kissing her roughly on the forehead. Then he hugged Lorraine and that was when Lorraine broke down. She buried her face in Jonathan's neck and he put his hand on her hair and held her. When she pulled back, her face was streaked with tears and makeup. She had smudges of blood all over her. "I was so scared," she said to him. "She wasn't moving. I couldn't wake her up." Her eyes were moving left and right, up and down, searching his face for something.

"Where is she?" he asked. "Is she still unconscious?"

"She woke up in the ambulance. They took her in for scans. Oh my God, Jon, it was awful. I've never seen anything so awful."

"It's okay," her father said. "It's going to be okay. You got her here, Lorrie. That's all that matters." He hugged her mother again and pulled Nessa in, too. They hugged, the three of them, and Nessa breathed in the scent of her mother and father together, and wondered if they could smell her, too—her guilt and her shame and everything else disgusting about her.

When they detangled themselves Nessa glanced at Simone, who was watching from a few feet away. Lorraine looked at her, too, and Simone took a step forward. "I'm so sorry," she said, mostly to Lorraine. "I can't even imagine how frightened you must be."

Lorraine nodded, wiping her eyes.

"Is there anything I can get you? Coffee? Something to eat?"

"No," Lorraine said. "But maybe Nessa would like something?"

All three of them looked at Nessa. She nodded, so that her mother and father might have some time alone.

THE HOSPITAL CAFETERIA was bright and familiar and Nessa had the feeling she'd been there before, though she had no memory of having been.

There was a mural on the far wall, an underwater scene with colorful fish and a treasure chest, an anchor plunging from the bottom of a ship.

She and Simone stood in line together. "What would you like?" Simone asked.

Nessa shrugged, glancing at the salads and soups, the baskets of apples and bruised bananas, the potato chips and candy and cookies, the oversized muffins in saran wrap.

She wasn't hungry at all, but she picked up a carton of chocolate milk, the kind they used to get with their lunches in elementary school.

"That's all you want?" Simone asked, and Nessa nodded. Simone took a bag of mini chocolate chip cookies from the counter. "How about we share?" she said. "Cookies and milk?"

"Okay," Nessa said.

Simone paid and they sat at a table near the windows. Outside there was a small courtyard, a few benches, and a manicured square of grass. It was nighttime, but with all the lights of the hospital, the courtyard looked as though it could still be day.

Simone opened the bag of cookies and shook them out onto a napkin. She ate one, chewing slowly, and then she pushed the napkin toward Nessa.

Nessa dunked a cookie in milk and took a bite. She put the other half of the cookie down and leaned back in her chair.

"How are you doing, Nessa? It must have been awful to see Tanya like that."

Simone was watching Nessa, but Nessa pretended not to notice. She didn't want to know what Simone was thinking about her. She no longer thought that Simone only liked her because of her father, but Nessa also felt certain that Simone spent far less time thinking about her than Nessa spent thinking about Simone.

"Nessa," Simone said, and when she looked at her stepmother, Nessa was surprised to see that Simone's eyes were wet, that her mouth was trembling a little. "Are you alright, honey?"

"I kicked her," Nessa said.

Simone looked back, wide-eyed.

"I kicked her down the stairs. It was my fault." Nessa put her head on the table and began to weep. She heard the sound of Simone pushing her chair back and then she felt Simone's arms around her. Simone held her, stroking her hair.

"It's alright," she whispered into Nessa's hair. "It was an accident," Simone said. "She's going to be fine." Nessa nodded into Simone's neck and then she lifted her arms. They held on to one another tightly.

2003

Tanya needed twelve stitches on the back of her head. The doctors told her that she had suffered a concussion, but other than that, she was going to be alright. They gave her medicine for the pain and every once in a while a nurse came in to check her vitals and have her count backwards from one hundred. They decided to keep her overnight just to be cautious.

Her family gathered around her bed, her mother and father on one side, Nessa on the other. Tanya didn't realize until later that Simone was waiting outside. It was strange, waking up, surrounded by the family she'd missed for so many years.

"How're you feeling, Tee?" Nessa asked.

"Tired," Tanya said. She didn't know how she could tell them she felt happy.

"Can you try to sleep, honey?" asked Lorraine.

"I don't know," Tanya said. "I kind of want to stay awake for a little."

"Does it hurt?" asked Nessa.

Tanya shook her head and then she started to cry.

"Sweetie." Her mother leaned over to hold Tanya's hand. "Oh, honey, it's okay. You're going to be okay."

Then her father started to sing the moon song.

Oh, Mr. Moon, Moon, Mr. Silver Moon, won't you please shine down on me.

Tanya rolled her eyes, but that was enough to make Lorraine and Nessa start singing, too.

Oh, Mr. Moon, Moon, Mr. Silver Moon, hiding behind that tree.

There stands a man with a big shotgun, ready to shoot if you start to run.

So, Mr. Moon, Moon, Mr. Silver Moon, won't you please shine down on,

Talk about your shining, won't you please shine down on me.

They finished and the hospital room filled with silence again. All four of them smiled. It felt good and sad. The easy way they fell back into being a family, and the easy way they'd fall back out.

Her father left shortly after. He hugged all of them, giving Tanya a few kisses on her forehead and cheek. "I'll be back to see you in the morning, okay, Tee?"

Then Lorraine walked him out, leaving Tanya alone with her sister.

"Can I lie down with you?" Nessa asked, and Tanya nodded. Nessa crawled into bed, squishing herself into the space between Tanya and the railing. "I'm sorry, Tee," she said.

"Me too," Tanya said. "I'm sorry, too."

"I'm the older sister. I'm supposed to protect you, not hurt you."

Tanya knew what she was talking about. It had only been two months since it happened, but now, in the hospital room, surrounded by her family and doctors, all of that seemed far away, like a nightmare that Tanya could barely remember. "You do protect me," she said.

"No," Nessa said. "I didn't."

The door opened then and one of the nurses, Kathy, came in, and Tanya was relieved to stop the conversation.

Kathy smiled when she saw the girls curled up in bed. "What a nice sister you have, Tanya," she said. "I'm going to prop you up a little bit now, okay?" Kathy pressed a button and the upper half of the bed rose to a forty-five-degree angle, Tanya and Nessa rising with it. "Now I want you to follow my finger. Keep your head nice and still." She moved her finger to the right and to the left, then up and down, and Tanya followed with her eyes.

"Perfect," Kathy said. "Now with your hand I want you to push back on mine." She lifted her hand out in front of Tanya and Tanya pushed. "Good, and now the other one."

Then Kathy looked in Tanya's eyes with a light and took her blood pressure, nodding. *Good,* she kept saying, and Tanya started to believe, then, that things were really going to be alright.

"Do you girls want the bed reclined again?" Kathy asked after she was done.

Tanya nodded.

"Okay. Ring if you need anything." Then Kathy left.

Tanya closed her eyes.

"Do you want to try to sleep?" Nessa asked.

Tanya nodded, and Nessa pulled up the blanket to cover them both.

"Will you wake me up in fifteen minutes to make sure I'm not dead?" Tanya asked, closing her eyes.

"Sure," Nessa said.

"Thanks."

Tanya dozed off then, and Nessa lay beside her, one of her hands on her sister's shoulder to monitor her breathing. When fifteen minutes passed, Nessa gently shook her shoulder.

"It's okay," Tanya said, keeping her eyes closed. "I'm still alive."

III.

On Monday morning, the courthouse is busier than it was on Friday. Nessa and Tanya and Lorraine find a bench near the back of courtroom 1. Each time the door opens, they turn and look, but it's never Jesse. Tanya instructs Lorraine to inhale deeply through her nose and exhale slowly through her mouth.

At exactly ten a.m., a court guard instructs everybody to rise and the judge walks in, the same one from Friday.

"I'm going to the bathroom," Lorraine whispers suddenly, and Tanya glares at her. "Hurry," she says.

The judge calls one case, another two-party hearing for a restraining order, before calling Lorraine Bloom and Jesse Wright up front.

"Go find her," Tanya hisses to Nessa, and then she stands. "Your Honor, my mother, Lorraine Bloom, is here, but she's in the restroom." Tanya's voice is unwavering.

"Fine," the judge says. "We'll come back to this one at the end."

Nessa doesn't see her mother in the lobby. She goes to the women's restroom and checks under the stalls for Lorraine's shoes. "Mom?" she says. "Lorraine?" she tries. No one answers.

Outside, the day has gotten warm and the sun surges hot against Nessa's dress. When she finally spots her mother, it's across the Mystic Valley Parkway, in a little parking lot, and Lorraine is standing with Jesse. Jesse is in a suit and tie, his hair wild in the breeze. He's talking and gesticulating, using up all the air around him, and Lorraine is listening, looking up at him.

Nessa makes a run for it, sprinting across the busy parkway, so that cars have to slam on their brakes to keep from hitting her. Someone curses loudly out their window. It's Jesse who sees Nessa first. He stops talking to stare in her direction. Then her mother turns around, following his gaze.

"The judge just called your name, Mom," Nessa says, approaching. Her entire body is shot through with nerves.

Lorraine doesn't answer.

"You're not going through with it," Nessa says. It starts out a question, and ends a statement.

"I'm not," Lorraine says. "Jesse and I are going to try therapy first."

"Nessa," Jesse says, and Nessa turns to him. He's crying. "I've been awful. I know you probably can't forgive me. But I'm going to get better, I promise you. I feel sick to my stomach about the way I've been. Your mom deserves the best," he says. "I want to be the kind of man she deserves. I'm going to make it up to you. I promise."

The anger that Nessa has been waiting for finally arrives—an escalation in her chest, a heartbeat so fast and hard it could've burst right out of her body. She could've hurt someone with her anger. She could've blasted someone apart with it.

"If I was Jesse's girlfriend," Nessa says to Lorraine, "and he had hurt me the way he's hurt you. If he had put his hands around—"

And then it strikes her to stop talking.

It's subtle, the shift she senses in Jesse. She wouldn't have noticed if not for the fact that she knows him well. There's the straightening of his back, the slight flare of his nostrils.

He's too dangerous, Nessa realizes then—with a fear that puts her anger to shame. It would be a mistake to repeat to Jesse what Lorraine has told her about him. It would be a mistake to get angry, to be reckless and emotional.

"If you think you can work things out, I support that." Nessa looks right at him, luring him with her softness and her weakness. "Jesse," she says. "Promise me you'll go to therapy?" She sounds practically flirtatious.

Jesse nods and allows his tears to bubble forth. He's back to playing sweet. "I promise, Nessa."

"I'm going to get Tanya," Nessa says, but when she turns around she sees that Tanya is already there, running across the parking lot toward them. She's crying. Loudly and sorrowfully—the only one of them that day whose tears are not manipulative. "Don't," she wails, and it's unclear who she's talking to. "Don't," she begs, and all three of them look down in shame.

W hen it dawned on Tanya that her mother and Nessa were not returning to the courtroom, she stood. She slid past the other people in her row, tripping over a purse at a woman's feet, muttered sorry. She glanced at the attorneys, safe and smug in the front, separated from the rest of the courtroom, and felt queasy with jealousy. That they were at their jobs; that after this they'd return to their offices and at the end of the day, go home and eat dinner, this morning long forgotten.

As she stumbled out of courtroom 1, she glanced back over her shoulder, with the crazy notion that one of the attorneys might notice her and catch her eye, maybe even run after her. Clearly something was not right. Clearly she needed assistance. And that was why they were here, was it not? To set things straight, to defend, to prosecute?

But nobody was looking at her, and Tanya found herself out in the lobby, alone and shaking. She leaned against the wall and listened to the indecipherable drone of the judge's voice inside. Then she hurled into action. She found the women's restroom and burst inside, bending down to check the stalls for her mother's shoes, for Nessa's. Nothing. So she searched the courthouse. She glanced inside conference rooms and offices she had no business looking into, down hallways and around corridors, getting only one strange look the entire time. She was dressed well enough to look like she worked there. She tried calling Lorraine and Nessa multiple times. Nessa's phone was still off. Her mother's was on, but she wasn't picking up.

A feeling came over Tanya then, as she hurried down the main hallway of the courthouse for the fifth time, and it was a feeling she'd had before, as cold and sudden as a blanket being ripped away in the middle of sleep. She was alone. She was not going to find her mother and sister in some back room. They had left the building and hadn't told her.

Tanya put her fists angrily to her cheeks and squeezed her eyes shut, willing herself to hold it together—pull it the *fuck* together—but a sound escaped, high-pitched and childish, and it was so embarrassing, Tanya lost her cool and gasped.

She rushed out of the courthouse like that, crying like a child, with her fists still up by her cheeks, and circled the building.

That was when she saw them across the street. It all clicked into place in one terrible instant: Jesse, towering in his suit, his arms splayed out in a grand, arrogant gesture, and Lorraine and Nessa with their faces turned up toward him.

Tanya didn't want to believe it. She picked up speed, breaking into a run, crossed the four lanes of traffic, which was practically suicidal.

Now, when Tanya draws near, they all take a step toward her. "Tee," her mother says, reaching for her, but Tanya lurches away.

She doesn't look at Jesse. She can feel his eyes, hot and proud, boring into her. After all these years, he's never seen her cry before. She turns to her mother and uses the only thing she has left.

"You're not a good mother," she says.

"Tanya—" Lorraine's eyes are naked with hurt, but Tanya stops herself from looking away.

"You left me alone in there," Tanya says. "I was looking all over for you. If you knew you were going back to him, you should have told me."

"I know," Lorraine says. "Honey, I'm sorry. I didn't know until just now. I wasn't—"

Tanya's heart plummets; she was hoping Lorraine was going to say that Tanya was mistaken.

"I need to go home," Tanya interrupts.

"Okay," Lorraine says, nodding. "Let's go home."

"No," Tanya says, viciously. "I need to go to *my* home. With my husband."

"Oh." Lorraine's eyes fill up with that helpless hurt again. "Of course. We should get going, then." She wipes at her eyes, and Jesse, who has been watching this entire conversation without moving, reaches out a hand as if to comfort Lorraine, but it's as if he's reached out and grabbed for Tanya.

Tanya jumps backwards.

For the first time, she actually makes eye contact with him. He's staring at her—his arm still extended toward Lorraine—his eyebrows lifted in anticipation.

Tanya collects herself. "Don't ever touch her in front of me," she says. When he doesn't respond, something swells huge inside her. "DON'T EVER TOUCH HER IN FRONT OF ME, JESSE. DID YOU HEAR ME?" She yells it, yells it so loudly that she surprises even herself.

"I heard you," Jesse says, lowering his arm.

She turns on her heel then and goes to the edge of the lot, waits for a break in traffic. She makes a promise to herself that she won't start to cry again until she's in her rental car alone, driving back to New York, with miles between her and her family. Crying in front of them had been a mistake. This whole weekend had been a mistake. The restraining order, the motel, all of it.

When they get to the car, Tanya goes into the backseat and slams the door shut. Lorraine starts the car and Nessa turns around in her seat and looks at Tanya, concerned. "Are you okay?" Nessa asks.

Tanya looks back at her sister and feels inexplicable anger. None of this is Nessa's fault, of course, but all of it, somehow, feels that way. Dan's face flashes in her mind then—the way it sometimes does without warning, triggered by a smell or the change of season or the way a man looks at her on the subway. But this time it's simply triggered by Nessa's face, by her sister's round, quiet, earnest eyes.

"I'm fine." Tanya looks away.

Her sister leaves not even half an hour later. Tanya hugs Lorraine and Nessa goodbye in the front hallway, giving out her cold embraces like obligatory handshakes. Lorraine kisses Tanya's cheeks and tries to reassure her with a smile, but Tanya has grown gray and stoic. She simply does not speak to Jesse or look at him, and he slinks off into the kitchen.

"Text me when you get home, okay, Tee?" Lorraine says.

Tanya nods without meeting her mother's eye.

"And tell Eitan I say hi," Lorraine adds, but Tanya doesn't respond.

Nessa walks Tanya to the car. The day has turned cloudy and Winter Street is quiet—almost ghostly—the neighborhood kids at school, the adults off at work, driveways empty, curtains closed.

"Tee, we did everything we could do," Nessa says, after Tanya's put her bag in the backseat. They stand, leaning against the car. "Mom isn't ready to leave him."

"It's not a matter of being ready or not. He strangled her, Nessa."

"I know," Nessa says.

"I'm not sure you do."

"Tanya, I'm just as upset about all of this as you are."

Tanya looks outraged at this. "You don't seem that upset."

"We're different that way," Nessa says. "I don't know how to get angry like you."

"What do you mean, *know how to get angry?*" Tanya cries. "Getting angry isn't something you choose to feel, it's a feeling that comes over you."

"It doesn't come over me the same way it comes over you."

"Well, what do you feel?"

Nessa shrugs helplessly. "I feel sad. I feel scared. I feel like you're mad at me and I don't know what to do to make things better."

"Why do you like Jesse?" Tanya demands.

"I hate Jesse. I *hate* him, Tee."

"Not when we were kids. When we were kids you liked him." She pauses. "You had a crush on him."

It's as though she's punched Nessa in the stomach. "No, I didn't."

"You did," Tanya says quietly, her eyes bright with accusation. "It was obvious."

"No. I didn't, Tanya."

Tanya shrugs and looks away.

"What do you want me to do, Tee? Do you want me to stay here with Mom and Jesse? I can quit my job and come live here." She's not sure, as she's speaking, if she's being sarcastic or sincere.

Tanya doesn't say anything.

"Look, I've been thinking of applying to social work schools anyway. I could move in with them during school and make sure he doesn't do anything to her. If that's what you want me to do, I'll do it."

Tanya exhales, exasperated. "You're a grown-up, Nessa. Do what you want."

"I don't know what I want! Why are you talking to me like this, like it's my fault?"

"I'm not blaming you. I just don't understand your choices sometimes."

"What choices?"

"I don't know. Everything." Tanya pulls out her phone and unlocks it. "Eitan's texting me. I need to call him back." It's obvious she's lying.

"Right now?" Nessa's on the verge of tears. She doesn't want her sister to go, leaving her and her mother and Jesse alone in the house, on this street.

"I need to go," Tanya says. "I want to beat traffic."

"I don't want you to."

"I have to. I have work tomorrow. I'm exhausted and I still need to drive five hours."

"I love you, Tanya," Nessa says.

"I love you, too."

"Are you sure?"

Tanya laughs, but her eyes are glazed over. She's somewhere else. "Of course I'm sure," she offers, and then she gets in her car and leaves Winter Street behind.

Nessa goes back inside and asks to borrow her mother's car. The drive is too quick. She parks across the street and checks her teeth in the rearview mirror, reapplies her lipstick. She experiences a pang of self-hatred, that she cares how she looks in front of him.

The moment she knocks on the door—the very same door—her stomach revolts. She glances back at the car. She needs a bathroom, and she needs one immediately. She could run away. Drive to a Starbucks, shit her brains out. Come back later, or another day.

But then the door opens and there's a woman looking at her from behind the screen. She's small with bleached blond hair, cut short around her ears. "Hello?" the woman says, raising her voice at the end, making it a question, and just like that, Nessa's stomach calms.

"Hi," she says. "I was wondering . . . is Dan here?" She hasn't planned how to phrase it.

"Dan?" The woman frowns. "I think you have the wrong house."

"Oh." Relief and disappointment flood her. "I'm sorry. I used to know someone who lived here."

"Really? My dad's lived here forever. He owns it. Eddie Wood?"

"Eddie Wood," Nessa says, absorbing the information: Dan is not Dan. Dan is a father. "Eddie. Of course. That's what I meant."

The woman smiles uneasily. "You're here to see my dad?"

Nessa nods.

The woman narrows her eyes. "How do you know him?"

"I used to live around here," Nessa says, and then, remembering the dog barking: "I walked his dog sometimes."

The woman's eyes widen. "Daisy," she says. "Poor Daisy. He had to put her down a few years ago. Cancer." She speaks softly, watching Nessa's face for a reaction. She's not beautiful, but she also isn't plain. Her mouth is expressive, more so than her eyes, which are hard and dark, heavily lined. She's one of those people who could be nineteen or forty-five, depending on the light.

"Oh," Nessa says. "I'm sorry to hear that."

The woman opens the door then and waves her inside. "My dad took it hard. I'm Heather, by the way."

"Nessa," she says, stepping inside. The hallway stuns her with its familiarity: the wood paneling, the low ceilings. The smell is the same: stale tobacco, a house that hasn't been cleaned for a long time, a hint of something citrus.

Heather leads her through the living room and into the kitchen, and Nessa follows, eyeing the furniture. There's the La-Z-Boy, the gray couch. The same blank walls, nothing hung. She wants to stop and stare, take out her phone and snap pictures, though of course she doesn't.

Nessa always envisioned Dan's kitchen to look like their own growing up, with linoleum countertops and a white tiled floor, windows that look out to a swamp and a school. She's pictured it countless times: Dan reaching into the refrigerator for the beers, prying them open with a bottle opener, or just using the countertop, the way Jesse sometimes did. She'd wondered if Dan had bought the beer in preparation for that night, or if he already had it lying around.

In actuality, Dan's kitchen is windowless, a galley kitchen. There are no signs that cooking is ever done there.

Heather pulls a photograph off the fridge and hands it to Nessa. A brown dog with a tight muscular body and an underbite. Daisy.

Nessa makes herself smile sadly. "Wow. Poor girl."

"Yup." Heather takes back the photo and sticks it on the fridge with a magnet. "My dad is resting upstairs," she says. "You know he's sick, right?"

Nessa shakes her head.

"Cancer," Heather says again, this time with an ironic shake of her head. "Lung." She pauses. "When was the last time you saw him?"

"Not for years."

"Well, you should know he doesn't look like himself. He stopped responding to chemo months ago. We're kind of just waiting it out." Her voice is harder than the one she'd used to talk about Daisy.

"I'm sorry," Nessa says. "How long has he been sick?"

"A year, now. He was diagnosed right after his fifty-eighth birthday."

Nessa's stomach lurches, her brain jumping into action, doing the math. That made him forty-five, she calculates, when he had sex with Tanya. She feels a twisting in her stomach, the sharp wrench of a screw being turned. "Can I use your bathroom?" she asks.

"Sure." Heather points to a door off the kitchen.

Nessa moves quickly, accidentally slamming the door behind her. She sits down right in time, her bowels emptying instantaneously. *Shit,* she whispers to the dank room. She's trembling. Her body immediately begins to hurt in that hot, shaky way an upset stomach hurts. Sweat forms on her upper lip and forehead.

Nessa closes her eyes and tries to recall Dan's face. What had she seen when he'd opened the door all those years ago? What had she missed?

She opens her eyes and looks around. There's a slow, steady drip from the faucet, a yellowed divot where the water has eroded the sink basin. Mildew has bloomed like bruises above the shower, crawling out across the ceiling and walls. The shower curtain looks decades old, stiff with soap scum. On the edge of the sink there's a purple toothbrush and a travel-sized tube of toothpaste, a blue retainer swimming in a cup of water. Heather's things, most likely.

Nessa flushes the toilet and washes her hands, opens up the mirrored medicine cabinet. Aleve, floss, a silver pair of nail scissors. She takes the scissors and slips them into her pocket.

Then an *um* floats out from the other side of the door, and Nessa can picture Heather with her hand up, deliberating whether she should knock or not.

"Be out in a minute," Nessa says loudly.

When she opens the door, Heather is standing right there. They look at each other. "Sorry," Nessa says, touching her abdomen. "My stomach."

"No problem," Heather says quickly. "My dad's in his room. I'm sure a visitor will do him good. It's been pretty quiet around here."

Nessa nods and follows Heather down the hall and up the stairs, imagining Tanya all those years ago, following Dan.

When they reach his room, Heather knocks twice before cracking open the door. "You have a visitor," she says, opening the door all the way. "Nessa. Daisy's walker."

Together they step inside. The room is dark and sour smelling; all the shades are pulled down. The only light emanates from a blue TV screen, stuck on a channel with no reception. Across the room a man is propped up in bed. Dan. Eddie. He nods mildly. "Oh," he says, and Nessa clears her throat.

"I'll let you guys talk," says Heather, and then she leaves.

Nessa approaches the bed. She is unprepared and terrified. In her pocket, she presses her thumb against the cool blade of the scissors. Heather is right; he does look different. The skin on his face droops and his eyes blink lifelessly, tucked away in their sockets. The hair on his head is sparse and patchy, whether from chemotherapy or age, she isn't sure. The only other time she saw him he'd been wearing a hat.

Nessa sits on the edge of the bed and Eddie regards her emotionlessly. She can tell he doesn't recognize her. She slips her hands under her thighs to keep them from shaking.

"You don't know who I am," she says. "Do you?"

Eddie furrows his brow, then shakes his head.

"We met years ago."

"What'd Heather say your name was?"

"Nessa."

"Nessa," he repeats. "I don't know any Nessas. None that I can remember. A Vanessa maybe, but no Nessas. Heather says you're a dog walker?"

And that time, hearing him talk: it comes flooding back. His reserve; his calm; the almost serene way he'd spoken to them that night. "How old are you girls?" he'd asked gently, the way an adult would ask a child. He'd seen them exactly the way they'd wanted to be seen. Two beautiful young girls, two variations of the same thing. *Your choice, take your pick.*

"Nessa is my real name," Nessa says. "When I met you, I told you my name was Lola." This time it's easier for her to talk. She pulls her hands out from under her legs and holds them tightly in her lap.

Eddie shrugs. "Doesn't ring a bell."

"You also met my sister," she says. "Layla?" But Eddie's gaze remains dull and indifferent.

"And you told us your name was Dan."

Something flashes in his eyes then: recognition, or maybe confusion. It's hard to tell.

Nessa glances across the bed. It has the sunken, lived-in stench of a bed that has become a home. Where he eats and naps and sleeps and passes the hours in between. "How old is your daughter, Eddie?" Nessa asks.

"Why," he says. His voice is flat, almost bored, like he doesn't care about the answer, but his body has stiffened.

"How old is she?"

"Why do you want to know?" He looks directly at Nessa, and it frightens her, even though his arms are weak and motionless by his sides.

She stands, her body humming from the inside out. "Do you remember the time you paid a fourteen-year-old girl one hundred dollars to have sex with you?"

Eddie's eyes widen. He stares at her, letting his eyes travel slowly from her face down her body. A muscle in his face twitches, as though trying to stifle some reaction.

"Get out," he says quietly, and the way he says it—she knows he knows who she is. He's remembering it.

Nessa takes a step forward so she's standing over him. Up close he's older and sicker and he smells. She searches his eyes for fear. "I want to know how old your daughter was when you raped my little sister."

And then he laughs, a thin, humorless laugh. "Get out of my house," he says, and even his anger sounds hollow, an old habit he carries around with him.

She reaches for the scissors in her pocket. "You should be ashamed of yourself." It's something she's said to him thousands of times in her head, and it feels surreal to say it out loud.

"What are you here to do?" he says. "Scold me?" And when she doesn't say anything he smiles. "*Kill* me?"

Nessa can feel herself beginning to unravel. It isn't fair how calm he is. He's supposed to be frightened. "How would you feel," she says, her voice rising, "if you found out that an old man had raped your daughter when she was fourteen years old?"

"I never raped anyone." He's no longer smiling. "And you think that girl downstairs is my daughter? She's not. She's just the greedy bitch who wants my money and my house when I die—which, lucky for her, is probably soon. Unless you want to help her out and kill me now." He raises his hairless eyebrows—it's the chemotherapy, she realizes—and leans forward. "Your sister wanted it," he says quietly. "She couldn't get enough of it. Right here on this bed. Moaning and groaning, begging me to—"

Nessa hurls the scissors across the room to make him shut up. They clatter against the wall and drop to the floor and he looks at her, dead-eyed.

And then, in one achingly clear moment, it occurs to Nessa how disturbing it is that she's back here, in this sick man's house, for the second time in her life. There is nothing he will say, she realizes, that will answer any question of hers. And there is nothing she could say or do—nothing—that will make this man, Dan or Eddie, whoever he is, feel remorse for what he did.

Nessa is wasting her time. He has started to talk again, watching her face, eager for an audience, as it's clear he spends most of his time alone. Silently, she turns around and walks out the bedroom door, shutting it behind her. She hears his voice falter then, finally, stop altogether.

By the time Tanya gets home her head is pounding, and when she walks inside her apartment and is assaulted by the smell of paint, it does nothing to help her mood or her head.

She stands in the doorway of her and Eitan's shared office, surveying the damage. Eitan has moved all their filing cabinets into the hallway and pushed the furniture—their two desks and desk chairs, as well as several bookshelves—into the middle of the room. The walls, all but one, have been painted a sickly yellow that reminds her of courtroom 1.

"Are you serious?" she says when she hears him come up behind her. She feels his hand on her back and she swats it away and whirls around to look at him. The last remains of a smile are melting off his face. Clearly he was thinking this would be a welcome surprise.

"You don't like it?"

"No, not particularly, Eitan."

"I thought you would."

"Why would you think that?" Her migraine is severe, her ears pulsing hotly on either side of her head like ticking bombs. There was an obscene amount of traffic on the Triborough Bridge, and for the entire five-hour drive she was bombarded with incoming text messages from her mother and sister. *Don't be mad; are you mad?* Asked in at least a dozen different ways.

Eitan looks dejected. "I know you had a shitty weekend. I thought this would cheer you up. I asked management and they said it was fine."

"*Shitty* is a kind way to describe the weekend I had," she says. "The paint fumes are going to make my head explode. Can you open a few windows?" She brushes past him and storms into the kitchen. "Please," she calls over her shoulder.

In the kitchen she pours herself a glass of water and searches through the drawer where they keep pain relievers. "Where the fuck is the ibuprofen?"

Eitan appears. "Tan—"

"Found it." She opens the bottle and shakes two white pills into her palm.

"Tanya, I'm not sure you should be taking that."

"Why not?"

"You're pregnant. You really should be taking Tylenol if you're—"

Tanya holds up her other hand. "Don't tell me what or what not to put in my body. You've put enough in there as it is."

Eitan holds up his hands in surrender.

"I have a migraine. And while you spent the weekend painting, I spent the weekend in a shithole motel trying to convince my mother not to go back to a man who strangled her to the point where her eye vessels burst— she had fucking bloody *eyes*, Eitan. And guess what! She went back. And please, Eitan, don't look at me that way."

"What way?"

"With your *God* eyes," Tanya says. His God eyes are his serious eyes, his kind eyes. "I don't want to cry. It's past the point of being cathartic. At this point it will just make me puffy tomorrow at work."

Eitan nods. "Okay," he says. "I get that."

"So please don't start acting all sweet; I really can't stand it right now."

"Okay. No crying."

Tanya doesn't answer. She swallows the pills and fills her glass with water again and gulps that down, too.

"How about food? You must be hungry."

"I'm starving," says Tanya. "I could eat your face."

"I can see that."

"What should we get?"

Eitan starts listing: "Mexican, Korean, Chinese, the sub place. What? Why are you making that face?"

"I went out to dinner with my mom and Nessa," she says. "I was a huge bitch. I left the restaurant while they were eating."

"You're a good daughter, you know that, right?"

"I told you I don't need a pep talk."

"I'm not trying to give you one. But you've gone through hell this weekend. And it's because you care so much about them."

Tanya sinks down to the floor and leans her head against the cabinet. "Nessa says my mom isn't *ready* to leave him. What's going to make her ready? Another injury? Another man? Another three weeks to think it over? I've seen enough of these cases to know—scumbags like Jesse don't change. And it doesn't look good for her if she keeps being wishy-washy in court. What the hell would you do if you were me, Eitan? I don't know how to get through to her that Jesse is playing her."

Eitan sits, too, leaning against the opposite wall, and she's grateful that he's not trying to touch her. "You know, this woman came into the hospital the other day with a broken wrist. Her husband threw her down the stairs. I looked in her chart and she's been to the ER four times in the last year alone. All DV. Baldwin was on call and he was talking with her, you know, telling her that she was in an abusive relationship and that she had to get out, that if she went back to him she was only going to end up back in the ER.

"And the woman just kept nodding, saying, *Yes, Doctor, I understand, thank you, thank you.* She was very agreeable and polite, you know—very gracious. So finally, Baldwin finishes his lecture and leaves. I go back into her room an hour later to discharge her. I don't think she recognized me or even realized I'd been in the room before with Baldwin. I asked her how she was feeling, and she said fine, and then I asked her if anyone was coming to pick her up from the hospital and help her get home—she was in a cast and on painkillers—and she just smiles and says, 'Oh, my husband is just across the hall in the restroom.' And I could have shaken her, Tanya. I was so close to saying something, and then I realized . . . this woman is being told all day, every day, what to do. At home she's being told what to do by her husband, and then when she comes in to get help, she's getting told by all these other men what to do." Eitan shrugs.

"So what did you do?" asks Tanya.

"I told her I was glad she was feeling better and to come back if there were any problems."

"And you think that's enough?"

"No," Eitan says. "Not really. But nothing that I was going to say was going to change her mind about her husband."

"It's different, though, Eitan. That's your patient. This is my *mom*."

"I know. And I'm not trying to say it's the same thing. I just think you're putting a lot of pressure on yourself to fix your mother's life. And I don't know if that's even possible."

"No," Tanya says. "You might be right." And she feels terribly sad then, thinking about how far away everyone is from everybody else. Instinctually, she puts her hands on her still-flat stomach, realizing it only moments afterward.

"Yellow," she says. "Why, of all colors, is that the one appointed gender-neutral?"

"I should have asked you first about painting."

"Yeah," says Tanya. "You should have." She closes her eyes. "So you think I should just wait for my mom to realize it on her own? Wait for her to be *ready*?"

"Do you have any other choice?"

Tanya opens her eyes and looks at her husband. She both loves him desperately and is irritated beyond belief with him, and she realizes that she'll probably feel this way about him countless times in the future.

"Probably not," she says. "Burritos?"

He smiles at her. "Order in or go out?"

"What do you feel like?"

"Let's go out," he says. "I need a break from the fumes."

THEY WALK THE FOUR BLOCKS up to the burrito place and eat outside, sitting beside one another on a bench across from a fenced-in playground. Tanya orders a pulled pork burrito with guacamole. Eitan keeps kosher, not out of obligation but out of habit—after twenty-some years of not eating pork and shellfish, it doesn't appeal to him.

Sometimes Tanya finds herself going out of her way to order pork when she's with Eitan as some sort of test. When is it finally going to piss him off? When is he going to want his Jewish wife?

Tanya goes back and forth on whether or not she's really Jewish. She was born into a family that called itself Jewish, and in some ways, that's been hard to shake. Lorraine married Jonathan beneath a chuppah, took and kept the Bloom last name. Her mother looks at home in the wedding photos, holding Jonathan's hand; up in the chair, laughing. The only hint of Lorraine's Catholicism is the prominent cross around Lorraine's mother's neck in the background of the photos. A mezuzah hung on their doorpost at 12 Winter Street for the first ten years of Tanya's life.

Lorraine was the one who used to drop the girls off at Hebrew school and pick them up each week. After the divorce, though, Lorraine stopped driving Tanya to Hebrew school on Thursday afternoons. Nessa's bat mitzvah, which was supposed to take place later that year, never happened. On Hanukkah they still lit the menorah and Lorraine would give them gifts, but without Jonathan there to lead them, they didn't sing the prayers. None of them knew the Hebrew well enough. After a while they stopped with the candles, and then eventually they were too old for gifts. Sometimes Tanya and Nessa went to Lexington for Passover seder or Rosh Hashanah, but usually Simone's family was there, too. It didn't feel like it used to.

Tanya has always associated Judaism with Jonathan—but she also associates Judaism with family, with togetherness, with childhood. Something to do with her mother and her sister and herself. To her, the memory of Judaism is a tender one, like waking up on a snow day as a kid—outside bright and glittering; inside, dark and warm with sleep.

"That's the safest I ever felt," Tanya told Eitan once. "Snow-day mornings. My parents outside shoveling, Nessa and me in our bunk bed." At his house in Lexington, her father has one of those electric snowblowers. Tanya doubts that Simone has ever shoveled in her life. She wonders if her father ever missed it—his life in Arlington. There were hardly any perfect moments, the four of them together. There weren't even very many good ones. It's not that her parents had fought so much. Mostly she remembers silence. Her mother making a joke—her father not laughing at it or feigning confusion. *I don't get it*. Her mother recounting a story from her day, her father not really listening—Nessa doing the listening instead.

But snow-day mornings, she thinks, were probably the best.

Now, though, she associates Judaism with Eitan. She probably doesn't even count, she thinks, with her Catholic mother, with her pork. But right now, sitting on the Upper West Side with her ex-Orthodox husband, Tanya does feel Jewish. And she has the strong sense that the child inside of her is as well—whatever the hell that means.

TANYA FINISHES HER BURRITO before Eitan even gets started on his second half, and she wonders why it's possible for her to eat this way in front of Eitan but not in front of her family. Eitan's always relished watching her eat. "I love when you want something, and then you get it," he's told her. He means food and sex—earthly pleasures. Things like a job, or a raise, or even a nice outfit—he wants all those things for her, too. But there's something about seeing someone you love satisfy a craving.

She remembers one time, early on in their relationship, watching him attempt to untie a knot. It was a drawstring on a sweatshirt of hers that had tangled in the wash. She'd grown frustrated with it and brought it to him, then watched as he delicately and patiently plucked at the fierce knot, until eventually it loosened and he managed to pull it free. She was taken aback by how aroused this made her—watching his fingers maneuver the string, the slight twitch of the veins in his hands as he did so. By the time he'd unknotted it, she so badly wanted him to touch her, to apply the same concentration and tenderness that he'd applied to that ridiculous drawstring, that she actually said to him, "Can we fuck?"—a sentence that Tanya had never uttered in her life, and has never uttered since. Afterward, when they were lying in bed naked below the waist, she told him about the string.

He listened intently. They weren't touching, but there was a humming in the space between their bodies. "You're so sexy, you know that?" he said.

Sexy and sex had always seemed like two separate things to Tanya. She felt sexy often—in the mornings, freshly showered and made up for work. When she delivered a smart argument; when she spoke her mind. At night in her glasses and underwear, reading before bed. Sex, though, brought up a whole lot of unsexy things for Tanya: There were the smells and the secretions, the hair in unfortunate places. There were unsexy sounds, ones that escaped before you were able to stop them. There were thoughts that passed through her mind during sex, that maybe in the moment were exciting, though afterward struck her as shameful, disgusting; pornographic.

Now Tanya turns to Eitan. There's a glob of sour cream on his chin. "You've got—" she says, pointing. They have an agreement: they will never not tell each other about food on their mouths.

He wipes it away.

"When I found out I was pregnant," Tanya says, "the first thing I thought was that I wanted an abortion."

Eitan swallows and looks at her, waits for her to continue.

"I came home ready to tell you that I was getting one. I walked in the door expecting to say, *Eitan, I'm pregnant and I need to get this nipped in the bud, stat.*" She pauses. "But you seemed so happy when I told you I was pregnant, like happier than I'd ever seen you. It made me feel terrible."

"I was happy," Eitan says hesitantly.

"I know."

"Do you still want an abortion?" he asks. There's worry in his eyes, though he doesn't look especially surprised.

"Sometimes," says Tanya. "When I was with my family I did. It seemed like having a baby was just going to make me more tied to them. Like, by turning into a mother, I might start to become more like my own. But then I came home today and saw you, and even though I kind of wanted to murder you, I also had this feeling, like, I can't wait to have a family with him."

"I know your mom has issues, Tanya, but she had you, and you turned out pretty fucking incredible."

Tanya suppresses a smile before flashing him a real one. "Valid point."

"Tanya, I don't want to have a baby that you don't really want to have."

"I do want to have a baby," she says. "I just think it's going to be a lot harder than either of us realize."

"I'm sure you're right."

"It has the potential to tear us apart."

"Why do you say that?"

"Because it happens all the time, Eitan. All the time."

"I don't know," Eitan says. "I think it also has the potential to be the best thing we've ever done."

On the bus ride back to Northampton, Nessa texts Henry. *Hey there,* she writes. *Getting back to Noho tonight. What are you up to?*

He responds immediately, which fills her with a relief so huge and sweeping that it embarrasses her. She can't bear the thought of spending the night alone. *What time?* he writes.

My bus gets in at 7.

I'll pick you up.

Cool, she writes back.

She leans back in her seat and closes her eyes.

She's still vibrating from her visit to Eddie's house, unsure of what to do with it. She'd expected to leave his house with something useful she might bring back to Tanya, but now, sitting on the bus, she wonders what that possibly could have been. An explanation? An apology? A corpse? She understands now that her visit to Eddie's house is not something that Tanya will ever have any interest in hearing about.

In the same way that Dan started out as a fantasy inside Nessa's mind, he will end with her, too. A sick, old man—malodorous and obscene, in a bed that she'd willed to life. This time she'll leave her sister out of it.

WHEN NESSA'S BUS pulls into the depot, Henry is already there, sitting on the curb in front of her car, smoking a cigarette. He's hunched over, neck bent, examining something on the sidewalk.

"Hey," she says as she approaches him.

He looks up, smiles. Puts out his cigarette and flicks it on the ground, stands, reaches out to take her bag.

"Thanks." She passes it over to him.

"No problem." He hands her the car keys.

On the ride home they don't talk much, but Henry keeps his hand on her knee while she drives. When "Beast of Burden" comes on the radio, he turns the volume up and smiles. He seems more relaxed than usual.

When they get back to her house, Nessa unlocks the door and he follows her inside. Her stomach feels light and fluttery, knowing that soon she'll be pressed up against Henry in bed.

"Do you want some water?" she asks as they enter the apartment.

"Sure."

She fills two glasses in the sink, watching from the kitchen as Henry drops her bag in the middle of the living room. He's wearing jeans and a maroon-colored button-up shirt. She's never seen him in a button-up shirt before and she wonders if he dressed up for her.

She joins him in the living room. "Here," she says, handing him a cup.

They both sip, watching one another, not breaking eye contact, even through the glass.

"So how was the trip?" he asks.

"Awful."

He bows his head then, and kisses her lightly on the lips. They stand, embracing. Nessa waits for him to ask her why, but he remains quiet.

"My stepfather strangled my mother," she says into his shoulder, and she feels a tinge of anticipation in the silence afterward. She wants a reaction.

He steps back. "Jesus. Why?"

Nessa looks up at him. "Does it matter why?"

"I guess not," he says. "Sorry that happened."

"Yeah. My sister and I went with her to the emergency room."

"Is she okay?"

"Sort of. I mean, she is now."

"People suck."

"That's kind of an understatement." Nessa is disappointed in his response. She wishes she could start crying, but she doesn't feel sad enough to cry. All she feels is restless and pissed off and a little bit aroused.

"You want to lie down?" he asks, and she nods into his shoulder.

Once in the bedroom he begins to kiss her for real—his mouth tastes like whatever he had for dinner and cigarettes—and he pulls off her shirt.

"Wait," she says, and she goes over to the windows in her bra to close the blinds. When she turns back around he's standing naked by the bed, a sheepish smile on his face. She's seen him without clothes a number of times, but this time she's struck by his imperfections. His stomach is round and soft, a middle-aged man's belly, and his erection peeks out from underneath. His shoulders are pulled forward from years of poor posture.

He strides toward her then, a hungry expression on his face. "Can you take this off?" he says, snapping her bra strap. His breath is bad and she wonders how he'd react if she were to say so.

She reaches behind her back and unhooks her bra, lets it drop to the floor. She almost pities him, watching him watch her. He seems mesmerized by her body.

They begin to kiss again and she reaches down and holds his penis, feeling it swell inside her grip.

He likes this and thrusts himself forward so he's pressed up against her stomach. Then his hands are all over her—on her chest and her rib cage, reaching behind her to grab her ass. She breathes hard in his ear, egging him on. She no longer knows if she's enjoying him, or if she's enjoying putting on a show for him, and after several minutes she decides that it doesn't matter *what* she's enjoying—only that it feels unbelievably good.

She allows him to guide her to the bed, his hands firmly pushing her backwards until she falls back onto the mattress. He climbs on top of her and roughly begins to touch her, forcing two fingers inside her vagina. He paws at her clit the way you might try to scrub a stain out of a couch cushion.

It hurts, but she doesn't want to throw him off by saying so—he looks

218 · HANNA HALPERIN

so excited, almost euphoric. She feels a little sorry for him; he has no idea how the female body works.

"How many girls have you slept with?" she asks, and when he smiles down at her, triumphant, she realizes he's taken the question as a compliment.

"Why do you want to know?" he asks.

She runs a finger down the inside of his thigh. "I just do."

"I've lost count," he says. "Forty, maybe fifty."

Nessa nods. It's more than she expected, and for some reason this turns her on.

"How many dudes have you fucked?" he asks, smiling.

"Twenty-seven," she answers honestly. "Counting you."

"Lucky twenty-seven." He drops himself onto her again, kissing her mouth and neck.

"Did you sleep with anyone while I was gone?" she asks.

He pushes himself up and looks at her strangely. "No. Did you?"

"No. I was with my family the whole time." She pauses. "Would you have been mad if I did?"

He shrugs, and then he seems to consider it. "I mean, it wouldn't have made me happy, but I wouldn't have been mad at you."

She nods and waits for him to ask her the same question, but he doesn't.

IT'S AFTERWARD, when they're lying in bed together, that her pity for Henry fades and affection takes its place. He seems calm, his eyes half-closed, running his hand up and down her arm.

"Have you ever gotten into a fight?" she asks. "Like, a physical fight?"

He opens one eye, glancing sideways at her. "A few."

"Like when?"

"In tenth grade I punched this guy, Adam Morris, in the face for calling me a faggot."

"Then what happened?"

"He punched me back. It broke out into this awesome fight in the cafeteria. We both got suspended." He lets out a loud, boyish laugh. "Have you?"

"I almost did today."

Henry grins. "Yeah?"

"Yeah," she says.

"What'd you do?"

"I came close to attacking an old man," she says, and when Henry starts to laugh again, she says, "Really."

"Why?"

Nessa shrugs and leans back onto the pillow, closes her eyes. She's never told anyone about Dan. She's never felt it was her secret to tell. In the moment, though, she desperately wants to tell Henry. She wants to see his reaction—anyone's reaction really. She has the feeling it will surprise him—maybe even impress him. On the other hand, she's worried he might just continue to laugh, think of it as one big joke.

Then, surprisingly, Henry kisses her nose, and Nessa opens her eyes.

He's staring unabashedly at her. She wonders if Henry is beginning to fall in love with her; the thought makes her chest feel warm and full. She decides that she'll tell him about Dan, about what happened fourteen years ago, and about what happened earlier that day. It's time to tell someone.

Before she can speak he smiles and says, "You're growing a zit."

"What?"

"Right there." He touches her face. "On your cheek."

"Um."

"Can I pop it?"

"Are you serious?"

"Please?"

"No." She throws the covers off and goes into the bathroom.

Nessa slams the door, suddenly on the verge of tears. She leans into the mirror and examines the zit, then glances down at her nakedness. Her body is red and splotchy from sex, almost allergic looking.

When she goes back into the bedroom, Henry is still in the same position on her bed.

"Why would you say that?" she demands.

He looks up at her. "Say what? That you have a zit?"

"Yes." She pauses. "It's rude. *You're* rude."

He looks taken aback. "Sorry," he says. "I guess I just feel comfortable around you."

She doesn't answer.

"Come here." He pats the bed next to him.

"Why?"

"Because."

Begrudgingly, she walks over to the bed and climbs in without looking at him. She leaves a foot of space between them and crosses her arms over her chest. "Just because you feel comfortable with me doesn't mean you can pop my zits." She's aware of how bratty she sounds, and she realizes that despite her anger, she's flirting with him.

"You can pop mine," he says.

She glances over.

He flips onto his stomach and reaches over his shoulder to swat at his back. "Right there," he says. "See it?"

She leans over and looks on his shoulder blade where there's a bulging whitehead. "I see it."

"Wanna pop that bad boy?"

"You're gross."

"But you want to, right?"

Despite herself, she laughs a little. "Kinda."

"Go ahead. Knock yourself out."

"Okay, but that doesn't mean you can pop mine."

"Understood."

"Fine. Here goes." With her fingertips, she pushes the surrounding skin and watches the pus form into a stiff white bead. After a few seconds, it explodes with a satisfying pop. "There you go," she says.

"It felt good, right?"

"You're a weirdo."

"Admit it—it felt good."

"It felt disgusting," she says, but she moves closer to him in bed, and lets her bare feet brush his.

D r. Louis Keller is shorter than both Lorraine and Jesse, with fuzzy gray hair sprouting out from the crown of his head and from his ears. He's wearing a short-sleeved button-up shirt and corduroys, more casual than Lorraine expected a therapist to dress, and smudged glasses, magnifying watery blue eyes.

"Thank you for taking the time to meet with us, Dr. Keller," Jesse says, shaking the man's hand.

"Lou," the therapist says warmly. "Please, call me Lou."

Lorraine is relieved. She likes Lou already.

He leads them into his office and tells them to sit wherever they feel comfortable. There are two matching armchairs, both faded green, and an ugly-looking polyester couch. Jesse, who's holding Lorraine's hand, leads them to the couch. They sit, and Lou settles across from them in one of the chairs.

"Jesse," Lou says, "I know we spoke a little over the phone about what's been going on with you and Lorraine, but now that we're all here, the three of us, why don't we start over? You can both tell me why it is you're here today. And take your time. Know that we won't get to everything today—not even close to everything—and that's okay. Therapy is a process, and today is just the very beginning." He smiles at Lorraine. "Lorraine, would you like to start?"

Lorraine glances over at Jesse, who squeezes her hand and nods.

"We've been fighting a lot recently," Lorraine says. "We've always had our ups and downs, but lately there's been a lot of downs. We . . . separated . . . last weekend. That was when Jesse called to set up the appointment. Things got really bad, but we decided we wanted to work it out. We've been together for sixteen years and married for ten."

Lou nods. "That's a long time."

"Yes," Lorraine says. "We love each other a lot."

"I can see that."

"I was thinking about this, Dr. Keller," Jesse says. "And I actually think a lot of our issues stem from loving each other so much—maybe *too* much. I've never cared more for anyone, and sometimes it overwhelms me. I just don't want to lose Lorrie. We wanted to come to therapy because we want to do everything in our power to make our marriage work. Lorrie's right, we've had our ups and downs, but I think that's part of any relationship, right? In my opinion, what it comes down to is how a couple *manages* those downs. That's where we've run into trouble. Me especially." Jesse is leaning forward with his hands on his knees in a way that reminds Lorraine of a sports huddle. "But coming to therapy," he goes on. "That was the healthy thing to do for both of us. So that's why we're here."

Lou nods and leans back in his seat. He isn't taking notes or even holding a pen and paper. "Great," Lou says. "Jesse, I think you're absolutely right that managing those downs, whether it be misunderstandings or an argument, or if one partner in the couple is having a rough time, is absolutely crucial. Lorraine, you mentioned that you and Jesse separated last weekend. Can you tell me more about that separation, and what led up to it?"

"Um, well, I applied for a restraining order."

Beside her Jesse stiffens.

"You did," Lou says, and she can't tell if it's a question or a statement.

"I didn't end up going through with it," Lorraine says.

"You should probably mention it was your daughter who convinced you to apply for the restraining order," Jesse says. "Your daughter who's always had it out for me, for whatever reason." He's looking closely at Lou while he says it.

"That's true," Lorraine says. "My daughter Tanya kind of talked me into it."

"Well, before we get to the order, why don't you tell me about what led up to it?" Lou looks at Lorraine.

"There was an incident in the middle of the night, when my daughters were home."

"That sounds like that's a good place to start," Lou says. "What happened?"

So Lorraine tells Lou about the conversation she'd had with Nessa and Tanya out on the porch that Jesse had overheard. She describes Jesse's rage and jealousy when he'd confronted her later that night after her daughters had gone to bed. She tells Lou that Jesse had hurled a bottle of soap across the room—but she does not say that he poured the soap all over her so that it had spilled into her face and eyes. At the point in the story where Jesse put his hands around her neck, Lorraine skips over this detail, telling herself that she'll arrive at it later; that it's only fair to let Jesse talk first, before saying everything—and especially that.

"He got really, really angry at me when he heard me talking about him. And my ex-husband," she says.

"Angry how?" Lou asks.

She looks down into her lap where her and Jesse's hands are clasped together.

"I got jealous," Jesse blurts out. "It was my own insecurity, my fault. I blew it out of proportion. I overreacted and lost control. It's something that I'd really like to work on. Instead of yelling and exploding, learning how to step back and talk calmly about my problems. It's something that I need help with." He leans forward again and lowers his voice. "My father cheated on my mother. I was exposed to my parents' issues at an early age. I don't think I've fully appreciated how that's affected me until now. He cheated on her—my father did—for their entire marriage. With many different women." He pauses then, as though he expects Lou to say something, but Lou just nods.

"I've had trust problems before," Jesse goes on. "Not that it excuses my behavior. But Lorrie's very attractive. I mean, look at her—she's beautiful. And I know how men's brains are, Dr. Keller—as I'm sure you do—being a therapist and all. I can't help getting protective."

"Thank you, Jesse. And please—call me Lou. All of that is important, I think. And I'd like to hear more, in particular about your family growing up. It sounds like a truly painful place for a child. First, though, I want to get back to what Lorraine was saying. Lorraine, can you tell me what Jesse's anger looks like to you? You said he threw a bottle of soap across the room?"

"Just like Jesse said," Lorraine says. "A lot of yelling and getting heated. A little aggressive."

"If you can, paint me a picture. Things you said, things he said, things you did, things he did. I'd just like to get an idea of what a fight between Lorraine and Jesse *looks* like, *sounds* like, *feels* like."

Lorraine nods, wondering how she's supposed to paint a picture with Jesse sitting right next to her.

Lou looks at Jesse. "Jesse, do you feel comfortable if Lorraine describes to me what the fight between the two of you was like, from her point of view?"

"Of course," Jesse says. He looks at Lorraine. "Honey, you can say anything."

A strong feeling takes hold of Lorraine, though she can't name it. "I don't really know how to describe it," she admits.

"I yelled at her that night," Jesse says. "I got in her face. My anger got the better of me and I—I shoved her." At this point Jesse's eyes fill with tears and he takes a huge breath. "I hate myself for doing that," he says. "I'm so ashamed."

"Thank you, Jesse," Lou says softly. "Thank you for sharing that. Lorraine, was that your experience, too?"

"He did shove me."

"Were you injured?"

"No."

"Have there been other fights where things have become physical?" Lou asks Lorraine.

"In a sense."

For an incredibly long minute, nobody says a word.

"I did have to go to the dentist," Lorraine says, unaware that she's about to say it before it's too late and there it is—hanging in the air like one of those giant red balloons in front of their house. Lorraine doesn't dare look at Jesse.

"Why did you have to go to the dentist?" Lou asks.

Lorraine is conscious of her face heating up. "It wasn't related," she says. "I had a cleaning scheduled. I was just remembering."

Lou takes a deep breath and when he speaks again, his voice sounds chipper, lighter. "Jesse, why don't you tell me about your living situation? When I spoke with you over the phone, you told me Lorraine had spent the night at a hotel but she was moving back in. How has it been going since then?"

Jesse lets go of Lorraine's hand and leans back against the couch. "She's back at home and things have been much better. This whole thing made me realize how much my marriage means to me and how stupid I've been, to risk losing it. I would never want to do anything to drive Lorrie away from me. I feel one hundred percent committed."

"I can see that," Lou says. "Tell me more, if you can."

AFTER THEY SAY GOODBYE to Lou and schedule another appointment for the following week, Lorraine is nervous walking to the car. She's worried she's said too much. But when they climb in, Jesse looks at her gently. "I feel like we're already making progress, don't you?"

Lorraine is so relieved that Jesse isn't angry that she reaches over the console and hugs him tightly. "I think we are, too," she says, and then she begins to cry.

"Why are you crying, baby?"

"You can't ever hurt me like that again, Jesse, okay?"

Jesse looks surprised. "I won't. I promise, Lorraine, I'm never, ever doing that again."

"But you've said things like that before. You've made promises that you haven't kept."

Jesse looks at his lap. "I know," he says. "I've fucked up so many times. I know I don't deserve all the chances you've given me." He looks up. "But, Lorrie, this time it really hit home. When you left . . . when that police officer showed up at our house. God, I died inside. But I get it now. I need to figure my shit out. Lorrie, I think I was really fucked up by my parents. Like, as a little boy, watching my dad fuck my mom up. I think any kid who sees that happening, he's—well, how can he not be a little messed up by it?"

"I know," Lorraine says. "I know it was hard for you as a boy."

"It was." Jesse's eyes fill with tears. "Those nights when you were gone, when you were with Nessa and Tanya and I was alone in the house, I just kept remembering things. There was this one time my dad came home. I must have been eight. He was piss drunk and he just went at my mom. I mean, worse than I'd ever seen it. She was on the floor and he was kicking her over and over in the stomach. He just wouldn't stop. I ran in and tried to get in between them and he hit me so hard I blacked out." Jesse touches his face: his chin and his jawbone. "He didn't let me go to school the whole next week 'cause of how bad I looked. I never want to be like that, Lorraine. I'm not that kind of man. I'm not my father. And, Lorrie, you're such a beautiful woman. Such a kind and beautiful woman. I don't know what I'd do without you."

Lorraine puts a hand on his leg. "Next time we meet with Lou I think you should tell him that story."

Jesse laughs a little then. "He's kind of an old geezer, Lou, isn't he?"

Lorraine pauses. She'd liked Lou and she'd thought Jesse liked him, too. "I thought he was nice."

"Yeah, he was nice. I guess I just don't necessarily see the point in paying someone to ask us questions like, *Tell me more,* and *How did that make you feel.* I feel like we could make just as much progress on our own, maybe even more, since we can really be ourselves in front of each other."

"But, Jesse, you said you'd do therapy."

"I know, Lorrie, and I'm doing it. I showed up today, didn't I? All I'm saying is I think any old fart could be a therapist if they wanted to. You don't need special training to do what the guy in there did."

"Maybe."

Jesse reaches over and squeezes her knee. "Let's get out of here. Are you hungry?"

Lorraine isn't, but she says sure anyway.

"How about Rocco's? You want to go to Rocco's?"

"Okay."

"Great," he says, starting the car. "Me too."

LATER THAT EVENING Lorraine misses a call from an unknown number and when she listens to the voice mail, she's surprised to hear the therapist's voice over the phone.

"Hi, Lorraine," he says. "This is Lou Keller calling. It was a pleasure meeting you and Jesse today. I wanted to ask you a question when you have a minute. Give me a call back when you have a private moment to talk." He leaves his phone numbers—both his office one and his cell phone—and she jots them down on a napkin. His message makes her nervous.

Lorraine waits until Jesse's in the shower that night to call back, and once she hears the water running, she dials Lou's cell phone number.

He answers on the second ring. "This is Lou Keller."

"Hi, Lou. It's Lorraine. Lorraine Bloom."

"Lorraine," Lou says. His warmth comes through over the phone. "Thank you for calling. Do you have a moment to speak privately?"

"Yes," she says. "I'm at home."

"Great. And is Jesse there?"

"He's in the shower," Lorraine says. "I could call back with him, if you wanted to speak with both of us?"

"No, I was actually hoping to speak just with you. If now's not a good time, though, we could plan something for tomorrow, maybe?"

"Now is fine," she says. "Jesse takes long showers."

"Alright then," Lou says. "This should really be a longer conversation, and I'd like to talk with you more face-to-face. But what I wanted to call to say was, I'm concerned about your safety, Lorraine."

Her heart begins to pound. "What?"

"Obviously we only got to the tip of the iceberg today, but I wanted to reach out, just to you, because to be quite clear and direct with you—and I wouldn't be a good therapist if I wasn't—I'm concerned about your safety." He pauses for a moment and when Lorraine doesn't say anything, he continues. "Couples therapy is an interesting thing. For some couples, it can do wonders. Really wonders. And for some, it doesn't do much of anything. But one thing that has to be in place, for couples therapy to work, is that there has to be an equal balance of power in the relationship. What I mean is, if one partner has more power over the other, couples therapy simply does not—*cannot*—work.

"In other words," he says, "if one partner is exerting power or control over the other, and I mean there are many different kinds of power— physical, verbal, emotional, sexual, financial even—that's going to make it difficult for therapy to work. Lorraine, when you were talking in my office today, how did it feel, telling me about the fights you've been having with Jesse?"

"It felt good, I guess," Lorraine says. She's humiliated. Did she do something wrong? Did she fail at therapy? She hadn't known it was possible to fail at therapy.

"Hmm," Lou says. "What felt good about it?"

"Getting it off my chest," she says. "Telling somebody else about it."

"Telling somebody else about what, specifically?"

"I guess the things Jesse's done to me."

"And what sorts of things has he done to you?"

"His jealousy," she says. "His anger. The times he's hurt me."

"Did you notice that Jesse did most of the talking today?"

"I guess," she says. "But I thought everything he was saying was important. He was apologizing, after all, and talking about his past. In the car after we left your office, he was telling me about this time he was a kid and his father came home—"

"Hold on to that for now. I do want to hear, but I also want to get to something else, while we still have time over the phone. Lorraine, what would have happened if you had told me why you had to go to the dentist?"

Lorraine feels her entire body go hot. "What?"

"What would have happened if you had told me today why you had to go to the dentist?"

She pauses. "Jesse would have been upset."

"Why?"

"He just would have. But, Dr. Keller—Lou—you have no idea what even happened."

"I don't need to know, Lorraine," Lou says. "I know enough to know it was bad."

Lorraine doesn't say anything.

"So if you had told me today what happened that made you have to go to the dentist, how would Jesse have reacted?"

"He'd be angry. Threatened."

"And when he's threatened, what does he do?"

Lorraine swallows. "He hurts me."

Upstairs she hears the shower turn off.

"I had to go to the dentist because he smashed my face into the kitchen sink," she whispers into the phone. "Three of my teeth fell out and the rest were bashed in. That's why I had to get braces." And then, even softer: "He just got out of the shower."

"Okay, I'll be quick, then. I'm going to tell you what I suggest. I don't think couples counseling is going to help your marriage, Lorraine, or you. Or Jesse, for that matter. If you don't feel safe talking openly with Jesse in the room—which, of course, you don't, because you'll be punished for doing so—therapy will be useless. Dangerous, actually. I think it's important that we continue to meet, though—you and me—and if you'd like, I can refer Jesse to his own therapist. Or, of course, if you want to see somebody else, I can refer you elsewhere. I'd like for you both to come in next week as planned, and I can present the idea of each of you meeting with individual therapists so we can make that transition without putting you on the spot. I don't know very much about what's been going on between you and Jesse, but my impression, from meeting with you today, is that you're not in a safe situation. Lorraine, if you felt unsafe, would you feel comfortable calling the police?"

"Um."

"Do you have somewhere you could go if—"

"I have to get off," Lorraine says. "He's out of the shower."

"Will you call me—" Lou starts to say, but Lorraine hangs up the phone.

For a long time, Tanya did not consider what happened at Dan's house rape. For a long time, she understood that night to be two things.

One, something that Tanya had wanted and, therefore, something she deserved.

And two, the night when something between her and Nessa broke.

Drinking beer in Dan's living room wasn't Tanya's first or even second time drinking alcohol. She'd drank twice before, both times in friends' basements, and both times, she'd kissed a boy.

Her first kiss had been with Matt Humphreys, and though she'd had nothing to compare it to, she knew it wasn't very good. Matt had vacillated between poking a lizard-like tongue in and out of her mouth and opening his own mouth wide enough to do a strep culture. After Matt left, she told her friends about it and the girls laughed, mimicking the awful kiss in the air with their tongues.

It was only a few weeks later when she'd had her second kiss, that one with a boy named Scott Meeks. Scott, who was cuter than Matt, and whose mouth had tasted like Skittles, had told Tanya that she was "one of the hottest girls in their grade" and though Tanya pretended not to care, she'd carried the compliment around with her ever since.

When the email from Dan showed up in their hottgirls@hotmail.com email account, Tanya had no interest in meeting up with a stranger to have sex. It occurred to her that she'd never actually wanted that; and though the idea had been kind of fun to think about, it had also embarrassed her—especially the way Nessa talked about it, with a dark, relentless sort of enthusiasm.

She'd wanted to get out of it, but Nessa had persisted and, ultimately, Tanya agreed to go. Her sister rarely looked that happy, and Tanya felt guilty, with her two kisses tucked away in her back pocket while her sister had never so much as held a boy's hand. So they emailed Dan back. They bought bras and underwear, walked from their house to Alewife, took the T to Central Square, and knocked on his front door.

It was only once they sat down in the living room, after Dan handed them beers, when a bud of desire sprouted up from somewhere deep and unexpected in Tanya. It was different from the desire she'd felt with Matt Humphreys or Scott Meeks. With those boys, kissing had felt like getting away with something—like cheating on a test or stealing a lip gloss from CVS. Things that Tanya, who was always good, always well behaved, did not do. Kissing those boys had been more about the moments afterward, once she was alone and could remember it in all its high school glory, when she could describe it later to her friends. Those kisses were a rite of passage—nothing more, nothing less.

But Dan stirred something in her, and beside Tanya, Nessa was stirred, too. Tanya could sense it, the self-conscious way Nessa kept touching her face and hair. Each time her sister spoke, her face turned beet red. The way Nessa was looking at Dan—with a petrified sort of wonder—reminded Tanya of the way her mother looked at Jesse. It unnerved Tanya—the unbridled, almost animal hunger that her mother and sister wore on their faces, as plain and forthright as noses.

And then Dan chose Tanya, and something spiteful clicked in her chest.

Nessa, upset, had fumbled getting up, and Tanya had watched her sister walk out, thinking, *Serves you right.*

She'd followed Dan upstairs, the beer like a trophy still in her hand. It wasn't until they were inside his bedroom, and he gently but firmly closed the door, that Tanya started to feel frightened. Dan turned on the lamp and sat down on his bed, then looked at her expectantly. She stared back, unsure of what to do. With Matt Humphreys and Scott Meeks, it had been an awkward dance of flirting and eye contact and tiny incremental moves closer to one another on the couch. Dan was a grown-up, though. Tanya understood this, now that they were in his bedroom. He didn't have posters or photos on his walls. The objects in his room were those of an adult's: a queen-sized bed, a television, a beige-colored shag rug on the floor.

"Can I see you?" he asked, and Tanya nodded, confused. She stood there for several moments more before Dan spoke again. "Without clothes, I mean."

"Oh," Tanya said. "Okay." Trembling, she put her beer down and undressed, unbuttoning her shirt and pulling off her jean shorts, until she was down to her lacy bra and underwear.

Dan looked at her, in awe, his mouth slightly open. If it had ended there, Tanya thinks to herself sometimes, it would have been okay. It humiliates her to admit it, but when she's honest with herself—which she isn't always—there was a part of her that enjoyed that moment. Standing in front of a grown man, watching his face go dumb with desire. She felt powerful. She felt, for the first time, sexy.

But then he stood and took off his own clothing—not with care or grace, but quickly, sloppily, his undershirt catching on his nose and ears, the cuffs of his jeans clutching his ankles, so that he'd had to bend down and tug them off. And his body—the mat of gray curls on his breastbone, his penis, which was large and erect and pointed right at her—terrified Tanya. He walked toward her and she knew that this had gone too far.

"Your body," he said, reaching into her bra to touch her tiny breast. And though she realized it was a compliment, she was flooded with shame.

He seemed to realize that she had no idea what to do and he led her to the bed and asked her to take off the rest.

And that was what she'd come all the way there to do—wasn't it? It didn't seem right or fair, or even possible, to say no at that point. It was already too late, Nessa out on the porch waiting for her, Tanya's shirt and shorts in a pile on the other side of the room.

So Tanya pulled off her bra and underwear and lay down on his bed. She closed her eyes and waited. Waited for it to start—for him to do whatever it was men did to women when they had sex with them; she didn't know. All she'd ever done was kiss.

But he didn't climb on top of her, or even touch her at all, and when she opened her eyes, he was staring at her.

"Have you ever given a blow job?" he asked, the same polite way he'd asked them if they'd found his house alright.

She shook her head no.

"Here." He took her hand then, pulling her up. "I'll show you how." He arranged her so that she was on her knees on the floor and he was sitting on the bed, facing her.

"It's just like kissing," he said, and then he took her face in his hands and pulled her toward his crotch.

"Open your mouth a little more," he said. She obeyed, tears burning in her sinuses, threatening to break through at any moment.

And then it was in her mouth.

"Curl your lips over your teeth," he instructed. "There you go. Good girl." He started off slow, but after a minute he began thrusting her face up and down with so much force that his penis jabbed the back of her throat and, without warning, she vomited and started, finally, to cry.

She looked up at him, relieved that she'd finally broken, relieved to finally be done. But either he didn't register the vomit or he didn't care. He tightened his grip on the sides of Tanya's head and continued to pump himself in and out of her mouth, the expression on his face taut and constipated. There was the taste of her vomit and the taste of him, and Tanya began having trouble breathing. She closed her eyes and focused on inhaling through her nose. That was when she stopped being able to remember very much.

She knows that eventually he pulled her up on the bed, that he forced his fingers inside her. Then climbed on top of her. When he penetrated her, she yelled out in pain, the first real noise she'd made the entire time, and he seemed surprised. "I'll go softer," he said, though softer hadn't hurt any less.

At the end he gave her money—five twenty-dollar bills, just like they'd asked for in the ad, and an extra ten, he told her, for a cab.

She dressed quickly and ran downstairs, almost tripping and falling, she was so eager to find Nessa, to throw herself into her older sister's arms. But when she'd come face-to-face with Nessa on the front porch of Dan's house, her sister's face streaked with tears, all of a sudden Tanya closed up. That was the only way she could think to describe that moment. She simply closed up; shut down. She no longer felt the urge to cry, and when Nessa tried to touch her and ask her questions, Tanya recoiled.

BACK AT HOME she saw that she'd bled through her underwear and a few days later her vagina hurt so badly, burned with such intensity every time she tried to pee, that she became convinced that Dan must have broken her in some fundamental, unfixable way.

When she finally went to the doctor one excruciating week later, the doctor prescribed antibiotics for a urinary tract infection.

"You're not sexually active, Tanya, are you?" her pediatrician had asked after the urine test had come back, and she'd shaken her head so vehemently that Dr. Essinger had laughed and patted her knee: "I didn't think so."

TANYA MET DYLAN STARR at a party shortly after. She already knew who he was. Everyone did. Dylan Starr was the captain of the lacrosse team. He was eighteen. He had bright blue eyes, a car, and a reputation for "going down" on girls. This phrase, once mysterious to Tanya, now triggered in her a sort of baffling comprehension.

When Tanya caught Dylan looking at her from across the room, she felt that surge of power she'd experienced at Dan's. She locked eyes with Dylan, smiled right at him, and then turned back to the girl she was talking to, knowing that he would find her later.

He did. "Tanya, right?" he said.

"Mm-hm."

"You play beer pong?"

"A little. Do you?"

"I dabble." He smiled. "I'm up next, want to be my partner?"

Tanya followed Dylan to the Ping-Pong table where cups of beer were arranged in pyramids on either end. When Tanya got the ball in a cup on her first try, Dylan whooped, giving her a high five before pointing tauntingly at the boys at the other end of the table. She was aware of people watching her—watching them—and it satisfied her. There she was, at the center of everything.

When Dylan missed two shots in a row, Tanya turned to him and said, "Guess lacrosse doesn't really translate to beer pong, huh?" and this made him laugh.

They kissed later that night in Dylan's car, Tanya straddling him in the backseat.

"Where'd you come from?" Dylan murmured.

"Ninth grade," she answered.

"You're a frosh?"

"You knew that," Tanya said.

"I didn't."

"Well, I am."

He bit his lip and looked at her, his blue eyes soft and drunk. "You ever given head?"

"Have you?" she asked.

He laughed. "I like you."

"You don't know me," she said, but she tightened her legs around him and dug her fingernails into his back.

SHE STARTED HANGING out with Dylan and his friends after school and on weekends. Her new social life made it so she could avoid facing her sister and mother at home, which was good, because she found she could barely stand being in the same room with either of them.

Her mother's life revolved, pitifully, around Jesse. It had for years, but it was only then that Tanya was able to articulate to herself why this bothered her, and it had to do with that hunger. She resolved never to need a man the way her mother did, and never to compromise her dignity for one, the way Nessa had wanted to—and the way Tanya had that night with Dan.

TANYA LIKED DYLAN. She liked the way it felt to walk through the hallways with him. She liked his confidence and his easy laugh, especially when he laughed at something she said, which was often. She liked watching his lacrosse games, how skilled and serious he was out on the field. She liked the way other girls looked at him—longingly—and the way they looked at her—with admiration.

She hated having sex with him, though. She did it partly because he wanted it, but also because she was convinced that if she had enough sex—*normal* sex, *fun* sex—the nightmare at Dan's house might eventually go away.

But the sex was not fun, and Dylan wanted to have it all the time. Usually they had it at his house. His parents were never home, and when they were, they'd have it in the back of his car or sometimes extremely quietly in his bedroom. They always had it the same way: Dylan on top and Tanya lying on her back, her legs curled around his waist. Sometimes he lifted her legs, propping them up against his shoulders, and sometimes she let him go down on her, though this made her uncomfortable. When he asked her to return the favor, she simply said no, and he didn't push.

He was always asking her if she had come, if she was close to coming, and what did she want him to do in order to make her come. His questions annoyed her. She could not be any further away from having an orgasm, but she knew she couldn't tell him this.

His insistence on making her come started to become a problem. He told her he wanted to slow down, to figure it out, to experiment. So eventually she began to lie. Within the first few minutes of sex she'd fake it, and then, relieved and proud, Dylan would kiss her, go at it for another forty-five seconds before finishing himself and collapsing on top of her. Then they could be done with sex for the day and move on to something else.

Tanya was fifteen by then—still under the age of consent in Massachusetts. From an outsider's point of view, the power dynamics were straightforward. Dylan was a senior; he was popular; he was male; he was the more experienced of the two. If an identical situation appeared on her desk at the DA's office, the verdict would be clear. Statutory rape, no question.

Tanya, however, did not feel taken advantage of. If anything, she felt she was taking advantage of Dylan. Dylan worshipped Tanya. He couldn't get enough of her. She liked him fine—she was attracted to him. But she didn't worship him and she certainly didn't love him. When he broke up with her during the fall of his freshman year of college, she didn't cry or even feel particularly sad. It came as no surprise to her.

SHE STILL HADN'T TOLD anybody about what had happened, though she thought about it every day. It was there in the front of her mind when she went to sleep, and there first thing when she woke up. Sometimes she'd be sitting in class and, without warning, a moment from the night would flash before her like a movie: Dan, naked, walking toward her. The saggy insides of Dan's thighs, the snarl of his pubic hair. The images themselves embarrassed her, consumed her; but the fact that she'd sought him out, that she'd felt proud—*excited*—when he chose her, wrecked Tanya. Nobody could ever know, she decided.

Meanwhile, Nessa had grown more sullen than ever, sleeping and eating in excess, looking at Tanya from across the room with sad, woeful eyes, practically daring Tanya to yell at her. Tanya didn't hate her sister, but she couldn't bear to be around her. It wasn't until Nessa left home after graduation to go on a road trip with her boyfriend that the feelings from that night with Dan began to fade a little. Dylan had broken up with her by then, and she had stopped hanging out with the popular crowd as much. She was more interested in the classes she was taking, especially an elective called Law and Civics, and teachers had started paying her more attention. She'd always gotten As, but it wasn't until her junior year that she began thinking of herself as smart. One day her Law and Civics teacher, Ms. Lowe, asked her where she was planning on applying for college.

"I have no idea," Tanya admitted. Her father had started to ask her this question, too, but each time he'd brought it up, it bothered her. He seemed desperate for Tanya to succeed, now that Nessa was off the grid.

The question felt different, though, coming from Ms. Lowe. Like validation, rather than something about her father's ego.

"You should start thinking about it," her teacher said to Tanya. "If you put your mind to it, you'll have a lot of options. And you know I'll write a letter of recommendation for you, right?"

"You will?" Tanya asked.

"Of course. You're one of my best students, Tanya."

"Where did you go?" Tanya asked.

"Smith," Ms. Lowe said. "It's a small liberal arts school in Northampton. All women." Her teacher smiled. "I know that's not always very appealing to some girls, but you work around it. It's never that hard to find boys, if you want to."

During her senior year Tanya applied to Smith early decision and she got in with a full merit scholarship.

College was a relief. It was good to be out of the house, away from her mother and Jesse, and surrounded by new people. The only men she came into contact with were professors and the occasional Hampshire or Amherst or UMass boy who came to campus to take a class. She rarely went to the parties at UMass on the weekends with the other girls in her dorm, particularly the straight ones who were looking to hook up.

She made it through her entire four years at Smith without having sex once. She thought about sex. In fact, she thought about it a lot. She wondered if she might be gay, and she experimented a few times, first drunkenly with a girl from her dorm named Emma, and then, for half a semester, soberly with Irene from her Modern Literature class.

Irene streaked her hair with mint green. She wore oversized tortoiseshell glasses and silver rings up and down her ears.

They bonded over their mutual irritation with another student in the class, a girl from Amherst, one of the dominating types with no self-awareness, who spoke too loudly and too often, always relating the conversation to something personal in her own life. Tanya and Irene started catching eyes with each other every time the girl spoke. Soon they began eating lunch together each week after class.

Irene was relaxed and confident. She was observant, especially about people, and Tanya enjoyed talking to her. It never felt like gossiping with Irene because she seemed to see the people around her so fully. She was an English major, with a creative writing emphasis. Tanya asked to read some of her work and Irene gave Tanya a story she wrote for her fiction class about a high school girl coming out to her parents. Tanya was impressed by her acerbic descriptions of people. She didn't sugarcoat things. In the story, the fictional father was fine with his daughter being gay, but the mother was not. Tanya's favorite scene was the one in which all three characters were at the dinner table together. It was interesting, seeing the particular way tension played out in another family.

"Is this about your family?" Tanya asked, and Irene had laughed. "My parents are under the impression I'm straight. How about yours?" Tanya didn't know how to answer. She could never imagine telling her family about Irene. She didn't tell her family anything about herself.

They spent several winter afternoons their junior year lying in bed together. Kissing a girl was no different, really, from kissing a boy. There was the thrill of being that close to somebody, the thrill of wanting and of being wanted. Without clothes and without glasses, Irene looked softer, and somehow it made the green in her hair less edgy and more tender.

When Irene put her hand between Tanya's legs, however, Tanya stopped her.

"Are you into girls?" Irene asked, not unkindly, after this had happened a few times.

"I don't know," Tanya said, although she did know, and she wasn't. "I know I like you, though."

"We can take it slow," Irene assured her. But eventually they stopped getting together, and by the end of the semester Irene had a girlfriend, and though she and Tanya still said hello when they saw each other around campus, their friendship faded.

BY THE TIME TANYA met Eitan, she'd grown to tolerate sex, even enjoy certain parts of it. To Tanya, sex was kind of like taking a shower in the winter. She dreaded walking into the cold bathroom in the morning, taking off her clothes, and waiting for the water to get hot enough to step in. But once she was inside, it felt nice. Warm, a little bit invigorating, like a reset button. But she was always relieved when it was over, and she could dry off and bundle up and finally start her day.

When she met Eitan, she'd been seeing another law student, Nate Oliver, for almost a year. Nate was serious and studious and, like her, a perfectionist. They joked that they brought out the elderly in one another—spending their days in the law library together, taking lunch and coffee breaks, holding hands on their walks to and from their apartments and the campus. They talked mostly about their classes and professors. When they had sex, it was on the rare night when neither one of them was up late working and always after a few glasses of wine.

But then she met Eitan, and something felt different. Tanya was drawn to Eitan.

Like Nate, he was driven, but he was less serious. He was playful. He made fun of her. And she was attracted to him.

Tanya loved Eitan's hands. The sureness of them, the mixture of confidence and gentleness in their movements. When she fantasized about Eitan, she fantasized about his hands. Sometimes she'd sit in class, imagining him touching her, and she'd get so worked up that, given the right pair of jeans, even the slightest movement—sitting up straighter, leaning forward— brought her close to orgasm.

It was the first time Tanya had ever had sex with someone she loved. And she told him this—the very first time they slept together.

"You love me?" He looked surprised. They had been dating for months at this point; but they'd done things backwards from their friends, getting to know one another first, before anything else.

Tanya nodded. "Does that freak you out?"

Eitan returned her gaze. "It makes me maybe the happiest I've ever been."

Still, though, she struggled. She desperately wanted to enjoy sex with Eitan, and she wanted to please him. But she was always relieved when it was over.

"Please tell me what you like," he'd ask, again and again, but Tanya was stumped. She was quiet during sex—quieter than she was anywhere else. His questions reminded her a little of Dylan, with his constant insistence that she finish. With Dylan, though, it had been a point of pride; her orgasm equaled his victory. Eitan's questions stemmed from a place of confusion and curiosity.

She didn't attribute her discomfort with sex entirely to Dan. One night didn't have that kind of power, Tanya told herself. And she'd be damned if she'd let one man—one sick, twisted man—have such an effect on her. No, the lasting effects of that night had less to do with him and more to do with something about Tanya and Nessa. Who they'd become sitting beside one another on Dan's couch. Not Lola and Layla—that was nothing more than fantasy, than play. It was something about *them*—their appetite: the way they let it get the better of them, the way it made them turn on each other. She'd always thought of her and her sister as fiercely loyal—they protected one another growing up. But that night, pitted against each other, they turned into the ugliest versions of themselves.

It was around then that Tanya went to Simone and for the first time told someone about what had happened all those years ago. Simone had insisted that talking to Eitan was necessary, and a few weeks later, Tanya told him. To her relief, Eitan responded calmly. He didn't demand to know Dan's last name, didn't cuss him out. He didn't cry or yell or look at her with disgust— which was Tanya's biggest fear.

For a month following their conversation, they didn't have sex. They held each other in bed, they hugged one another tightly, but they both kept their clothing on and their hands to themselves.

Then one night Tanya reached for him in bed. "Is this okay?" she asked, letting her hand wander down the plane of his stomach, over the front of his boxers.

He turned to her and nodded.

For a while they lay like that next to one another, Tanya's hand skating the surface of his body, Eitan still, except for the rise and fall of his chest, beside her.

When Eitan finally reached over, his hand tracing the waistband of her pajama pants, Tanya exhaled audibly, relieved.

"Is this okay?" he asked, and she nodded, closing her eyes and moving closer to him.

They continued like this. Before each further movement, they asked each other if it was okay. Before they removed one another's clothes, before they used their hands or mouths to touch one another, before Tanya rolled on top of Eitan and guided him inside her.

TANYA NO LONGER BLAMES NESSA for that night. But when Nessa told Tanya that she'd driven to Dan's house, when Nessa suggested they report Dan after all these years, Tanya began to play with the idea of responsibility again in her mind. In a way, it would be easy to blame Nessa; easier, even, to blame Lorraine. She'd thought sometimes of telling her mother what had happened to her. Not for comfort, but out of anger. *You left us alone. Look what happened.*

It would be too awful, though, seeing her mother's face. Anger burns quick. Once the anger was gone, they would have to live with that knowledge forever between them. She thinks how hurt Lorraine had looked when Tanya had told her she wasn't a good mother outside the courthouse. Lorraine made it impossible to talk to her—her mother's hurt and sadness and neediness louder than anything and anyone else around her. Except for Jesse, of course. When it came to Jesse, Lorraine paled in comparison.

But here was Nessa, all these years later, still wanting to blame Dan, as if Dan had anything to do with it. There was no evidence of that night, no hospital visit, no rape kit—and even if there was, Tanya had no interest in pressing charges, in testifying. She never wanted to see Dan again.

Tanya has the feeling sometimes that her sister lived in an alternate universe—a fantasy world. That somehow, during that night, Tanya had been sucked into her sister's head, dropped into a world in which she'd never really agreed to go.

Or maybe, Tanya sometimes thinks, it was more complicated than that. Maybe Nessa had opened up something in Tanya's own mind—somewhere Tanya had never wanted to open up. That little bud of desire. That feeling of pride. There were some things better left sealed.

"Nessa drove to Dan's house," Tanya blurts out that night in bed to Eitan. It's strange, saying his name out loud, and for a moment she's scared Eitan might not know who she's talking about, but when her husband rolls over and looks at her, she sees that he does.

"Why?" Eitan asks.

"No reason that makes any sort of sense."

"How do you feel about it?"

Immediately Tanya wishes she hadn't brought it up; she's not interested in having a conversation about Dan. "I don't feel anything one way or the other. I just think it's pretty fucking idiotic."

"Thinking something is pretty fucking idiotic is a feeling, I'd say."

"Thanks, Dr. Phil."

"Just saying," he says, reaching for her hand under the covers.

"*Just saying*," Tanya mimics, squeezing his hand back.

When Tanya thinks about the kind of mother she wants to be, she knows she wants to be different from her own. She wants to be the kind of parent who never lets her child see any of her own sadness or anger or loneliness, because she knows how much it hurts to see that in your own mother. How stifling it can be; how impossible it becomes to have any of your own feelings. She knows it's impossible, though. That if she tries to mask all of that from her child, she'll just be hiding. And the truth is—children are smarter than that. They'd see right through her.

Really what she wants to be is a mother who isn't in pain. She wonders if such a woman exists.

L orraine doesn't tell Jesse about Lou's phone call. Things with Jesse are going well, and she doesn't want to rock the boat. There's an easy quality that's come over them that Lorraine hasn't felt in years. Jesse seems to be seeing things clearly. To be seeing her clearly. That part of him is there—she knows it must still be there—but together, the two of them, they will fend it off. They will control it. If anybody knows how to control it, it is Lorraine.

Lou called back twice that week and left voice mails both times. She hasn't returned his calls. The night before their second appointment, Lorraine decides that the only choice she has is to cut things off with the therapist before Lou messes things up with her and Jesse.

"I was thinking about what you said last week," Lorraine says to Jesse, that night in the kitchen. She's preparing dinner and Jesse is at the table paying bills. "I think Lou is an old geezer."

Jesse looks up, surprised. "You do?"

"Yeah. I don't think I even want to go back tomorrow."

"What made you change your mind about him?"

"I don't know," she says. "I was thinking about it and it's just a lot of money to sit there and have a conversation."

Jesse smiles and turns back to the checkbook. "Yeah, no shit."

A pang of uneasiness passes through her.

"I still think we should talk, though," she says. "Just you and me."

"Of course."

He folds the check and slips it into an envelope, then brings the envelope up to his mouth, carefully licks the edge.

"Like maybe we could talk right now," she says.

"I'm kind of in the middle, Lorrie."

"Okay. After you're done?"

He looks at her, irritated. "I spent all day working. Can we do it when I'm not so tired?"

"Yeah," she says. "Sure." She turns back to the stove and prods the onions in the pan. She tries to push away her uneasiness, but it's hard to shake. It's something about the way he said, *No shit.*

Lorraine turns off the burner and is about to transfer the onions to the saucepan when Jesse comes up behind her and slips his thumbs into her belt loops.

"I want you," he whispers into her hair.

She smiles. Ever since she's come home they've been having a lot of sex. Good sex, too. "Okay," she says. "Let me just get these into——"

"No," he says. "I want you now."

"Give me a few minutes," she says.

He reaches between her legs. "I can't wait."

"Jesse, this is time sensitive——"

"I don't care about the sauce."

He wraps his arm around her waist and fiddles with the button on the front of her jeans. "Shit," he mutters, tugging at it, but he can't get it through the hole, so Lorraine reaches down and undoes the button herself.

He yanks her pants down, and then his own. "Bend over," he says roughly, and she bends over the counter, her arms outspread.

She isn't ready, and it hurts.

"You feel so good," he says, breathing hard in her ear.

"So do you." She squeezes her eyes shut and tries to focus on feeling good, but Lou's face keeps getting in the way, so she gives up on feeling good and opens her eyes, concentrating on the red of the linoleum counter, the way it's faded in some spots and bright in others. In one section of her mind she's thinking about the sauce, calculating how long she has before it's ruined. In another section of her mind, Lou is still there, watching her from above, his kind eyes big and filled with disappointment.

It's only a few minutes before Jesse finishes and shudders against her. "Jesus," he says into her hair, and she moans softly in response.

He takes a step back and zips his fly.

"I'm going to put these in the mail," he says, walking over to the table.

She's still bent over the counter with her pants down by her ankles when he leaves the kitchen.

Sally pads in then, as though she was waiting for them to finish before entering. Lorraine sinks to the floor and Sally nestles her head in Lorraine's lap, whimpering. They sit together like this until Lorraine hears the front door close and Jesse's car start in the driveway.

Gently, Lorraine stands, pulls up her pants, and fishes through her purse for her phone. She finds Lou's cell phone number and composes a text message. *This is Lorraine Bloom,* she types. *We can't come in to see you tomorrow, but I'd like to schedule a time to come see you on my own. I think you might be right about Jesse. Please call me.*

After sending it, she deletes the outgoing text from her text messages. If Jesse looks through her phone, there is nothing he can use against her.

THE NEXT EVENING, Lorraine and Jesse sit together on opposite ends of the sofa. The day has passed uneventfully, though there's been a slight yet perceptible downward shift in Jesse's mood. Neither one of them has brought up the therapy appointment, and three o'clock came and went without comment. Lorraine's checked her phone several times, but Lou hasn't called or responded to her text message. She tries to convince herself that he must be busy, that his silence is not something to read into, but she can't help but feel let down by the therapist.

Beside her, Jesse is flipping channels, abnormally quiet. "What do you want for dinner?" Lorraine asks. Her voice sounds nasal and she can feel Jesse's irritation, like a silent alarm.

He shrugs, his eyes glued to the TV, identical little screens reflected in both eyes.

"How about pizza?" she says. "Andrina's?"

"Fine."

"The white pizza?"

"Sure."

Lorraine stands, grateful for a task to get her out of the living room.

"Wait, Lorrie." Jesse's voice lifts a bit, and for a moment she thinks his mood might pass. "Let's do pepperoni. It's not a pizza if it doesn't have to-mato sauce."

She nods. "Okay."

"With extra cheese."

"Sound delish," she says, a little too brightly, and he rolls his eyes and turns back to the TV.

Lorraine makes the call from the kitchen. Maybe he's hungry, she thinks as she waits for someone to answer. Maybe he just needs some food in him.

After she puts in the order she stays in the kitchen cleaning so that she doesn't have to sit with Jesse in the living room. She opens the fridge and a smell wafts out, thick and dank. She begins to pull things out. Everything, it seems, is expired. There's raspberries fuzzy with mold, dark green lettuce, slime against a plastic bag. She finds a Tupperware container full of chicken and green beans that's been shoved in the back of the refrigerator for so long that she's scared to open it. When she pulls out an empty carton of milk, she's hit with sudden anger. It's been years since she's seen Jesse clean.

"Where are they?" Jesse calls from the living room.

Lorraine glances at the microwave clock. It's been almost forty minutes since she placed the order. "I'll call them," she says.

When the doorbell finally rings, twenty minutes later, it's almost nine and Lorraine hurries to the door, Sally padding along behind her.

The delivery boy, a scruffy teenager, smiles bashfully at her. "Sorry for the wait," he says. "I went to Winter Lane instead of Winter Street."

"That's okay," Lorraine says. "An easy mistake to make."

The boy reaches down and scratches Sally's ears. "Yeah," he says. "Turned out 12 Winter *Lane* was having a party. They tried to get me to leave the pizza with them."

"Ha," she says. "Thanks for holding on to it. How much do we owe you?"

The boy glances at the receipt stapled to the box. "Fourteen dollars and sixty-eight cents."

"Sure, let me just grab my purse—"

"I got it, Lorrie," Jesse says, appearing in the doorway.

She nods and takes the pizza from the boy and leaves Jesse to pay the kid.

"Thanks, man," she hears the boy say to Jesse. Then the front door closes and Jesse strides into the kitchen, smirking. "Flirting with the delivery guy?"

Lorraine stops herself from making a face. "No."

"Is that why you put on makeup?"

"I didn't put on makeup," she says.

"Sure you did. Look at your lips, all red."

"I didn't."

"I saw the way he was looking at you." Jesse is smiling, but his eyes are sharp, barely blinking.

"He wasn't looking at me in any kind of way. He was fourteen, Jesse." She nods toward the table where the pizza box is sitting. "Should we eat while it's hot?"

"Don't play dumb, though. Who'd you put on lipstick for?"

"I'm serious, Jesse. I didn't put on any lipstick."

"Come on." He's standing close enough now that she can see the bluish tinge of his contact lenses.

"Even if I had put on lipstick," Lorraine says, "it wouldn't be to seduce the pizza delivery boy."

"It looks good on you, that shade of red."

Lorraine tries to walk past him, but Jesse blocks her. He leans forward and presses his lips to hers.

"Do you want to eat?" she asks, tilting her head away.

"Yeah."

Lorraine walks across the kitchen and pulls two glasses from the cupboard. She's fuming. Lou was right. Of course Lou was right. She'll call him again, she decides, maybe even later that night while Jesse's in the shower. Angrily, she pops ice cubes out of the trays and drops them into the glasses, then refills the empty trays with water and slides them back into the freezer.

When she turns around Jesse's face is hardened with rage and Lorraine's stomach clenches.

"What's the matter?" she says.

Jesse takes the pizza box from the table and shoves it in her face. Her heart sinks. The pizza is white.

"Fuck," she mutters. "I don't know how that happened."

"It's not that hard to figure out. Obviously you ordered the wrong pizza."

"I can run over there," she says.

Jesse thrusts the box back on the table. "It's fucking nine o'clock, Lorraine. By the time you get there and wait for them to make a new one, it'll be ten."

Lorraine glances at the dog, who is lying in the doorway, watching, her eyes moving back and forth between them.

"I can throw something together now," she offers. "I have that cheese to make—"

"And what?" Jesse interrupts. "Just throw this pizza away?"

"I'm sorry, okay?" She pauses and thinks back to their therapy session, when Jesse talked about stepping back and talking calmly about his problems rather than exploding. "Jesse, it was an honest mistake. And you said you wouldn't talk to me like that."

"Do you know how much you've put me through, Lorraine? Does it even occur to you the kind of month I've had with all of your *shit*? A police officer showing up at my door, for God's sake?"

He has that look in his eye and Lorraine knows there's no reasoning with him now.

"I saw the text messages from the shrink on your phone, by the way." He smiles then, and fear settles over Lorraine like a fog. "About coming in to meet with him alone, *as soon as possible*." He takes a step closer. "You're so desperate for attention that you're even wanting it from some short ugly therapist who probably hasn't been laid in decades. You know he gets off listening to other people's sex lives, since he doesn't have one of his own." Jesse's eyes have hardened completely. "Lorraine, do you understand where you'd be without me?"

In her peripheral vision Lorraine eyes the living room. A plan is formulating in her mind. She'll insist on going to get another pizza and take Sally with her. In the car, she'll call Nessa. She'll drive straight to her daughter's house in Northampton that night. She'll call Lou, too, explain that she never received his text messages, that Jesse must have gotten to her phone first. And the next morning, she'll call Tanya. She'll tell her daughter that she needs to make another plan; a restraining order isn't going to keep Jesse away.

All she needs now are her wallet and her keys. Her purse is on the armchair in the living room. She takes a small step backwards. "I'm going to get another pizza."

"Don't bother," Jesse says, taking another step toward her.

"I'll be right back, Jesse."

"No." Jesse seals a hand on her shoulder. "Stay."

"Okay. I'm just going to run to—"

And then, before she has time to realize what's going on, her face is on fire. Her hand flies to her cheek and she holds it, the flesh hot and ringing in her palm.

"Don't think about leaving."

Sally has materialized by Lorraine's side, pressing her warm, old body against Lorraine's leg. Lorraine tries to swallow, but her mouth is too dry, and for a second she gags, unable to breathe.

Usually when Jesse turns this way, Lorraine relinquishes her body to him. It's better than trying to resist. Sometimes she even eggs it on. The sooner it happens, the sooner it will be over, and the waiting is almost always worse than what follows. Physical pain no longer scares her. She hates it; she dreads it——but she knows how to close her eyes and wait for it to be over. It's simply a matter of time. Time until he loses steam. Time until he has to go to work. Time until they reach the far end of the room, and she's pushed up against the wall with nowhere left for them to go.

Today is different, though. Today she wants to leave before he starts. She cannot stand the pain today. She *will* not. She's barefoot, but she won't bother with shoes or a jacket. All she needs is her purse from the living room.

Jesse is gripping her by her forearms, his breath hot and stale and alcoholic.

"Let me go," she says, and then she hurls herself into him with all her strength. Jesse tumbles backwards, shock etched into his eyebrows and mouth. She's never done that before. Lorraine seizes the moment and runs from the kitchen to the living room, her breath knocking noisily in her ears, Sally staggering behind her.

She leaps toward the chair where her purse is, but the seat is empty, and it's then when she remembers that her purse is upstairs. "Fuck," she says. Frantic tears prick at her eyes.

She starts to run to the front door, but Jesse's there and he's cornered her, wedging her against the couch. He slams his body against hers, and she tumbles to the floor, landing hard on her tailbone. She yells out in pain.

Jesse is above her, red and panting, eyes wild with hate. Because he hates her, she realizes then, in a moment of terrifying clarity. He despises her.

He begins to beat her, shoving her across the floor with his arms and legs. The air is ringing with Sally's howls, each louder and more desperate than the last. Lorraine has curled up into a ball, her arms over her head, the sounds of Jesse's fists against her, of Sally's protesting, of both of their breathing and yelling and crying filling up the house. Eventually they'll cross the room and Jesse will push her against the far wall and there won't be anywhere else to go. She looks through her fingers to see how close they are to the wall and she begins to count in her head. *One Mississippi, two Mississippi.*

"How much longer?" the girls used to ask on car trips, and she would say, "One hundred Mississippis." And they would start counting, sometimes making it all the way to one hundred, but usually getting bored and abandoning the counting, which had always been the point.

Ten Mississippis, she tells herself now. Ten until they reach the wall and it's over.

She's on eight when she feels a hard blow to her side and head—the wall—when Jesse's breathing slows, when her own breathing no longer sounds like somebody else's, someone heaving into a microphone. For a moment, sound stops altogether—pain stops; fear stops. Even Sally takes a breath. They're done. Lorraine puts her hand to her face. Her nose is bleeding and her mouth is, too, where her braces have smashed up against the insides of her lips. There's a sharp pain pulsing above her left hip. She looks up at Jesse.

She's crying and she opens her mouth to say something—this is usually the part when the softness comes back in Jesse's eyes. But before she has the chance to speak, Jesse's hands are around her neck, squeezing. She swats at him with her arms, but she's on the floor and he's above her, and she's powerless.

The room is dead silent, except for Sally, her moaning strange and eerie all by itself. This, more than anything, scares her; all that quiet. Lorraine is starting to see stars and Dr. Reimer's face has appeared in her mind: *Tell me about the stars, Lorraine,* he's saying, and she's saying her daughters' names in her head, *Nessa Tanya Nessa Tanya,* like a chant or a prayer, or maybe an apology. Help me, she's screaming, but her screams are silent because Jesse's hands are around her neck and she can't breathe and now she really is seeing stars. Hundreds of them, thousands of them, twinkling against a pitch-black sky.

It's a Friday and the pub is packed with people. The music—something loud and melodic—is throbbing in the walls, the floor, the glasses on the bar. Nessa is on her second rum and Coke and Henry is finishing up his third Guinness. They're seated at the corner of the bar, leaning in to hear one another. Nessa's cell phone is in her purse, which is slung over the back of her chair, so at eleven p.m., when the calls start coming through, she doesn't hear them.

"We all lost touch after high school," Henry is saying. "Or I lost touch, anyway." Nessa nods encouragingly. She's asked Henry about his friends, and with little prompting from her, he's been talking about them with more emotion than she knew he was capable of. "Now most of my buddies are married and having kids," he says.

"Is it all over Facebook?" she asks, smiling.

Henry grins and takes another swig of beer. Glances in the bartender's direction. "Yup," he says. "If I see one more goddamn professional photo shoot for babies . . ."

Nessa laughs.

"You want another?" he asks, nodding to her glass.

"Sure." She pushes back her chair. "I'll be right back."

She walks to the bathroom, aware of Henry watching her walk away. She smiles, remembering the way he looked that morning, naked and wrapped in her floral sheets, his bare feet sticking out off the end of the bed.

They've spent every night together this week, and earlier this evening, Henry asked if she wanted to go out to get drinks at the new bar that opened up on Main Street. She said yes, happily. It is, technically, their first date.

In the bathroom there's a line and Nessa pulls out her phone, and that's when she sees that she has twenty-four missed calls. Most of them are from Tanya, but some of them are from her father, some from Simone, and a handful from various unknown numbers. Terror takes hold and Nessa's stomach plummets.

She runs out of the bathroom into the bar, shoving people out of the way. She's aware of the pounding music and the looks people are giving her as she pushes past them, but all she can hear is the blood between her ears— like a heartbeat, an underwater sort of death march.

Outside, it's cool and it's started to drizzle. Tanya answers on the second ring. "Nessa," she says breathlessly, and Nessa can hear in her sister's voice that something is terribly wrong.

"What happened?" she says.

"Are you alone?"

"I'm with Henry. What is it?"

"Mom." And then Tanya starts to wail.

Nessa's body turns cold from the inside out. She clutches the phone. "What happened, Tanya?"

"He killed her."

Nessa drops to the ground. It's as if there's a string running the length of her body and someone tugged hard on that string—through her head and down her torso and stomach and one of her legs, coming out the back of her knee.

"What?" she says, though she's unsure if she's said it aloud or in her own head. On the other end, Tanya is sobbing, unable to speak, and Nessa grips the phone to her cheek. She's kneeling on the pavement, several feet from the entrance of the bar, and people are walking around her, their voices loud and distant at the same time. Her heart feels large and oversized in her chest, beating so hard she might pass out.

"Watch it," somebody says, stumbling over her.

"Tanya," Nessa says, and her own voice is like a dismembered thing. "What are you talking about? Where did you even hear this?"

"The hospital," Tanya cries. "The police called."

Nessa shakes her head into the phone. "Give me their number. I'll call. He must have hurt her again. Where is she? Is she at Somerville Hospital?"

"Nessa," Tanya heaves through tears. "She was already . . . when they got there."

"When who got where?" Nessa demands.

"The police. The O'Briens called 911 when they heard sounds coming from the house."

Something dark and heavy is descending over Nessa. "Tanya, are you sure?"

"I'm sure."

Nessa tastes it first—the hot sourness in her mouth, the rum, and then the sick. She vomits onto the pavement.

Behind her someone says, "Did you see that? That chick just barfed."

Her ears are ringing and she can't hear Tanya anymore. Her sister's voice is far away, just out of reach.

Then Eitan is on the phone, and Eitan's voice is louder, right in Nessa's ear. He's explaining to Nessa that Jesse has been arrested and is at the hospital, but that he'll be transferred soon to the jail, where he'll be held without bail, that they need to go to Boston where they will identify . . . He pauses there. Then he's saying things like *You won't be alone* and *We'll get through this.*

Henry appears in the parking lot then, with Nessa's coat under one arm. When he sees her, bent over on the pavement, he runs to her, a panic-stricken look on his face. "Eitan, I have to go," Nessa says into the phone, and then she stands, shaking, the string still there threatening to pull at any moment.

"What happened?" Henry says, and Nessa falls against him. "Nessa, what happened?" he urges. He's holding her and rubbing her back.

"He killed my mom," she says into his neck. And that's when she starts to cry. It's a deep and terrible crying, a noise an animal would make—not a human. Certainly not her. "How did this happen?" she says, and she pulls back to look at Henry, who stares back at her with alarm.

He pulls her close then. She's sobbing into his shoulder and he's stroking her hair and her back and the sides of her face. She can feel his chest heaving against hers. She hears Tanya's voice over and over again—the words she said—and she tries to think of a way to make them not true.

THE NEXT HOURS are a blur of phone calls. Jonathan and Simone both offer to come get Nessa in Northampton, but Nessa refuses—she can't bear the thought of seeing her father—and so she tells them that Henry will drive her to their house in Lexington the next morning. That night she packs a bag: a dress for a funeral, two pairs of pants, three pairs of pajamas, one skirt, and not a single top. Enough underwear for two weeks. Sneakers and a coat too heavy for May. She forgets toiletries entirely.

Henry gives her something to fall asleep and she takes it, not bothering to ask what it is, and she falls into a horrifying sleep, waking up every thirty minutes. She cries in her dreams and every time she opens her eyes.

Images flash through her mind—ones of her mother that are so terrible that she scratches at her arms, digs her fingernails into her flesh to keep herself from fully seeing them. At three in the morning she goes to the bathroom and, for the first time since Tanya's phone call, looks at herself in the mirror. Her reflection makes her so sick with loneliness that she has the impulse to call her mother. She goes so far as to pull out her phone.

Henry stays over, and in the morning, they get in his car. He has his license back now and it's the first time he's driving her instead of the other way around. Nessa leans back in the passenger seat and stares out the window. They don't speak on the ride, but something silent and close radiates between them. At one point, Henry nods toward the radio and asks, "Is this okay?"

Nessa nods. She hadn't realized there was music playing.

"You alright?" he asks at one point. "Actually, that's a stupid question. Sorry."

They stop at a gas station in Sturbridge and Nessa watches out the window as Henry pumps gas. He keeps one of his hands in his jeans pocket and the other gripping the pump. His lips are chapped and there are reddish acne scars on his cheeks. She wonders then if she's in love with Henry, and she imagines what it would be like if she and Henry were to get married. She pictures them having a pack of children, all boys, who'd grow up to be just as big and tall as their father. She imagines herself in a kitchen, serving huge plates of meat to her family of boys. Henry in a suit coming home from work, bending down to kiss her cheek. It's a strange but comforting thought.

After Henry finishes pumping gas he goes inside the mini-mart and comes back with cigarettes and Swedish Fish.

"Want one?" he asks, holding out the pack of Camels.

She nods. Between the two of them they smoke the entire pack by the time they get to Lexington.

WHEN THEY PULL into her father's driveway, Tanya and Eitan's rental car is already there. Nessa turns to Henry. Tears come and she blinks them away.

"Do you want to stay?" she asks.

"Here?" Henry glances at the house.

Nessa nods. "The funeral is on Monday."

"I don't know." Henry looks down at his lap. "I have to work this weekend."

"Do you think you could stay just one night?"

Henry looks uncomfortable. "I would, but I'm actually supposed to work this afternoon." He eyes the clock. "I gotta book it back there by two."

"Okay," Nessa says, and the image of Henry and their giant sons floats away like a balloon that's escaped a child's fist. "Well, thanks for driving me," she says, a new layer of grief descending upon her.

"No problem." Henry reaches over and takes Nessa's hand. "Also, I feel really bad asking, but do you think you could throw me a few for gas? I'm not getting paid 'til next week so I'm running a little dry."

Nessa reaches for her purse on the car floor. She feels nauseous again. "How much?"

"Fifteen okay?"

She pulls her cash out and counts. "Twelve is all I have on me."

"That'll work."

"Okay."

"I'm really, really sorry about your mom," Henry says. He leans over the console then and kisses her quickly on the cheek. "See you when you get back?" he asks.

"Sure." She climbs out of the car and pulls her duffel from the backseat, throws it over her shoulder. "Bye," she says, as she slams the car door, though she doubts Henry can hear her.

INSIDE, HER FATHER'S house is muggy with grief. The air is thick, as though it's reached some sort of saturation level, as though Nessa might actually choke if she breathes in too deeply. She wishes she could turn around and run after Henry's car.

But then Tanya appears in the front hallway, and Nessa is stopped short by her sister's appearance. Tanya's eyes are so swollen that she looks as though she's had an allergic reaction, and her cheeks are red and raw, painful looking, just shy of bloody. The expression on Tanya's face is filled with such unimaginable terror, all Nessa can do is open her arms and take her sister in. Tanya weeps into Nessa's shoulder.

"It's going to be okay," Nessa whispers, holding her sister's shaking body. "I'm here and we're going to get through this." She doesn't know where these words are coming from, or, for that matter, the calm she suddenly feels, but she understands now why she's here, and what her role is, and that in itself is a relief. She's here to take care of Tanya.

Tanya has collapsed against her and is crying with such physical force she starts to gag.

"It's okay," Nessa says, and she leads Tanya into the living room, where she sits her on the couch. Kneeling before her, she takes Tanya's hands. "Breathe, Tee. Concentrate on breathing. Inhale, okay?"

Tanya draws in a ragged breath and Nessa nods. "Good. Now exhale slowly."

She leads Tanya through this, one breath at a time, until her sister has stabilized. At some point she becomes aware of other people in the room. Once Tanya is breathing normally again, Nessa turns around.

"Sweetheart," her father says, and Nessa sees that her father and Simone are crying, too. When her father hugs her, he says, "I'm sorry," and Nessa isn't sure what he's apologizing for.

Then Ben appears, solemn and quiet, and Nessa hugs him. Her little brother doesn't say anything, but he rests his head against Nessa's neck, and she feels dampness in his eyes, though he holds his tears back the way an adult would.

"Ben," she says, and the softness of the syllable is strangely comforting. She sniffs sharply and contains herself, letting her tears sit like screens over her eyes, blurring her vision and giving her something to concentrate on.

It's only when Sally pads in, the dog's eyes sad but watchful, that the unbearable heaviness of last night returns. The dog looks around the room, confused, unsure of where to go. But she goes to Nessa and Nessa kneels, taking Sally's face in her hands. Up close Nessa sees that Sally has aged since she saw her just twelve days ago. The fur on her muzzle and nose is whiter and thinner and her eyes are even more bloodshot than before. Sally nuzzles her nose deeply into Nessa's lap, making small, unfamiliar childlike noises.

THAT NIGHT THE WEIGHT of her sister's body beside her in bed is enough for Tanya to close her eyes. They're lying beside one another in the guest room, in a bed freshly made, the linens soft and clean smelling. The hallway light slips in beneath the crack under the door, stretching along the length of the room.

Tanya's body aches. Her throat, her lungs, her abdomen, all the muscles in her neck. That morning, the first without her mother, she woke with her eyes swollen shut, and for fifteen minutes she couldn't see, feeling around with her hands like a blind woman, yelling Eitan's name. She thinks of killing herself—throwing herself in front of an oncoming train, swallowing a bottle of sleeping pills. She tells herself it's the baby that's stopping her.

When she and Eitan arrived at her father's house in Lexington that morning, it was as though showing up to a distant relative's house—an aunt and uncle she sees once in a while at holidays and family gatherings. Tanya attempted to hold it together, but when Simone tried to hug her, murmuring something sympathetic, Tanya pulled away from her stepmother, disgusted by the smell of Rose Noir, the sound of Simone's voice, the way her stepmother had worn her hair that day, clipped back with a tortoiseshell barrette.

Simone had made a small noise—shock or distress—and Jonathan had quietly suggested she wait inside.

"I can't look at her right now," Tanya told her father, and Jonathan had said he understood.

Nessa was the only person Tanya had wanted to see.

"I don't know what I'd do without you," Tanya whispers to Nessa that night in bed.

"Me neither," Nessa whispers back.

"I'd kill myself," Tanya says. For so long Tanya has been scared of turning into her mother, but now that her mother is gone, Tanya feels unhinged, free-floating. She feels that she barely knows herself.

Nessa turns over and looks at her. In the dark, her sister's eyes glint. "Don't, Tanya," she says. "Promise me."

"I won't," Tanya says. "I promise. You too."

"I promise," says Nessa.

"I can't even look at Simone."

Nessa nods. "Don't punish yourself by cutting yourself off from her."

"It's not that I'm punishing myself," Tanya says. "I feel guilty."

"Guilty about what?" asks Nessa.

Tanya pauses. She wonders how she could possibly explain to Nessa everything she feels guilty about.

"I know you guys are close," Nessa offers. "It doesn't bother me."

"I'm not any closer to her than I am to you or Mom. She's more of a friend. It's something totally different."

"I know," Nessa says.

"She's never going to be a mom to me. She never was one and she never will be." Tanya can feel herself start to cry again.

"I know," Nessa says. "It's okay to be close to her. It's a good thing."

It's a lie, though. Tanya has fantasized about having Simone for a mother ever since she was in high school.

Tanya allows Nessa to put her arms around her. For a few minutes they lie quietly, listening to the house hum. Eitan is downstairs sleeping on the pull-out couch and Ben's asleep in his bedroom next door. The master bedroom is at the end of the hall. Tanya's been inside only a handful of times, usually to get toilet paper from underneath the bathroom sink, or to use the full-length mirror on Simone's closet door.

She imagines knocking on their bedroom door, Simone opening it, wearing her pajamas, something expensive and feminine. Would Simone take her in her arms? Would they crawl in bed together? No, of course not. They hug but never for more than a few seconds, and always with space between their bodies. They've sat on a bed together, but never under the covers and never lying down. When Tanya was a girl, Lorraine used to sleep with her in the bottom bunk on nights she didn't want to sleep alone. Tanya used to resent her mother for those nights. "It wasn't normal," she remembers complaining to a Smith friend. "She had no boundaries."

On the nightstand Nessa's phone vibrates and Nessa untangles herself from Tanya to reach for it.

"Who is it?" Tanya asks, though she can tell by the expression on Nessa's face that it's Henry.

"Henry," Nessa answers.

"What'd he say?"

"*How's it going.*"

"What are you going to say back?"

"Nothing." Nessa puts her phone back on the nightstand.

"How was he last night?"

"He was good," Nessa says, though she sounds uncertain. "He stayed with me the entire time."

Tanya is about to ask why he isn't here now, but she stops herself. "Did you sleep last night?" she asks instead.

"In and out. Did you?"

"Barely. No."

"Just close your eyes," Nessa says. "And every time you wake up, just squeeze me."

"Okay," Tanya agrees. It seems an odd plan, but somehow it also makes sense.

When Tanya was younger and couldn't sleep, Lorraine used to rub her back and play with her hair. There was once a time when being touched by her mother wasn't unbearable, but soothing. Tanya would give anything to be comforted by her mom right now—to let Lorraine know it was alright to hold her.

The next day, when they step inside their house on Winter Street, the smell of their childhood—their mother—hits Tanya with a force that's physical. "Fuck," she says, fighting tears. "How the fuck are we supposed to do this?"

"We just do it," says Nessa.

Together, they go straight upstairs, avoiding the living room and kitchen, where there's still yellow caution tape up from two nights ago when the police showed up to the house after the O'Briens called 911.

The door to their mother's bedroom is open and Lorraine's room looks like it always does. The bed is made, but hastily, and there's a pile of clean laundry at the foot of the bed, still waiting to be folded. The shades on the windows are open and afternoon sunlight pours in, illuminating free-floating dust in the air. Lorraine's purse sits slumped in the chair next to her bed. Her laptop, left open, is beneath it, the screen black and smudged.

Nessa walks bravely over to Lorraine's closet. "What do you think she would want to wear?"

Tanya joins Nessa, dreading the smell of her mother's clothing.

"What about this?" Nessa asks, holding up a blue dress. It's short-sleeved and linen; comfortable looking.

Tanya takes the dress from Nessa and examines it, glances at the tag inside. "It's Gap. We're not burying Mom in Gap."

"Oh," says Nessa. "Let me look for her Chanel and Gucci then."

"Shut up," Tanya says. "What about this one?" She fingers the skirt of another dress, this one long and emerald, a silky fabric. It's elegant even on the hanger.

Nessa's eyes grow wide as she reaches out to touch it. "Jesse bought it for her."

"Then fuck it," Tanya says, anger detonating in her chest. She yanks the dress off the hanger and throws it as hard as she can against the wall, but it's airy and lands in a calm, whispery heap, so she hurls the hanger across the room instead, where it hits the window with a dull thud and then clatters to the floor. "I fucking hate him. I hate him so much."

Nessa nods. "I know."

"Why the fuck did he do this?" Tanya wipes at her eyes and nose. She is so tired of crying. Her face hurts from it; the flesh on her cheeks stings.

"Let's take a break," Nessa says.

"And do what?" Tanya says, irritated by her sister's composure, and at the same time grateful for it.

"I don't know, get some air. Maybe you want to call Eitan?"

"Who will you call?" Tanya asks, and though she doesn't intend it to be cruel, it comes out sounding that way.

Nessa shrugs. "Henry," she says—and this, more than the stupid dress, is what sends Tanya over the edge.

"Okay," she says through tears, "I'm going to go outside and talk to him for a few minutes."

"Good," Nessa says. "I'll be up here."

OUTSIDE, Tanya walks down their driveway and surveys the neighbors' houses. It doesn't look like a street where a homicide would happen. There are gardens out front and signs of children in the yards: bicycles, sidewalk chalk in driveways. Tanya finds herself climbing their own porch again, but this time, ringing the O'Briens' bell.

As kids, Tanya and Nessa used to prank the O'Briens, ringing their doorbell and then running away, hiding behind trees and watching them open the door, look sternly down at their front stoop where she and Nessa had left a little object: a block of moldy cheese, a maxi pad, one time a demonic-looking rubber mask of George W. Bush's face.

When Tanya goes to ring the O'Briens' bell, she has the ridiculous idea that the doorbell might be some sort of portal—that by pressing it, she'll transport herself back in time, to when she and Nessa were girls and Lorraine was still alive. She presses it—the same white rectangle of plastic—then hears the familiar chime from inside the house. This time she doesn't run away but stands on the doorstep and waits for the door to open. When it does, it's Mrs. O'Brien who's standing there, and when she sees that it's Tanya, the old woman blinks and then wordlessly opens her arms.

Tanya hesitates but allows her neighbor to embrace her.

"Tanya," Mrs. O'Brien says, and it occurs to Tanya that it's the first time they've had a conversation as two adults. "Come in," she says.

"I can't stay for very long," Tanya says, following Mrs. O'Brien inside. "My sister is waiting for me."

"Of course. Sit, please," she says, motioning to the kitchen table. "Tea?"

"Thank you," says Tanya. She sits and looks around as Mrs. O'Brien puts the kettle on the stove. She's never actually been inside the O'Briens' house, and she's surprised by how different their house looks from her own. It's meticulously clean and decorated in deep greens and reds, like a hunting lodge. Mrs. O'Brien sets out several boxes of tea on the table and then sits across from Tanya to wait for the water to boil.

"I just wanted to ask . . . ," Tanya starts to say, but Mrs. O'Brien nods and puts a firm hand over Tanya's.

"I know," she says. "Oh gosh, I've gone over the night a million times in my head."

"What happened?"

"Bob and I were in bed. Honey, we've heard noises before, coming from your mother's house, but not like that."

"What did you hear?" Tanya asks.

Mrs. O'Brien looks at her and seems to be contemplating whether or not to answer. "Yelling," she says. "A lot of yelling. Both of them. And the dog. I told Bob to go over there and I called the police."

"Bob went over there?"

Mrs. O'Brien looks down at the table. When she looks back up, her eyes are rimmed red, and Tanya has the sense that Mrs. O'Brien has been crying a fair amount about this. "He did. Not fast enough. I'm so terribly sorry.

"He tried CPR. Chest compressions. Mouth-to-mouth. Everything he could."

"Was he still there? When Bob arrived?"

"Jesse, you mean?"

Tanya nods.

Mrs. O'Brien's eyes flash. "He was."

"What was he doing when Bob got there?"

"I don't know that you want to hear this."

"I do."

Mrs. O'Brien squints, as if in pain. "He . . . what Bob said was that Jesse had . . . injured himself. He was bleeding out."

"Where? Where had he injured himself?"

Mrs. O'Brien touches her wrist. "Here," she says. "And his throat." She clears her throat.

Tanya's stomach clenches with this new information. "Jesse tried to commit suicide?"

"Well, I can't say for sure. But it appeared to Bob that, yes, he attempted to."

Tanya laughs but the sound is strange and humorless, and Mrs. O'Brien looks startled. "I'm glad it didn't work," Tanya says. "I'm glad he didn't get out of it so easily."

"It's terrible," Mrs. O'Brien says. "It's the most terrible thing."

"What happened when the police showed up?"

"Bob says they revived him. He left in an ambulance almost immediately."

Tanya feels jumpy. Almost giddy. That Jesse tried to kill himself further indicates his guilt; his cowardliness. She feels the way she does when she discovers a new piece of evidence, or a particular argument, when working on a case. Though it's not joy that she feels, thinking about Jesse sitting in a jail cell without access to a razor or a gun or a rope, it's relative to joy— relief, vindication.

The kettle boils then, and Mrs. O'Brien stands.

"I'm sorry," Tanya says, standing, too. "I should get back to my sister."

"I hope I haven't upset you. Oh dear, it was a tragic thing that happened to your mother. It should never have happened."

"Thank you for calling the police," Tanya says. "And Bob. Please thank him for going over there. For trying."

"I wish more than anything we had gotten there sooner."

"It's not your fault," Tanya says firmly.

"Still . . ."

Together they walk to the door and Tanya turns to look at her before leaving. "Will you come to the funeral on Monday?"

"Bob and I will both be there."

Tanya nods. "I'm sorry about ringing your doorbell when we were kids. You must have hated us."

For the first time, Mrs. O'Brien smiles. "Honey, there are so many things to hate in this world, and you kids playing wasn't one of them."

"Still, we must have driven you crazy."

"A little. Nothing we couldn't handle. We still have that George Bush mask somewhere. Sometimes Bob wears it on Halloween when he answers the door for the trick-or-treaters." She laughs, though her eyes are sad.

TANYA RETURNS TO THEIR HOUSE, and this time when she walks inside, the smell doesn't bother her as much. The news about Jesse has filled her up. She walks upstairs, burning with new anger and energy, ready to tell Nessa, but she stops short in the doorway of her mother's bedroom.

Her sister is across the room, standing in front of the full-length mirror, though her eyes are closed. She's wearing Lorraine's emerald dress.

"Ness?"

Nessa opens her eyes and they look at each other in the reflection.

"Do you mind?" Nessa asks. "If I keep it?"

Tanya goes over to the bed, suddenly exhausted. She lies down. "I don't mind."

Nessa comes and stretches out next to her. For several moments they lie without talking. Tanya wants to tell her about Jesse, but she knows her sister will only be more upset by the news.

"You look pretty," Tanya says instead.

Nessa opens her eyes and for the first time that day, she tears up. "Really?" she asks.

Tanya nods and Nessa looks away, embarrassed.

"You're pretty, Nessa. You've always been pretty."

Nessa squeezes her eyes shut and shakes her head. "Mom thought you were so pretty. I could tell when she looked at you she was always kind of amazed." Nessa is crying freely now. "When you got married she was in awe. You should've seen her face, Tanya. She couldn't stop looking at you."

Tanya looks at Nessa. "Mom thought you were beautiful, too, Ness."

Nessa shrugs and stares up at the ceiling. "How am I supposed to get married without her here? How am I supposed to have kids?"

Tanya thinks about her own child, a tiny secret the size of a raspberry in her belly, and wonders if this is the moment she's supposed to tell Nessa. But she pushes the thought away and rolls over to look at her sister. "I'll be here. I'll be here for all of that."

Nessa blinks, her eyelashes slick. "I think I found an outfit. It's not a dress."

"Can I see?"

They sit up and Nessa retrieves a pair of olive-green pants and a black cashmere sweater from Lorraine's closet. "It's casual, I guess," Nessa says. "But it's really nice."

"I like it," says Tanya. "I think she'd like it, too."

"Yeah," Nessa says, wiping her nose. "Me too."

Tanya pulls the blue woolen throw blanket at the foot of the bed over herself, even though it's warm that day, especially upstairs. They've had the blanket forever. It's as familiar to her as the smell of their house, as the feel of the stairs beneath her feet.

She rolls over and looks at Nessa. "Can I have this blanket?" she asks.

A strange expression comes over Nessa's face and for a moment it looks like she might say no, and the thought horrifies Tanya—that they could possibly fight over their mother's belongings. But Nessa only nods.

The morning of the funeral, Tanya wakes suddenly from an old recurring nightmare she hasn't had in years. In the dream she's walking up an endlessly high staircase with no risers. She keeps slipping, each time coming dangerously close to plunging through the open space. The nightmare usually ends when she does finally slip, flailing awake with a gasp.

This morning, though, there's no relief in waking up. Her life has become a nightmare. The stairs—she'd choose that over her mother's funeral, any day.

Beside her, Nessa is also up, staring at the ceiling, a look of disbelief on her face.

"I want this day to be over," Nessa says.

The last few days have been a whirlwind of activity and planning, and it makes sense to Tanya now, why people have funerals. The funeral, in actuality, has little to do with Lorraine. It's for the people still alive. It gives them structure, a to-do list. In the last seventy-two hours they've met with a funeral home director, they've met with the rabbi, they've selected a casket for Lorraine to be buried in, they've ordered bagels and cream cheese and two hundred dollars' worth of lox for the shiva, they've made countless phone calls, they've had arguments over which flowers to order, ordered the flowers.

Now everything is ready, and all there is left to do is mourn, and Tanya knows that once she starts crying today, she won't be able to stop.

"I'm going to take a shower," Nessa says, sitting up in bed.

Tanya watches Nessa undress, pull off her T-shirt and shorts, flick her underwear off her ankle onto the floor. She walks naked into the bathroom attached to their room. Usually Nessa is shy about her body around Tanya, changing quickly with her back to her. Today, though, there is ease in Nessa's nakedness, in her slow walk from the bed to the bathroom.

While Nessa's in the shower, Tanya gets out of bed and goes downstairs to find Eitan. She hears quiet conversation coming from the kitchen, and she finds Eitan and Ben sitting across the table from each other in their pajamas, eating cereal.

"Morning," Tanya says from the doorway.

"Hi," Ben says.

And Eitan: "Come sit."

"Is it only you two up?" she asks.

"Your dad's outside on the porch," says Eitan.

"I'll be right back."

She finds her father outside, already dressed in his suit and kippah, though the service doesn't start for another two and a half hours. She realizes then, in the harsh sunlight, that he's grayed substantially. There's tiredness in his eyes, a resignation. He looks, for the first time in his marriage, significantly older than Simone.

Jonathan turns to her and gives her a quick, fierce hug. Already he's been crying.

"Did you get the bagels?" Tanya asks.

"We picked everything up this morning. Camille is coming over at nine to set the house up." Camille is their housekeeper, a woman who comes every week to clean.

"That's good."

"How'd you sleep?"

"Okay," Tanya lies. "You?"

"I barely slept. Ben came in and woke Simone up in the middle of the night. First time he's done that in years."

"How much does he know?"

"Not much," her father says. "He knows that your mom died, but not how. He asked, though. Simone told him it was an accident."

Tanya nods and looks out into her father's backyard. It's teeming with equipment—a soccer net and a smattering of small orange cones, a swing set, a batting tee. The entire property is surrounded by trees—enormous, towering trees that must be hundreds of years old. It's hard to believe that her father and Simone own all of them.

"How are you doing, sweetie?"

"I mean, not great," she says, irritated by her father's use of the diminutive.

"Is there anything I can do?"

"Unless you can go back in time, not really."

"I loved your mom, Tee," he says. "I always have."

Tanya turns and gives her father a sharp look. "You don't cheat on someone you love."

He seems surprised and looks down. "What I did wasn't right."

"You chose a different life," Tanya says. "And you have one, with Simone and Ben." She gestures to the backyard. "And that's okay—it was your choice. But you left our family. And right now, this isn't your loss."

"Tanya, I'm not saying it is. I just want to be here for you and Nessa. I love you two more than you can imagine."

Tanya looks at her father. His left eyelid is quivering and she can't tell if it's a twitch or if he's about to cry. "You left us, Dad," she says, holding back tears herself. "You left us alone with Mom and Jesse."

"Tanya, you have to believe me, I didn't know he was like that," Jonathan says. "God, if I had known, I would've done something. It kills me that—"

"What would you have done?"

"Well." He pauses. "I would have talked to your mom about it. I wouldn't have wanted you and Nessa in the house if—I keep thinking—he never touched you, did he?"

"Jesus, Dad, no."

"Because if I knew the extent of—"

"Why would she have listened to you?" Tanya cuts him off. "You're off with your new pregnant wife and you call Mom up and tell her to break up with her boyfriend? How do you think that would've gone over? No. When you cheated on her and left her, you gave up the right to give her your opinion."

"There's no easy answers, I know. I'm sorry, though, that I let you down." Tanya shrugs, suddenly exhausted by the conversation.

"It's okay that you're angry at me," her father goes on. "I can handle that."

"I don't know what you want me to say."

"You don't have to say anything."

They sit for a few minutes in silence. Inside they can hear Eitan and Ben, their voices soft and indistinct, floating out from the kitchen.

"He knows," Tanya says.

"What?"

"Ben knows. He's ten. He's a smart kid."

Jonathan seems to consider this. "You might be right."

"Kids pick up on stuff. They understand things even if they don't know how they understand."

Jonathan closes his eyes and nods slowly, and in his suit and kippah he almost has the look of praying.

"Dad, I'm pregnant."

Her father opens his eyes and whips his head to look at her. She nods and his eyes widen into two green pools. "What?" he says. He draws her in then, hugging her so tightly that she gasps. He begins to cry, and Tanya can't tell if it's from happiness or sadness, though the line between the two seems not to matter.

"I love you so much," he says, and for the first time since she was a child, Tanya says it back.

After the funeral, a small gathering of family and a few of Lorraine's friends come back to their father's house for an abbreviated shiva. Simone is in the kitchen with Camille, cutting and toasting bagels, and everyone else is gathered in the living room or the den, talking in soft voices. Nessa goes back and forth between the kitchen and the other rooms, helping to bring in food and clear away used plates and cups.

Lorraine's closest friends, Wendy and Marcy, have offered multiple times to help. "Sit down and rest," they've told her, but Nessa refuses. She likes having things to do. She doesn't have it in her to sit in a puddle on the sofa, the way Tanya is.

Her sister is curled up, small as a girl, Eitan diligently by her side. Tanya's face and lips are raw from crying, her eyes naked. Nessa doesn't know what to make of Tanya's tears. She wasn't expecting to be the stoic one, the only one to speak at the funeral. When it had been Tanya's turn, her sister had collapsed against Eitan, so distraught that Nessa worried Tanya might need to leave the room.

People have been dropping food off all day, and it's Nessa who's been answering the door and accepting condolences, fielding questions. People want to know the details of Lorraine's death.

"Where is Jesse now?" they ask. "What's going to happen?"

One of Lorraine's coworkers just came out with it: "Do you mind if I ask what he did to her?" she said to Nessa, sidling in close.

"Yes," Nessa answered shortly, and the woman, surprised, nodded and left soon afterward. Details are getting out, though. Nessa's watching it happen. She can read on people's faces how much they know. Their expressions soften—they look at Nessa and Tanya with stunned disbelief and pity.

A couple hours in, Nessa goes down to the basement where her father and Simone keep extra paper goods. She's searching through the storage closet for more napkins when she hears Wendy and Marcy talking on the other side of the wall.

"The thing is," Marcy is saying, "I wasn't really surprised." Marcy lowers her voice and Nessa strains to hear. "Wendy, when I got the phone call, it was almost like I was having déjà vu. Like it had already happened."

"I know."

"God, it sounds awful to say, but I was almost expecting it."

"I think we all were," Wendy says. "Think about all the times we talked to her about this very possibility, Marcy. We were begging her. And you know me. I don't *beg*."

"Jesus. I feel sick with guilt."

"Marce. Blaming ourselves won't do anyone any good. It has nothing to do with us. You know that, right?"

"I just keep thinking about that last time. The way I stormed out. I was so frustrated with her."

"Well, she was frustrating!" Wendy's voice rises in protest. "She wasn't seeing anything clearly. She never could with men. With Jesse especially. That's not new, Marcy. This was a long time coming."

"And the girls. I feel so bad for them."

"Nessa seems so cut off," Wendy says, her voice changing in tone. She sounds relieved, to be talking about Nessa and not Lorraine anymore.

"I was thinking that."

"Do you think she's high?"

"Right now?"

"I don't know. Could be. She seems so blank."

"I wouldn't blame her," Marcy says wryly. "What a fucking miserable day."

"And when she spoke. It was strange, don't you think? She looked almost in a trance."

"God, and it's weird seeing Jonathan. What a fucking prick."

"With that hot new wife."

"Well, not new anymore."

"She's hot, though. Jesus."

"Lorraine would have hated this," Wendy says, laughing bitterly. "Us sitting around with them, eating bagels and lox. And don't get me started on the Jewish stuff. It's strange. It's bizarre, is what it is."

Nessa steps out then, gripping the package of paper napkins.

"Nessa," Wendy says. Both women gape at her, stunned expressions on their faces.

"What's wrong with you?" Nessa hisses, surprising herself with the venom in her voice. "If you knew she was in trouble, how could you not tell me? I could have done something."

Marcy's eyes are huge. "Honey, we're just—"

"Don't call me *honey*, Marcy. You don't get to make things better by calling me that."

"Nessa, none of us knew how bad it was—"

"You talk about my family like we're characters on a TV show. My *hot* stepmom. My *prick* dad. My pathetic mess of a mother. And to make assumptions about me. Just because I'm not spilling my guts and crying my eyes out doesn't mean I'm not feeling things. Why are you even here? If you're here to judge us and make yourselves feel better—that this isn't your fault—you should go."

Marcy has started to cry softly, wiping at her eyes with a wadded tissue she's pulled from her purse, but Wendy's face has hardened and when she speaks there's an angry edge of condescension in her voice. "The truth is, Nessa, we were all in denial about what was going on with your mother and

Jesse, how bad things had gotten. But what happened to your mom is only one person's fault, and that person is Jesse. Putting blame on yourself, or on—"

"I don't blame myself," Nessa interrupts. "Why the hell would I blame myself?"

Simone appears in the doorway then, and they all turn to look. Her stepmother is holding a fancy-looking bagel cutter in her hand and turns worriedly from Nessa to the other women. "Is everything okay?" she asks.

And that's when Nessa drops to the floor. She's crying from the pit of her stomach, as though her body is trying to rid itself of something impossible, like an organ. The women run to her. That's why they're here, after all. To soothe, to hold, to love. But she hates these women. She wants nothing from them. All Nessa wants is her own mother.

Nessa gets a bus back to Northampton. She tells everyone she has to go home for work, which is a lie. Dr. Janeski has told her to take as much time as she needs. Her father and Simone have told Nessa she can stay with them as long as she'd like and Tanya has practically begged her to come back to New York City with her and Eitan. Nessa considers it, but painful as it will be to be apart from her family, it's more painful to be with them.

And besides that, she wants to see Henry. They've been texting every day since the morning he dropped her off in Lexington, and since she's been away from him, she's thought about him almost constantly.

Nessa was upset that first day, when he didn't stay with her, but her anger faded quickly. He'd texted her that night, and despite her hurt, it felt frighteningly good to see his name pop up on her phone. A few days later he'd asked her: *When are you coming home?*

Home. It was such a loving word.

THAT EVENING SHE SHOWERS and shaves her legs and her bikini line. She does her makeup and spritzes perfume on her wrists and neck. There's an unopened bottle of wine in the back of her cupboard and she sticks it in the freezer, then searches her closet for something to wear. She finds a pair of black jeans she hasn't fit in for years and a black top with short lace sleeves.

She's lost weight. She hasn't been on a scale, but she guesses it must be ten pounds or so. Her body looks different. She looks less like herself and more like Tanya.

Since Lorraine died, food has tasted strange and chemical, too bright— like a headache in her mouth. The very act of swallowing makes her nauseous. She's also been smoking cigarettes, further curbing her appetite. Smoking gives her an excuse to go outside, to leave whatever unbearable roomful of people she's in at the time.

Henry is supposed to be at her house at eight. At seven forty-five, Nessa is dressed and waiting. At eight thirty, she texts him. *Where are you?*

Sorry, held up, he texts back. And then, several minutes later, *On my way.*

At eight fifty she hears Henry's car in the driveway and she glances at herself in the mirror before walking to the door to greet him.

When she opens the door, Henry is standing with his hands shoved in his jeans pockets. He's wearing an old sweatshirt and when she leans in to hug him, she can smell beer on his breath.

"How's it going?" he says, when they pull back.

She doesn't know what she was expecting, but it wasn't this. She pushes her disappointment away and leads him into the living room. "Would you like a glass of wine?" she asks.

"Sure."

In the kitchen, she pours two generous glasses and watches as he settles onto her couch.

"How was it?" he asks, as though she'd gone to a concert.

She shrugs and hands him a glass. He sips right away, and this angers her, that he doesn't wait for her to sip first.

"You doing okay?"

"Not really," she says.

For the whole time she'd been in Lexington, she'd been narrating the events to Henry. There's my mother, she told him, privately in her head. There's my mother's body. But now that she's with him, she has no idea what to say.

Nessa downs her wine, eager suddenly to get into bed. She wants desperately to be held. She wants to feel his giant hands on her new, unknown body. Her stomach is flatter and her face is slimmer and her smallness, especially in comparison to his largeness, makes her feel unlike herself. He could wrap his arms around her and she could simply disappear.

The single glass of wine hits her hard and she starts to laugh.

He looks at her, unsure whether to smile. "What's so funny over there?"

She shrugs and puts down her empty glass. "I just feel kind of wasted."

"Yeah?"

She moves closer to him on the couch.

He finishes his own glass and sets it down on the floor.

"Are you drunk?" she asks.

"Kinda."

She climbs onto his lap, straddling him, and wraps her legs around his waist. "I missed you," she whispers.

"I missed you, too." He slips his hands under her shirt, moving them up and down her back.

"But actually," she says. "Like, I actually, genuinely missed you."

"I really missed you, too."

They begin to kiss and Nessa drapes her arms over his shoulders, running her fingers through his hair. She's waiting for the feeling of disappearing, that almost dreamlike state she goes into during sex, or that period of touching right before sex. The high that it brings, the anticipation, is almost better than what follows.

But the high doesn't come. She can't shake the feeling of terror. It's all there, everything that happened. She wonders, sorrowfully, if it will always be there.

"Let's go to my bedroom," she whispers.

Henry stands up, with Nessa still in his arms. And this seems to work—*there* is the high. The feeling of disappearing.

She feels like a little girl being carried by him. She buries her face into his neck and breathes him in. Closing her eyes, she allows herself to enjoy the walk from the living room to the bedroom. She allows herself to enjoy the feeling of slowly being lowered onto her mattress, like a child being put to bed.

She keeps her eyes closed while he undresses her.

"You look different," he comments.

"How?"

"I don't know. Smaller maybe." He kisses her shoulder. "You look so pretty."

The words melt her. "I missed this," she says.

"Me too."

When he finishes undressing her, he begins to undress himself. She listens: the zipper of his fly, the rustling of his jeans, the gentle sounds his clothing makes when it lands on the floor.

"You know what I really missed?" His voice is soft and close to her ear.

"What?" she says, eyes still closed.

"This."

He takes her hand and pulls it toward him, then wraps her hand around his erect penis. Nessa opens her eyes. Nausea dances its familiar dance in the pit of her stomach. She jerks her hand away and sits up.

He frowns. "What?"

"I didn't want you to do that."

"Um. Okay. It kind of seemed like you wanted to . . ."

"Wanted to what?"

"Fuck."

Nessa stands, yanking the blanket off the bed, pulling it over herself. "Why do you have to use that word?"

"Fuck?"

"Yes."

"I didn't mean anything by it."

"Why can't you be nicer to me, Henry? You're not very nice to me."

"Sorry," he mutters. "I knew this was a bad idea."

"You knew what was a bad idea?"

"Sleeping together. After what happened to your mom."

"Don't talk about my mom." She looks at his naked body splayed out on her bed and feels disgusted. His penis lies deflated, a soft little mushroom against his thigh. She takes the alarm clock on her night table and hurls it at his crotch.

"Jesus," he says, throwing his arms down to cover himself.

"Is that what this is?" Nessa says. "I'm just someone you're sleeping with?"

"I like you," Henry says, but he's no longer making eye contact with her, and his face has morphed into something cold and unknown. "I'm attracted to you. But I'm not like . . ." He pauses. "Trying to be in a relationship. I kind of get the feeling that—"

"Shut up," she interrupts, and she turns her back to him. "Get out."

"Will do," he says promptly, and his voice is laced with relief.

When Dr. Janeski shows up on her doorstep with a massive lasagna, Nessa's first thought is, Did Dr. Janeski make that lasagna herself? Does Dr. Janeski even *eat* lasagna?

"Nessa," the doctor says, pushing open the screen door. "Honey." And then, to Nessa's surprise, Janeski wraps one slender arm around Nessa, the pan of lasagna under the other arm, and kisses her on the cheek. *Honey.*

She's dressed the same way she does at work, in all black, with heavy silver jewelry that matches the color of her hair. Her posture is impeccable. Thin and petite without being frail, she reminds Nessa of an elegant insect.

"Thanks for coming, Dr. Janeski."

"Of course, Nessa. And call me Janet, okay?"

Nessa nods. "Do you want to come in?"

"Only if you'd like me to. Am I disturbing you?"

"No, no. Come on in. My place is a mess."

Dr. Janeski shakes her head warmly, averting her eyes of the cluttered hallway and the living room strewn with blankets and mail and half-empty water glasses. "Don't worry for a second," she says.

"Would you like something to drink?"

"No, thank you, Nessa. Shall we sit for a few minutes?"

"Okay." Nessa leads Janeski into her kitchen. Tupperware is piled on the counters and her sink is filled with dishes. There's a funny smell coming from somewhere that she hadn't noticed before, but now that Janeski is here it announces itself immediately. They sit at the kitchen table and Nessa brushes a few crumbs off the edge. "Sorry," she says again.

"Please." Janeski waves her hand and leans over the table and looks deeply into Nessa's eyes. "Nessa. I was *heartbroken* to hear about your mother."

"Yeah," Nessa says softly, and then, without warning, she bursts out laughing. It's something about the way Janeski said the word *heartbroken*—as though Janeski had known Lorraine, as though the psychiatrist's heart had actually broken apart at the news, which, Nessa knows, is not the case. They'd never met.

Janeski watches her, unfazed.

"God, what's wrong with me," Nessa says, covering her mouth. "I don't know why I'm laughing."

Janeski shrugs, smiling. "That's perfectly normal." She continues to sit, waiting for Nessa to say more.

She wonders if this is what it's like to be a patient of Dr. Janeski's. The freedom to say or do anything, and just have her sit there and take it. Most of Janeski's patients are young women, students from Smith with pretty hair and smart eyes, dressed in expensive jeans with holes ripped stylishly in the knees. They sit in the waiting room on their phones, waiting for Dr. Janeski to come get them, and when she does, they stand expectantly, anticipating Dr. Janeski's smile—her warmth—which she doles out to those girls but never to Nessa. Then they emerge fifty minutes later, looking flushed and energized, as though they've just had sex or won money from a scratch ticket. Their lives are important, Dr. Janeski tells them. Their suffering real.

"It's nice of you to come," Nessa says. "Don't you have patients?"

"It's Saturday," Janeski says. "Of course I wanted to come see you. I've been thinking of you so much, Nessa. How are you doing?"

Nessa shrugs and, to her relief, her eyes fill with tears. "I'm not doing well," she admits. Nessa hasn't slept for days. She nods off sometimes, but never for more than twenty or thirty minutes at a time. And she dreads waking up—the realization all over again. She can't bear the thought of crawling into bed, of changing into her pajamas, brushing her teeth, pulling the covers over herself, so she avoids the bedroom and has taken to sleeping on the couch with the television and the lights on.

"Are you sleeping?" Dr. Janeski asks, reading her mind.

Nessa shakes her head.

"How about eating?"

"Sometimes."

Janeski nods. "It's important to eat a little, even if you don't have an appetite. Can I fix you a plate of lasagna?"

"Okay."

Janeski stands and Nessa watches the psychiatrist navigate her messy kitchen, pulling open the drawer with the knives and then washing a plate from the sink, drying it with a towel, then carefully extracting a healthy-sized portion of lasagna from the pan. Janeski puts it in the microwave and takes a step to the left so as not to be hit by the carcinogenic waves.

"A few bites," she says, putting the plate down in front of Nessa. "Whatever you can manage."

Nessa escorts a steaming bite of cheese and sauce into her mouth. "Thank you," she says, swallowing. "It's good."

Something about the way Janeski is squinting at her, nodding continuously, is putting Nessa on edge.

"Why is it normal to laugh?" Nessa asks.

Janeski bows her head admiringly, as though Nessa's question is brilliant. "You're in shock, Nessa. How could you not be? You, both you and your sister, have just suffered a tremendous trauma. Grief is a stress on your body and your emotions. Laughter can be a release from some of those stresses." Janeski smiles and tilts her head. "I once had a patient who couldn't stop burping after her grandmother died."

"And sleeping," Nessa says. "Why do you think it's so hard for me to get in bed? I don't even want to walk into my bedroom. The thought of turning out my lights . . ."

"Hmm. Have you slept in your bed at all since this happened?"

Nessa shakes her head.

Janeski's eyes move from right to left, thinking. "Bedtime is such a hard time of day. How often did you speak on the phone with your mother, Nessa?"

"Almost every day," Nessa lies.

"What time?"

"I guess usually at night."

"So no wonder you don't want to go into your bedroom at night! It's too painful. Of course it is. Nessa, have you been talking to family or friends over the phone? And if you don't mind my asking, do you have a therapist?"

"No," Nessa says. "I don't have a therapist."

"Well, if you'd like, I can refer you to someone. I know some truly lovely clinicians in the area. A few who specialize in grief."

"I don't think I can afford to see a therapist."

"I have several colleagues who I'm almost certain will be able to work out a sliding scale with you." She smiles graciously, as though the generosity of her colleagues reflects well on her.

"Maybe," Nessa says. "Dr. Janeski?"

"Yes?"

"Is it normal, during grief . . . to have promiscuous sex?"

Dr. Janeski doesn't bat an eye. "Certainly."

Nessa looks down and rubs a finger back and forth over a scar in the table. "He wasn't very nice to me," she says softly.

She can feel Janeski watching her, waiting for her to say more.

"It was that guy . . . Henry?" She looks up. "From your office. Henry Alden."

Janeski nods slowly and though she doesn't say anything, she doesn't move a muscle.

It feels important to Nessa that Dr. Janeski know that Henry wasn't nice to her. In fact, she wants it to be Janeski's fault.

"When did this happen?" Janeski asks. "With Henry?"

Nessa shrugs. She knows she should be careful not to give up too much information. "A few days after the funeral."

"Is this a new development, with Henry?"

"He ran into me at the bus stop, asked to bum a cigarette."

"I didn't know you smoked."

Nessa shrugs, expressionless.

"Anyhow," Janeski continues. "He must have recognized you from the office?"

"I guess."

"Did you recognize him?"

"Not at first."

"Well, it doesn't matter, not now. But yes, Nessa, engaging in promiscuous activity, in dangerous risk-taking, is all, I imagine, related to your grief." Her tone has become wholly professional—the Janet who cooked the lasagna has vanished. "There is someone in particular, a Dr. Roberta Hughes, who I think would be an excellent match for you. If you'd like I can give you her number and give her a call today to let her know you'll be reaching out."

"I probably can't afford to pay more than fifty dollars a session. Especially right now."

"Something you can discuss with Roberta. I do believe she'll try to arrange something with you, though I don't want to speak for her."

"I appreciate it, Dr. Janeski, I really do. And the lasagna. I'll eat more later." She nods to the plate where the lasagna sits, now cold.

"Of course. You know that if you need anything you can call me, right?"

"I know. Thank you."

Janeski stands. "When you're ready, you'll sleep in your bed. And if you'd like, you can call me and we can talk. Only if you're comfortable, of course. I want you to know I'm here for you. We've gotten close over the years, haven't we? I care about you, Nessa. I care about you tremendously."

"I care about you, too, Dr. Janeski."

"May I give you another hug?"

"Sure."

They hug. Up close Janeski smells like a bar of lavender soap.

"Here," Janeski says, opening her purse. She hands Nessa a card. "Here's Dr. Hughes's number."

"Wait, so is it Dr. Hughes or Roberta?" Nessa asks.

The psychiatrist's eyes flash. "Something you should probably ask her."

"Will do." Nessa walks Janeski to the door. "See you later, Janet."

AFTER JANESKI PULLS out of the driveway, Nessa storms down the hallway, into her bedroom. It's a mess, still thrown apart from that night she'd raided her closet in search of a dress to wear to her mother's funeral. Her anger, which she imagines as a big, blood-filled ball, dense as a tumor, flexes its muscle inside her stomach.

She sits on the floor and calls Tanya.

"Hey." Tanya's voice emerges almost immediately from the phone, as though she has been waiting for Nessa to call.

"Hey."

"Are you crying?" Tanya asks.

"No. Fucking Janeski just showed up at my house."

"Really?"

"After two years of working for her, she asks me to call her Janet. What the fuck does that mean? I've earned it—now that Mom's gone?"

They don't say the word *dead* to each other. They don't use the past tense. Not because they're in denial, and not because it upsets them; but they both worry about upsetting the other.

"I don't know," Tanya says. She sounds distracted. "She's a bitch. But she was probably just trying to be nice."

"And then during our conversation I kept calling her *Doctor* Janeski. I probably said it five times, and she didn't correct me once. And then she tells me about some shrink she thinks I should see and she refers to her as both *Dr. Hughes* and *Roberta* practically in the same breath. She's a sadistic, manipulative fuck, that's what she is. She's probably a terrible therapist."

"That's fucked up," Tanya says into the phone. And then, fuzzily, "Eitan, can you check the oven?"

"What are you guys eating?"

"Lasagna. Eitan's mom is here. She brought it over."

"That's what Janeski brought." In a flash, Nessa is overcome with loneliness.

"Ness, can I call you back? Bina, like, just got here."

"Sure." She tries to sound upbeat, pretends that this doesn't hurt.

"You okay? You don't sound good."

"I'm fine," she says.

Nessa hangs up the phone and starts to sob.

Tanya hangs up the phone and puts a hand on her belly, breathes in, counting to three, and breathes out, counting to five. *My mother is dead.* It's the sentence that's been running through Tanya's head every second of every day since it happened. Her mother was a victim of a heinous crime, which makes Tanya a victim of a heinous crime as well. Tanya has no interest in being a victim. She has no interest in being a survivor. Even those words—the gentle way attorneys use them when they're around clients, always careful to hear which one the client prefers, as though it makes some huge difference—infuriate her.

Jesse is sitting in a jail cell in Concord, Massachusetts, waiting for his arraignment. And if Tanya has anything to do with it—which she will—he'll remain in a jail cell for the rest of his life.

She's been speaking to Nessa every day on the phone since the funeral, usually multiple times. They don't speak directly about what happened. Instead they speak about the people who've reached out to them—old boyfriends and distant relatives, friends from summer camp, elementary school teachers. They talk about what they're eating for dinner that night, the tuna casserole that Nessa's neighbor brought over that instantly stunk up the apartment, the entire loaf of chocolate chip banana bread that Tanya ate in one sitting. They complain about their various physical ailments—headaches and stomachaches, aching muscles. They've both been experiencing tooth

294 · HANNA HALPERIN

pain. They watch old episodes of *Friends*—their favorite TV show as teenagers—and sometimes they watch the same episode together over the phone, dipping in and out of conversation, laughing at the same jokes. That's one thing that's surprised Tanya. Despite how sad they both are, she and Nessa laugh often with one another.

She still hasn't been able to tell Nessa about the baby. Nobody in her family knows, except for her father, who has promised to keep it quiet for the time being, even from Simone.

So here she is, carrying this literal secret, heavy with guilt. And all she can think is that it isn't fair to Nessa. Tanya has a whole other family. A brand-new one, waiting in the wings. It doesn't make the pain any less, the loss any smaller, but it dampens it. She'd be lying if she said it didn't dampen it.

ON HER FIRST DAY back at work, Tanya finds a pale green envelope on her desk; inside, a card: *With Deepest Sympathy,* it reads, in lavish cursive, signed by everyone at the courthouse. Most people have written little notes. *Thinking of you. Praying for your family. Let me know if there's anything I can do.*

No doubt it was Marjorie who bought the card and circulated it around the office. Marjorie is the mother of the courthouse, the one who brings in cupcakes for birthdays, who organizes the Yankee Swap in December, who always remembers the names of everyone's spouses and children. Tanya tucks the card back inside the envelope and puts it in her desk drawer, then opens her laptop and begins scrolling through the docket for that morning. The words swim on the screen in front of her and the image of Lorraine in the casket resumes its now-familiar spot in the forefront of Tanya's mind.

Her phone vibrates on her desk—it's an unknown number, a telemarketer probably, but she grabs it.

"Hello?" Tanya says into the phone.

"Hi, is this Tanya?" asks a woman's voice.

"This is she."

"Hi, Tanya, this is Lily calling from Graze Salon. I was calling to see if you wanted to reschedule your appointment with Amanda from a few weeks ago?" The woman's voice is loud and bubbly, blissfully unaware of the recent events in Tanya's life.

"Oh," Tanya says. She'd forgotten all about the appointment. She fingers a lock of her hair and examines the ends, which are dry and starting to split. "Yes," she says. "I'm glad you called."

"Great," the woman chirps. "When can you come in?"

"What does she have next week?"

"Amanda will be out on maternity leave starting next week, but I'm happy to set you up with another stylist then."

"Really?" asks Tanya, surprised. She thinks back to her last appointment with Amanda and tries to remember if she'd looked pregnant, but she can't recall. "Does she have any openings this week, then?"

Tanya hears the tapping of computer keys. "Amanda just had a cancellation tonight at six thirty. Would that work?"

"Perfect," Tanya says, though this means she'll have to leave work early. "I'll see her then."

She hangs up and jiggles the touchpad on her computer, stirring it to life.

There's a knock on the door. It's Patrick McConnell, a hotshot defense attorney. "Tanya," he says. "I'm sorry for your loss."

"Me too," she says.

He comes over and gives her a quick but warm hug, and Tanya can smell his shampoo and the coffee on his breath, his expensive cologne.

He steps back. "I had no idea your mom was sick."

"She wasn't," Tanya says. "Her husband killed her."

Patrick looks positively shocked and Tanya is relieved. Before long, everyone will know and maybe they'll leave her alone about it.

"Jesus Christ," he says thickly. "I don't know what to say. That's fucking awful, Tanya. That's terrible."

"Yeah," Tanya says. "I know. You don't have to say anything."

"What the fuck is wrong with people?" He shakes his head.

It's ironic, of course. Patrick defends people like Jesse all the time—though mostly people with a lot more money than Jesse. It's how Patrick affords his cologne, his neat, pressed suit, his twenty-four-hour doorman apartment in Murray Hill, complete with a roof deck and an elevator that opens right up into his living room. He hosted the holiday party that December.

"People are monsters," Tanya says.

Patrick kneels down and looks straight at Tanya with huge, fearless eyes. "Tell me what I can do," he says. "And I'll do it." Patrick's confidence radiates off him, as strong and expensive as his cologne. If she ever murdered someone and needed an attorney, Patrick McConnell would be the first person she'd call.

"Thanks, Patrick. I wish there was something."

"You think of something, and you call me, okay?"

Tanya nods. Up close she notices that his lashes are long and dark, almost feminine. "Okay," she says. "I will."

AMANDA DOESN'T FEEL the need to fill the silences the way other hairdressers do, asking Tanya about what she's up to that weekend and is she planning any vacations soon, whether she's seen any good movies lately.

She is pretty and plump with milk-white skin and colorful tattoos curling out from the cuffs of her sleeves and the neckline of her top. Every time Tanya comes in, her hair is different—one month stick straight and burgundy red, another month a dark, severe bob. The last time it had been long and flowing, like a mermaid's, down her back.

When she comes to retrieve Tanya from the front waiting area of Graze later that evening, Amanda is wearing a stretchy black dress that hugs her impossibly huge belly. Her hair is pulled into a loose ponytail, a few loose tendrils framing her face. Tanya is stunned by how pretty she looks.

"Wow," she says, standing. "Congratulations. You look beautiful."

Amanda smiles, and they hug as best they can with Amanda's stomach between them. "I don't feel it," Amanda says. "I'm one big walking bladder."

Tanya laughs. "When are you due?"

"June fifteenth on the dot," Amanda says. "I'm scheduled for a C-section." She grazes her hands over her stomach. "Little squish is ready to come out. I can feel it."

Amanda leads Tanya through the salon, past rows of chairs and mirrors, where people are seated in various stages of getting their hair done. The room is loud with the whir of hair dryers and, underneath it, indistinguishable pop music.

Tanya sits at Amanda's station and Amanda wraps a black smock around her, fastening it in the back. She pulls Tanya's hair out and splays it over her shoulders. "It's gotten long," she comments, running her fingers through it.

It feels good, Amanda's hands in her hair, the expert way she gently unknots the ends with her fingers.

It occurs to Tanya that the hair on her head is the same hair that was there when she'd last seen her mother. That by cutting it, she'll be ridding herself of that forever. The thought makes her tremble.

"So what are we doing today?" Amanda asks.

"Maybe something different," Tanya says, her voice so steady it surprises her. "What do you think would look good?"

Amanda takes a step back and cocks her head, examining Tanya's reflection. "How would you feel about going shorter?" she asks. "Not too short, a little above your shoulders, long enough to pull back still. We could do angles, some piece-y layers framing your face. Add some volume. It would really make those big eyes pop."

"Okay," Tanya says. "I trust you."

"Oh, goody." Amanda smiles. "This is exciting."

As Amanda washes Tanya's hair, Tanya closes her eyes, focusing on the hot water on her scalp, the feeling of Amanda's fingers as she scrubs shampoo through her hair, the pressure of the sink basin against the back of her neck. She's not crying, but she's close, and it's the enormity of Amanda's belly that keeps her from breaking down. She wonders if the babies can sense each other, each warm and safe in its own womb, but only a few feet apart.

Amanda wraps a plush towel around Tanya's head and leads her back to the chair.

"I'm pregnant, too," Tanya blurts out, as Amanda starts to rub her hair dry with the towel.

"Oh my God!" Amanda's face lights up and she leans down and hugs Tanya. "Oh, sweetheart," she says. "That's incredible. How far along are you?"

"Only two months," Tanya says, nodding toward Amanda's belly. "I've got a long way to go."

"Two months," Amanda muses. "Are your boobs killing you?"

"Not really. They're too puny, I think," she says. "I've been having terrible morning sickness, though."

"That's the worst," Amanda says. "You gotta eat. Just a little something bland like crackers. It's much worse on an empty stomach."

"Thanks," says Tanya. "So do you know if you're having a girl or a boy?"

"A girl." Amanda beams. "We're naming her Rosie, after Curt's mom."

"Rosie. That's pretty."

"Rose Elizabeth Campbell."

Then Amanda starts snipping and Tanya watches as her hair falls to the ground in dark, wet clumps. She tries to push away the thought that she's doing something wrong, something violent, and she turns her attention to the mirror and concentrates on Amanda's reflection, the beach ball of Amanda's stomach.

"Is Curt excited?" Tanya asks.

Amanda nods. "Over the moon. He'll be the best daddy. But poor little girl, he's going to be so overprotective."

"Yeah?" Tanya asks.

"He's already said she's not allowed to date 'til she's eighteen. Look up for me a little?"

Tanya tilts her chin up.

"What about your beau?" Amanda asks. "What kind of daddy's he going to be?"

"Eitan will be a softie. If anyone's going to be the bad cop, it'll be me."

Amanda smiles. "He must be a nice guy."

"He is," Tanya says.

"Excuse me for one sec, honey, okay? I'm going to grab some leave-in conditioner."

"Sure," Tanya says, and Amanda waddles off.

Tanya looks down at all her wet hair scattered on the floor. Across the room there's a woman with a broom, sweeping hair into a dustpan. Quickly, Tanya steps down from the chair and kneels, grabbing fistfuls of her hair from the floor. It's wet and sticks to her fingers, but she empties palmfuls of it into her purse, brushing it off so it lands in clumps on her wallet and keys and lipstick.

"I'm sorry, Mom," she whispers, like a crazy woman.

When Amanda returns, Tanya is back in the chair, the snippets of hair safe inside her purse.

"Do you want a boy or a girl?" Amanda asks as she rubs the conditioner into Tanya's damp hair.

Tanya pauses. She's supposed to want a girl, she knows. But the truth is, she's terrified of bringing a girl into a world where Donald Trump is president, where men like Jesse and Dan exist.

"A boy," she answers honestly, and Tanya is relieved when Amanda doesn't look surprised or ask why.

For the rest of the cut, Tanya closes her eyes and she and Amanda settle into their familiar quiet.

"What do you think?" Amanda says, a little while later.

Tanya opens her eyes and stares at her reflection. She looks pretty—her hair especially—and terribly sad. "I love it," she tells Amanda. "Thank you. It's really great." She forces herself to smile.

"It's fun, isn't it?" Amanda says, fluffing Tanya's hair a little with her hands.

"It is," Tanya agrees.

"You think your husband will like it?" Amanda asks, and Tanya is surprised to realize that the person she was thinking about liking it was Patrick McConnell from work.

"He'll love it. I can't wait to see his face. Thank you."

"You're welcome, honey."

Amanda takes off the black smock and Tanya stands, brushing a few stray strands from her lap.

SHE LEAVES AMANDA a ridiculous tip—almost forty percent—and walks out of the salon into the May evening. It's practically luscious outside—the air warm and fragrant with late spring, the sky mottled with pinks and oranges and blues, like something tropical and sugary. Her head feels light. She can smell her own hair the way you might catch a whiff of someone else's—as something separate and distinct and a little bit exciting.

She stands there on the sidewalk, panicked—the familiar feeling that now comes over her whenever she doesn't have a specific task at hand, when she's alone, or when she sees something beautiful, like the city and the sky. Her body seizes up, the same way it did the night when she got that call from the police. She wonders if she'll ever be able to shake it—the feeling that the unthinkable has happened, that it can never be undone.

Tanya heads in the direction of Central Park, not wanting to go home to her empty apartment. She walks east down Seventy-Sixth Street, then turns left, making her way up Central Park West, through families and groups of vendors and tourists. She watches as people pour out of the Museum of Natural History onto the stone steps, holding up their phones to take pictures of the sky. The trees lining the park are dark and full of sun, like syrup, dripping through the leaves, dappling the sidewalk with light and shadow.

She envies these people; the pleasure they're getting from the sky, from their jaunt through the museum. It seems impossible to Tanya that something as simple and perfect as a sunset in the city will ever bring her joy again.

Tanya pulls out her phone and calls Eitan at work.

"What are you up to?" she asks when he picks up.

"Things got really busy here," he says. "Are you just leaving?"

"I left a while ago," she says. "I'm on Central Park West across from the museum."

"How was it being back?"

"It was okay," she says. "Do you want to meet me here? Maybe we can get dinner?"

"I wish, babe," Eitan says. "It's going to be a few hours before I can leave."

"No problem," Tanya says.

They hang up and Tanya scrolls through her phone. She pauses at Patrick McConnell's name and stares at it, trying to imagine what it would feel like to press it.

Probably she would get his voice mail.

His voice has been going through her head all day. "Tell me what I can do," he'd said, "and I'll do it." He'd sounded so certain, as though there was an answer, as though there was something to be done.

With an abandon that's entirely foreign, Tanya presses his name and holds her phone up to her ear. It rings, once, twice, three times, until the sound of Patrick's voice mail comes through: *You've reached Patrick McConnell. I'm unable to . . .*

Relieved, and slightly breathless, she hangs up.

Several moments later, her phone vibrates in her hand, and when she looks down, it's Patrick, calling back.

"Hi!" she answers, her voice emerging stupidly animated, and she actually winces at the sound of it.

"Tanya. I missed your call." His voice is deeper and more serious over the phone.

She considers playing dumb, blaming it on a butt dial. But all she says is, "Yeah."

"How are you?" he asks, and there's softness in his question.

"I'm fine," she says, trailing off.

"Where are you?"

"Upper West Side," she answers. "Across the street from the Museum of Natural History." She pauses. "I could use a drink. But I'm not drinking these days."

"Funny," he says. "Neither am I. How about a walk through the park, then, before it gets dark? A pretzel?"

"Alright," she says.

"Give me ten minutes. I just need to send this email and then I'm jumping in a cab."

"I'm not interrupting you?" Tanya asks.

"Not at all," he says. "Be there soon."

TANYA WAITS FOR PATRICK on a bench near the entrance of the park. She knows what she's doing is foolish and potentially irreversible, but she also seems to have entered some sort of fugue state. Whatever comes next, she feels, is not entirely up to her. Besides, she tells herself, there's nothing wrong with calling a friend and taking a walk through the park. Though he's not really a friend.

Across the street, a taxi pulls over on the museum side of Central Park West, and Tanya watches Patrick emerge. There's something almost presidential about the way he unfolds out of the car, sunglasses on, surveying his surroundings. He crosses the street in wide, lean strides and when he sees her, he removes his sunglasses and raises his hand in greeting.

"I'm glad you called," he says, as he approaches. "I've been wondering all day how you're doing."

They embrace, which feels strange, the second embrace that day, but this one they linger in a little longer.

"You got your hair done," he observes, stepping back.

She tucks her hair behind her ears.

"I like it. It suits you."

"Thank you," she says. "Should we see about that pretzel?"

"Absolutely."

Together they walk toward the entrance of the park. Tanya wonders then about Patrick's girlfriend. She's met her, Selena, a handful of times, but only in passing and briefly at the holiday party Patrick hosted. Blond and trim, she's an attractive woman, in the same wealthy way Patrick is: a body that's professionally trained, skin that shines with good health and diet, never a hair out of place. They have the look of people who can afford to take cabs everywhere; never any sweating or weather involved.

"How long have you been sober?" Patrick asks.

Tanya looks at him, surprised. "What?"

"You said you don't drink anymore."

"Oh," Tanya says. "Well, I—"

"No need to answer if it's personal. Next month I'll be two years clean."

"That's great, Patrick," Tanya says, sincerely, though she's taken aback. "I'm not. Well. I don't have a problem with alcohol. I'm just not drinking."

"Gotcha," says Patrick. "I was going to say, you didn't seem the type."

"The alcoholic type?"

Patrick smiles. "You're very measured."

"Am I?"

"I mean it as a compliment. Cool as a cucumber." Patrick points toward a food stand advertising pretzels and ice cream. "Shall we?"

They walk toward the stand. "I'm not always so cool, you know."

He looks at her, interested.

"I do impulsive things. I make mistakes."

"Well, you are human after all."

"I am," Tanya concedes.

"What's the most impulsive thing you've ever done?"

Tanya glances at him. He's not flirting with her, she doesn't think. He seems to genuinely want to know.

She wonders if Patrick has been to rehab, if he goes to AA meetings. It's hard to imagine Patrick McConnell in a church basement, sitting on one of those metal folding chairs, listening to a circle of people share their stories.

Still, there's vulnerability in admitting this to her, and she realizes that he must trust her, at least enough to keep his admission confidential.

She thinks about kissing Patrick, what it would be like. *There* was something impulsive, something stupid. It would be fun, kissing Patrick, who was handsome and confident, who might whisk her away to an alternate reality. Afterward would be torture, though. Telling Eitan, or not telling Eitan. Either way.

"Calling you was impulsive," she says. "Not the most impulsive thing I've ever done." She smiles wryly. "I'm not that dull. But, well, I didn't put much thought into it. I felt the urge to reach out—to you. And I did."

"I was surprised to see your name on my phone," Patrick says.

They've reached the food stand.

"I'd like a pretzel, please," Tanya says to the vendor, the presence of a third party a relief. "With mustard."

"Make that two," says Patrick, and the man pulls down two massive pretzels and hands them over along with little tubs of yellow mustard. Patrick insists on paying and they walk over to a bench down the path. The trees are all in bloom, and when they sit, Tanya looks up at the light green buds against the candy-colored sky.

"You know I've never eaten a New York pretzel?" Tanya says.

"Never?"

"Nope."

"Well, what do you think?"

"It's good," Tanya says. "Salty. Better than I imagined." She glances down at her hands, holding the pretzel, the sparkle of sun glinting off her wedding band and engagement ring, and then over at Patrick's hands—bare. He seems to notice her staring and he puts the pretzel down in his lap and turns slightly to face her. "So why'd you have the urge to call me?"

"I felt lost," Tanya says.

Patrick nods, as though this makes sense. "You must be going through hell."

"Yeah," she says. "I don't feel like myself." She sets her own pretzel down on the bench and holds her hands in her lap. When she glances at him, he's looking at her softly.

"I was happy when I saw your name on my phone. *Tanya Bloom*," he says, smiling a little. "I was so flustered that I didn't pick up."

"I was flustered when you called me back," she admits.

"I know neither one of us is drinking. But if you're interested, I do have some excellent pot I'd love to share with you. It's medicinal. I've found it to be pretty soothing, if you're into that."

"Oh," says Tanya.

"We'd have to go back to my apartment. We could smoke it on the balcony."

Tanya's only smoked pot once in her life, her freshman year at Smith with a group of students in the West Quad, and she can't say she enjoyed the experience. There was the passing of the joint from mouth to mouth—unsanitary—and all they'd done afterward was order pizza and watch something stupid on television. Everyone seemed to find all the same unfunny things funny, so finally Tanya had left, thinking she probably hadn't inhaled properly.

But when she returned to her dorm and tried to read "The Yellow Wall-paper" for her Lit class, she found she couldn't concentrate and her mind kept moving in unfamiliar circles. So Tanya set the book down and turned off the overhead light and put on music: Joni Mitchell's album *Blue*. It was the type of music Nessa would have listened to in a moment like that: kind of sad, kind of romantic, kind of lonely.

Was she lonely? she remembers wondering, lying in her dorm room that Friday night. The rest of the campus was occupied. Gathered together in various groups, dancing, playing drinking games, passing joints. In some rooms people were probably kissing or close to kissing; having sex or close to having sex. Across the West Quad, the group of kids she was just with were probably watching another show, still laughing.

"Sure," she says, turning to Patrick, her stomach a mess of nerves. "Why not."

So they barrel down Lexington in the backseat of a cab, past Hunter College and Bloomingdale's and the Chrysler Building. The cabdriver is aggressive, as if he knows what they're doing is illicit, and that Tanya, given too much time, might change her mind. He weaves in and out of lanes, tears through yellow lights, wastes nobody's time. She and Patrick are both quiet, watching New York fly by out their windows. When the driver slams on the brakes for a pedestrian and Tanya is flung forward against her seat belt, Patrick casts out his arm, as if to stop her from flying through the windshield. "Careful," he says sharply to the driver, but the driver says nothing in response.

They're dropped off in front of Patrick's building, a high-rise on Madison Avenue, with a wide green awning out front. The doorman smiles, nodding kindly and opening the door for them.

"Thanks, Rudy," Patrick says, stepping back to allow Tanya in first.

"No problem, Mr. McConnell."

Tanya enters the air-conditioned lobby. Everything is white marble and spotless. There's a lounge area with crisp modern couches and a cream-colored rug, floor-to-ceiling mirrors lining the walls across from the elevators. She's been there before, of course, that December for the work holiday party. She'd arrived drunk, with Eitan. She remembers taking the elevator up in their winter coats, holding hands and laughing to each other about the over-the-top lavishness of the place.

It feels so different this time, sober, and arriving with Patrick. She wonders what Rudy thinks, if he thinks anything at all. They step inside the elevator and Patrick presses the button for the eleventh floor.

"How long have you been here?" Tanya asks.

"Two and a half years," Patrick says. "I'm thinking of moving downtown, though."

"This isn't downtown enough for you?"

"Nah. It's boring up here."

"What about Selena? Where does she live?"

"She's in Brooklyn now. Williamsburg." He rolls his eyes.

"You don't like it there?"

"No. To put it lightly."

"Me neither," Tanya says. "I could do without the man buns and the Amish beards."

Patrick laughs as the elevator doors open. "Here we are."

His apartment is as exquisite as she remembers: an open floor plan centering around a living room the size of Tanya's entire apartment. Stunning views. "You've been here before, right?" he asks.

"For the holiday party. You have a beautiful apartment."

"Oh, thanks. Please—make yourself at home. Can I get you a water or a seltzer? Soda?"

"Water's good."

"Great. And if you don't mind I'm going to change quick—I'm still in this shirt from work and I've just about sweated through it."

"Go ahead," Tanya says.

Patrick disappears and Tanya wanders into the den. There's a huge brown leather couch catty-corner to a love seat, a low-rise coffee table scattered with newspapers and *New Yorkers*. The opposite wall is entirely floor-to-ceiling bookshelves, filled to the brim with books. She scans the titles—mostly law books and nonfiction, a full set of encyclopedias, anthologies of essays, biographies, a handful of novels.

Patrick appears several minutes later, this time in jeans and a white T-shirt, and Tanya feels her body react—that unmistakable pulse of pressure between her legs. She's attracted to him.

"Judging my library?" he asks.

"A little."

"And?" he asks.

"And what?"

"What's your takeaway?" There's a small smile on his face. He's holding a plastic baggie of marijuana.

"You read mostly men," she says.

"Ah."

"And the women you do have seem to write cookbooks." She pulls one of the books off the shelves—*A Traditional Irish Table* by Cathleen Kelly. "Do you cook?"

Patrick laughs. "My mom gave me that. I have no idea why."

Tanya smiles and slides the book back in its place. The word *mom* makes her weak with sadness.

"Do you mind a little tobacco?" he asks.

Tanya glances at the baggie and an image pops into her head, clear as day: Patrick drinking whiskey from a crystal tumbler at his holiday party in December. She remembers because he'd thrown his arm over Eitan's shoulder and offered him a sip.

"Man, don't be drinking that," he'd said, meaning Eitan's beer, "when you could be drinking *this*. Here, try mine." He handed Patrick his tumbler. "Johnnie Walker Blue. I'll have Taylor fix you one."

She wonders if the whiskey that night had been a slip-up, or if the two-years-sober thing he'd told her in the park was a lie.

"I'm sorry," she says to Patrick now. "But I just realized the time." She holds up her phone, as if for proof. "It's later than I thought. I really should get home."

"Oh, really?" Patrick says. And though he keeps his smile securely on his face, there's disappointment in his eyes, maybe even a touch of agitation.

All of a sudden, Tanya is trembling. She thinks of Eitan uptown, on the eighth floor of Lenox Hill Hospital, and then she thinks of her baby, and she's overcome with relief for her small, delicate family.

"You okay, Tanya?"

"No," she says. "I'm not. And I don't think smoking that is going to help me."

Patrick quickly stuffs the baggie in his jeans pocket. To Tanya's surprise, he looks ashamed. "Look," he says, "I don't know what you're going through. Not at all. But if this means anything, Tanya, you're one of the strongest people I know. If it were me, I'd have downed the entire liquor store by now." He shakes his head a little. "People get through things their own way, and I'm sure you have your things. But from where I'm standing, you're a fucking champ." His voice has changed from the assured tone he used to answer his phone, from the seductive one he used with her down in Central Park.

This voice—she can hear the boy in Patrick McConnell. Not in a juvenile way, but rather—for the first time, he sounds vulnerable. She wants to thank him for this, but she knows it will only embarrass him, that she risks losing this side of him altogether.

"People keep saying I'm strong," she says instead. "As if I've had a choice in all this. But I didn't. It just happened. I'm not being strong. I'm just being."

Patrick shakes his head resolutely. "But look at yourself. You're back at work. You got your hair cut. You made the wise decision not to smoke with me." He smiles. "You're on a roll."

"True," she says. "I mean, I can barely look at a tree without bursting into tears."

"Hey." He shrugs. "That's most people on a normal day. Give yourself a break."

ONCE OUTSIDE, TANYA BREATHES in the evening air, grateful to be alone. She doesn't feel the need to call anyone and tell them where she just was, what she almost did. Not Eitan or Nessa or Simone. There's nothing to confess; no apology to make. Almost is not the same thing as doing. Almost is not a crime.

She walks to Times Square, a place she normally avoids with a passion, though tonight it doesn't bother her. The garish lights and the flashing billboards, the swarming tourists with their souvenirs and selfie sticks, make it seem almost like a different country. It aligns with the oddness of the rest of her night.

She catches the 1 train uptown. The subway is quiet for a Monday evening, with plenty of open seats, but Tanya chooses to stand. She watches the other passengers. Most are plugged in: listening to music or reading or scrolling or tapping their phones. Some are just closing their eyes.

The secret knowledge of her baby—that she is not alone in this city, on this train, in her own body—comforts her in a way it hasn't before. She wonders if the little person inside of her has a consciousness yet; if the baby has any awareness of being carried around to all these wildly different places: the courthouse and Graze Salon, Central Park, Murray Hill, Times Square, and now, underground and zooming uptown—Fiftieth Street, Columbus Circle, Sixty-Sixth Street, Seventy-Second Street, all the way up to Seventy-Ninth Street. Can this tiny little soul sense it—she wonders—what it feels like, going home?

IV.

It's eight a.m., mid-August, and already the city is sweltering, hot air coming up from the vents in the sidewalk like breath. Nessa hauls her suitcase out from the underbelly of the Peter Pan bus and heads toward the subway to catch the train up to Tanya and Eitan's apartment.

She stands in a long line to buy her MetroCard and when she finally gets to the kiosk, it takes four tries before the machine reads her credit card. When it finally spits out a yellow pass, it feels like an accomplishment.

The trains are packed. Nessa is pressed shoulder to shoulder between a big-boned man who seems to be falling in and out of sleep and a professionally dressed woman with AirPods in her ears. Nessa is close enough to hear the woman's music, something harsh and syncopated. She clutches her suitcase between her legs and looks around at all the New Yorkers and the tourists, everyone fairly quiet in their own worlds.

When she gets off at Seventy-Ninth Street, the city is calmer than downtown. There are people walking dogs and pushing strollers, and rather than heading in every possible direction, they seem more at the mercy of the city's grid. Nessa walks from Broadway to West End Avenue and then up four blocks to Tanya's apartment.

"Hey!" Tanya's voice crackles over the intercom, once she's rung up. "Come up."

The door buzzes and Nessa pushes it open, dragging her rolling suitcase over the threshold of the doorway, then up the two flights of stairs.

Tanya is waiting for Nessa at the door of her apartment. There's a round, unmistakable melon-sized bump beneath her sister's shirt.

"Look at you," Nessa says, overcome. She only learned about Tanya's pregnancy a month ago, when Tanya called to ask if Nessa could come be with her when she found out the sex of the baby.

They hug and it feels different with Tanya's belly between them, a third little person.

"Holy shit," Nessa says. "You're going to be a mother."

"The poor, innocent child."

Nessa kneels and presses her hands to Tanya's belly. It's warm and firm. She puts her ear against Tanya's stomach and knocks gently with her knuckles. "Hey there," she says. "Who are you in there?"

THAT AFTERNOON NESSA and Tanya sit together in the waiting room at Tanya's ob-gyn. "So what do you want?" Nessa asks. "Boy or girl?"

"I don't care," Tanya says. "As long as it's healthy and happy—"

"Oh, come on. Don't feed me that. I won't tell—"

"No," Tanya interrupts. "Because if I tell you and I end up with the other one, you'll always know."

"Why does that matter? It's not like I'll tell the kid."

"I'm not saying."

"Fine. I know what you want anyway."

"You don't know," Tanya says. "But don't say it. Don't jinx it."

Nessa purses her lips and picks up a parenting magazine. On the front a beautiful woman with blond hair is holding a blond-haired baby, smiling widely into the camera. If it weren't for the child pressed up against the woman's cheek, it could have been an advertisement for toothpaste.

"This is going to be you," Nessa says, holding out the magazine.

Tanya rolls her eyes.

Eitan rushes in then, sweaty and bright-eyed. "There were major delays on the 6," he says, collapsing in the chair next to Tanya. "I literally ran here all the way from Fifty-Eighth."

Tanya smiles curtly. "Time to get back to the gym, huh?"

"Does she always talk to you like that?" Nessa asks.

"Pretty much."

"It's for his own good," Tanya says, patting Eitan's knee. "I don't want him to have a heart attack on me."

"Tanya?"

All three of them look up. A nurse is standing in the doorway. "Come in."

IN THE EXAM ROOM, the nurse takes Tanya's blood pressure and temperature, her height and weight. "Change into this gown, please," she tells Tanya. "With the front open. Dr. Townes will be with you shortly."

"Turn around while I change," Tanya instructs Nessa and Eitan, after the nurse leaves and shuts the door.

"But you're a beautiful pregnant woman," Nessa says. "I want to see."

"*Turn.*"

"So what do you think it's going to be, Eitan?" Nessa asks, as they both turn around to give Tanya privacy.

Eitan exhales thoughtfully. "This morning I woke up certain it was going to be a girl. But then on my run here I got this really strong feeling that it's a boy. I don't know," he says. "I really don't know."

His eyes are almost childlike with excitement, and Nessa wonders what it would be like to be with a man as good as Eitan. A man who treats women kindly, and not because he wants something in return.

Men like that have never expressed an interest in Nessa. For a moment she feels furious, but then the doctor comes in, and Nessa pushes the feeling down, quick and tidy.

Dr. Townes is short with round, pink cheeks and a rounded pink nose. "You've got your whole crew with you," she says, shaking Eitan's and Nessa's hands.

Then she examines Tanya, rubs ultrasound gel on Tanya's belly, and gently moves the probe over the bump. "So you want to know the sex of the baby?" Dr. Townes asks.

Tanya glances at Eitan and then at Nessa. She nods at the doctor. "We want to know."

Dr. Townes smiles. She likes this part. "You're having a little boy."

Nessa's stomach sinks. She looks at Tanya and her sister's eyes well up.

"Oh my God," Tanya says, starting to cry. She's gripping both Nessa's and Eitan's hands.

Eitan bends down and kisses Tanya's cheeks and hair. "A boy," he says, beaming. "We're having a boy."

Nessa steps back so that Tanya and Eitan can hug one another.

The doctor and Nessa and Eitan leave the room, and finally, Tanya is left alone with her baby. The first real, private moment she'll ever have with her boy. She puts her hands on her belly, and for the first time since she's become pregnant, she speaks out loud. "You're my son," she tells him. Not in a baby voice. It's just a sentence. Tanya is relieved.

She walks over to the window in her hospital gown. The room is cold, colder by the glass. They're on the fourteenth floor, and from above, the cars in the parking lot and the ambulances lined up by the curb look miniature, like a child's playset.

The sky is filled with impossibly huge cumulus clouds, so bright and textured they look artificial—the kind of clouds that if you were religious, or perhaps a child, might make you think of heaven. Tanya looks from cloud to cloud.

"It's a boy," she says, and this time it's to Lorraine. Lorraine, who should have been there in the room with them. It hurts Tanya's breastbone—a deep, physical ache—that her mother will never meet her son or hold him in her arms. Tanya's son will never know Lorraine's voice.

Tanya doesn't linger at the window, though. She doesn't believe Lorraine can hear her. Her mother's absence is absolute.

Tanya gets dressed. She leaves the room and walks down the hallway of the doctor's office, which has become familiar, almost homey, these past few months. Before pushing open the swinging door that leads into the waiting room, she peeks through the small windowpane, where she can see Nessa and Eitan sitting beside one another. Nessa has one of the parenting magazines open in her lap, and she's reading aloud.

Tanya smiles, watching Eitan. He's trying so hard to contain himself as he listens to Nessa. His lip is quivering—he's suppressing a grin, and he's jiggling his foot with anticipation. He looks like a boy stuck indoors on a warm day—glancing out the window every few moments, anticipating the air and the sun and the wind and the grass. A boy who can barely stop himself, so strong is his desire to jump out of his seat and race around until he can't anymore, until he collapses on the grass with exhaustion, his nose and his cheeks and his chest humming with warmth. She can picture him then as a young boy with his kippah, davening next to his father on Saturday mornings, his huge eyes taking up half his face, and the thought leaves her breathless. Little Eitan with all that boundless energy.

They are starting something new, together; she and her husband. Something decidedly different. It's optimistic, of course; maybe foolishly so. It's what every young couple thinks when they start out: gathering from their pasts what they'd like to pass down and tossing away the rest. It's bound to be messier than they anticipate. When they tell their little boy about his grandmother, eventually they'll have to tell him about Jesse, also. When she sings their son the moon song, it'll be something more than just a lullaby. There will be grief there, too, but that doesn't mean she won't sing it.

Tanya pushes open the door then, and Eitan and Nessa both look up.

"There you are," Nessa says. "Tee, have you thought at all about what kind of birth you want to have? I was just telling Eitan—I know the whole midwife doula thing isn't really your style, but I actually think you may want to consider a *water* birth."

"Maybe," Tanya says.

"Why are you laughing?" Nessa asks. She smiles.

Tanya shakes her head. "I don't know," she says. "It's hard to explain."

It's easier to be alone in New York City than in Northampton. In a college town, everyone, it seems, is in love. All those perfect green quads. The ever-constant Main Street with its hemp stores and coffee shops. Couples crowding the sidewalks with their romance.

In New York, people walk alone, rushing past one another. After Tanya's doctor appointment, Nessa heads off by herself to the Met. Her loneliness rises up like heat, mixing with all the other loneliness in the city, and becomes part of the collective. As she walks across Central Park toward the East Side, she feels herself becoming part of something bigger. It's practically religious, though it has nothing to do with God.

When she reaches the East Side, she walks the ten blocks up Madison Avenue toward the museum, past outrageous storefronts—Ralph Lauren, Vera Wang, Gabriela Hearst—past apartment buildings with uniformed doormen standing patiently in the doorways. The sidewalks are wide and clean; tulips burst up in orchestrated color along lines of locust trees.

Inside the museum, the lighting is white lace, angelic. She makes her way through the exhibits as if in a dream, stopping to look at paintings that catch her attention and passing by the ones that don't. She likes the art with people in it the most; isn't interested in the abstract or the surreal. She's drawn to the pieces that tell a story. She finds herself narrating the art in her mind, as if to another person, and she's aware, again, of her own deep loneliness. She's not bothered by it—she's lived with it for so long. Rather she's struck by it. But here in the museum, in this city, surrounded by all this beauty, Nessa is at home in her loneliness.

She stops in the gift shop on her way out and buys an overpriced sketchpad and drawing pencils and emerges back into the day with her new supplies. She takes the subway downtown, the hurl and clatter of the train a drastic shift from the stifling tranquility of the Upper East Side, and gets off at Bleecker Street.

She buys an empanada from a food truck, then settles in a park to eat and draw. The park is small, with minimal green space and a smattering of benches along a paved winding path. Across from her are two teenage girls on another bench. One of the girls is holding a white box from a bakery in her lap, which she opens to reveal two perfect cupcakes—vanilla cake with pale pink frosting. Nessa watches the girls. They spend a lot of time admiring the cupcakes, giggling to one another. When they start to eat, Nessa puts down her empanada and pulls out her pad and begins to sketch. One girl is eating the frosting first and the other one starts from the bottom, leaving the frosting for last. They're turned slightly toward one another on the bench, as if to watch each other enjoy the cupcakes, but they are no longer talking or giggling, so Nessa knows they must be close. Close enough to be able to eat in each other's presence without feeling pressure to entertain one another at the same time.

They finish their cupcakes and get up and leave before Nessa has even finished sketching the skeleton of the bench and one of the girl's figures. She puts down the pad. The drawing does not resemble girls eating cupcakes in the slightest. Nessa finishes her own food and thinks about Tanya's baby. How when you're born into a family, you're born into this very specific kind of sadness. It's part of you before you even enter the world. This little boy already has so much history—not that it will ruin his life. But it will be a part of him. Even if Tanya decides to never tell him any of it. As Nessa glances across the park, and beyond to the city streets, she thinks about all the people carrying around things they have no idea they're carrying around. She wonders what's inside her—all the things she doesn't know about.

She wonders how motherhood will change Tanya. She knows her sister is scared. She can see it in Tanya's eyes—that veiled panic. Nessa doesn't know why it keeps happening this way—that her little sister is the one to grow up before her, that Nessa always seems to fall behind. Tanya still seems to need her, to want her there. There is comfort in that.

Nessa opens the sketchpad again and turns to a blank page. She pivots on the bench and begins to sketch a tree; behind it a fence and some tenement buildings. Windows open, air conditioners busting out, curtains and blinds—some pulled open, some closed. In one window sits a cat. She has the most fun drawing the windows, like making a pattern but with small, important differences in each repeated shape.

"You an artist?"

Nessa looks up, over her shoulder.

A man is standing behind her bench, peering at her drawing, a cigarette hanging from his lip. He is wearing a dark coat, too warm for the day. His head is shaved, but his stubble is silver. He is attractive, though in need of a shower.

"No," she says, turning the page quickly to a blank one.

The man smiles at this. "You're shy," he says. "Why?"

Nessa looks at him again, harder. His eyes are shining. She tries to understand what she is seeing on the man's face; what she is feeling.

"You want one?" he asks, pulling out his pack of cigarettes. "Artists smoke, don't they?"

Nessa realizes then that she's been inhaling deeply through her nose, sucking in the cigarette smoke, as if she were a smoker who'd recently quit, aching for one more puff. The smell has always reminded her of someone, and now, she realizes—probably always—it will remind her of her mother; more so than of any man.

Nessa considers saying yes. Smoking with this stranger. Will the smell transport her? she wonders. Will it make her feel closer to her mother? And giving herself over to the man, which she feels herself longing to do—it would be so easy—will it make her any less lonely?

"No," she says. "I don't smoke." And then before he can make more conversation, Nessa stands up and leaves the park.

SHE WALKS FOR A LONG TIME, watching the city change from block to block, from neighborhood to neighborhood. The air cools as the sun slowly sinks from the sky, dropping behind the buildings. Her body starts to ache. First her lower back and then her legs. The shoes she's wearing are rubbing against her heels and the tops of her pinky toes. For a while she's able to ignore it, but soon it's all she can think about, the little blisters she can see in her mind's eye, growing pinker and shinier and more painful by the minute. She forces herself to keep walking. When she reaches Times Square, the city explodes—in color and in scale—and the blisters on Nessa's feet explode, too. She ducks into a Duane Reade and buys Band-Aids and plasters them all over her feet.

It's dark by the time Nessa stops for dinner and she is light-headed from hunger. She orders the steak.

"Anything to drink?" the waiter asks.

"Just water."

When he brings her food she has to stop herself from making noises while she eats; it is that good, and she feels so satisfied. She eats too quickly and leaves her plate clean.

"Room for dessert?" the waiter asks.

Nessa glances at him. She wishes he wasn't so cute—dark, youthful eyes, and a playful half smile. She reminds herself she'll never see him again. "Yes," she admits.

He brings her the dessert menu.

Nessa orders a nine-dollar slice of cake. The cake is so beautiful that for a minute she just stares at it. Thinking of the teenage girls in the park, Nessa pulls out her sketchpad and begins to draw the cake—the contoured icing, the plump raspberries, the dollop of homemade whipped cream. She draws the plate it's on, white china with a drizzle of chocolate, and, beneath the plate, the checkered tablecloth. She draws the lip of her purse, the curve of the shoulder strap, the edge of the Duane Reade bag, which are piled on a corner of the table.

When she finally begins to eat, she realizes how full she is from the steak, but she isn't one to waste dessert. She finishes it, slowly, the entire thing.

"Can I get you anything else?" the waiter asks, clearing away her empty plate. "Coffee or tea?"

"Just the check, please," Nessa says.

She leaves a hefty tip for her cute waiter, and exits the restaurant, full and sleepy.

WHEN NESSA FINALLY makes it back to Tanya's apartment, it's almost eleven.

The intercom crackles and then Tanya's voice emerges. "It's fricking late, Nessa."

"Let me up," Nessa responds.

The door buzzes and Nessa opens it, flying up the stairs.

Tanya is standing grumpily in the doorway of her apartment. She's in her pajamas, her hair pulled into a bun, her glasses perched on her nose. She's wearing her retainer. Beneath her T-shirt, her sister's stomach swells.

"Did I wake you up?" Nessa asks.

"What does it look like?"

"Sorry."

Tanya shrugs, but a hint of a smile peeks through. "How was your day?"

Nessa steps into the apartment, which is chilled from central air. "It was nice."

"Yeah?"

"First I went to the museum—"

"*Shhh,*" Tanya interrupts, pointing to the bedroom. "Eitan's sleeping."

"Sorry." Nessa lowers her voice to a whisper. "First I—"

"Wait, wait," Tanya says, ushering them into the living room. "Let's sit."

Nessa steps out of her ruined, bloodied shoes and unzips her shorts, which began to feel uncomfortably tight after the cake.

Tanya turns on the lamp beside the couch and they both sit, Nessa leaning against one arm, and Tanya against the other.

"Here," Nessa says. She unfolds the blue throw blanket that's draped over the top of the couch and smooths it over both their legs. "Do you have enough?"

"Yeah," Tanya says. "But my feet are cold."

"You can put them under me if you want."

Tanya makes a face. "I'll pass."

"Fine."

"Actually." She reconsiders.

Nessa lifts her hips off the couch and Tanya slips her feet underneath.

Nessa tucks the blanket under their legs so they're enclosed in it together; swaddled. She remembers back to the afternoon in their mother's bedroom, two days after Lorraine's death, when Tanya had asked to keep the blue blanket. Nessa had almost said no. She had so many memories of that blanket, and as soon as Tanya had asked for it, Nessa had desperately wanted it, too. But somehow, she'd managed to pull back; she'd stopped herself from saying so. Now, sitting across from Tanya, she's relieved that she did.

Tanya pops her retainer out and sets it gently on the coffee table, then pulls the blanket up to her chin and leans forward, her eyes bright with expectation.

And in that moment, Tanya looks so much like she did when she was still a girl—before she wore makeup, before they'd ever let each other down—that Nessa can feel it, a weightlessness in her chest. The sensation of starting again.

Acknowledgments

First I want to thank my agent, Margaret Riley King, and my editor, Allison Lorentzen. Without these two brilliant women, this novel wouldn't exist. Margaret believed in this book before it was a book and has been advocating for it since the very beginning. Her sharp insight helped shape it into the story that it is today. Her dedication means the world. Thank you to Allison Lorentzen, for her wise and thoughtful editing. It's rare to find an ideal reader, and for me, Allison is that. It is a true honor to work with her.

Thank you to everyone at Viking who has done so much to bring this novel into the world. I'm grateful to Carolyn Coleburn, Bel Banta, Camille Leblanc, Lindsay Prevette, Nora Alice Demick, and Mary Stone. Thank you to Lynn Buckley for designing the beautiful cover. Thank you to Sophie Cudd and Haley Heidemann at WME.

The seeds of this story began at the MFA program at the University of Wisconsin–Madison. I'm forever grateful to my Wisconsin writing family— Danielle Evans, Jesse Lee Kercheval, Judith Claire Mitchell, Piyali Bhattach- arya, Christian Holt, Will Kelly, Lucy Tan, and Jackson Tobin—all of whom have read drafts, multiple drafts, or pieces of the novel along the way.

There are certain writing teachers whose feedback and encouragement made a profound impact. For me, those teachers are Amelia Kahaney and Judith Claire Mitchell. Thank you for your generosity and for taking my writing seriously. Also, for being there in moments of discouragement.

Thank you to everyone I have had the privilege of working with at Emerge and CONNECT. Thank you for the work you do to end domestic violence and the difference you make in people's lives: David Adams, Susan Cayouette, Ted German, Zack Moser, Erika Robinson, Teresa Martinez Mc-Callum, Maria Ciriello, Jennifer Neary, Heather Arpin, Sara Townes, Isadora Brito, and Haven Huck. I have met so many people doing this work whose stories and strength I am forever changed by.

Thank you to Lizzy Schule and Mike Broida for being early readers and for excellent notes that I returned to again and again. Thank you to Kevin Jiang for long talks about writing and life; to Rebecca Luberoff and Laura Olivier for the walks and talks; to Linda Kilner Olivier for the Arlington memories; to Jenna Bernstein for being a creative soulmate on the Island. Thank you to Andrew Ding who is a good friend and always provides honest and helpful feedback on my writing. Thank you to my grandmother, Joan Halperin, who was one of the first readers of this novel and who encourages and inspires me.

My sister, Sofia, and my brother, Gabe, are my closest friends; I'm so happy that I'm related to you. Thank you to my dad, who taught me how to listen. And to my mom, who showed me to find beauty and creativity in the unexpected things. I am tremendously lucky to be your daughter.